The Deadwood Encore

Kathleen Murray was born in Carlow and educated at Trinity College Dublin. She has published work in *The Stinging Fly*, *Dublin Review*, *Prairie Schooner*, *Winter Papers*, and various anthologies. In 2007 she was the first Irish winner of the Fish Short Story Prize, and she was a finalist for the 2011 Davy Byrnes Short Story Award for her story 'Storm Glass'. *The Deadwood Encore* is her first novel.

The Deadwood Encore

Kathleen Murray

HarperCollins*Ireland*

HarperCollinsIreland
The Watermarque Building
Ringsend Road
Dublin DO4 K7N3
Ireland

a division of
HarperCollins*Publishers*
1 London Bridge Street
London SE1 9GF
UK

www.harpercollins.co.uk

First published by HarperCollins*Ireland* in 2022

1 3 5 7 9 10 8 6 4 2

A catalogue record of this book is available from the British Library

TPB ISBN 978-0-00-852419-7

Typeset in Bembo & Hero New by
Palimpsest Book Production Ltd, Falkirk, Stirlingshire

Printed and Bound in the UK using 100% Renewable Electricity
at CPI Group (UK) Ltd

MIX
Paper from
responsible sources
FSC C007454

This book is produced from independently certified FSC™ paper
to ensure responsible forest management.

For more information visit: www.harpercollins.co.uk/green

For my parents Nancy and Ollie

Contents

Begin the Beguine

And we suddenly know what
heaven we're in . . .

So said Perry Como, comrade in arms in the eternal choir of
seventh sons, and so say all of us. As the train crosses the
county border heading towards my old home town, the clack
clack of the iron wheels sings out begin the beguine begin
agin, begin agin. Sets me thinking, the way a place begins at
an invisible line. In a way a story is no different. How can I
begin to tell the story of how great a love and all that
malarkey? More to the point, how do you know the end?
That's the million-dollar question. For once you get started,
there's no surer thing than you're heading toward an end. But
you can't have the full knowledge of the end until the end
delivers itself. Then it's beyond you. No better man than
myself to make that proclamation given my own sad demise:
died, as far as I can make out, on the 2nd September, four
year ago, leaving behind my wife, Josie, generally known as
the Mater, and seven healthy offspring. My last moments
occupying a human body were spent hurtling over a humpback

bridge with my son Mossy cursing like a sailor at the wheel beside me.

Now I've been returned in a manner of speaking. But not to myself. I'm residing in a little wooden statue. Some quare perspective I've been granted. You see certain things when you're where I am, you know a few particulars and yet you've no will to exert. No will and, more importantly, no desire. You're at the vagaries of whatever takes a hold of you. What's taking a hold of me now is the sounds of this train, and me resting here in my niece Lena's belongings. Follow me up to Carlow, tie a yellow ribbon on it, for I'm going home.

Here's an article of truth, as we were brought up on. You might have heard it said that Carlow is famous for one thing: the last wolf in Ireland was kilt here. You might know about it because of the annual Wolf Night, a night of music and dancing, scallion eating and all kinds of carnivality.

Carnivality, that's my word. I don't know am I plucking words out of the air or are they blowing into me, for words I'm not overly familiar with is swirling around my head like a dust cloud. Are they gathering themselves up to make up a story, or only flying through me on their way to another destination altogether? Either way, it doesn't really matter, the wherefore or the why.

That's a lesson I'd already learned full well as a young fellah anyways. When I inherited the power of healing from my father, never thought of questioning the why or the how, just accepted it. Puts me in mind of Frank, my youngest, my seventh son. Forever worrying at things, each new anxiety a pebble dropped in the lake, just rippling out and out til he has himself mithered.

I'm being taken out of this moment on the train, back to that last wolf as if my spirit has a kinship with his. I seen him clear as anything, a rangy looking beast, roaming through the woods, skirting the dancing master's ground at Useann Park, rank with human smell. Then away up the side of Mount Leinster crossing to a rocky outcrop that looks over to Bunclody. No sense of county borders in that fellah's head, only trails to be covered and scents to be tracked. He's having his final meal, his last supper. It's the sweetest meat he could savour, let's say a full-grown rabbit.

He leaves go of a lonely howl. Waiting for the sound to return, perhaps another male prowling the territories of Laois or Wexford or, even better, the yearning cry of a female matching his keen desire. Waiting, poised, head raised, ears flat back, ready to turn in any direction and lope off. A barn owl swoops low, breaking into his line of sight, a rustle in the heather nearby as small creatures make themselves smaller, stiller. Silence. He roams through last darkness til morning, his final dawn. Returns to his den.

There's John Watson waking up, breaking the ice around the goatskin in his window frame, see what type of day is presenting itself. A bright day in Ballydarton, 1786, and he's ready for another crack at facing down the nemesis who's been plaguing his livestock. His two wolfhounds sleep on, the twitching paws drawing patterns in the ash spilled out across the hearth.

That wolf can't know he's the end of a line stretching back to when the island was dense with oak and elm. Like most history before we polish it up, his final hours are plain out: waking up, stretching stiff limbs, lapping up fresh meltwater. The satisfaction of his own piss flowing down a tree trunk, pooling over hard earth. Then the baying of hounds on the air, freeze low to the ground, the arms of a spruce trembling above him.

3

Funny auld scene for me to be in the thick of. As the clock has run down for me, I'm lost in time and yet here I am, occupying a few precious moments in the skin of a wolf. For all I know I could be stuck here for eternity.

My present condition, as best I can make out, is to be thrust into certain places. I'm fully in them, yet I'm over and outside at the same time. I'm all of it: that wolf's ears alert to the growl of the hunting dog; the sharpness of the frost on the leaf; the lightness of ash falling through the grate. My heart is a sky littered with stars. So that'll give you a sense of how there's no beginning nor end to yokes for me. It's some quare trip, this limbo eternity business.

I'm striking out in another direction altogether now, whilst remaining in the same spot. There's a very few souls, when they hear mention of Carlow, will retrieve a different scene altogether, dredged up from the depths of the grey matter. The first electric street lighting in all of Ireland, wasn't it switched on in Carlow town?

That's a fact, and as we used to say, facts are your only man. Though I'm in a prime position to dispute this having gone well beyond the fact of life and death, as commonly understood.

1891, the year when electricity began singing through the wires. Wires held up by wooden poles that were felled in woods near Stradbally, brought by horse and trap and erected by none other than one Patrick Whelan, the great-great-grandfather of yours truly. Generally known as Patta. So there he is, the bold Patta, felling trees goodo, building his own guillotine, professionally speaking, as far as I can make it out. Because his job up to then was gas lighter for the town. Not too much known of him, a third son. Or maybe fourth. Of little note til you hit the magic number seven in our family.

Beginning of the end for him, electricity. He took it on board - change, that is - left for Newfoundland. You have to keep moving or you'll be caught standing still.

Parnell himself was in town for a meeting, ended up being the guest of honour at the switching on of the lights. A symbol of the new and free Ireland, Parnell declared. The launch of light-filled streets for Carlow and the end of Patta's livelihood. That's the kind of conundrum you come up against in life. You take things in one direction and the pull is against you completely. You're heading north and you find yourself facing south. My thoughts are stretching in and out like an accordion but there's a story here to follow, so I may pull in my horns and strike for home.

I'll state one final thing that surely nails the Carlow colours to the mast and sets it apart from other, unremarkable, Irish counties. There's another reason for Carlow to limber up, nudge aside Longford, Roscommon, brush off wee Louth and Leitrim. The largest dolmen in the continent of Europe is located in a field near Carlow town.

That's right, heading towards Kernanstown, on a hillside, plain as you like, no fuss or frills, three massive boulders; three holding up a back-breaking fourth, balanced within an inch of its life. The Brownshill Dolmen.

Fair enough, nothing like the situation in Sligo where they say you can't cross the road without tripping over a megalithic tomb. Meath, another case in hand. Queuing up to catch the magical ray stretching its golden fingers down the passage at Newgrange and you're within a stone's throw of the ancient hill of Tara.

That's not Carlow. One very big dolmen. That's some resting place for a body. Capstone one hundred ton and change they say. Hard to be sure because you can't prop it on a scales, but people who know these things have affirmed its reputation. That dolmen took some effort to put together. We don't do things by halves. Nor overdo it. Build one, leave it alone, move on.

Beginning and endings. Like the guts of a story. I always thought it was fairly simple; you told a story through plain telling it, beginning, middle and end. Or if you had the talent, maybe write it down with pen on paper. But I seen now there's many a road leading into a tale and out. I'm in the strange position of being the pen and the paper; the ink running through it; the eye catching it; the mind reanimating the flat black and white into a spectacle. Reanimate, there's another word I wasn't overly acquainted with in my former life. It's true, though. Once you try and shape a story, it's like opening a door that'll revive the past and rouse a future. Forget about the present, it disappears. Nothing less than that. Hard to describe, even to myself, but there's some story needs to come out of all of this palaver. I thought I'd reached the end, as you do when you die; thought that whatever happened, or didn't, wasn't nothing to do with me any more. Now I'm wondering is this the end of my own story or the start of someone else's? Or are we all tangled up in a middle that goes on and on?

And we suddenly know what
heaven we're in,
When they begin the beguine

I Need You

Tuesday afternoon, a good-looking young wan with a scrawny whelp of a child arrives at our back door.

'Mrs Whelan here?' she asks.

'No,' I says. The way she's staring at me, I'm thinking I might have a blob of chicken curry on my chin or something. So I rub the chin, and my nose just in case, and the young fellah starts copying me.

'Is she due back?' she says.

'Impossible to tell with the Mater. Travels to the beat of her own drum.'

'It's for the cure.' She stands there, adjusting her bag. The strap stretches her top off her shoulder a bit and you can see her collarbone. There's something very even about that bone.

'It's actually me you're looking for,' I says, then I feel the red starting up from my neck at the thought of maybe laying hands on her. Well, not on, but a couple of inches over whatever affliction she has. 'The mother is more spirit guides, tea leaves and that.'

'I must've picked it up wrong. May as well give it a go seeing as we're here. Ringworm okay?'

Ringworm can be tricky enough at the best of times and I'm still waiting for the best of times to arrive. They say by the time he was five year old my father had the full gift; his father could drain an infection off a man with the whack of his left thumb by age ten. My great-grandfather didn't show any sign til his sixteenth birthday and then he'd lift Lazarus from the grave. If Lazarus' death had anything to do with circulatory issues, I mean. I was holding out hope for my eighteenth birthday but that's come and gone nearly two year and I'm only getting joy out of warts and the odd rash. It'd be easier if the Da was still around to give me a steer.

'Grand. Come on in,' I goes. 'Where is it mostly? We do see a lot on the stomach.'

'Not on me,' she says, giving me daggers. 'Him. On his leg.'

'I could do warts as well while you're here,' I says trying to make up a bit of ground. 'If the child has any. His hands?'

The young lad looks up doubtfully at his mother.

'Conor, show the man your hands.'

The boy rips his fingers through the air, like a tiger.

'Knock it off.'

He straightens them out, giving me the middle finger first, then unfolding the others. Dirty fingernails and there's some kind of hangnail situation going on with the thumb but no sign of a wart.

'Looks all clear. Though they can be dormant.'

'Dormant warts?' she says, sounding interested.

'Yeah,' I says, trying not to be too showy. 'It's kind of my thing. At the moment. You specialise in one area and then expand out.'

'Oh.'

'Like if it was joints, I'd be doing knees and shoulders. Hips.' Hips comes out too strong, like I'm thinking about hips. 'Or an ear nose throat fellah.'

They're both staring at me and my mind says shut the fuck up but my mouth says, 'Well you have to see what emerges, what comes out, over time. Every generation is different, so you never know. You probably heard of my Da, Billy Whelan, well-known for digestive stuff, skin afflictions, general pain relief. A bit of everything really. There's a lot looking for immune system stuff now and that's a new field. In a way. Though there was always, you know, hay fever. And stuff.'

'Warts?' she goes.

'Yeah.'

'All warts?' she says.

'Yeah.'

'Genital?'

'What the fuck?'

She gives me the hairy eyeball, 'Language please,' and nods at the young fellah who's pulling a scab off his elbow.

'That's not really my thing,' I says.

'Well,' she says. 'It's nobody's thing when you think of it. So the ringworm cure?'

I direct her towards the sitting room for our kitchen can be in any state.

She indicates an area, back of the kid's knee. I put my hand out, hover it and close my eyes. Usually I think of football scores, or calculate the odds of something happening, but today I remember this one time when I asked the Da if there was special words inside his head when he was giving the cure. He laughed but he didn't say what the real prayer is, just started to sing, something about touching a leaf or the sky, a baby crying.

9

'Finish it for me, Frank,' he said.

I'd heard him sing it a million times so I put my head back and gave it some welly, '*I believe.*'

'There you have it son.'

This other day, after I seen him do five or six different cases, all varieties – a leg ulcer, rashes and a twitch – I asked, 'What do you say, Da? Do you say different things for each one?'

He looked down at me like I was a tiny burr sticking to his trousers. 'I say, "clear the way, I'm coming through".'

'You say that to who, their leg? God?'

'I'm not really in an ongoing conversation with him. But if I was, I'd tell him, *Dream along with me, I'm on my way to a star,*' and he burst into a full-blooded rendition. Of all the singers, he favoured Perry Como because of their shared history: both seventh sons with the gift. You'd think that'd make me his favourite son, me being seventh and all. But no, it was Bernie, my twin brother. They were forever messing, dancing around the house, singing.

When I open my eyes, they're both staring at me, the woman and her kid. I must've lost track of time. 'It's a tough one,' I goes. 'Hang on.'

I get this rag from the kitchen, an auld dressing gown the Mater cut up into small squares. Before I go back in, I squeeze some lemon juice onto the material. The Mater's a massive fan of lemon juice. She uses it for everything: her hair, cleaning sinks, her elbows, the works. I haven't any good reason to believe it'll do the business with the ringworm but it won't do any harm either.

'Can you get him to pull down his sweatpants?'

The boy looks appalled.

'Relax,' I says to the kid. 'I'm not a paedo. As far as my personal life goes, strictly females, 18 to 26.'

I've never actually been close to my upper limit but I reckon your woman must be mid-twenties, based on the kid.

'Is that an IQ or an age requirement?' she says, giving me a look that'd freeze warts quicker than liquid nitrogen.

I rub the cloth on the patch of ringworm.

'What's that?' the kid says.

'It's a kind of relic. In the family, way back.'

'Smells like an air freshener,' she goes, wrinkling up her nose.

'Smells like lemon drops,' the boy adds, doing exaggerated sniffing with his nose.

'Yeah, we keep them in a special lemonwood box. This is a quare tough one. You'll need to come back three days in a row. I'll be in around six tomorrow and Wednesday.'

She purses up her lips as if she's thinking about her alternatives. What's to think about? Chances are she's been through every other remedy before she came to us – most people have.

'Okay,' she says.

The thought of being at the receiving end of her sarky attitude again gives me a quare shiver inside. Fuck it if the ringworm persists; I'll cross that bridge when I get to it.

'See ya tomorrow so,' she says.

As we're walking out of the sitting room, I hear the back door creaking. It's the Mater; she must've come in through the lanes. I quickly steer your woman and the kid out the front.

When she's going down the path, I call out, 'I didn't catch your name.'

Without turning around she goes, 'June.' The foxgloves and Sweet William are leaning in, nearly rubbing off her hip as she goes out the gate. June. And it's May. June in May. It's like an ad.

The Mater sticks her head into the hallway. 'Thought you'd be at work.'

'I'm on earlies this week,' I say. 'Bad case of ringworm there.'

The Mater gives a me a look that tells me exactly where she thinks ringworm sits on the scale of human suffering.

'Very quiet at the mill,' I says. 'Reckon I'll be back to part-time soon.'

I see June's left a fiver on the side table. The Mater always does a big spiel about how she can't take any money when she does a reading or talking to the spirits, but if the person wants to make a donation, fair enough. I couldn't be bothered to do the whole blah blah, I usually say it straight out, according to how much I think they're good for. But I wasn't going to hit June up, in case she didn't have any cash on her. Or worse, if I'm not successful. I slip the note into my pocket. The Mater turns quick as anything, her eyes raking the table. Too late, Mater. I pull a couple of odds from my pocket, go over to the donation jar. I drop a two-euro in. She continues her staring at me. I fish around, pull another two-euro coin out, and drop it in too. So that leaves me with one euro for my efforts and another two sessions with June. And the kid and his ringworm. I wish it'd been warts; I'd be feeling much more secure.

I pass my reflection in the hall mirror, rub a hand over my skull. The hair's a bit random. For some reason, Bernie comes into my head. This morning, running to get the Kavanagh's bus to Dublin, the way he was swishing his hair. He may as well wear a neon sign on his head that says G–A–Y.

'We'll have a pot of tea,' the Mater says.

She settles herself at the kitchen table. I sit opposite her; put my hands palm down on the table, the way the Da used to.

'Would you not put on the kettle?' she says.

I get up again and fill the kettle. I busy myself getting the mugs and milk out, don't bother sitting back down.

'Have you heard from your brother today?' she goes.

'No.'

'He's not back yet. He was due in off the 4.30 bus and he's not answering his phone.'

'Maybe he missed it. Sure he can get the Bus Éireann instead.'

'Have you noticed anything recently?'

'What?'

'Bernie's not himself, Frank. Very up and down.'

I had noticed for a fellah that likes to go out, he's been laying fair low. Since he dropped out of college, he doesn't be hanging out around town as much. Takes the odd trip over to Kilkenny, some new crowd he's got in with there, that's about it. Suppose he's gone a bit secretive.

'Bit quiet, alright.'

'Why do you think that is?' She looks at me, shrewd out.

'Maybe a chemical imbalance in his brain.'

'Ah, Frank.'

'Well that's what you read. He's either flying high or in the doldrums.' And, I don't add, he's getting more gay by the day, if that's humanly possible. 'Maybe he should finish his course?'

'His head's not in the right place for college. They said he can always go back when he's ready. He won't even have to repeat the whole year, only the one or two subjects.'

I don't get why he left. When the Da died, Bernie went a bit off the rails, but he still managed to stay in school, sit his Leaving Cert. I couldn't see the point. Some mornings I was too tired to get out of bed, not to mind putting on a uniform. Ended up hanging around Uncle Murt's yard for a while, fixing up bits of furniture and helping him with the key cutting

13

and shoe repair business. After a while, I got work in the sawmill and Bernie got a place in Carlow IT college.

The Mater takes a strand of her hair and, delicate as you like, tucks it into the headgear. That woman was born for the stage. She's taken to wearing a turban-type yoke recently. Since she attached a massive crystal to the front of it, the whole thing keeps creeping off her head onto her face.

'I got a call from Murt,' she goes. 'His Lena is coming back.'

'I thought he'd kicked her out for good. Tough love and all that.'

'No, she ended up in some, I don't know, commune in Mayo. But she's coming home. Big into art now. She's some mad notion of taking over his shop, turning it into a gallery.'

Carlow's a small place and it's hard to avoid anyone, especially if they're family. That's all I need, Bernie and his ups and downs and now Lena and her antics showing up.

'What does Murt think?'

'She's his daughter and it's her home. At the end of the day family's family.'

Uncle Murt's as decent a skin as they come. When his marriage broke up, Janine, his wife, hooked up with some horse trainer in Naas and took Lena over there with her. She grew up with big gamblers, little jockeys, and bent bookies. Once she got thrown out of the third school, she got shipped back to Murt. Why they had to put her in the same class as me was a total embarrassment: smoking these cigarillos instead of fags, wearing a flat hat constantly, even during PE.

'I'll try and call over to him this week.'

'That'd be nice, Frank.' She lets out a long breath and nods at the kettle. 'That's not all.'

'What else?' I says, boiling it up again and wetting the tea bags. I hunt around the press for a few biscuits.

'We need to do right by each other,' she goes. 'By the family.'

This is turning into a pink horse of a different colour. I sit back down. To brace myself for whatever she's on about, I take a grip of a spoon and focus all my energy on it, Uri Geller style.

'By the family?'

I'm trying to work out who exactly she means. There's only herself, myself and Bernie left at home since the Da's accident. The other four lads are down in Australia, and Mossy's taken off on a spiritual journey that involves him not using technology. He's incommunicado bar the odd postcard.

'There's things stirring, son, I feel it in my waters. When your father passed, I thought some of the boys might come back but they're gone for good. Maybe Mossy'll come home eventually. There's Bernie's situation and yourself . . .' She pauses here, gives me a hard look. 'It is what it is. Going forward.'

The fuck is she on about? Bernie's depressed, needs to get his shit together. Get a job or go back to college. No biggie. I'm ready to assume the mantle of the seventh son of a seventh son, once the particulars of the gift fully reveal themselves. A bit of faith in me from my own family would go a long way. Right then her phone beeps.

'Thank God.' She lets out a big sigh. 'It's him. He's got a lift down with some girl he met in Dublin. He might be late in.'

I'm rubbing the handle of the spoon up and down but it remains straight as a die, not a bend in sight. I can see my head in the bowl part, blurred and upside down. My eyes get bigger and smaller as I move it around.

'You've zoned out,' she says.

'Haven't. If it's money you're on about, I'm getting a fair few shifts at the mill. Once the gift comes through fully, it could be a nice earner. I know the Da didn't like charging, but people has more disposable income now and–'

'That's not what I mean, Frank. All I'm saying is—'

Her mobile starts ringing. She answers it: Cissy Agar, her best pal. She only lives across the green; they could shout over at each other if they had a mind to but they're always on the phone. Cissy does dressmaking and zips and she has the measure, literally, of everyone in the town. The Mater gives me the nod to say we're done talking for now.

I start thinking about June coming back with the young lad tomorrow. Better make sure I'm in decent time from work to have a shower. Hope the ringworm isn't gone any worse or I'll look like some loser.

The cure is supposed to shift naturally from father to the seventh son; maybe the timing was off with the Da dying so sudden. Fucked up the handover so to speak. I always pictured myself slipping into his shoes, the way people were rocking up to our door, putting their health and their hopes in his hands. Wherever you'd go, a pub or a match or anywhere, people mightn't say anything direct but the respect, it was in their faces for what he did, the relief they got. I used to imagine it was me accepting their thanks, humble-like, same as him. Now I'm faced with a simple case of ringworm. Should be a piece of cake and it will be. But I wish I felt more certain inside myself I can cure it.

I bring the spoon closer to my face until it's resting right over my eyeball. A teaspoon is just the right size. Such a simple yoke for lifting sugar and yet you could take your eye out with it if you're not careful. The Mater reaches across and grabs the spoon off me, gives me a right rap on the knuckles. Time to go.

Keeping the Balance

Wednesday morning at the mill, I'm hanging for the break to get a cuppa into me. Last night Bernie came in at all hours making a racket in the kitchen as per usual. At least I'm by myself on the forklift, moving a load of planed spruce to the sheds; I can take things handy enough.

Come half ten, the lads are having a game of whist in the canteen. They try and get me to join in but I want to have my tea in peace. I sit in next to Hopper McGrath and watch him play out the hand. There's none sharper at the cards than my best mate Hopper, especially when he's holding nothing of value. You'd never guess: the shoulders are real relaxed. He's always saying that: ease out the shoulders, then go in hard. Once they're finished, the lads started shifting around.

'What's the story, Whelan?' Hopper's cutting the cards fancy, accordioning them in and out.

'Nothing.'

'How's Bernie these days? Up to anything interesting?'

If someone else asked, I'd think they were only digging for

dirt. People do love to be passing comment on other people's business. But I don't mind Hopper asking. He's nearly like another brother to me, and to Bernie. We grew up together, same class in school, all three of us. Til me and Hopper got fucked out.

'I don't even know what he's up to half the time,' I says. 'He's in his room all day with the curtains closed, like a shut-in. Then he arrives down to the kitchen, a rucksack full of I don't know what, heading off to Dublin or somewhere. I seen a wig sticking out under his bed the other day.'

'A wig? Something wrong with his hair?'

'No. He said it belongs to some friend who's acting in a show.'

The door of the canteen opens and Dennis the boss heads for the coffee machine. He looks stressed out. Hopper knocks back the last of his tea, gets up to go.

'Did you ever come across this girl, June?' I says, casual. 'Long brownish hair, twenties, kid about five or six?'

'Is she the one working in the bookies, on Tullow Street?'

'I don't know.'

I'm in and out to Ace Bookmakers the odd time. But if June works there, how did I not notice her before? I couldn't have seen her and not felt what I felt yesterday. Because if I did, then maybe yesterday was nothing. The doubt starts to creep in.

'What is it?' Hopper goes. 'Your face's dropped like a bag of kittens in a fucking well.'

'Nothing.'

The hooter is going off by the sheds and we pull on our gloves.

'The lads are going for a drink later,' I says. 'You going?'

'No, I was thinking of heading to Athy tonight. Moose heard

18

there's some metal band playing a set in Fitzpatrick's. He's getting some quality blow from a cousin in Waterford.'

'How are you getting to Athy?'

'I told you Ruth asked me to keep an eye on the house while they're in the Canaries. Keith's a new Lexus sitting in the drive.'

'They're letting you drive the Lexus?'

Seems highly unlikely. His sister Ruth's so far up her own arse she could brush her teeth from the inside out. Puts on airs and graces like she never grew up on the same estate as us, treats Hopper like a bad smell. Though they must be on speaking terms again.

'Not exactly, but I know where the keys are. David, their youngest, he's breeding those Russian red hamsters. I promised him I'd look after them. I said I might have to rush a pregnant hamster to the vet in an emergency.'

'Emergency?'

'The way they can turn on their babies, massacre them. So he told me where the keys are.'

'A bit risky, no licence or insurance or nothing,' I goes.

'I wouldn't go into town.'

'Nah, not really interested anyways.'

All that afternoon, I'm thinking about June. Just having a kid doesn't necessarily mean she's got a fellah. More likely I suppose. I should get a better suss today once I get talking to her. But if it gets awkward she'll still have to come back for the third appointment. No, say nothing til then.

That evening, when it gets near six, I'm standing in the hall listening to the Mater heating dinner, chatting away goodo. She'd talk to the wall. Literally. She has a whole variety of yokes around the house she has full-scale conversations with.

I've come in and she's chatting to the teapot, pausing every so often as if it was answering back. I asked her a while ago, 'Any joy contacting Da, from beyond?'

'Not a dicky bird. Maybe he hasn't landed yet.'

That's a new one on me; I presume she didn't mean limbo or hell for she's very à la carte when it comes to religion. The Church never gave the Da much respect for his skills; competitive edge there from the local clergy. I was sorry I asked for I could see by her face she was disappointed. Why wouldn't she be, with all these randomers – from Mrs so-and-so's dead aunty Mary to some foot soldier in the GPO – using her head as a personal message board and a deafening silence from the very one she wants to hear from.

The bell on our front door can be dodgy so I'm keeping an eye out the window for June. Bernie's upstairs, prancing around his room. I've warned him not to come down. He's liable to be in any state. He should've gone off to Australia, joined the brothers, mad bastards as they might be and all.

This waiting is getting me a bit edgy so I start going through numbers: the brothers' ages, working out what age each one'll be when I'm twenty-one, then go up from that; when I'm sixty-three, same age the Da died, what age would Lar be or Senan?

Is that another voice with the Mater? I have a quick check in the hall mirror, give a rub to my hair, wipe a few crumbs clinging off my T-shirt onto the ground. When I walk into the kitchen, the little kid is standing there with some other woman.

'I was just on my way in to you,' your woman says. She's a bit older than June and kind of hippyish-looking but in a clean way.

'Alright,' I go.

The kid makes a face at me; I can't remember his name. The woman says goodbye to the Mater and follows me with the kid in tow.

I go over to the Xbox, pretend to be switching something off.

'Where's June?' I ask, keeping my back turned as I can feel myself going red.

'She's off,' the woman says.

'Off what?'

'Off what?' The kid mimics me and starts to piss himself laughing. 'Off her rocker like you.'

'Conor, take it easy,' the woman says and there's a toughness in her voice you wouldn't guess from the long hair and the flowery blouse and all.

I act natural and go ahead with getting the cloth out. 'Same routine as yesterday,' I says to the boy. He pulls a face at me but he's wearing shorts today, so he sticks the leg out. I think the ringworm is less pink. Although I've been wishing so much it will be, I could be imagining it.

The whole time I have my hand over the leg, giving it a rub with the little cloth, I keep trying to think of something to say. Your one is so busy on her phone she doesn't even look to see what I'm doing. Then I notice. How did I not see yesterday, scars down the back of the kid's leg. Old scars though he's not that fucking old so, Jesus, he must've got them when he was only a rug rat. Straight white lines; must've been a belt or a strap.

No gaudy scars pops into my head. Weird line. Nothing gaudy about scars. My own scars, all gotten fair and square: one under my left knee from the tricycle that time; the long one on my wrist from the chicken wire on McDermott's pigeon loft. Appendix scar. Some amount of accidents happened in this house. I was only small when Lar, the eldest brother, cycled off the shed roof one time for a dare. Senan was an accident waiting to happen, always crashing into something, pegged the whole kitchen table over when his legs got tangled in it. But none of us got beat at home, that's for sure.

The kid's staring at me; he knows I've noticed. He's not so full of himself now.

'Is that it?' It's the hippy woman.

Whichever of them owns the young fellah, you wouldn't take them as the type to take a belt to a child. Maybe that's why there's no mention of a father.

'Sorry, yeah. That's it.'

'Great, thanks,' and she's over, leaving a fiver on the mantelpiece. At the front door, I ask her will she be bringing him tomorrow. She says he'll be here.

After the hippy woman and the kid leave, the Mater calls me into the kitchen. She's on the move.

'Frank, do us a favour. I need to go over to Cissy's for a few hours to help her with the costumes. Are you around?'

'I don't know. Why?'

'Bernie's a bit low in himself. That appointment he had in Dublin. I should've gone with him.'

'What appointment?'

'Frank, if you're interested in his wellbeing why don't you ask? He tells me nothing,' she says, putting on her jacket. 'I want to make sure he'll have company. Cissy's doing a fitting for the children's choir for Wolf Night. I'm giving her a dig out with the cutting. Very tricky. Those Kiernan triplets, big as houses and only in high babies. She's to put an extra panel in the side.'

'What's for dinner?'

'There's pizzas in the fridge. Deep dish. Should be safe

enough if you lift the ham off. I need to get started on the ears.'

The Mater is a star when it comes to scoring us top-class dinners. She hasn't cooked in years, since she started work in Morrissey's Supermarket. Whatever way she manages it, there's always a few pizzas that slipped down the back of the cooler or a frozen shepherd's pie that got accidently unfrozen.

Once the Mater's gone out, I go see if Bernie wants me to throw one in the oven for him. He has the bedroom door locked, won't even answer me. I can hear him snuffling around. When he's in good form, there's no one like him. He'd have you sick laughing. But he'd drive you to drink when he gets like this. I'll do him one anyways.

He's still not down when I finish the first pizza. I'm only having a taste of the second one when Hopper messages me about going out, just local. I know the Mater asked me to stay in with Bernie, but if he's going to spend the evening in his room, what's the odds if I'm here or not? I text back and Hopper's over pronto. We're ready to head when Bernie comes down in a dressing gown and sweats.

'Alright, Bernie,' Hopper goes.

'Alright, Hopper,' Bernie goes, turning his back on me to get the ketchup down from the press. I think he's got eye make-up on.

'We're going for a pint. You want to come?'

I could kill Hopper. Bernie'll drag us all down with his mood.

'He's alright,' I goes.

'I wouldn't mind,' Bernie says. 'Where you going?'

'The usual, Waxy Doyle's.'

'Alright,' he goes, shovelling the rest of the slices in. Back he goes upstairs to change. Fuck. When he arrives down the face is washed, hair gelled, good to go.

'Nice shirt,' Hopper goes.

Bernie's well chuffed. It's a new one; must've got it in Dublin. Patterned but very fitted. Which on some would look like fuckwankery. But he can carry it off. At least it's not the one he came down in the other day: as close to a girl's blouse as you could get.

Hopper keeps talking the whole way into town, ignoring the vibes between Bernie and me. I wish I hadn't agreed to go for a drink at all. Waiting to cross over at Kennedy Avenue, these fuckwits in a Toyota pass by, blaring out Slipknot or some such shite. One of them rolls down the window.

'Fucking faggot,' he shouts and fucks something out the window at Bernie. It catches him on the arm, bursts down the side of his shirt. A milk carton. Who drives around drinking fucking milk?

'Scurvy cunting muck savages,' Hopper roars after them and pegs his Coke can at their back window. It splashes off the car but they're gone.

'Do you know them?' I says to Bernie.

'No.'

How the fuck could they pick him out, only standing there?

'I think I'll give the drinks a miss,' Bernie says, trying to wipe the wet off with his other sleeve.

'Forget about them,' Hopper says. 'Come on for one.'

'Yeah,' I go, though I'm a bit torn.

'Nobody'll even notice,' Hopper goes, despite the fact you can see the whole side of the shirt is soaked.

'Maybe another time.'

'This town'd wreck your fucking head,' Hopper says.

'Yeah,' Bernie goes and turns back. 'See yis.'

If that was me, I'd go home, have a good look in the mirror and change every fucking bit of myself til I disappeared. I'd fashion myself into something that could carry me around without sticking out. Not Bernie. He puts the chin up and heads off, cool as you like.

'It's like the Dark Ages around here,' Hopper goes. 'We need to get well out of it this summer.'

Then he's off on one of his hobby horses: if we could just get a few bob together for the flights, places like Brazil or Alaska, we'd have no problem getting work. Always big plans with Hopper; just never has the moolah to back them up.

Before we turn down Mardyke Street for Waxy's, Hopper announces he has to check the house alarm over at Ruth's first.

When we get there, he heads for the hamsters in the laundry room. No new arrivals. He's a look around, to check on things. Then I cop it; he's after the car keys.

Sure enough, once he's locked up the house and we're back out, he takes a car key out of his pocket.

But when Hopper points the fob at the car, it doesn't respond. I try it too – no go. Eventually we cop it; they're not the keys for the Lexus. Of course they weren't going to leave an opportunity like that in the way of Hopper. It's for Ruth's Honda Jazz, parked around the side. Hopper takes it in his stride.

'We could take a quick run over to Athy, check out this band,' he goes, pushing back the driving seat of the neon-green Noddy car, adjusting the mirror.

Why not? Bernie's probably going to spend the evening back at the house, moping in his room. I feel bad for him, but he's got a bit difficult recently. Stopped hanging around with me and the lads last year; didn't ever ask me to come along to any college nights. I think he thought I'd be an embarrassment in front of his new crowd. Since he dropped out, he won't hardly talk to me. Just a ball of misery rolling around the house. Apart from when he takes off to Kilkenny or Dublin for an overnight and comes back all buzzed. I'm not saying I didn't miss him a bit at first but that's the way it is now.

I'd say he's already gone online telling everyone about how shit his life is, and this town is the pits and his brother is . . . well, whatever he says about me, I don't care. And if Hopper drives sharpish, we'll be well back before the Mater gets in.

'Go on, so.'

It only takes about twenty minutes to get to Athy. I'm shitting we'll be pulled over by a cop but Hopper's cool as a breeze, even eating a load of Ruth's chocolate Eclairs I found stashed in the glove compartment.

We park up behind the church and head to Fitzpatrick's. It's practically empty, no sign of a gig. We have a quick drink anyways and, on the advice of the barman, try the Esquire next. No joy. We move on and end up in the Widow's Legacy. There's a card game going in one corner and a group of women having some kind of stitch and bitch in the other. This one comes up, orders a vodka and Coke. She's a knitting needle tucked in behind her ear, good-looking but definitely into her thirties. Hopper prefers older women. I don't know how old, but I do know for a fact he went home with your one who manages Duane Jewellers in the Brookfield Shopping Centre. She's classy looking but she was in Senan's year in school, which'd put her in her forties if she's a day.

Hopper starts discussing the finer points of needlework with her. Then he goes over to check out the jumpers and the bootees they're knitting. He's not drinking but I'm hoovering up the pints. I keep thinking of those shitheads with the milk. Should've tried to follow them, maybe. A woman from the knitting group come up for an order, smiles at me. Her earrings are huge, big hoops. I remember June had earrings and an extra one at the top of her right ear. I can picture that one – a gold spike – but I can't be sure one way or another what the others were like. Keep thinking of her ears.

I must've fallen asleep in the car on the way home. Next thing I know, I'm sitting on my own front doorstep. Stand up, have to sit down. Lost my keys again. Hopper's throwing pebbles up at Bernie's bedroom window.

'Quiet the fuck down, Hopper. Mater'll fucking swing for me if I wake her up.'

We must be making a bit of a racket because Eithne Agar, Cissy's daughter, comes across the green.

'Eithnehellogoodnight.'

She's ignoring me, whispering with Hopper. I catch a few words: 'ambulance', 'fight' or something like that.

Turns out Bernie was carted off to St Luke's in an ambulance, half-conscious. Went out drinking after we left him. To the Old Vic, biggest dive in town, got stuck into an argument with some group of lads. Maybe they gave him a going-over outside or maybe he fell on the way home. He was bleeding a fair bit; something about his wrist too.

'You mother's up the walls,' she says to me.

'Why didn't she text me?'

'She tried to.'

I check my phone. It's out of juice. Piece of shit.

Hopper turns the car round, gets me back in and we head off to the hospital in Kilkenny. He stops at some petrol station, sorts out a strong tea and a stale pastry to get me half-sober.

'You alright, Frank?'

'Yeah. Not like it's the first time he's put us through the wringer.'

The first time Bernie ended up in A & E was nearly two year ago. We were in Newbridge, the Mater and me. After the Da died, she'd gone more into the spirit communication side of things than the tea leaves; she was going all over the county, even up to Wicklow, Kildare, everywhere. Building up a fair reputation she was until Bernie's antics started taking their toll.

That night, he was mincing around town, getting into all kind of shit that was avoidable. These lads kicked him so hard in the stomach it ruptured his spleen. When I seen him all hooked up in the hospital, I nearly lost my life. I thought my heart was going to stop I was so scared for him. But you'd be surprised what you get used to.

The Real Deal

'What are you doing here? Where's the Mater?' The first words Bernie says to me from his trolley in A & E.

'She got a lift home with Hopper. You were asleep.'

I don't tell him about the bollocking the Mater gave me in the corridor for going out for a few pints and leaving him in the house by himself.

'You smell like a brewery,' he goes.

'Speak for yourself. The nurse said they'll let you go once the doctor does his rounds in the morning. Why didn't you go home? You were looking for trouble, going to the Old Vic. Keep up this craic, you'll be the first at something.'

'What?' Bernie goes, twisting away from me on the trolley, nearly ending up in the lap of an auld one shaking all over like she's possessed.

'The first brother to go six feet under.' I'm only trying to lighten it up but it's coming out wrong.

'I'll always be the first,' he goes. 'Between you and me.'

'By four minutes,' I answer. 'Which, considering the difference between sixth or seventh place, is a world apart.' Usually that puts a halt to his gallop. Getting born on his coattails meant I'm the one to inherit the gift. 'Bernie, you have to get a grip.'

He's dead quiet.

'You don't have to stay in Carlow. Or Ireland even,' I says. 'Why don't you go over to the lads in Australia? It'd be more your scene. Senan'd get you a job no problem.'

'On a building site?'

'You'd get into a restaurant or a hairdresser's or something.'

'That's so stereotyping. Anyway, the Mater needs me around.'

'Not while you're putting years on her with your carry-on. You're all over the shop.'

I could see I was getting to him by the speed of the heels rubbing up and down on the bed-sheet.

'Dr Evans, he's a specialist, he said . . . the lists—'

'Hang on,' I says. 'What specialist? What're you on a list for?' I haven't a bogs what he's referring to.

'I need to tell you.'

'The fuck're you on about? They said you've a sprained wrist and a bang on the head. That's all.'

'No, Dr Evans in Dublin. He's for . . . and the assessment . . .' and he drifts off.

It's weird watching him asleep. I'm trying not to pay attention to some of the stuff that's going down in the A & E, especially the bodily noises in the next cubicle. I must have nodded off myself because when I open my eyes he's watching me. He seems a bit more compos mentis, so I ask him what happened. Turns out he saw a car parked up near the Old Vic, recognised it and decided to go in. Sits up on a barstool in his stinking milk shirt. Right beside the muck savages that threw the carton at him. Ordered his vodkas and Red Bull, drank them and left. He thinks they followed him out, jumped him.

I don't get it. Why he has to stick his neck out all the time. Why didn't he ring me and Hopper; we could've backed him up. Or pulled him out of there.

'It's more than you think,' Bernie says. 'I'm not a . . . because I've been . . .' His voice is getting a bit slurred. He closes his eyes and I think he's fallen back asleep.

'I'm a woman,' he says, eyes still closed. 'Inside.'

I'm not sure I heard right.

'What? You're no more a fucking woman than the Marlboro Man.'

He says nothing for ages. Then he whispers, 'The Marlboro Man was gay.'

'Shut up,' I says, and give him a dig in the arm. He's off his face on whatever painkillers they gave him. I tell him to try and sleep, I'm going out for a smoke.

He knew well I'd google it, and sure enough as soon as I go out, I check Marlboro Man. There was loads of them, most died of cancer. One, maybe two was gay as well.

I get a bottle of Coke from the machine in the waiting room. There's a young one in the horrors over on a chair, holding her stomach and letting out high shuddery moans. An old couple are waiting real quiet, not speaking, staring straight ahead. His face is grey and his hands are gripping his knees. Her lips are moving all the time. Then I cop it; she's praying. There's bad shit going down for people and that idiot of a brother of mine is just walking into trouble like it's a hot bath.

I head back in and stand beside him until he wakes up. 'Look.' I drop my voice to thwart his neighbour on the next trolley. She got the rattles under control anyways; now she's practically hanging off the side, earwigging. This is turning out

31

to be way more interesting for her than sitting at home with her cat, watching *Coronation Street*. 'You've had a bad night. You need to cool off, get your head straight.'

'I know where to get hormones,' he whispers. 'On the internet.'

'What the fuck,' I says. 'They could sell you any auld shite. I don't know what you were at in Dublin. It's unbalanced you.'

'You're the one needs to work on your balance, not me,' he says, facing away from me. 'You know the earth's always turning 'neath ya.' Less than a minute and he's conked out.

They discharge him about eight in the morning. A couple of stitches and a badly twisted wrist. We both dozed on and off for the night, which was a relief cos I don't know what to be saying to him. I did say he brought this on himself, putting it up to those lads. And I let him know how he put the heart crossways in the Mater; maybe that's what's shutting him up. Neither of us mentions the other stuff he was going on with.

Hopper rang to see if we wanted him to collect us, but I've sorted a lift from Ma Byrne who's coming off night shift in the canteen. She's dying to get the inside track on what happened, but Bernie pretends to be asleep in her back seat and I'm saying nothing. When we get home, he heads straight to his room. The Mater ignores me, goes up after him.

I only get about two hours' kip; I've some head on me when I wake up. I'll be dead late for work, again. Two mugs of tea, strong as tar, piece of toast and I'm still not right. The Mater comes down and takes the slice I just buttered. She's as cool with me as if I dosed Bernie myself.

'I'm thinking of calling in sick,' I goes.

'Really? With people in this house genuinely ill.' She indicates the kettle with her head.

I get up and brew her up a fresh pot.

'No need for you to be here,' she goes. 'I'm off today anyway so I'll stay with him.'

As if that was why I was going to stay home. I'm fucking exhausted. But I can't be doing with sitting listening to her cooing over him all day and me getting the bum's rush.

'See you later, son,' is all she has to offer, not even looking at me as I'm heading out the door.

I get another bollocking at work, this time from the boss for being late. I don't want to tell him why. But Hopper must've said something because later in the canteen Dennis comes over, tries to talk to me about some football match that's on the box tonight. Fuck that.

The noise of the saws is cutting sections out of my brain. Every time I think of what Bernie was going on with last night, it's like an impossible sum. It literally doesn't add up. We all suspected Bernie was gay, before he even told us, so no big surprise there. He was always mad into different stuff to me, to any of the brothers; going all emo, painting his nails and shit. Loads of blokes do that. He even mimed a Beyoncé number for our school concert in second year. It was fairly good too; no RuPaul but whatever floats your boat.

But this woman thing is a whole different ball game. I don't know what to think about it. He told me he'd gone to see a counsellor in college a few times but what's the story with this doctor in Dublin?

I get it that it's his life and all but why can't he go along the way it is now? Adrian Kelly in the chipper is gay but he's not rubbing your face in it. Even plays midfield for Éire Óg.

I nearly take the corner off the office prefab when I'm turning the forklift. Junior Hennessey is dossing by the back of the skips, so I swap over with him. He's thrilled; been dying to get driving since he started last month. I do some general tidying, then skive off behind the sheds. I'm hanging for a kip and eventually knock off around half three.

The Mater is in the kitchen, a bit dressed up, packing her handbag.

'Where's Bernie?' I goes.

'He tried a bit of lunch earlier. Gone back to bed; he's very shook.'

I have a look around the fridge, pull out a block of cheese and a tomato. 'Might have a little lie down meself.'

'Are you staying home now?' she goes.

'Yeah. I'm totally done in.'

'You can keep an eye on him. I have to go out.'

'I can't see through his bedroom door.'

'Don't be smart, Frank,' she says, 'it doesn't suit you. Don't abandon him this time.'

She's still hopping at me. Not that she's taking on any responsibility for staying late at Cissy's, stitching their auld wolf ears, catching up on the gossip.

'What's for dinner?'

She's put my dinner in the oven for later, and one for Bernie.

'Don't be picking the chips off his plate. He's only after staring death in the face.'

'Of his own accord.' While she's sharp as a tack dealing with grieving widows or hopeful virgins, giving them a steer with the spirits, when it comes to Bernie, she's too soft by fucking half. She needs to get some perspective on his shenanigans.

'It's not his fault,' she goes. 'I think he was Kenneth Williams in one of his past lives.'

'Jesus, that was a quick turnaround,' I says, doing a rough calculation in my head.

'That man's aura was putrid,' she goes on. 'That's why he wasn't in the *Carry On* Christmas specials.'

'Mother, leave it out with the fucking auras.'

That's only her jealousy coming through. Apart from the fact she's all but colour blind, the aura business is covered off by two sisters in Graiguenamanagh who've been in the game for years. Last year when Bernie went low, she had to cancel a session she was to give in Tinryland and got replaced by the Colour Me Aura Beautiful sisters. She hasn't been asked back since.

'You can't see it, Frank, but he's very vulnerable. He was thrown off by that doctor in Dublin.'

'What kind of doctor was that exactly?'

'I couldn't rightly get a handle on it myself. I think the counsellor in college sent him. Get him sorted out before he goes back to his studies. Whatever's going on, he's not himself.'

She doesn't know the half of it. I have a root around the medicine tin for painkillers.

'Nurofen Plus is it?' she goes. 'Behind the washing-up liquid, under the sink. I'm afraid where Bernie's head might take him. Better safe than sorry.'

She's not on the right track at all.

She checks her watch. 'I suppose I've time for a quick cup.'

As a peace offering, I'm allowed to make her a pot of tea. She's dying to tell me where she's going. Turns out Lena got home yesterday but she left some luggage at the station. The Mater's going with Murt to get it, out of pure nosiness.

'Why doesn't he tell her to sling her hook?'

'It's not that simple, Frank. Blood is thicker than water. She's a very artistic nature, from the Whelan side. That's half her problem right there.'

I fill myself a big mug of tea. 'My head is lifting. I'm going up.'

As I pass her chair, she takes a grip of my arm. 'Love you, son.'

'Yeah, I know.'

I knock on Bernie's door. He's his headphones on, tucked up in bed like it's the middle of winter instead of a sunny afternoon.

'You alright?'

'I'm grand,' he says. 'Before you say anything, I don't regret it. I'll drink in whatever pub I choose. I'm not stepping back for a couple of goms from the arse end of Timahoe. This is my town.'

I can't stop staring at the bandage on his forehead, knowing there's five stitches underneath it. He says one fellah tried to stick a clothes hanger in his ear. Seems unlikely that there'd be a clothes hanger on the road outside the pub. I suppose anything is possible. They did have a carton of milk in the car, so you never know what you're dealing with.

I know I should be bulling over the lads who did this to Bernie, and I am. But looking at him there in his bed, scrolling through his messages, for all the world he could be nursing a regular hangover. It's him I'm furious at, for putting us through this. It's constant the last few years: picking fights or having his stomach pumped. Hanging out with weirdos who spend half their time in the nut house.

'If all you wanted was a drink you could have gone with me and Hopper,' I says.

'I need a lot more than a drink. Do you not remember what I told you last night?'

I tell him I was half-cut at the hospital, and he was totally out of it. I'm hoping he'll leave it at that. I'm shattered. But no. It's like he thinks we had some big conversation in the hospital and I'm all up to speed and everything's hunky-dory. He starts explaining to me how he didn't know, but at the same time he always did, and then he was in this group in college, a gay group, and he knew what was possible, what he needed to do. He's bursting to tell me what it was like for him as a kid, as if I wasn't there. Saying what a relief it is to talk. Going on about this group he's going to in Kilkenny and a woman, she's transgender, he stays with sometimes in Dublin who runs some kind of hostel, or dosshouse or whatever.

'I know you, Bernie,' I says, 'and you're gay, which is fine by me. And everyone. Maybe it's just . . . you're not yourself.'

'Exactly,' he goes, pointing his finger at me. 'I'm not.'

He always turns my words back on me in an argument.

'It doesn't make sense. It could be a mental health thing,' I says. 'Why don't you leave it go for a while?'

'I can't.'

'Why not?'

'Time. That's why. I want to start living my real life now. I know who I am. I don't want to look back and have spent my best years in a shell of myself.' Now words are pouring out of his mouth, floating past my head. What he's talking about, it's like someone off the television, not my twin brother, Bernie. This doesn't square off with our lives.

Then he sits up and says he has to ask me something straight out. 'Frank,' he goes, looking directly at me. 'I need to know if you have my back.'

I've always had his back, the same way he had mine. But I don't get what I'm in for with all this. Doesn't even wait for me to answer, starts talking about other people, how fucking amazing they all are, all backing him cos he got beat up. This is completely different from putting on an act on stage, or prancing around in the Mater's housecoat, lip synching to Beyoncé. I keep thinking about a programme I saw last year, I think I might even have watched it with him, and there was men who were women, gay and straight. With kids some of them. Was he sitting there beside me thinking he was somehow like them? Some of them even having surgery. He's not saying that, but would he actually go that far, not be himself any more?

He stops, says I never answered him.

'Of course,' I say to shut him up. 'I've got your back.'

'No matter what?'

'No matter what.'

That seems to satisfy him.

'Apart from when you're picking fights with knuckle-draggers,' I goes as I walk out. 'You're on your own then.'

I pull across the curtains in my room, throw myself down on the bed. Thoughts are creeping around my head like black spiders. At least I'm here, going for a kip in my own room, and Bernie's still breathing in his. How is he always so clear-cut about everything? What if I'm as positive about what I believe? Bernie, you're my brother, end of story. How'll that work?

The Da was gone so quick, walked out the back door with Mossy, got into the car, never came back. Pure accident; everyone said so. Tyre burst, car swerved and the side of the bridge gave way. There, then gone. I always seen us working side by side doing the healing, him explaining things to me, maybe me driving him around when he got older. Then taking over. That whole future, gone too.

Four month later, Mossy disappears without a trace right when we could have done with a dose of his madness around.

He told the Mater he couldn't stay in the house with the guilts. When someone is gone, completely out of the blue, it gets in on you that it can happen again, anytime. If Bernie was to actually go through with this shit, I'd lose my twin on top of all that. That's too much for any one person to have to take.

Curing the Kid

My phones buzzes. Hopper: *Everything ok?* I text back: *yeah talk later.* I must've fallen back asleep because next thing I know I get a message from the Mater: *dinner in oven check bernie ringworm 6.*

What time is it? 5.45. Shit. June and the kid, due at six. I need to freshen up. I tear off the T-shirt and put on a clean one. Then I take that off and put on a short-sleeve shirt. Fuck, I'll have to change the sweatpants if I'm wearing a shirt. I have the pants off when there's a knock on the front door. I'm busting to go to the jacks. I spot a pile of clean laundry – nice one, Mater – grab a fresh T-shirt, pull back up the sweats.

Rinsing my hands when I hear another knock. I can't believe I forgot June was coming. Or not. Probably the hippy woman again.

When I open it, the kid is standing there. Beside him is June.

'You look surprised,' she says.

'Kind of in the middle of a thing,' I says.

She's knockdown gorgeous. The young lad pulls a flower from the Mater's trellis around the front door. 'Wanna give her a flower?' he smirks.

'Conor, leave that alone,' she says.

They go into the hallway and I try to concentrate, but I'm in a heap, no two ways about it.

'No shoes,' the kid goes.

'Yeah, I was changing. Not long in from work.'

'Nice,' June says.

'What?'

'Kicking your shoes off after a long day.'

The kid is doubled over and I give him a hard look.

'I used to run,' I says. 'Barefoot. I mean feet.' I turn around because I can feel my neck going red. 'I'll get the cloth. Go on into the front room.'

I go into the kitchen and get the cloth from the box. When I come back the kid is after taking down a medal from the shelf over the TV. 'What's these?' he says.

She stands up, puts her phone away. 'Conor, it's not okay to go through other people's stuff. You don't like it when PJ goes through your cards.'

'It's okay,' I says.

She takes the medal off him, goes to put it back. 'There's loads here. You must be some runner.'

'They're mostly my brother Bernie's. But a few are mine. If you count the relay medals probably close to a good few.'

The lad has his leg stuck out before I even ask. 'Look, mister, it's nearly gone.'

Only a faint red circular shadow on the skin. Nice one.

'Tied a knot in that divil's tail,' I says, giving him a wink.

I get to work on the leg, and as I'm doing that, my head starts to melt inside with how that feet conversation went. I mean, I did run, true, but I'm not actually the person who won most of those medals. Maybe I won two per cent, which makes it a, what, ninety-eight per cent lie? Though I used to help Bernie train, cycle alongside him down the Barrow track. That's probably worth a few per cent of any medal there. I was the sub for the relay team and I did take part in a couple of heats. That puts me back around a sixty, seventy per cent lie. If I tell the truth now what would I even say?

She's sitting on the couch and she has her hair done different this time, more tied back but still loose.

'Seems like you have the gift, alright. I'll have to keep you in mind,' she says. 'Always some rash or scabies. Constant battle against nits. If you could sort them out, you'd make a fortune.'

Jesus. She's no shame that's for sure. Most people would die before admitting to their kids having scabies. Or nits. She's as cool about it.

'How many have you?'

'Sorry?' she says, distracted by the phone again. 'Five at the moment.'

At the moment? I feel sweat starting to collect on my forehead. It's quare hot already; when was the last day it rained, properly rained?

'You alright?' she says.

'Yeah, I'm grand. It's turning into a decent-looking summer, isn't it?'

She's so embarrassed for me talking about the weather, she walks across the room to inspect the Mater's collection. We hardly notice it, but it is something to look at, takes up a whole wall. She collects all kinds of crap; has hundreds of different objects, all pushed together on the shelves. She gets stuff from all over the place, a lot of it from Murt. Then June puts her hand around this yoke. The Mater swears it's a hair straightener from a hundred year ago, but Bernie claims it was for some other less hygienic purpose altogether. I hope she doesn't ask me about it. She picks up an old glass milk bottle, puts it back in the exact same spot.

'This is amazing,' June goes.

'She started it years ago. It's kind of unstoppable now.'

'Does she buy things online?'

'No, she won't buy anything.'

There's a whole set of rules to the Mater's collection that make sense to her and her alone. For example, she won't buy anything to go on the shelves. Has to come to her in some other way. But even if you buy her something for a present, she'll decide if it goes up. Not even to do with it being the most expensive thing. All Mossy's postcards since he left have made the cut. Her latest favourite is bits of worn-out glass from a beach in Australia Lar sent home.

'Where did she get the shelving unit?'

'I made it up for her. I work up at the mill. We do a bit of bespoke stuff for customers. Well, I don't usually but . . . I can.'

As a piece of furniture it's not something that's to everyone's taste but I did fit it up exactly to what the Mater needed. A few little details here and there to give it a lift. She got some surprise when she came down that day.

'It was for her birthday last year.'

'Was it a significant one?'

'Yeah, and she was a bit low. Bernie, that's my brother, he got all the lads to make an effort.'

The Mater couldn't believe it, only expecting I'd get her the usual bunch of flowers from the garage. She was fair thrilled with that set of shelves, though it's only wood and a few dowels at the end of the day, but I did put a good bit of work into it. Got a few nice lengths from some church pews Murt had in his scrapyard. Myself and Hopper took the old shelves down when she was gone to bed and fitted this in. Even took photos so I'd be able to put all her stuff back in exactly the same places.

The lads sent a bottle of champagne and some kangaroo poo from Australia. Chocolate the poo was, but she got a good laugh out of that. Another of Mossy's postcards arrived too, a photo of himself on a fishing trawler and a mad poem he made up. Postmarked from Morocco. He had a big, long Al Qaeda-type beard. The Mater keeps expecting to see him on the news in Syria or Iraq, but that eejit could as easily be holed up with the Holy Ghost Fathers in Kiltegan.

'Are you okay?' June says. 'You look exhausted.'

I say I've a few things on my mind, mumble something about being in the emergency last night.

'You were in A & E?' she says, looking concerned.

'No.' There's no way I'm getting into all that shit about Bernie. 'With a mate. Turned out to be nothing in the end.'

In place of going on with that line of conversation what comes out my mouth is, 'Is your friend not around?'

'What?' she says.

'The other woman. Your . . .' I end up saying 'your friend' again.

'Come again?' she says, looking at the kid as if he's behind this turn of events. He throws an exaggerated shrug.

'From yesterday.'

'Marissa?'

'I didn't catch her name.'

'We work together. In the kids' project on Barrack Street.'

'I'm not following you.'

'KidsAlive. I'm a youth worker.'

Scabies, nits, loads of kids. I have it now, that new place for fucked-up kids. Hennessey was only talking about it at work the other day, saying Caroline Reilly's young fellah was going to some place on Barrack Street to sort his head out after his da going off with his ma's sister. The kid's totally gone off the rails; drove a ride-on lawnmower through the Lidl car park. Nearly took the legs from under some auld one, knocked her trolley into the bollards. Hennessey does drag racing near Gowran Park, and he bumped into this crew there with a gang of kids. How is that going to help? I said. We'd have been given a slap across the head and out splitting logs for a week. Though Hopper says the mother's eating the sleeping tablets; out of it, day and night. He said that child is all but rearing himself at eight years old. Let him blow off some steam on a racetrack, he goes, rather than pegging bangers in letterboxes.

Anyway, June probably had to go to college to train to be whatever she is, and that puts her right out of my league. I can't think of nothing to say. So I says, 'Do you do the drag racing? With them?'

'What?' She and the little fellah are staring at me like I've lost my marbles right in front of them.

He does the big exaggerated face and repeats the word dragggg real slow as if it's a foreign language.

'I'm finished here,' I says. 'He should be grand now.'

They both make to go pronto. When they get to the front door, she starts to fumble in her handbag. 'Well thanks,' she says as she gives me a tenner.

'Right. See ya round.'

'I had a fiver ready in case it didn't work.'

'Feel free to bring him back if you're not happy.'

The kid is already outside the gate, shouting at a gang on the green playing football.

'I'm only kidding, Frank. See you.'

She turns to go and I relax. It's easier to look at her when she's not facing me. Outside the gate, she turns back and catches me staring.

They're gone. I stay at the door for a minute. The garden is looking great. The Mater has a whole heap of flowers that she got a few years back and they're after spreading out like mad. On a bright day they fair sparkle, white and golden. Near hypnotise you.

Something about a summer's day like this; everything so vivid, the smell of grass, kids whizzing around on scooters and bikes, owning it like summer was specially designed for them. I get a rush from it all before the bag of hammers in my head starts up again something woeful. Too many ups and downs in twenty-four hours and a hangover to boot.

Once I've the plate of food zapped, I go back into the front room with a two-litre bottle of Coke, pull the curtains against the light and settle in for a zoned-out evening channel hopping.

Return of the Da

The day after a session, when I'm in ribbons, there's no better spot than slouched down in the Da's old armchair, watching the box. I'm flicking between a documentary about rap music in Miami and football's fifty funniest moments, which I've seen loads of times before. But there is something satisfying watching a multimillionaire footballer trip over his own feet or have the elastic in his shorts snap.

I must've dozed off cos next thing Bernie has the control took out of my hand and is sitting on the couch with a box of Heroes and a bag of tortilla chips. He's a bit crocked with the wrist bandaged up.

'Alright, bro?' he says.

'Who gave you the chocs?'

'Got them for meself. Self-love, buddy, that's the name of the game.'

'Wanker is another name for it.'

'Actually they were on special offer. The Mater brought home three boxes, one each. Here' – he throws me over the bag of chips – 'you look like you need these.'

I work through the chips and Bernie flicks from one thing to another. At least half the programmes he checks out I wouldn't be arsed with. But I haven't got the energy to argue the toss.

'Watch a film?' he goes. He seems to be back to himself, acting like everything is normal between us.

'Not stupid shit,' I say. 'Or anything foreign.'

He picks out an old comedy we used to watch loads, *Tropic Thunder*. Good one.

Sometimes as a hangover starts to lose its grip, but I'm nowhere near back to myself, I enjoy that feeling. I'm totally zoned out, can't really concentrate on anything for more than a minute and that's a relief. Like I didn't do myself any favours with June today, but I haven't got the energy to dwell on it.

We fly through the first box of chocs, are arguing about who'll go into the kitchen to get the next one, then out of the blue Bernie goes, 'What was that kid in for earlier?'

I knew he was listening up in his room.

'Ringworm. Sorted.'

'The ringworm. And of course the warts. Any sign of anything else emerging, gift-wise?'

'What do you mean?'

'Well,' he goes. 'The Da was well past warts by the time he was, you know, what, ten, eleven? Onto the ulcers and tumours and stuff.'

'I'm actually thinking of doing veruccas too,' I says back. 'It's different for different people.'

'Not people, bro. Comes out in sons, seventh sons.'

'What're you going on about? That's me, the seventh son.'

'You're definitely a full-blooded son. More thinking of the seventh bit.'

'Laurence, Pat, Mick, Senan, Mossy,' I goes. 'Five. You, six, and four minutes later, me. Seventh.'

He's been spending a good bit of time with the Looney Tune brigade, fair enough, but Bernie usually makes sense. Then he goes all dreamy, wraps his legs under himself on the couch and starts singing all high, '*I am your sister and you . . .*'

'Except you're not my sister,' I goes.

'Thing is, irrespective of who knows it, I am. Puts you back in sixth-son position.'

I'm looking at him and he's looking back at me. People usen't be able to tell us apart as kids with the same haircuts and all. So this is challenging for me, watching a version of myself look back at myself, knowing that he doesn't even think he's himself. Very fucking trippy.

'But you're mistaken, Inspector Morse,' I says. 'How is it, if I'm not the seventh son, that I'm already showing evidence of the gift? Didn't you see the *lámh* of James McHugh two weeks ago? A gnarly toad. Three days later, hands of a virgin.'

Bernie is doing something with a chocolate wrapper, making a folded-up bird yoke.

'The placebo effect,' he says. 'It's common in conditions such as warts. It's probably a big effect in most conditions actually. Power of persuasion.'

I don't really get him, but my mind is racing at this stage. Fair enough, warts is only warts. Then I remind Bernie of Cissy Agar and the shingles last winter. A ring of fire around her waist, she said. You don't expect them to disappear over-night, and she'd already started on the antibiotics, but she definitely said I sped things up.

'I'd say it's more the power of seven than persuasion,' I says.

He shrugs. 'The Da definitely had something special going on, I'll give you that.'

He doesn't say it but I know what he's implying. The Da had something special and you don't. He can't seriously be thinking that I don't have the gift because he's just decided not to be my brother any more. Trust him to complicate my life; he's always a step ahead of me in complicated stuff.

'Look,' I says. 'I don't know what you're going through with your identity stuff and all that, but in terms of the gift, that's something very essential about our family. Going back generations.'

'Frank, no one gives a shit about the gift stuff, only you.'

'And all the people who come to me for the cure.'

'That's right; queues out the door day and night.'

'The Da gave a shit. Out of respect for him, at least keep your business and mine separate.'

'Sadly for you, I can't,' he goes. 'You need me to be your brother for you to be the seventh son. I'm not. I never was, Frank. In a way I could be doing you a favour.'

'How's that?'

He says maybe it'll take the pressure off me; I won't have to see if I measure up to the Da. A whole load of thoughts go through my head real fast. Just believing something doesn't change things, make them true, does it? Like, the Da and the Mater took him for a boy, so that has to count for something. He's their son. He's not actually changed anything permanent about himself. Yeah, fine, express yourself with the long hair and the way he goes on, be camp as Christmas if that's what you want, but anyone can do that and then change again. But I say nothing because Bernie has a way of chipping away at your arguments til you're only left with what he thinks. He's always so clear about things, same even when we were small. He'd know straight away, *I don't want to go here, I'm not doing that*. The way he's talking about this stuff, I can see he's convinced he's not my brother. Bernie'd be the very person to convince the world black is white.

Where'll that leave me if he does? With five older brothers, not six?

I get the remote and higher up the volume. I don't have anything more to say and he shuts up too. I feel like if we go on with this conversation, it might go anywhere. Those places words can take you where you can't get back.

He starts doing this thing with his head, shaking his hair from side to side. It's nearly shoulder length, but he's got some kind of flick to it.

'What did you do to your hair?'

'Got a blow dry,' he says.

'Where?'

'What's it to you? Looking for a recommendation?'

'You didn't go to Kayla's? She's a gob like a bursted slipper.'

The Mater's a regular at Kayla's Kutz, as much for the gossip as the haircut. Kayla'd have the news spread across town like butter on toast: 'Bernie Whelan, not only gay, he's a woman.' It's not like I give a shit, but there's people in this town just waiting for anyone to show up a bit different so they can cut them down to size. It wouldn't just be Bernie; I'd have to take the flak as well. I'm his twin brother, for fuck sake. We were swimming in the dark together before we took our first breath. That's solitary confinement with one other person for nine months. Even after we got born, we were inseparable up until the last few years. I suppose with the Da dying, everything changed. Maybe not being kids any more would've changed things anyways.

'I'm only messing,' he says. 'I did it myself this afternoon.'

'What?'

'My hair.' He's swishing his hair, looking at me all serious. 'Did Da ever say anything to you?'

'About you?'

'No, about you.'

I'm thinking what to say back to this when the door opens. The Mater.

'Forget it,' he goes. 'As long as there's people, there's warts, right?'

She comes right into the middle of the room, drops her bags and plants herself right in front of the widescreen. 'Lads,' she says. 'There's light and there's light.'

Bernie starts pointing the remote around her to turn the sound up. But she snatches it out of his hand and flicks the TV onto mute, quick as.

'In the middle of watching something,' he goes.

'You can record it. All good things come to those who wait.' She waits, looking at us. We wait.

'We're waiting,' Bernie goes.

There's something odd about her. She has a new headpiece on, some pointy yoke in goldish material, but it's not that. Her face is different; softer-looking or something. Maybe she had a makeover.

'The light, lads. Only the whole room was lit up, all the pieces on the table floating on light.'

'Where's this?' says Bernie.

'Murt's kitchen.'

'Did he fit the underpress lights?' says Bernie, not really paying attention.

She ignores him and ploughs on. 'The way it was pouring in, you could only really see the outlines; all different shapes and sizes. Like being reborn into the light.'

It's not the first time the Mater has come back from Murt's with her head spinning. Murt always had the shoe repair and key cutting business in the garage at the side of the house, but ever since Janine left, he's been filling up the rooms with more and more shit. Now his whole sitting room and the shoe counter is a kind of huckster shop. He even got a sign made up outside: *Murt's Emporium*. Or d'Emporium to the rest of the world. And he's a yard full of more stuff across the back lane. He's gone mad into house clearances and auctions. You never know what you'd find in his kitchen: a set of silver trays he's polishing up, or some animal hide being cleaned and stretched out. Occasionally he finds something on his travels he thinks'll suit the Mater's collection. Last year it was this auld glass statue he gave to her, of a cockerel. Gabriel Windhawk she named it, uses it to make contact with the other side. Her personal spirit guide.

'Did he have something for your shelves?' I says.

'Frank, you're not at the races,' she goes.

Eventually we get the full story. The whole thing started when Murt and the Mater went to the station. When they get there, Lena's already there with Locky Dunne the station-master. He's helping her move a load of boxes. That right there will tell you exactly what a manipulator Lena is, for I've seen Locky hide down behind his counter and there's wheelchairs nearly having to build their own hoist to get on to the train. Renowned as a man who wouldn't work to warm himself.

Murt wasn't exactly expecting all this gear and Lena wasn't expecting the Mater, and there's a bit of a to-do about it, and the Mater ends up sitting in the back with a wooden crate on her bad knee.

When they got back to Murt's, the stuff that came out of the boxes was statues, a few paintings, abstract, and generally a load of tat. It appears Lena's been living in a therapeutic community for the past six months, doing art and growing lavender; now she's back to try and muscle in on Murt's business.

'What's a therapeutic community?' I goes.

I can see the Mater's not sure herself. 'Well, whatever it is, there's no drink or drugs and they get up very early with the sun. Not so much in the winter. They hibernate. No internet. I don't know do they even use mobile phones. That's why she was out of contact for so long.'

'Christ on a bike,' I says.

'Fucking hell,' Bernie adds.

Lena claims the stuff is genuine spiritual articles. There's a Child of Prague, now sporting a babygro and dreads, apparently the exact same size as the actual Child of Prague.

'Bit on the small side,' Bernie goes.

'They had his body shrunk, for relics,' she shoots back before launching into more descriptions of the pieces.

'Why would they shrink a child's body?' I says when the Mater draws a breath. 'More to the point, how?'

'The same way you shrink anything. Heat, steam.'

She's some talent for making up shite on the hoof. I do start to laugh and I can see Bernie is trying not to. She ignores us.

'They're into upscaling yokes,' the Mater says.

'Descale it?' Bernie, distracted, cos he's snuck the TV sound back on but low.

'Up-something it. Paint it, decorate it,' the Mater goes. 'Like they'd put sequins on a statue of the Blessed Virgin Mary, a feather boa. That kind of thing.'

This is exactly the kind of mad shit I'd expect Lena to come up with. And of course there's a catch. She promised her mates they'd make a few bob offloading this junk through d'Emporium. She wants Murt to clear out his stuff, put their shit in the front window for Wolf Night.

Anyway, the Mater recognised a couple of familiar faces: the roundy belly of Buddha under a Batman costume; then the tall dark one, Martin De Porres, with a tutu and pearls.

'But as soon as he came out of the box my eyes were drawn to him,' she says. 'Barely hanging on the edge of the table he was, with Padre Pio's elbow giving him a puck.'

She couldn't help herself, she says, she reached out and touched the face.

'Murt?'

'No, the arsing statue, you eejit.' Heading out to the hall, she starts singing, '*The first time ever I saw your face.*' She returns with a shopping bag and takes out this lump of wood.

I hunker down to get a closer look. In case you're imagining a movie-star-type bust or a real authentic Jesus-looking statue, that is not the situation here. If there's an ugly tree in the world of statues, this one didn't just hit every branch on the way down, he was cut from the fucking stump. He's literally a piece of wood that is very crudely carved with a face and a tiny body. If you look closely, I'd say the head and body are not all the one. The back of the head looks like it was sawed offa bigger piece and someone has attached a little collar with crow feathers glued on. It's touched up with poster paint, blue around the eyes and two stripes on each cheek, as you'd paint on your faces playing cowboys and Indians.

'What saint is this?' I goes.

'This is well before saints were invented,' she says, looking proud as punch. 'Trust your father to sidestep that one.'

'What's the Da got to do with it?' Bernie goes.

'I never thought I'd fall in love again. With the same man. So lightning can strike twice, boys.'

'Looks like it struck that particular branch a few times,' Bernie goes.

The Mater plants herself in front of Bernie, face like thunder. 'That's no way to speak to your father.'

'What the fuck?'

We all look over at the crude little yoke on the carpet. Fuck me if I don't get this sudden flash it's watching me. Then it's gone.

So the Mater is convinced the Da's spirit is lodging in this little figurine. And typical of Lena: as soon as she copped the Mater really wanted it, she wouldn't let it go. In the end, while Murt and Lena were having a massive blow-up, the Mater tucked it under her oxter and slipped out. She was walking out of that house with it, one way or another.

'So, boys, you can welcome your father home,' she goes. With that, she picks the little statue up, flounces off into the kitchen.

Sixth Son of a Seventh Son

The Mater doesn't come back in to us before she goes upstairs. She must be pissed off with our reaction or maybe she's gone up for a cosy night with her log of love. I don't really know what to think. Bernie says it'll wear off after a few days.

'Did you see anything, in the statue, like?' I ask.

'Course not. Anyways, what harm if it keeps her happy,' he goes, turning the TV up. 'Welcome home, Deadwood Da.'

'What?'

'You know, *the deadwood stage is a-headin' on over the hills,*' he sings.

Trust him to remember the words; that was one of the Da's favourite songs. The Deadwood Da. Good one.

'She misses him, doesn't she?' I goes.

'Yeah. That's love I suppose.'

I notice one of Bernie's trophies lying on the ground behind the couch. Maybe the kid was planning to pinch it.

'That woman who was here today with the ringworm kid,' I says, 'she was very impressed at your medals and stuff.'

'Was she?'

'June. She works with kids. Disturbed kids or if they're in trouble. That kid isn't hers.'

Bernie gives a shrug, starts flicking the channels without settling on anything.

'I'd say it's interesting work,' I goes.

Although I've said hardly nothing, Bernie sits right up in his chair and stares at me. 'Now that you mention it, I did see her, cos I was looking out the window when she left. I noticed her lowlights. Nice cut too.'

I'm not sure what lowlights are; I get my phone out to look it up. But Bernie has the bit between his teeth now.

'So you found her interesting. That's interesting. Maybe she's finding you interesting too, Frank. You know where mutual interest can lead to? If you get the finger out.'

I ignore him, scrolling through loads of images of hair, very fake-looking compared to June's.

'What about Lena?' I says to change the subject. 'Sounds like she's arrived back with a bang.'

'I'm surprised. Word on the street is she assaulted some fellah at that addiction place. The farm, over near Tullow. That's why she had to leg it to the arse end of nowhere.'

'What? Where'd you hear that?'

'Dunno. Just talk.'

We watch a reality thing for a few minutes, about one lad and ten women on a desert island. Crap, until this one girl steals the food, climbs up a tree and spies on the others while she's stuffing her face. She's class. It's not that late but we're both yawning, wrecked after last night. He heads up and I follow him soon after.

Lying in my bed – my room is sandwiched between Bernie's and the Mater's – I can hear the two of them: her with her call-in shows, shouting out at the radio; him listening to his music and singing away. He must be wearing earphones; in fairness he can sing better than that. Then I recognise the song, *Float On*; he's belting it out. Thinking of us down at the running track, pumping ourselves up with that tune when we were younger, and look where things have got to now.

I throw a shoe against the wall. 'Shut up.'

'Fuck off.'

I throw a deodorant at the other wall. 'Ma, take a pill.'

Even when they quiet down, I can't get to sleep, though. Bernie's done a number on me. Typical him, messing with my head. It keeps nagging at me; what if my gift is coming to a standstill because of Bernie's situation?

The last thing I need creeping into my head is the doubt. When some auld one rocks up to the house with their eczema or knee pain or whatever, I need to believe in the cure before they ever do. That's why the Mater is getting to be so successful. She is one hundred per cent, no taking the piss, convinced of her ability to communicate with the other side. I see it even when she's chatting to her collection on the shelves. Always cracking jokes with these tiny glass animals, flirting with the robin in the top hat, discussing clothes with the octopus with diamond eyes. Then her voice goes nearly shy talking to the little abacus. She says it has great intelligence, the brain of a Chinese philosopher. Sometimes she's so convincing, I nearly think I hear them talk back. Nothing's simple around this house. My mind is fair racing at this stage. It's the one thing the Da always warned me against, overthinking.

'You think too much, Frank, and it's not your strong suit,' he'd say to me. 'It's all in the doing of it. Don't think, just do it.'

Ever since he's gone, I see the Nike swoosh everywhere and *Just Do It*. All good and fine if you're Ronaldo; bit different if you're me.

I want to go to sleep but I'm quare thirsty and the mouth's as dry as a sponge. I decide to head downstairs, brew a pot, maybe do a bit of toast. As I'm passing the Mater's room, the door is open and I catch a glimpse of the statue sitting on the floor facing out at me. I wouldn't mind having a good look at it, by myself. She doesn't even stir when I go in and lift it.

Waiting for the kettle to boil, I prop it up on the draining board. Whatever way the light catches the contours of the wood, the eyes are looking dead straight at me.

The Mater said look into the eyes and she's right. Bernie said it's to do with the distance between the eyes and the nose, some scientific thing about we're drawn to look at eyes and mouths and if you stretch the eyes out to the side like this carving, they make you a bit a dizzy. Especially if the nose is lower than it should be. You see it in the odd human face. I have to say he might be on to something. Like Evan who works behind the bar in Squire Maguire's is weird looking but you can't stop looking at him as well. Angela McCann at the checkout in Tesco's, she's ugly as all fucking get out but when she says, 'Do you have a Clubcard?', even if you only catch her eye for a minute, you kind of can't stop. It's not too bad if you're only looking at half her face but once she swivels around to take your cash and the two eyes are facing you, well. First you think you can't see the two together, they're so far apart and her nose is after taking a hike south, but then the whole thing pulls you in like a weasel circling a rabbit and you'd nearly give her a twenty instead of a ten.

Mug of tea in one hand, I lift the statue in the other and carry him to the table. I know it's mad but there's no one there to take the piss out of me.

'How's it going, Deadwood Da?'

I start by telling him about how things have been; Mossy leaving and the Mater being down in herself for that first year, not making any effort to go out until Murt got her sorted with the job in Morrissey's.

He's staring at me like this is all old news. Between the tea and the chat, it's relaxing. The Mater's right; there's something about this yoke would definitely put you in mind of the Da. I shut up talking while I have a root around the presses for a bit of chocolate. When I sit back down, he looks at me and I get this feeling he's trying to tell me something.

'Is it about the gift, Da? Do you want to tell me something about being a seventh son?'

Nothing back.

I don't know why but I start telling him about Bernie. The stuff he was going on with in the hospital and afterwards. 'Thing is, Da, let's say Bernie is some class of a female inside himself, that probably cast a shadow over me, even if I didn't know it. No wonder I'm stuck on warts and ringworm.'

As soon as I've said it out loud, I feel like I'm ratting on Bernie. Would I say that to the Da if he was really here, sitting across from me at this table? Probably not.

'Sometimes I used to be wondering if you had any doubts about me when you were here, you know, before. And it's stuck with me; how you never got a chance to say straight out you believed in me.'

Why does he need to know all this now? He died not knowing, thinking he had seven sons. Thinking I was his seventh and the gift got passed on to me, the way it was meant to. That's what really matters. What he believed, what I believe. Not what Bernie has to say about anything.

So I start telling him about today, June and the kid and the warts. I end up more describing June: how she carries herself, a bit standoffish but like she might be stopping herself laughing. Hopefully not at me. I'd say she's a good laugh. I know he can't move his face but there's something more alert now in the way the Deadwood is facing across to me.

'Thing is, Da, I wish I could ask her out. I haven't done too well on that front so far. I'm up for shifting, same as any fellah, but it starts to get in on me, that I'm under a certain obligation to carry on the family tradition and all that, produce seven sons. Every time I get going with a young one, the thought'll come into my head and it wrecks the buzz totally. Like fucking Rainman, I start calculating how many years it'll take us to have seven kids, ideally seven boys in a row. And if I had baby girls instead of fellahs, unless we had twins or triplets. Up to me oxters in nappies and shite and what would that cost? What if we tried using the cloth ones from the old days? Not for to be hippies or anything, but to save a few bob, would she go for it? Doing the figures in my head trying to make sure I'd have a sound case to put forward.

'At that stage, even though I wouldn't have said nothing out loud, they seem to pick it up offa me, the fact I don't have the clutch fully engaged. I know I think too much but when you stop for a sup and think, "She'd have to produce seven kids," Jesus, you do take a hard look at a girl. Sometimes trying to get a bit of kip at night, figures start floating in front of my eyes. I see them, little baldy-heads in nappies riding on the back of woolly sheep, bronco-style, clearing the gate between one field and the next. Presume that was never an issue for you?'

He was always laughing at me through his eyes and fuck me if this tarted-up fire log isn't doing the same.

Love in a Home

You'll be welcome wherever you roam!
You can tell when there's love in a home!

It can be nice here in the kitchen perched up on the table when the rest have gone to bed. As the song goes, a table and chair have their own way of smiling and asking you sit down, stay a while. I never noticed much before the way the light does come in over the sink when the moon is up. Every object takes on its own particular dimension then, clothed in a white shroud. The sugar bowl and the jug and the teaspoon on the counter, they look like a set when the light draws them together. The draining board, a silvery ice rink with a few upturned mugs stranded, waiting for the lift at breakfast and the next hot drop of tea. Some quare yokes are lying around: a ball of string and tweezers. They do look right ominous, out of place, the moonlight sharpening the edges.

It can darken too as sudden as anything, clouds passing over, blotting out the scene. Obliterating the specificity of the situation. Another word I never used before, specificity. But I'm not afraid of anything now. I was always known as a brave man, physically and mentally: on the roads, on the pitch, in any company. But like many a man, I carried my limits inside of me. A word like that, specificity, I'd've never had the courage to throw it into a conversation lightly. Now I seem to be expanding in all directions. Specificity; a flake of skin falling off the hide of language. Nothing to me now; I'll give it a run out, once at least.

When you're just an object, in my case a block of wood, the elements play on you in a way they couldn't when you were alive, full of pumping lungs and pulsing veins. Take the dawning of the day; first light rising up and up til it's flooding in the window. When I was alive, up early on a bright morning, I'd say, 'It's a beauty. Come on, up and out, lads. A day for hanging out the washing, Mater.' But I'd hardly take a minute to really let the light play across me, bathe me the way it does now. I'm awash day and night with light and darkness, confined to my little wooden barracks. Same with noises: the creaking of the floorboards, the fridge humming and sighing behind me, an occasional rustling outside the back door as a night hunter, cat, maybe fox, passes by. At the mercy of it all and a merciful thing, this life after death.

I'll give it a lash, describing my current situation, though the whole of it is beyond my reckoning. I've acquired no particular insight into the nature of the spiritual world since my demise, none beyond what you might gather any day you draw a breath and realise it at the very self-same time. But, in the most lovely way, that doesn't matter to me in the slightest. If I've any advice to offer from the great beyond it's this: you'll welcome what life throws into your lap all the more if you've no expectation of understanding it.

For myself, I'm ensconced in a piece of wood currently touted as some kind of artsy statue. But prior to this, the self-same statue was propping up the leg of a couch in a bedsit in Castlebar. I'm more than happy to have progressed from that. Considering the many artefacts lying around, I could have ended up in a china teapot or a deckchair. So to have some class of a face for people to look at is quare good luck. Consequently, they're all talking to me and treating me with exceptional care.

That song, you know the one about tying the yellow ribbon on the old oak tree, never made me feel much of anything, more a singalong kind of tune. But I've a different take on it now because it's my truth too: *I'm comin' home, I've done my time.* Wondering does anyone remember you or even care? Though it occurs to me maybe I'm only starting my time now.

Now I've got to know what is and isn't mine. The family is still coming through for me; the Mater picked me out of the line-up of likely lads sitting on Murt's table. Now Frank's got up in the middle of the night to come down and pour his heart out to me. He's all tangled up in hisself as per usual. Even now, I can hear him back in his bed, twisting and turning like a dog with fleas.

Back to my own situation, I'm not the first occupant of this particular log. Certain yokes, as I have now ascertained, cycle the spirits home. A sort of carriage disconnected from the engine, shunted into a siding before the last push for the end of the line. I'm not referring to Padre Pio's gloves or a splinter from the auld crown. Quare ordinary yokes'll do the job. I gather man-made materials - for example, plastic toys, batteries - do not have the correct affinity to house a human spirit, even short-term. So if you've any fear of dimensions beyond what you can see, you'd be as well to build your house on top of a landfill, for there's not much shifting there, seen or unseen. Though, even as I'm talking it out, there's probably a breed of earthworm or cockroach that can digest auld plastic and shit it back out as something better. Once that comes to pass, I'd say you could end up being rehoused, post-passing, in any kind of receptacle. All that's required is something that fits into the turn of seasons, beginnings and ends, to make it fit for purpose.

Anyway, enough about the wooden shell I'm occupying. I sense time drawing in around me, that I won't be here long. No more than a story coming to its conclusion. There's a satisfying certainty about an end, especially after the bullet dodged, an arrow sidestepped, death defied. You succumb to it eventually. I had a cousin near Myshall and his face contorted for years with the palsy. But as the final breath escaped him, a sereneness took over his long-boned features, like a melancholic greyhound.

So, things are stirring around the old home fires. Only embers, but with the gentle breath of enquiry from my son Frank, they are to be reignited. From where I'm sitting you see things clearer. Take Bernie, for example. Boy girl man woman, like the finest whiskey, drain it from a jam jar; it won't affect the taste. A decent soul and, whatever way life pans out, Bernie'll find love. For it was forever spilling out of that child.

Frank, however. Setting my auld wooden noggin on the kitchen table, looking at me as hard as if I was still alive and he's the serious little *gasún*, trying to work out how the cogs turn inside my skull. Trying to figure out the magic, beyond the healing, the whole magic of just being. Let it be, let it be. Letting it be, that's the struggle for poor Frank. What I contributed to his unease, I can't say; all I wanted was that he'd be free to be himself. Who that self turned out to be and whatever it carried – gifts or talents or weaknesses – was all of one to me. I was determined that'd be the gift I'd pass on to him, a love for who he was, not what he could do.

You're dead right, Mr C.:

You'll be welcome wherever you roam!
You can tell when there's love in a home!

What's the Key?

Hate it first thing in the morning when you're trying to get out the door for work and you can't find your shit, your keys and all that. The Deadwood Da is on the table watching me. Which doesn't help when you're under pressure. I throw back a cup of tea, lob the cornflakes bowl into the sink.

'Any idea where me keys are, Da?' No joy. I may get a new set cut. I go up to Bernie's room and give a rap on the door. 'Gis a loan of your key, Bernie.' But no answer.

I'm grabbing a chocolate bar from the press when the Mater comes down. She looks worn out.

'Off to work, son?'

'Yeah. Although it's dead slow. He had us cleaning out sheds yesterday. At least it's Friday.'

She pours herself a cup of tea, then moves the Deadwood over beside her.

'What time you in?' I ask.

'Not til eleven. I want to make sure Bernie's up. He's to get a script from Dr Clarke.'

'I've lost my keys again. Tell him I'm taking his bike. Mine's flat.'

I'm looking for my wallet in the pile of jackets on the chair so I'm not fully tuned in to her, but she's going on about people and she might even make a complaint to the guards.

'About what?'

'Those lads throwing stuff at Bernie, that pushed him to the edge. Even if he can't remember exactly what happened afterwards.'

I should let it go right there. I mean we're all tired after the session in the hospital and the Mater turning soft on a bit of wood. But I can't. 'He can be his own worst enemy,' I says.

She's staring into her mug of tea. No reaction.

'Maybe he should look at, I don't know, a change of scene or something.'

'Bernie needs the support of his family, first and foremost.'

'For what?'

'He's having a crisis of some sort between dropping out of college and his form is off. The doctor has him on some class of anti-depressants, Frank. The same thing they put Olivia Byrne on; she couldn't even work the remote control. She told me she was stuck watching some heavy metal channel all day. Couldn't hardly get off the couch to switch it off.'

'All this has an effect on other people, too. Chances are I'd have a better run at developing my gift if there was bit more stability, or something, around me.'

Nothing back from the Mater.

'I'm worried for your sake more than anyone's,' I goes. 'You could do without all this shit.'

If she only knew the half of what's coming down the line with Bernie.

She gets up, looks at herself in the microwave door to put these big earrings in. 'Aren't you doing alright at the mill?' She starts to tidy up the table, putting a few dishes into the sink. 'You're good with your hands.'

I've no intention of spending the rest of my life there, feeding the hungry maw of a woodchipper, hands splintered, driving a forklift from one end of the yard and back. Going out the back door I have a last go. 'This isn't the right place for Bernie. He'd be happier in a city. If the Da was around, I think he'd say the same.'

She's some cool customer. She has this way of inhaling, as if the air is distilled in her nose before it reaches the lungs. She does her long sniffing thing a couple of times. 'You don't worry one bit about me. If he had anything to say,' she goes, giving a nod to the Deadwood, 'he'd say the only thing needs fixing around here is your attitude.'

It sounds ridiculous but there's something about that auld lump of wood that draws you to look at it, as if it's partaking in the conversation. Both the Mater and I turn our heads in that direction at the exact same time. Not that the Deadwood is one bit like the Da, who had a great head of wavy hair, black as anything and a grey lick going through it. His nose was kind of wide; the nose on this is ugly out. And yet there's a solidness to the wooden face that'd remind you of the Da somehow.

'Maybe we're looking at the end of the line,' she goes, talking more to the Deadwood than me.

'What d'ya mean?'

'I don't know did it ever show up this late in past generations. The gift, Frank.'

That's a low blow; she's still holding it against me for Bernie ending up in hospital. The Da always said that confidence was half of the cure anyways. Maybe if people around here showed a bit more confidence in me, that'd be some help.

'Be nice if I'd someone around who actually knows something about the gift. I'm left trying to carry this whole thing on my own.'

'Well, if you feel I've nothing to offer, despite living with your father for forty-odd years, talk to your uncle Murt,' she huffs. 'He's a Whelan through and through.'

With that she's gone out to the hall to get her handbag.

We're not due to finish work til five, but come lunchtime the boss, Dennis, tells me, Hopper and Hennessey to knock off early. Fair enough, there's not much going on.

When I get home, the Mater's still at work and Bernie must be gone out; I can't get in. I check for the spare key under her wishing-well planter but I must've lost that one too. I text the Mater in case there's another spare around. She says come down to Morrissey's and get hers.

Richie Morrissey is outside the supermarket, patrolling the empty car park. 'How ya, Frank.'

'Alright, Richie.'

Ever since the council put in parking meters, people have been using Morrissey's as the best place in town for free parking. Richie's obsessed by it: noting down licence plates of people coming in; writing letters to the politicians; trying to get the council to put up a barrier. Turns out now Kehoe's Cleaners next door might have a legal claim over a section of the car park. They've started to leave their laundry vans there; it's heading for all-out warfare.

'Did you hear about—' Richie starts, then he's gone like a flash as a white van pulls in at the far end.

Inside, the Mater is restocking the baked goods section.

They've asked her not to wear the headgear at work, tone down the amulets and crystals, but she's making a stand with the earrings, big red hula-hoops.

'You're addicted to these maple pecan slices,' she says. 'Third time this week. Would you not have some fruit? Blueberries is on special.'

'Not here for that. I told you I need the house keys.'

'You can have them, but only if you take a run over to Murt's directly to get a copy cut.'

'Grand.'

I'd been meaning to ask him about the statue anyways. Maybe I'll pick his brain about the family history, the Bernie situation. She fishes a key ring out of her pocket. It has a little straw figure attached to it. Another new gewgaw.

'Don't lose that. Murt gave it to me. It was dug up with the bog body, at Croghan Hill. They found this little maneen clenched in one hand, a hank of human hair in the other. And a pound of butter.'

'Thousands of years ago and they were weighing butter in pounds and ounces?'

She should stick with the facts. She does okay with the tea leaves, but it'll be her downfall the way she gets carried away with the spirit stuff. She's going grand and then she'll put her own skew on things. I can tell when she's moved over from whoever she's communing with to her own imagination, as plain as crossing a ditch. Unnecessary.

'Well they didn't have a deli counter and a scales,' she goes, 'but it was a significant piece of butter.'

She goes back over to the racks of pastries. I put the key and the straw yoke in my pocket and have a gander up along the shelves.

There's nothing like the smell of fresh baking. I close my eyes and take a deep breath. Maybe I will take a couple of those maple slices, bring one up to Murt. He's a quare sweet tooth, always sucking on a toffee or a lemon drop.

'Frank, would you ever use a tongs like a civilised person?'

'Later.' I head off with the pastries and the keys.

Back out in the car park, Richie is standing at the exit, roaring at a laundry van speeding off. His face is puce and he's shaking his fist. Hidden depths of passion. The Mater's been saying for years he has a fancy woman stashed up the county somewhere. It's hard to believe, such a dry-looking man, always checking shelves and counting boxes and not much interests outside the business. They say you shouldn't judge a book by its cover. Speaking of books, the Mater pointed his woman out to me once at a 'Voices Beyond the Great Divide' session over in Hacketstown.

'That's her, a librarian,' she whispered before the session got started. 'They say she's the only thing keeping the mobile library open.'

Looking at the blonde hair piled up and a low-cut red blouse bursting its buttons with the effort of what it's expected to contain, I could imagine the mountainy lads salivating at the sight of the mobile library van climbing the crest of a distant hill.

'Well, they do say reading broadens the mind,' I said back to her, just as the lights went down.

Cycling over to Murt's, I kind of drift off thinking of the great divide between myself and June. How I'd have to be punching well above my weight to ever go out with someone like her. Though Richie's bit on the side looked well out of his league. Makes you realise how you don't really know what anybody wants. Especially when it comes to feelings. Like what if it had turned out that June did have a fellah and that was her kid? And just say for argument's sake she was interested in me. Would I go for it? It's a matter of bad luck timing in some ways if you meet the right person but in the wrong order. Or worse, what if I was with someone else, had a couple of kids, and I met June and realised we were perfect for each other? You'd like to think you wouldn't make a fucking eejit of yourself. Like Richie Morrissey. Or worse, make a fool out of your wife. But it's one thing to say what's the right thing for a person to do, another thing to find out if you're that person or not.

d'Emporium

When I get to Murt's, he's sitting outside, soaking up the afternoon sun. He's a new table and matching chairs with fancy metal legs set up on the footpath.

'How's it going, Murt?'

'Frank, I haven't seen you in an age. All good here. And yourself?'

'Not bad.' I hand him the key and the bag of pastries. 'I need keys cut again.'

'Was expecting you over last week. Did you get my message about the washstands?'

'Forgot.'

'They'll go down a bomb once they're stripped and varnished.'

Of all the brothers, Murt was closest to the Da. He's good craic, though he's seventy-five if he's a day. I don't know why, but he always has time for me. Before I got work up at the mill, I was helping him out: house clearances, going to a few auctions, the car boot sales too.

'Coffee, Frank?'

'Lena around?'

Hope she's not. The way she turns her head to one side when she's talking to me, as if I'm some kind of a mongrel. Cocka-fucking-poodle yourself.

'No. She's off meeting friends. This group she's got herself into, Mytopia. Seems to have more branches than the GAA. Apparently they've land rented past Ardattin for growing lavender.'

'Go on, so, I'll have a cuppa. Tea, mind.'

Everyone's gone mad for coffee; even some of the lads at work are pushing for a proper coffee machine. But I'm sticking to the tea.

He lifts a tall silver pot off the table, shows me the handle fashioned like a snake, the tiny spout a pair of lips. 'From the Czarina's trousseau. It's possible Rasputin drank his own urine from this very pot.'

'A trousseau?'

'Much good it did him. Would you not try my coffee beans? Venezuelan.'

'No, you're grand; tea bag'll do me. Lyons if you have one.'

I sit back, look at the big trees across the street, oak and beech. Although they've made complete shite of the footpath with their roots, you do get a lovely bit of green light coming through and loads of birds singing. Where Murt lives is on a side street that twists its way down to the river. The buildings are all old, mostly residential, a few shopfronts scattered in between. He's the key cutting and leather work behind a counter, on the right of the door. It's a bit chaotic: shelves of odd shoes and scraps of leather; belts hanging by buckles; handbags stacked up. His machines for keys take up the length of one wall. Recently he's knocked the other wall out into what used to be his living room and extended the garage through. Still a bit rough-looking but that's where he keeps the antiques and second-hand stuff.

'Have a look at these.' He comes out with a mug of tea, indicates a number of objects on the table. Tarnished metal pins and some kind of pliers, all rusty yokes. I pick up a sort of animal horn, greyish-white, about as long as my hand, cut flat at the wide end, all smoothed out.

'Over a thousand years old. Uncovered at one of the first Viking settlements in Ireland.'

'How did it get from there to d'Emporium?'

He nods his head from side to side as if he's in between a yes and a no, although it's not really a yes or no question. 'A few things came my way,' he goes. 'I might hang on to that. I like thinking about some Viking lad, filing it down of a summer day, thinking about whatever they had to be thinking about. Same as us probably: dinner, the family, keeping warm, what's beyond the next hill.'

'Did this come with Lena's stuff?' I ask, putting it back down on the table.

'No, I acquired that meself. Lena and her friends are into more self-expression. Decorating rather than restoring. Top marks for effort.'

'How is she?'

'She's quare exercised about a few of my business matters right now. She'd be better off minding her own health and wellbeing.'

From the shade of Murt's advertising sandwich board, Crystal ambles out, puts her two paws on his knee.

'Miss Madam is ready for her snack.' Before he goes inside, he tears off a big corner of the pastry and hands it to the cat.

She devours it, eyeing me up all the time. She stops at the door, rubs herself up and down against Lucky, the life-sized black Labrador statue. Used to be at the old post office with a sign around his neck: *St Francis's Society for Deaf and Dumb*

Boys. The paint's worn off the top of his head from kids putting coins in the slit in his noggin.

Murt's singing away, some song about Venezuelan coffee and women. While he's puttering about, I start wondering about Venezuela. Not that I could even point it out on a map. Is it near Mexico? It could be right at the bottom of South America. Doesn't matter. It's not like the people there would give a shite if the whole of Carlow was toppled by a hurricane or massacred by a madman. I suppose what matters to you only depends on where your feet are planted.

'If you've a bit of free time coming up,' Murt calls out from inside, 'there's a renovation: school in Killerig. The Currans are doing it. A few nice desks going out in a skip if we're passing. Varnish them up, they'd sell handy enough.'

I know he's been trying to nudge me towards working with him. But I keep putting him off. The mill is okay. I was waiting til I turned eighteen, see if the gift'd get stronger in me. Or I'd find one particular ailment that was mine, like eyes or something. That'd establish me. Maybe it's not going to be til I'm twenty-one. Maybe it's not on the cards at all with all the shenanigans in our family. To shake off the doubts I try to imagine myself in Venezuela. Be a lot hotter than here and beyond that . . . no, I can't think what it'd be like. Or living in the North Pole, that's easier. There'd be an igloo; Bernie'd be preening himself in one corner, the Mater in her snowshoes, heading over to Cissy Agar's igloo for the latest gossip. Hopper'd be revving up outside, trying to get me to go snowplough racing or some such messing. What if June was there? Probably not enough fucked-up kids to be minding so she might be a flying doctor, if they have them up there. And me? I can't think of nothing for me. Though I like the whiteness of it all. I'd like that.

There's a whisper from behind me. Murt. 'Don't look around. What he's up to?'

What the fuck. I hadn't noticed but behind a tree opposite is a fellah, hat pulled down over his face. When he notices me watching him, he shifts around a bit.

'Is it Old Man Qualter?'

'Him, alright.'

Everyone knows Ronan Qualter from lying down in the cathedral, squirming his way up the middle aisle to the altar. He's there seven days a week before he goes to work, flat out, face to the floor. Had to be barred from communions and confirmations.

'Is he coming over here?'

'Sure is,' I says.

'Fuck him. Bring in that coffee pot and the brooches.'

As soon as your man sees me move, he picks up his step. I gather up the stuff and bring it in to the shop.

Qualter steps in.

Murt straightens himself, pushes his hair back, redoes his ponytail slowly. 'Looking to get some shoes stretched, Ronan? Though I hear Shaws have lovely sandals in for the summer. The children's section.'

This seems to have hit the mark; Qualter reddens immediately. I look at his feet and, sure enough, they're tiny. How he doesn't overbalance on them is a miracle for they're barely feet at all, more like paws.

'That advertising board outside. Signage. You need planning permission for that,' Qualter goes, sticking his chin out at Murt. 'This is a residential area. There's wheelchairs, prams.'

'Well,' says Murt. 'Eileen McCabe from number 16 did a test run on her motorised wheelchair. She's no problem traversing the footpath.'

'Another complaint into the council, you'll be in trouble.' He's getting rightly worked up. 'This is a change of usage, and you can't deny it.'

Murt says nothing.

Before your man turns to go, he drops an envelope on the counter. 'A copy of my letter to Mr Lowry, county engineer.'

'What?'

Then Qualter stands at the front door, taps his fist on Lucky's head. 'Have you a licence?'

'To what end?' says Murt.

'You have to have a licence if you're collecting for charity.'

'Licence, me arse,' Murt says.

I burst out laughing at the two of them and Qualter scuttles off.

Murt slugs back his coffee. 'That bastard won't be happy til he's sucked the joy out of Christmas. Come in for a minute.'

'What's all that about?'

He tells me the trouble is Qualter's moved in next door; inherited the house from his aunt Sylvie Kirwan. She liked the odd glass of sherry, or three, in the afternoons and Murt didn't mind either. Your man is convinced Murt fleeced her of some old family heirlooms. And he doesn't like the cut of Murt's jib, in general, says it brings down the tone of the neighbourhood.

'He's trying to get the residents' association all riled up about my business. He has me crucified; in and out to the council complaining.'

Of course, Murt has taken a few liberties in terms of turning the whole ground floor of the house into a business. He reckons the best solution long-term is to renovate his shed in the lane behind and set his equipment up there. 'And I could concentrate more on the antiques. It's a handy little money-spinner, Frank, the keys and shoes.'

When we go into the kitchen, I nearly forget what's just gone down. It's a zoo in there: stuff piled on the table and chairs. The Mater did not do the situation any justice. The first yoke I pick up, they've taken the head of crucified Jesus and put it on a Barbie doll. There's a statue of Mary holding a baby with fake fur all over its body. Feathers and sequins are falling off everything from St Patrick to Padre Pio. Compared to this stuff, the Deadwood Da is looking pretty good.

'Fucking hell. No fear she'll be asked to decorate the crib this year.'

Poor Murt looks a bit lost.

'Are you going to sell this stuff on Wolf Night?' I says.

'We're at a bit of a stalemate. I don't want to discourage her. But she's highly strung. Like her mother.'

He reckons putting these on display will aggravate things, give Qualter more ammo. The keys and shoes are okay, but he doesn't have permission to be running a full-scale antiques business, not to mind a freakshow art gallery.

'There's still some that believe in the crime of blasphemy,' Murt goes.

He says he could apply for planning permission, get the shop and the yard set up proper. He has enough money to do it, but it'd take time. 'I'm not a young man any more. I need to go full legit or jack the whole thing in. Of course, there'd be no point unless I had someone to work with me, take it over eventually.'

'I suppose Lena could run it for you then?'

'She'd never be able for it. You've a good eye for it, though.'

'I don't know anything about business or that.'

'You'd pick it up quick enough.'

He selects a blank key from the rack and secures it in the machine vice. Once it's cut, he hands me the new and old set of keys. 'Did I hear something about Bernie getting into a bit of bother?'

I fill him in on Bernie's trip to A & E.

'He needs to find his groove,' he goes, rolling the antique horn around on his palm, wrapping his fist around it like a dagger. 'Takes a child a while to grow into a skin be times.'

'You don't know the half of what he's growing into,' I says. 'He's all over the shop.'

Murt has a tray of old jewellery on the dresser and he brings it over to the kitchen table. He starts sorting through the pile, picking an odd one out, setting it aside. 'Sounds like he's got under your skin.'

'Well, someone's always left picking up the pieces.'

Murt says that it was Bernie ended up in A & E, not me. No one's holding me responsible for Bernie's wellbeing. Suggests that maybe I should have a think about where things are at for me.

Why is it being put on me as if I'm the problem? I wasn't planning on saying anything to anybody, but it comes out in a rush. I tell him some of the stuff Bernie was saying in the hospital.

He listens, sipping away at his coffee. But he doesn't seem that thrown by the facts of what I'm telling him. 'It's good that Bernie was able to confide in you,' Murt goes, polishing away.

I'm not sure he's getting the full picture: that Bernie is actually talking about physically changing himself, living as a different person. Or the same person but a completely different version in terms of not being a fellah any more.

'How's the Mater expected to cope with this?' I says. 'He could show up anywhere around town. Shops, pubs. Anywhere. Tesco's, Morrissey's, the dole. Not just dressed up. He's planning to change everything. How he looks, his hair. I mean everything.'

'Well, I wouldn't worry too much about her. Your father coped with it,' Murt goes, holding a silver chain with a big green pendant up to the light. 'So I expect she'll manage.'

It takes me a minute to get what he just said. 'The Da?'

He says nothing.

'You think he knew?'

'I know he did. Your father seen every stripe of humanity at one stage or another. Bernie wasn't the first woman got trapped in the wrong body. These things happen.'

'What about the Mater? Does she know?'

He takes his time, placing the necklace into its own little box.

'I don't think so. Billy wanted Bernie to tell her himself when he felt the time was right. I didn't think it was my place to bring it up with her after your father passed. It's Bernie's story to share.'

'What do you think about it?'

'I imagine he has a hard road ahead of him, whatever way he goes about this. So I've no intention of adding to that.'

I can't believe it. So the Da knew all along. Trust him to guess it. Murt's even implying the Da accepted Bernie. When you think about it, of course he would. Bernie who could do no wrong.

I must have a face on me because Murt reaches over, pats my shoulder. 'Your father saw that you had a great talent for getting on with people,' he says. 'He knew you'd good hands. Good heart. That's the main thing.'

This is some quare gunk to get. Cos this means he might've thought I wasn't a real seventh son. Not in the straightforward way he was and his father before him and going back forever. No wonder he was always trying to avoid my questions, fobbing me off when I wanted to stay with him and he was healing people.

'The main thing? Is it? Like that's worth shit.' I've heard enough. I put the key in my pocket and head out the back door.

Instead of going straight home, I go into the yard at the back of his house. Since I was a kid, I loved rooting through it. Stacked up inside the gate is a dining table and chair set I haven't seen before. Nice wood, maybe walnut. More doors and window frames, another ride-on lawnmower. I wouldn't mind having a look at that engine. In the corrugated shed is a whole load of old washstands.

I recognise two massive mirrors from a pub clearing we did last year. I used to think if you got around to sorting the stuff out, you'd make a decent bit of money. Now it all seems a bit shoddy. Broken down. Useless. Stuff that was valuable to someone once and it's ended up in a pile here.

Cycling home down Barrack Street I get held up by a red light and a convoy of young wans and buggies heading to the park. I look across the street and coming out of the old library building is your woman the hippy and some fellah with massive dreads. If that lad was working in the mill, he'd need a hairnet for the beard alone, else he'd be sucked in, chipped, spat out in two seconds flat. So that must be where June works, the youth club place. I watch the two of them pull down a metal shutter over the big window and head on. June appears out a side door, bends down, fits a padlock to the shutter. I'm waiting to see if she looks over. Then I think of me, ordinary Frank Whelan with no talent or gift whatsoever, waving a bit of cloth over the young fellah's leg and taking cash off her for doing it. It's mortifying. I pull in behind a parked van.

When she goes to follow the others, she hops a bit. Leaning up against the wall, she takes her sandal off, shakes it out.

All the way home, I keep thinking about that stone lodged

between her shoe and the sole of her foot. Even a tiny pebble, it's so annoying the way it gives you a little jolt each time you stand on it. Reminding you it's there every time you take a step. You think you can keep going but no, that little yoke is enough to stop you in your tracks. Won't let itself be ignored.

What I've just heard from Murt, it's reminded me of something. Small enough thing but it's grigging me. This one time the Da and Murt did a big cleanout of some auld one's house and he brought home a sports bag full of magazines. First off, I thought they were going to be *Match* or *Shoot*, even *Beanos*. No. It was all these women's magazines. He said they were for the Mater, but he gave Bernie the bag. I looked through a few of them for the problem pages and sex tips. But it was mostly fashion and make-up and shit. After Da died, Bernie was fixated on those magazines. He'd spend hours on his bed poring over the photos. *Vogue* I think was the main one, not that I was allowed near them. It's burning into my head, the Da coming in the back door and me and the Mater and Bernie sitting at the table, all wondering what he had for us, him getting us to guess. Those stupid fucking magazines.

I'm cycling home that fast it's making my eyes sting.

Warts and All

When I come in the back door, I see Bernie's taken over the kitchen again, his stuff spread out across the table. He's looking at himself in a mirror, drawing a black line under his eye with a pencil. He's the last person I want to see right now.

'You missed a bit,' I says.

'Where?' he goes, smacking his lips together, blinking his eyes.

'Shaving. Under your left ear.'

'Fuck off. There's buffalo wings in the fridge. Extremely spicy, though.'

Once he mentions food, I realise I'm hungry. I put a few wings in the microwave and bang on the kettle. When I reach over to get a fork from the draining board, I manage to knock the spoon out of the bag of sugar, catapulting a line of grains across the counter.

'Fuck sake. What's up with you?' he goes. 'You're pacing around. Just sit down would ya. Making me nervous.'

The microwave pings and I take the wings out. The first bite and I scald the roof of my mouth. Then my lips go massive and numb with the spiciness. I'm nearly crying with the pain. Bernie's laughing at me but at least he pushes his glass of milk across the table. Once my mouth and the wings cool off a bit, I get stuck into them again.

'Murt was asking how you were doing.'

'Didn't know you were over at Murt's.' He's busy again with his face, turning his head this way and that way. 'Why're you staring at me?'

'After you being at the hospital and all, he was hoping you were okay.'

'Did you tell him I'm grand? Still have my good looks, that's the main thing.'

'He was talking about the Da.'

'What about him?' He's packing all his stuff away. There was messages coming in on his phone the whole time and now he starts tapping and typing away.

'The Da talked to Murt about you.'

'What about me? When?' He's still looking at the screen. But I can tell he's paying attention now by how his body is gone still and he's just scrolling up and down the screen.

'Why didn't you tell me the Da knew? The other night when you were talking about it all.'

He just shrugs, closes up his mirror.

'He must have been gutted when he found out,' I goes. 'Did he catch you dressed up or something?'

'Fuck sake, Frank. No, I told him.'

'What?' I can't believe it. We were only kids when the Da died. Could Bernie have been thinking like this back then?

'I told him. He got it. Said it was fine by him.'

'He said that? Fine by him? If you were his daughter not his son?'

'Not in so many words. But pretty much, yeah.'

I can't swallow the food in my mouth. I try make my throat suck it down but it's stuck. I go over to the bin and spit a gobful out. I'm trying to catch my breath.

'You alright, Frank?'

'A chicken bone. What did he say?'

'I was crying a bit and I think he might have cried for a minute. Gave me a hug.' Bernie's staring down at his hands. 'The thing he said was he wanted me to have happiness in my life, whatever it took. Cos I brought them happiness.'

'What did the Mater say?'

Silence from Bernie now. I push it a bit before he'll admit it; she still doesn't know. Says that it's complicated. He starts to explain but I say forget about it. Not interested. I dump the rest of the wings in the bin and rinse off the plate. Before I go out of the kitchen I take a good look at him. He's busy clipping his nails into a saucer. It's weird, right, but I have this moment where I see him not as my twin, but as this completely separate person. Of course, everyone has their own secrets and shit, but I see he has this special way of taking up space in the world like he owns it. Doesn't ask anything of anyone else, just goes his own way. Probably the fact the Da knew gave him that. Not that I ever thought him being gay made him unhappy or less than me. But I suppose I thought people seen him as the odd one and me as normal. Normal, except I was going to inherit this gift thing that made me special, stronger. Turns out he's perfectly grand with who he is and now I'm left with nothing. And the Da knew it all along. That's the worst part.

It's a quiet enough weekend, especially since the Mater is still fair put out with what happened to Bernie in town. For some reason she's still blaming it on me, for not going home with him. At least she's over at Cissy's mostly, stitching up the costumes; keeps her out of my hair.

Hopper's on to me Saturday, trying to get me to go out, but I could do with a weekend on the down-low. I need to get a bit of cash together cos I'm dead broke after the session the other night.

The other thing is I want to spend a bit of time around the Deadwood. The Mater doesn't seem to be as taken up with him as the first few days, so he's turning up all over the house, propped up on the kitchen table or the floor of the front room. Thing is, I've started getting some weird vibes whenever I pass him. I thought I heard his voice once or twice and when I turn around, I catch him looking directly back at me.

Although I don't know exactly what I feel about him now. The way he said nothing about Bernie and how he treated me as regards the healing. Knowing he knew is making me feel different about everything: myself, our family, stuff I thought was nailed-down solid facts.

Tuesday evening this woman rings, leaves a voicemail asking about the healing for her father in Tinahely who's had the cataracts done. He's nearly blind again and won't go back to the doctor. I hear the Mater ring her back, tell her the Da has passed on. She doesn't even mention me, recommends Marty Duffy in Bagenalstown.

'Why didn't you tell them to come over to me?' I ask her when we're sitting down for our tea.

'Who?' she goes.

'You know who. Your woman on the phone.'

'Eyes are very tricky. Even your father'd tell you.'

'Aye, aye,' Bernie goes, nodding at the Deadwood.

The way the Mater bypassed me without even asking, and

she's done the same before. She doesn't believe in me. The Da must have told her I didn't have it. Even if he didn't tell her why. Everyone knew it before me. My brain keeps twisting round, like a screw getting tighter each time it turns. Tightening around this one fact: it's over for me, the whole seventh son thing.

'Speaking of eyes,' the Mater goes. 'Some commotion today.'

A whole display of chocolate chip cookies got knocked over in Morrissey's by Peadar Lacey's new guide dog. The Mater's share, forty packets, are in a box on the front porch. In date and all. So we can have broken biscuits for breakfast, dinner and tea if we like.

She's fair put out on Peadar's behalf. 'I said to him when I was cleaning it up, what make of dog is that at all? He says to me, "It's a Labrador." It's no more a Labrador than I am. Couldn't guide its nose to its arse.'

'That's a cruel trick to play on a blind man,' goes Bernie, throwing a big handful of chocolate chip crumbs into his gob.

After tea on Wednesday, Eithne Agar comes in with her warts. The whole family were regulars when the Da was alive, in and out to our house with aches and pains and whathaveya. Eithne is the only one still comes to me.

She usually waits til the hand is fair covered, but there's barely three or four on the left finger and two on the right palm. Small enough yokes too.

'You've barely showing there at all, Eithne,' I goes.

'I know,' she says. 'It was grand when I was working in Conlon's, just taking orders over the phone. But I started in Tynan's Butchers last week, in the cash booth. Collie Tynan says get these sorted cos it puts the customers off.'

'Fair enough.'

He told her to go get them frozen off but she said she'd prefer to go natural. I feel a bit of a fraud. She'd probably have as much luck with these if she rubbed a pork chop over them. But she's here and it's not like she pays, so she won't be out of pocket one way or another.

'I'll have a go anyways.'

She chats on about the job and stuff around town. I don't have much to say. Quicker this is over, the better.

'How's Bernie?' she asks on her way out.

'Alright.'

I forgot Eithne took Bernie to her debs. For a fellah who was gay and now is going down this woman route, he got through a fair few girls. Has he even given a minute's thought to where's it going to leave them if he decides to change?

'Tell him I was asking for him,' she says.

'Will do.'

'When're they off to London?'

'Who?'

'Thought I heard your mother saying something to my mother about a trip,' she goes, turning puce. 'Anyways, see you later.'

'See ya.'

London my hole. He can hardly afford a bus ticket to Tullow. He's probably upstairs listening.

I shout up, 'Bernie, your girlfriend says hello.'

No answer. I get a Coke from the fridge. The Deadwood is on the window ledge catching a big ray of the sun blasting through the window. Lovely evening out, the kind where the Da'd be pottering around the back garden digging his veg or fixing something, even after putting in a full day on the roads. Why not? I stick him under my arm and bring him with me to the gazebo. Me and Hopper built that gazebo for the Mater last year and she does enjoy sitting out there of an evening. It was part of our plan – well, Hopper's plan really – to get leftover wood from the mill and build garden furniture. Make a bit of extra cash. Forget why exactly we gave it up.

We're soaking up the heat out there, me and the Deadwood. I start telling him about Eithne. He was always mad about her, loved when she'd come over with Cissy. Maybe cos he didn't have a daughter.

'Although that's not as black and white as it seems, is it, Da? Not according to Bernie. And Murt. When exactly did you know about Bernie? He says you'd already guessed before he told you. So if you knew that, you must've had your doubts about me from the get-go. Remember when I was small, I thought I could make a bruise disappear if I touched it, like a puddle drying up. Or waving my hand over Bernie's cut knee, trying to close it up. The look you'd be giving me. It's mad, cos today with Eithne I acted the same as usual. Wasn't any different from before. Maybe cos I've never felt anything in the first place. I was only ever copying what I saw you doing. But I never knew what was going on inside your head.'

The sun is making me squint, so I shut my eyes for a minute. 'Why didn't you say anything to me? Is that why you made your way back? To tell me in person the jig is up?'

I must've dozed off because a roar from the kitchen wakes me up. I run back. The Mater.

'What the fuck?'

'He's gone,' she says. She sinks into a chair. 'That malicious bowsie Lena. I'll swing for her.'

'Fuck sake, I thought someone attacked ya. He's down with me.'

She leps up, her eyes blazing at me. 'What are you doing with him out there? Carving him into bits?'

She doesn't have one bit of trust in me. Fuck her. She'd never think this ill of the other fucking eejits. I'm the runt. The lads in Australia, pictures on Facebook every day practically, holidays in Bali and bungee jumping in New Zealand and Senan's motorbikes and still they can't make it home for Christmas, when all the Mater wants is to see them again. Now Bernie has to crawl up on the fucking cross. I'm left to take the brunt of it.

I get the Deadwood Da. Put him slap bang in the middle of the kitchen table. Say nothing, go out into the garden to cool off. The Mater follows out with a white Magnum for me and a Cornetto for herself.

'I didn't mean to hurt you, son, but I don't know if I'm coming or going. When I first saw that statue I thought, sure as I live and die, your father's returned. Now I think I've lost it again. I don't know am I going a bit doolally.'

'G'wan. Gis the Magnum before it melts.'

She sits in beside me in the gazebo. Because the legs ended up a bit uneven, we're both a bit squashed into one corner. Then she lands it; Eithne was right, they are going to London, herself and Bernie, for a few days.

'What? He's going to London?' I says. 'He can't even afford to pay for a round.'

'Don't be like that.'

'When's this all happening?'

'Not until Sunday. Only for a few nights.'

'This is un-fucking-believable. Ye've been planning this behind my back.'

'Didn't you say he could do with a change of scene?' she goes. 'For his mental health.'

'He's not handing a penny up to you. And what about me?'

'Look, I haven't seen your aunty Eileen for years. Her Anthony is nearly fully confined to a wheelchair so they're not coming home anytime soon. Anyways, I think yourself and Bernie could do with a break from each other. Ye were the best of friends growing up. Now—'

I get up before she finishes whatever she was going to say. She was barely speaking to her sister Eileen a few years back. I bite off the end of the ice-cream and leave her there.

When I pass through the kitchen, I'm drawn to look at Deadwood. It's quare difficult to describe what it is about him, but he can hold your gaze as steady as anything.

'Things have got totally unbalanced since you're gone, Da. Remember the way this house used to be heaving with the lads here, and people knocking in for the cure. Now the Mater and Bernie is all cosying up and I'm being cut loose. I could just go any which way and who'd give a shit one way or the other?'

Talking to him steadies my head a bit. That's what the Da used to do. He'd say himself that was a major part of the cure, helping people get a grip on themselves, disease and all, even if it wasn't going to go away. Get a grip on their whole selves and hold onto a bit inside. I know cos he done it for me too.

'It's not on, Da,' I goes.

I nearly hear his voice saying back to me, 'Let it settle, son. Let it go.'

The World of Work

I'm glad there's no one except me up early Thursday morning. Last night I stayed up in my room so I didn't have to listen to Bernie and the Mater making their travel plans behind my back.

I grab a quick slice of toast and marmalade and head to work. When I get there it's mad busy for a change. I end up on the forklift moving a load of tiling battens to the old warehouse. Around half nine I park up behind the sheds for a smoke. Back there you've only the track between you and the Barrow. Nice to be sitting high up; you get a good view downriver, where the water widens out and splits in two.

A couple of coots appear, bobbing along, then one disappears under the surface, pops back up with a gulp further on. Probably doesn't even know he's a coot. No clue regarding the fact he's the plainest-looking bird. Nice work, floating along, getting your grub as you go. No waiting for a pay cheque or thinking about the future. Birds never really have to work. Nor any animal. Except I suppose sheepdogs. Probably horses. I start thinking of animal jobs, elephants in India I seen on

TV dragging tree trunks. Lot of working animals, not to mind insects: worker bees and ants. Probably other insects organising themselves into work crews too. A hooter goes off in the sheds; breaks the grip of categorising animal jobs in my head.

Driving across the yard I'm thinking of the Da, working for the council all his life, laying roads, trimming the hedgerows, filling in potholes. Knew every highway and byway backwards. He loved it, said he did anyways. Though now I've a better idea how work does go hard on you, I'm not so sure it was as easy as he made out.

He always had a couple of nixers on the go, himself and the lads. He'd have a house to drop into, some visitation he'd promised; the whole crew'd go along. Dinky Driscoll, his best mate, was mad into his fishing. If they were near a river, they'd drop him off with his gear. The Da'd often come home, throw a sack of perch in the sink. He'd barely have time to wash his hands and there'd be someone waiting in the hall with their ailments. At times it'd be dead obvious what was wrong with them, yellow pallor or a rash, but others'd look same as you or me.

Never imagined I'd be working a job like this. When you have a gift, it's like having a musical talent, a great voice. Some only use it for their own entertainment, singing in the pub or at family parties, then others make a living out of it, going on TV shows and talent competitions. The Da seemed happy with his job in the council, just putting his talent for healing to the service of others. After he went, the idea grew in me that, once the gift showed itself, I'd make it all my life and livelihood. In a weird way, it'd make me closer to the Da. Not that I was trying to bring him back or nothing. I was just waiting for something to happen that would turn things from shit back to good again.

The Mater was fair shook when the Da went. But she pulled herself together, got a job. She'd say a person needs work, not just for the money. That's her, in her pink pinny, under fluorescent lights all day. Her little acts of rebellion, jangling her loop-de-loop earrings, sneaking me out the odd croissant or bag of chicken wings. She says she likes working in Morrissey's. I suppose it's paying for herself and Bernie's jaunt over to London. Every time I think about that, it grigs me again.

I'm sitting there when Hennessey comes around the corner. 'You'd better get your arse into gear. The boss's wondering where the fuck you are.'

When I go over to the office, Dennis pops his head out. 'The very man. Busy now. Come back over at one, will ya?'

'Alright.'

When he sticks his head back in, I ask Janice behind the desk what's up, but she shrugs.

Quarter to eleven, I knock off for break and join Hopper in the canteen. We have a few hands of whist with the lads, then I say about the meeting with Dennis.

'He wants to see me as well,' Hopper goes. 'Janice came over to tell me, the scarf wrapped across her face like a terrorist. She's paranoid about the dust.'

'Whatcha think it is?'

Hopper shrugs. 'Probably health and safety shite. Whatever it is, bring a few matchsticks to prop your eyes open. You know the way he drones on, bore the head off a dead bee.' Then he drops the voice to tell me he's got some important info on my love interest.

'What're you on about?' I hadn't said hardly nothing to him about June.

'You have to admit, when love hits, it hits,' he goes. 'You said she worked in that youth club, right? You know Simon Connolly?'

'Which one is he?'

'Connolly's Cabs. Two years ahead of us in school, the real white hair. Barely on the right side of albino.'

'Oh yeah. Why?'

Turns out your man Connolly's driving a minibus for the place where June works. She's from Waterford originally, went to college there. She shares a house in Avondale Green with two teachers. Enjoys the odd bottle of vino with the girls in Sami's Bistro and goes home most weekends because, get this, he goes, 'She's the goalie for her local camogie team.'

'Probably going out with some GAA head in Waterford, so.'

'No,' he goes, raising his pint. 'Single apparently.'

I'm not surprised she's a goalie. I can imagine her concentrating something fierce, roaring at her backs to cop the fuck on. You'd want someone as cool-headed as her in goal. Dangerous though, hurling. I start thinking about some young wan giving the sliotar a right belt with a hurl; the impact of the ash on the lump of leather and cork; then the acceleration – what, maybe a hundred miles an hour – coming straight at her face. I know they have the head gear and everything but how fast can the eye see and–

'Earth to Frank, come in.' Hopper gives me a knuckle on the side of the head. 'You're gone *Full Metal Jacket*. I know by the way your jaw is hanging.'

I was never much into sports. Thinking back to the running, I did enjoy it though I was heavier than Bernie, slower. That can be a bit disheartening when your brother is always between you and the finishing line. But you have to respect a woman who'll put herself smack bang in front of a speeding ball for her county and club.

'Anyways so what about it?'

'Simon tells me they've a work do next Saturday in Waxy's and your woman June is going. So you've a couple of days to get yourself in shape, so you can ask her out when you bump into her, accidentally on purpose.'

I know I should be glad, but it seems like more pressure to be heaped upon me when I'm at a bit of a low point already.

As the morning goes on, everyone has an opinion on why we're been hauled up to the office. The lads in the sheds think it's probably something to do with the card games getting a bit serious. Seems that Mick Dougan lost a week's wages on forty-fives. His wife rang the front office; she threatened to arrive up with the kids. But Hopper and me weren't involved in that, not at the latter stages anyway. Charles Egan, who never has nothing good to say about anything, thinks the place is going to close down. If Eddie Farrell was around we'd know what was going on, being the union rep and all. But he's in Corfu for two weeks.

I have a wander over to the benches where the girls from the office have their smoke. They go mysterious quiet when I ask about the meeting, start talking about where they're going out at the weekend. Cliona, a pain in the arse at the best of times, turns to me, 'Wouldn't you be as well to get back to the sheds and at least be seen to do a bit of work?'

Fuck sake.

One o'clock. It's like being back at school. Myself and Hopper outside the office. Janice and Cliona in the front office are as busy as I've ever seen, heads down.

When Dennis brings us in, he cuts straight to the chase.

'Got a call from McGraths's during the week. They're putting a go-slow on that housing development at the back of the fire station. I'd say they'll be in receivership before the end of the summer. Thin edge of the wedge.'

McGrath's Developments is one of our biggest customers. Dennis is looking at the two of us, nodding his head like we all agreed something. I focus on the picture he has on the wall: a photo of himself and his two kids on a rollercoaster. You can see he's having a great time, laughing like a maniac, but the youngest fellah on the outside looks like he's going to puke his ring up. Why would you blow that up and put it on your wall? How do they take those photos anyways? Must be an automatic trigger on the track. Next thing I hear him saying, 'We're going to have to run with this, lads.'

What the fuck did I miss? I don't know what to say so I keep my trap shut.

Hopper's well on the case. 'Why us? We have our Safe Pass; both us can drive the forklift, do the machines, anything. You get more out of us than most of the crew.'

'Last in, first out.'

'Junior Hennessey started well after us,' I says, though they're never going to get rid of him on account of his father being the local cop.

'Look, it's temporary. If it picks up, you'll be the first to get a call. But Pauline was in yesterday evening going over the figures and I wouldn't even feel confident what's coming down the road for me.'

There's bit of back and forth. I haven't much to offer. It's the first time I've got fired in my life. It doesn't feel as bad as you'd think.

'We'll need something to be getting on with,' Hopper goes. 'It'll be weeks before the labour comes through.'

Dennis pulls out the bottom drawer of his desk and takes

out two envelopes. 'There you go, lads. P45s and everything in there.'

He's our marching orders all ready. Fucking hell.

'If you want to knock off a bit early this afternoon, take a bit of time to sort out your stuff.' Then he takes a roll of notes from his pocket and peels off a couple of fifties, hands them over to Hopper. 'Split that between ye and say nothing to nobody.'

'Talk about putting you in the mood for the weekend,' Hopper says as we're walking over to the lockers.

There's a fair few lads hanging around having a smoke, waiting to hear. I go for a slash when Hopper tells them. Once they find out, everybody heads back fairly sharpish, like our bad luck might be contagious.

Hopper has a joint in his pocket and we decide to walk out the Barrow track, have a smoke. Enjoy the first few hours of freedom.

Something about an envelope I can't resist opening, even if it's only my wage slip. I rip it down the side. When I look at the docket, I say to Hopper there might be a mistake. Way more than we usually get.

He gives me a dig on the arm. 'The extra's holiday pay and shit,' he goes. 'Ease his guilty conscience. It's a shame for you.'

'Why?'

'You're better suited to waged work than me. I'm more of an entrepreneurial spirit.'

Not sure how to take that.

'Did ya see that picture of Dennis's kids?' Hopper goes.

'Yeah.'

'Got me thinking,' Hopper goes, 'about this corpse of mine.'

'What're you on about?'

That's the thing about Hopper, says right out loud whatever

101

mad shit he's thinking. 'Remember that poem from school?' he goes. 'The little brother in the coffin.'

I know the one he means, like you couldn't help but get that one: *a four-foot box, a foot for every year.* Ma Cole, our English teacher, was mad about poetry. Even made us learn off a few lines, though it's not obligatory.

'Standing in that office, listening to him shiteing on, I started measuring out my own body. Mentally, from the toes right up along, and imagining I was in a coffin. I could feel it. As though I was going to suffocate, it was so real.'

Maybe it's being around wood all day, but I imagine an oak lid myself, pushing down on me.

He grips me, looks me dead straight in the eye, 'We should head off somewhere. Courtown. Or Tramore. Dive in the fucking sea. Imagine screaming with the cold, our pelts shrinking with self-fucking-preservation. Running up and down the beach to dry off. Have a few cans, shift some young one from Dublin who wears perfume they don't even sell around here.'

There's something about Hopper that has a want for living large, bursting out of his skin. Even back when we started school, he'd rip his copybook with the speed of the crayons and bite every toy in the classroom to see how it felt. Now he'll put in a day's work and still have a maw on him to drive halfway across the county for a gig or some new one he fancies.

We look at each other and leg it. Like we're mitching off school again. The two of us race down the track, laughing our arses off, shoving each other into the reeds.

I was expecting the Mater to be quare disappointed for me when she hears the news. But when I go in the back door, she's left a note propped up against the Deadwood. Says Bernie is gone to Kilkenny and she's headed to Aghade with Cissy Agar to get rabbit skins off a man, for the costumes.

I heat up a bit of leftover shepherd's pie and I'm watching TV when there's a call from the back door. Eithne in again. She reckons there's been noticable shrinkage of the warts.

I go through the motions, but my heart's not in it. I say there's no need to come back again for a third go; it's sorted.

When I tell her about being laid off, she's not one bit surprised. Apparently loads of lads has been let go over the last few months; she says half the town is surviving on cheap mince. Hardly a steak going out from one end of the week to the other. I suppose it's not too bad being broke over the summer, but come the winter I'd go off my rocker.

She's getting on okay in the butcher's. Starts telling me about Old Man Tynan, the grandfather. Gone a bit senile but he wanders in occasionally. They have his original apron hanging up on the door. They don't give him a real cleaver, just an old toy machete painted silver, let him chop away at lambs' livers and chicken fillets in the back room. When he heard I was curing her warts, he piped up with some *raiméis* about my father being a butcher's apprentice as a young fellah.

'Don't think so,' I says to Eithne.

'Not in Carlow,' she goes. 'Some other place. He was very definite about it. Did something happen and he gave it up, came back home?'

'Nope.'

'The old man's a bit off his trolley,' she says. 'Sawing away goodo as serious as anything.'

After she goes, I'm watching the end of my shepherd's pie have a second spin in the microwave, wondering if the Da was a butcher. Who knows, he could have been; probably loads of his life I know nothing about. The Deadwood is sitting pretty on the draining board. I point my fork at him. 'A butcher, no less. The secret life of logs. Got my eye on you.'

The way he's staring back, you'd swear he's the one got his eye on me.

Big Ears, the Brothers, and Waxy's

Friday morning I'm not planning on getting up early, seeing as I have no job to go to. But the Mater is roaring at me from the kitchen in case I've slept it out. She doesn't know the news; herself and Cissy didn't get back til all hours last night. I come down for a cuppa, fill her in on me getting laid off.

'Well if it's not one bloody thing it's another.'

She says she'll talk to Richie about getting me a few shifts at Morrissey's but she can forget about that. No way I'm stacking shelves and wearing a fucking pinny.

'What about window cleaning?' she goes. 'Or there's quare good money in tree surgery. Margaret Ryan's young fellah, he's a whole load of logs drying out the back, ready to sell once the weather turns. Would you think of a computer course?'

'You're only saying random shit now. Don't worry about it.'

Once she's gone, I fill a mug of tea and head back to bed. But I can't get to sleep and it's too early to do anything. Eventually I get up, mooch around. I take Bernie's face cream down from the bathroom shelf, try a bit, on my cheeks and nose, to see what's the go. Maybe I'll get my hair trimmed. Nothing fancy. Yeah, that's a plan.

On the way back from the barber's I dawdle along but there's hardly anyone around town. Anyone who is out and about seems to be busy going somewhere.

When I get into the house it's dead quiet and I wonder did Bernie come home last night at all. I have a hard look at the new haircut in the hall mirror. And my face. I'm fairly average-looking. I try smiling and nodding. Right as I'm glancing away, I notice my ears. They seem massive, like joke ears you put on over your real ones. When I straighten up and look head-on it's not so bad. But when I turn to one side there's definitely something odd-looking. Must be the way Gerry cut my hair. I've been going to him since forever but he's easily distracted by the horses. I could tell he was scanning the *Racing Post* and the razor going goodo across my skull. He's gone too high behind the ears, that's what's wrong. As if he was trying to make a feature of them or something. It looks like a mowed lawn with an ornamental fucking ear in the middle.

Not the kind of setback I need today. I'll have to keep my head straight-on tomorrow night when I'm talking to anyone, especially June.

I fill a big bowl of cornflakes and go into the front room. I'm flicking between wrestling and some baseball game from New York. When they hit a home run and the camera pans across the rows, everyone is roaring like one beast, forgetting themselves. I like watching crowds at sports things, thinking, what if I was there instead of here, one voice in a stadium of thousands, a different me in a different life.

Then they're showing the Australian football. Maybe the accent of the commentators puts it in my head to ring the lads. I hardly ever do; if the Mater skypes them, I might stick around and say hello. I suppose cos there was a big gap between the first four brothers, then Mossy, Bernie and me, we're not all that close. Having said that, family is family, and someone should let them know what's going on around here; me getting laid off and Bernie's carry-on.

I know Pat's moved in with Lar since his marriage broke up. I think the Mater said Senan's pitched up in Melbourne too since he left Tasmania. Back with the second wife. Or first. She's not too clear and I've a feeling it's number three. I'll try Pat; he's usually the best for answering.

'Hey, it's me.'

'What's up, little bro?' Pat says. 'Everything okay?'

'Yeah, all good. It's–' But before I get to say anything, someone's thrown a cushion in front of Pat's face.

'Knock it off, you wanker.' Then he goes to me, 'What're you doing, growing your ears?'

'What?'

'Must be the angle, your ears look massive. Come here, Lar,' he shouts. 'Look at Frank's ears.'

Then someone yanks him from the chair, and my screen fills up with Lar, and a head of dyed blond hair. 'G'day, bro,' he goes. 'What'cha think of my *gruaig*?'

'Twenty years ago, maybe. Or thirty. Listen, was the Mater talking to ye lately?'

'A bit. What's up?'

'Well, Bernie ended up in the A & E again.'

'Yeah, I heard he'd a bit of dip in form, alright.'

'Bit more than that.'

'I think you've inherited Murt's ears. No wonder he keeps the hair long.'

'You know he's still out of college and all?'

'Yeah, I know,' Lar goes. 'Pat was chatting to him.'

There's a delay in our voices going over and back and the screen is freezing up a bit. It's not clear to me by Lar's expression is he hearing anything.

'I got laid off.'

'You thinking of coming over, Frank? No problem getting you set up with a bit of work.' He waits for an answer, then someone behind is shouting across the room.

'Look,' I goes, 'Bernie's gone beyond the beyond. Taking tablets and shit. He might be a . . . a trans—'

'What?'

'A girl.'

Lar turns around; someone's switched on music in the background. 'Lads, Bernie's got a girl,' he shouts.

'No, you knob.'

'That boy doesn't know if he's coming or going.'

I try to explain but there's this sudden loud ringing in the background.

'What's that noise?'

'The smoke alarm off again. Pat's left the grill on. Hang on. Have to knock it off before the sprinkler comes on.'

Lar gets up and I wait a few minutes. They must've forgot I'm still there because someone picks up the phone and puts it somewhere else in the room. I'm looking at a crate of empty beer bottles and a basket piled high with laundry. And a wall, somewhere in Melbourne, Australia. Thanks for the support, lads.

I head up to bed early, wishing this Friday would come to an end and I could sleep away half of Saturday. No such luck. Eight o'clock in the morning the Mater has me wide awake with her clattering around. She's on an early shift. I wait til she's left before I go down for breakfast. I'm putting on a few slices of toast when Bernie comes down, puts a load directly from the washing machine into the dryer.

'The Mater'll kill ya if she sees you using the dryer on a day like this,' I says.

'I need stuff for London.'

For something he managed to keep under wraps for the past month, now he can't stop talking about their trip. They've been cooking up this London holiday since well before his latest 'dip in form'.

The day drags on; everywhere I go in the house, Bernie's right there, packing up his suitcase, then taking stuff back out again. The mad thing is, though his announcement about his trans thing got right in on my head, when he's right there in front of me, I keep forgetting about it. Then it comes back. It's the exact same as when the Da died; I'd wake up some mornings and I'd forget for a second. Or I'd come home from school through the back door and think he'd be there. Before it'd sink in again.

I'm trying not to obsess too much about meeting June tonight. She's bound to say something about the healing, ask me stuff about it. What can I even say? It was a mistake? We got a bit mixed up with the number of boys in the family? Explain about the placebo effect and offer her money back? That'll go down a treat.

Eventually I get stuck into the Xbox and that passes a few hours. The Mater comes home from work with a couple of microwave dinners for this evening, new vegetarian range. Bernie doesn't want any, so we split the lamb pot. Then I try the beef and kidney pie. It's alright; whatever is posing as lamb or beef none of us can make out; Bernie reckons it's a kind of mushroom. I'd do the pie again, but I'd give the lamb a miss.

They'll leave in the morning and be in Eileen's by lunch-time. Bernie's all thrilled cos she's booked them tickets for some big show. The Mater's going on about the last time she went to London, about fifteen year ago, on a boat. She's trying to get me involved in the conversation. I don't ask one question because I don't want to know.

She loads up the freezer and packs the cupboard with snacks. It'll be the first time I've the place to myself. She's fussing a bit about what I'll do and if I've any plans.

'I think it'll be good to have a bit of space to meself for a few days,' I says. 'To think.'

'Oh no,' she says. 'Don't be sitting around thinking, Frank. That's the worst thing you can do. Get out and enjoy yourself.'

'As it happens, I'm heading out tonight.'

'I thought you'd stay in,' she goes. 'Our last night and all.'

'I'd already made plans. With the lads.'

I can see she's a bit put out with me going out on her last night, but I can't tell her about June or she'll have my head melted with questions.

After tea I've a quick shower and shave, put a bit of gel in the hair. A clean top and jeans and I'm good to go.

Hopper knocks in around half seven.

'What the craic, Mrs Whelan?' he goes.

'I could complain but who'd listen?' she says.

While I'm getting my wallet and jacket they swap all the latest gossip. He's like an auld one the way he goes on, telling her he saw Richie Morrissey dropping a certain woman at the train station in Newbridge. She's telling him all about London and how they're going to see where Eileen works. Eileen's a cleaner in some fancy hospital, but you'd swear it was a major tourist attraction, the way the Mater's going on.

On the way into town, I tell Hopper he's an eejit to be listening to the Mater and all the guff she goes on with.

'She asked me to keep an eye on ya this weekend. Doesn't want you mopin' around.'

He's annoying me now. Like I'm the poor sap everyone has to take care of. I'm a bit on edge thinking how it'll go with June. Change of topic'd be better all round, so I ask him about the Deadwood Da. I'd told him about the statue but this evening was the first time he'd actually seen it.

'I don't know,' he goes. 'To be honest, I didn't really get a close look.'

'Something about it, though?'

He doesn't answer straight off. Not like Hopper to hold back on his views. I don't know if he believes in all my family stuff – me having the gift of the seventh son and the Mater's psychic stuff – but he never takes the piss out of us. I should tell him I probably don't have the gift, but I don't want to get into it now.

'Something right lively about it. I couldn't say I seen your Da in it exactly. Maybe because you put it in my mind, you know the way a lot of that stuff is – well, we're suggestible beings.'

'What stuff? Who's suggestible?' I'm not letting that pass.

'Fuck sake. It must be yer woman has yer nerves all jangly. Relax the fucking kaks, Frank.'

'Fuck off. It's not that at all, if you want to know.' I've had enough people having a go at me without him joining in. 'Certain information I found out,' I says, 'changes a lot of things for me.'

'What things?'

'Tell ya another time. But I'm not sure June is going to be all that interested in me.'

'She is. So don't start getting all turned in on yourself now.'

Heading down Tullow Street, he brings up the subject of the Deadwood Da again, trying to make conversation. I've nothing to be saying.

'I was thinking of the origin of that statue,' he says. 'Eskimoish.'

'Oh yeah?'

'Some class of totem pole.'

'Lena got it in Mayo. Never heard of Eskimos pitching up in Ballina.'

'I'm thinking further afield. Eskimo Indians,' he goes. 'Them lads, American Indians, they wouldn't have any sense of borders. Like, how would they? They're following the buffalo, roaming across the land. So a lot of them were in and out of Canada regularly. And some of them crossed paths with the Eskimos who were coming down south, hunting wolves and shit. Intermingling of the species and they ended up making up the Canadian-type Indian.'

'You're well up on your geography anyways.'

'Yeah,' he goes. 'Used to have a map of the world on my bedroom ceiling. Always planning new trips: Alaska, Peru, India. Must have taken after my mother.'

I let him rattle on about ways you can travel cheap from one country to another, if you know the right people, til we get to Waxy's. Our crowd are there already – Moose, Dermot, and Carl – securing the best spot at the end of the counter, across from the door out to the smoking area. So loads of people passes us, going in and out.

The lads have lots of suggestions what myself and Hopper should do in terms of spending the cash from the mill.

'Did yer mother not see it coming, you getting laid off?' Moose goes. 'Thought she was supposed to be psychic.'

Hopper gives him a dig, makes him get the next round in. I keep trying to think what to say if June asks me about my family or my job, but I can't get one simple sentence fixed in my brain.

At least watching Chrissie behind the bar is a distraction. She's way faster than the lads and her balance is something else. At one stage she has three pints in her hand and does this 360-degree turn and dip to avoid Macker, who gets wild confused once it's busy. Whatever she says to him, he turns puce, then she winks at me, which does him in altogether. I'm laughing at the two of them, better'n TV, when someone squeezes in beside me.

'I'll have whatever you're on,' June says. 'Though they do say laughing to yourself, first sign of madness.'

I nearly choke on my pint. 'Oh, how's it going?' I say. 'Didn't know you drank here.'

She says nothing.

'Usually,' I go on. 'Or do you usually drink here?'

'Work night out. I'm not around much at the weekend. Unless I'm working. I tend to go home.'

'Me too. I mean, this is my home. Not here obviously. In the town.'

'The man with the hands,' she says. 'Do you have them insured?'

'What?'

'Like Madonna's boobs. Insured for millions.'

I don't know if it's the drink or what, but my mind has completely slowed down, the opposite of what it usually does. Her words are so clear, like there isn't loads of other noise around. Her eyes have black pencil make-up that makes them extra long and then turn up like a cat. Her real eyes are like a picture inside a black frame. Green.

'Insured?' I go.

113

'You know, tools of your trade and all that.'

I have no idea what she's talking about.

'Is that how you make your living?' she goes on. 'Do you have another job?'

Shit. The very fucking day when I cease to have another job she asks.

'Do you want a drink?' I says. The words do not seem to have come out of my mouth.

'Well, I'm in a round already, but thanks. Another time'd be great.'

For some reason I notice her ear. Her hair is sitting perfectly behind her very lovely ear. Did I say that out loud? Sweet Jesus, please no. I touch my own ear, which seems to have grown even bigger since I left the house.

'Absolutely,' I go. 'Definitely another time.'

She puts in an order of about six drinks. Chrissie has it all on the go sharpish. As the vodkas and mixers and pints start to line up, I ask if she wants a hand carrying them down.

'No, you're alright, mate,' a voice comes from behind me. Aussie accent. The big hairy fellah. He reaches in and takes about four glasses. His hands are massive. She smiles at me, puts two mixers in her handbag, and lifts the rest.

'Thanks. See ya,' and she follows after him as he forces a path through the crowd with his huge hairy head and his big hairy face.

The rest of the evening is a bit of a blur. I'm chatting away with the lads but I'm trying to keep an eye on where June's crowd is. The place clears out a bit around half ten; loads of people trying to get into TeeDee's Nightclub before eleven, get the last of the two-for-one shots. Hopper and myself hang on.

'How'd you get on?' Hopper goes.

'Alright. Good. Might be meeting up for a drink.'

'Nice one. When?'

'Didn't exactly say.'

'Did you get her number?'

'No.'

'Fuck sake, Frank.'

As they're calling last orders, Hopper's trying to get me to go to TeeDee's. Macker is starting to collect the glasses, wipe down empty tables.

I spot June putting her jacket on, heading for the far door with a crowd. Watching her gives me a sinking feeling of another thing that didn't quite go right.

'Hang on,' Hopper goes and heads for the jacks. On the way, I see him get himself into some conversation with the big hairy bloke and June. They're laughing at something. When he comes back, he drains the last of his pint and hands me a bit of paper. 'Nice race of people, Aussies. Here you go, bro.'

'What's that?'

'The magic number. June's. Ask her out. She's interested in you and she's free tomorrow. She's never seen a dolmen.'

'What's a dolmen to do with it?'

'Don't ask.'

Her phone number, written on the back of a receipt. He wangled a number out of her, just like that. How he got the conversation turned around to the dolmen is beyond me. I haven't been there myself since I was a kid. It'd be weird to take her to look at a pile of rocks in the middle of a field, but if she wants to see it, I suppose it could be amazing as well.

Hopper's decided to go on to the club, but I don't want to end the night there, prefer a bit of time to myself. As we're splitting up at the corner, he says he'll drop around tomorrow and make sure I use that phone number.

Walking home through the town, it's mad. I feel like I've been drawing on pure oxygen ever since she stood at my elbow and said hello. When I breathe now I can feel the air filling my lungs like balloons in my chest. Maybe it's the drink but I see everyone more vividly: the buzz they're on, wrecked and high, feeling good, looking good, primed for a night of dancing and shifting.

Leaving the crowds behind, turning on to Syne Alley, the town feels like it belongs to me. In the doorway of McCabe's Opticians there's a couple laying into one another. Behind them the pairs of glasses in the window are calmly watching them get it on. A car cruises by, the bass line bouncing back off the walls so strong you can nearly see waves in the air.

By the time I come around the courthouse I've left most of the action behind, but the feeling is still with me. I look up. Although you can't really see any stars I feel how massive the sky is over me, over everyone.

What was June going on about, something about my hands? I stretch my fingers, clench, unclench my fist. Maybe she thinks, cos of the seventh son shit, I have some special sensitivity, a magic touch. The man with the hands.

What'll she think of me when it turns out I've no special gift? Just having regular hands doesn't hardly elevate me above ninety-nine per cent of the population. What was I thinking? There's nothing special about me. Or my hands. Carrying on like a fucking eejit over with the kid. Bits of old cloth soaked in lemon juice that any fool could rub on their own leg. Three times. Taking money for it. Talk about false pretences.

By the time I get through the queue at Fast Dan's Takeaway I'm sure of it. She'd never go out with me, especially when this comes out. I get a bag of chips, put my hood up, and make for home. May as well peg her phone number into the nearest bin. But I don't. I close my fist around it, keep a hold of it deep in my pocket.

Mater Under the Gazebo

The light's on in the kitchen when I get home but there's no one there. I'm looking in the press for ketchup when I catch something out of the corner of my eye. Something's crawling around at the end of the garden. Couldn't be Bernie cos I heard him up in his bedroom when I came in; probably still packing and unpacking. I take the Da's putter out from under the stairs, thinking it's some messer up to no good. I'll give him a hole-in-one and the rest of it too.

When I step out, next door's sensor light comes on and I see the Mater down on her belly, squirming in under the gazebo. With the slant on it, I wouldn't feel fully confident she mightn't get herself stuck. She's something wrapped up in newspaper that she's pushing under.

'What the fuck?'

She reverses out, arse first, top speed. 'Jesus, Frank, you nearly gave me a heart attack.'

'What are you up to?'

She scurries back up the garden and in the back door, pronto. I follow her. She's sitting at the table catching her breath when I get in. I fill the kettle while she picks at my bag of chips.

'Pass us the vinegar, there's a good lad.'

'What're you up to?' I ask, pushing the ketchup across the table. 'I'd thought you'd be in bed.'

She makes me wait til I have a pot of tea brewed and she has half my chips gone.

'Murt dropped over earlier with a few odds and ends for Eileen,' she starts. 'Earrings and a brooch. Antique.'

Apparently he's quare upset because Lena is up to high doh, threatening all kinds against him if he doesn't display her artworks and some lavender-related products in d'Emporium on Wolf Night. I don't even ask what lavender's got to do with it. And as well, she's raging against the Mater for taking the Deadwood.

'Don't mind her,' I says. 'That's just resentment for the way Murt keeps an eye out for us.'

'Don't mind who?' Bernie says from the doorway. He comes in, twirls a fistful of my chips around a pool of ketchup and then does the same with another handful while the first ones are still in his gob.

The Mater gives him a quick rundown on events leading up to her decision to bury the Deadwood under the gazebo til she gets back from London. She's dead set against Lena getting it back.

'Why don't you take him with you?' I says.

'Of course I would,' she says. 'But we need to keep a bit of room in the suitcase for shopping.'

It's odd. She was all about the Deadwood the first night she came back from Murt's; now with her big trip coming up, he's to be set aside, quick as all get out. Come to think of it, I don't even hear her talking to him at all.

'Won't he be there to keep you company, Frank, when we're gone,' she goes.

Maybe she's picked up on the connection between me and the Deadwood.

'Whatever.' I'm distracted, trying to think back to before I stepped inside this house, the way I was feeling talking to June. I make a move to go.

'Hang on there, son,' the Mater says, swirling the leaves at the bottom of her mug. The three long twists, the 999 of the teacup world.

'Mater, what're you doing?'

She shushes me and dumps the last bit of black tea into the empty milk carton. She stares hard as anything into the mug. Taking her a while.

'Give it here, I'll have a look,' says Bernie.

'Since when can you read the leaves?' I goes.

'Since forever.'

He's peering into the cup for what seems like ages. He might be goofing off; I can't see is his eyes closed, because his hair is falling around his face.

'The chain there. A cross, I think, and wind,' he goes, before drowning the rest of the chips with vinegar.

'Yeah, blowing out your arse,' I goes.

'That's some combination,' the Mater says. 'Quare times ahead.'

She has a quick look at it herself. 'Often seen fire or water, indicating travel, but there's something in that wind. Winds of change.'

She looks up at me as if she's about to say something but then shakes her head. 'I may go to bed. Early start tomorrow.'

As she passes me, she gives me a quick hug. 'Night, son. See you next week. Try and have a bit of fun.'

'See you in the morning.'

'Probably not. We're getting a lift dead early,' Bernie goes, using the sharp knife to take the skin off an orange in one strip. 'Half five or something.'

'Thought you were getting the airport bus up at eleven.'

'Richie Morrissey arranged with the lads to pick us up,' Bernie says. 'We'll get dropped directly to the airport. Harry's taking us in the brewery truck.'

Harry Morrissey, Richie's son, who can do no wrong. Surprised he's not dragging a trailer full of sick puppies to the vet's as well. Three years ahead of me in school, science nerd, mad into The Doors. Before he'd even sat his Leaving, himself and one of the Elm Drive Bolgers, another geek, were selling home brew. Wasn't bad either. Then they took over one of the old warehouses down by the river. They've set up a local brewery. Called it *Scalater 88*. The name is everywhere now: sponsoring the football team, running a music festival in Tullow, started making gin this year as well.

Bernie's a bad case of the munchies; starts going through the presses, eventually settling on a bowl of Coco Pops and a beer.

'How'd you get the money together for the trip?' I ask him as I'm getting up to go.

He doesn't look up. 'The lads gave me a few quid.'

'What lads?'

'The brothers.'

'Pat? Lar?'

'Yeah, and Senan. And for the Mater.'

I'm gutted. I could've done the poor mouth on the phone about being laid off and all. Seems like the whole lot of them is conniving against me.

'They don't know what you're about.'

'Actually, they do, cos I told Senan. It's no big deal over there. He's working with a trans plumber from Cork. She transitioned on the job.'

'Did what?'

'You know, went through the whole thing. Transitioned, from male to female. So, no biggie.'

'On a building site? I doubt it. Even in Australia.'

That reminds me, I still haven't asked him what's the deal with him not telling the Mater about him being a woman, inside, all along. She's usually the first port of call for all his ups and downs.

The minute I bring it up, he gets quare busy looking for chocolate digestives in the press. Eventually he mumbles something about wanting to tell her when she has a break from work, when she has time to process.

'So when she's on her big trip to London, you're going to land that on her?' I says.

'I wouldn't put it like that, but yeah, I think it might be a good time.'

Good luck to the two of them.

I go into the back garden for a smoke. As soon as I take a few steps out, McDermott's light comes on again. Everything's lit up for a few seconds. You can't get any peace anywhere. I settle into the gazebo and spark up. Funny to think the Deadwood is a few feet below, buried under my backside.

'What're you back for, Da? To take care of unfinished business? The Mater always says that's what keeps her tea leaves and angel readings ticking over: unfinished business. It's what draws the spirits back and the punters in. I know you went sudden but seems like you had plenty of time to tell me what was going down if you wanted to. You bottled it. Not like you. If you're back to provide a bit of moral support for the biggest let-down of my life so far, don't worry about it. I can take care of myself.'

A light comes on upstairs, Bernie's room. Can he see me? No, he's only having a smoke out the window. Weird watching him blowing a big stream of puff into the night, staring up into the sky.

'Smoking kills,' I say in a deep voice.

Bernie sticks his head right out the window. 'Who's that?'

I step back into the garden and the sensor goes on again.

'Fuck you, Frank. You'll have the whole road up.'

'Here, gis a drag of that.'

He takes a pull, then drops the spliff out the window. It falls onto the coalbunker. I have a few drags standing at the back door, thinking about June. Imagining if she had ended up coming back here, having a smoke in the garden with her. I wouldn't say she smokes, on account of her being into sport and all that. I keep dead still for a few minutes. When I take a step to stub the fag out in a plant pot, McDermott's light comes on again.

'Call it a night, Frank.' Bernie sticks his head out above me. 'It's like a fucking disco out there.'

Don't Fence Me In

Send me off forever but I ask you please,
Don't fence me in

And yet here I am, facing into the fence between ourselves and McDermott's, buried under a bloody gondola on legs. I'm wrapped up like a portion of chips in yesterday's news, a smattering of soil on top of me.

Something very . . . not funny, what's the word? Ironic, I'll give that a run out. Something very ironic about being buried twice. Even Jesus didn't end up six feet under a second time. I'd've preferred if the Mater'd put me in the attic for safe keeping, or under the bed. How and ever.

There's some that'll wonder about aspects of the great hereafter that I'm omitting from my telling. The reason I'm not saying much is because it's hard to grasp when you've lost your bearings in terms of time and space. The force of gravity is exerting no pull so I can't say much about the physical elements of being dead. What I seem to tune into is not dependent on my location. It might be the case that if my fate and that of others is intertwined, I'm drawn into those

124

scenarios, be they past or present. Seems to be turning out that myself and Frank have unfinished business to take care of, not, as I presumed, the Mater and I. My life, in so far as this is a life, is not tied down to the here and now. I drift outside of time and then get sucked into a moment, one beat of life is my own heartbeat. I'm seeing things in my past as if they're running parallel to now. It's not like when you're alive, how you remember. Memories are stories reeling out behind you and your imagination gives you a steer towards the future. Remembering and imagining, they're as conjoined as a single drop of water.

The way I'm getting it is, there's no eternity because there's no time. You know how you'd say, 'I've all the time in the world'? I have all the time in the world now and there's no time. So make of that what you will.

Were you ever afraid of an emptiness at the heart of everything; this world, life, your own self? You were right in a way; there is nothing. Nothing like what you knew and nothing matters. But it's grand. It's absolutely grand stretching off in every direction and dimension.

I know this'll end. While I'm enjoying my encore there's someone in the wings, hands on the ropes, ready to lower the final curtain. Bit by bit the knots are loosening. With every twist and turn, my spirit's freeing itself. The one tie that binds me still, not vengeance or retribution. Love. Frank's asking me why I'm here. I'm asking the same thing myself because there's a whole heap I don't know. But the more he gets stuck into answering the question 'Why am I here?' for himself, the more he opens hisself up to the unknown and unknowable; things will start to shift. For me and him. I wish I could tell him I'm not here to add to his worries about the gift. It's complicated and right now I can feel it all hanging in the balance. I can't influence him but he needs to get moving. Not sit around thinking, no.

On the upside I'm here to witness first love. Frank and June. Got me thinking back to my first love, meself and Letty. I've an inkling that therein lie the seeds of my current predicament.

I was born and bred in Carlow, schooled here up to a point, spent most of my life inside the county borders. But early in my life, I wanted to go a bit of distance, get a perspective, you might say. I mostly wanted to get away from my father's will. He was determined to mould me into something approximating the twisted shape of himself. My mother, always my ally, she got me an apprenticeship in a butcher's. Not too far away. That's where I met Letty, fell in love for the first time.

In the end I was only gone a short while before my father hauled me back. I never left my home town again. For a short journey, it caused some grief. I never saw Letty again. My father told me she went to Glasgow. Into service with a well-off family, washing and cleaning, taking care of their babies. Yet even with all the slants and views I can get now on any given situation, I can't see that.

Here I am run aground inside this statue, hoping I'll be flung into her life as it progressed and be gifted a picture of her at a dance somewhere swirling around, maybe married with a rake of children under her feet, or just staring out a window dreaming on a summer day. Why can I not see her life as it unspooled?

So, that's a bit of unfinished business needs taking care of and I've a sense I need Frank's help to do it. That's the nature of families, always handing down your concerns to the next generation. Spreading out the sorrows and the joys; any open wounds does be shared out as well.

You think your heart is constantly at the centre of operations, pounding away in your chest, but that's not the case at all. The heart has gone, left you a million times over by the time it gives its last drum roll. It's got its own journey to make, its own maps to chart. Slipped out in the night, travelled over continents, leapt across a room, into a storm; defied logic and time. When Letty comes to me now, it's not a heart beating the way it did back then. It's red tracers all around me, drawing another type of map, a criss-cross of paths laid down by wants and fears; journeys not taken, imagined, hoped for, dim but there all the same. Funny the way I'm open to a new way of seeing when I've lost the power of sight; turned into a new class of being and I'm no longer here.

Send me off forever but I ask you please,
Don't fence me in

Lena Cuts Katie

I wake up about ten. When I go to the jacks, the doors to the Mater and Bernie's rooms are open, beds empty. They're gone. Downstairs the kitchen's in a heap, mugs and bowls piled in the sink, flakes and milk spilled on the table. They must've been in a rush, couldn't wait to leave. I put the kettle on, get myself sorted with a cup of tea. But there's only a dribble of milk left, not enough for me to have a decent portion of cereal. I have a root in my jacket for a smoke. Ordinarily I wouldn't want one this early but there's an empty feeling around the house. Of course, the Deadwood is at the end of the garden; I could dig him up. At least I'll have him to myself for a couple of days; chance to thrash a few things out.

As I pull out the fags, a scrap of paper drops onto the floor. June's number. I pick it up, put it in front of me. If I ring that exact sequence of numbers, she'll answer. Or her voicemail might kick in. She'd probably say, 'Hello, who's that?', because she doesn't have my number. Then what? Identify myself, say something about last night? That's it; I can't think of nothing else to say.

I could ring her from another number; I think there's still a phone box at the post office. If I called her from there, I could just listen to her voice. A weird thing to be thinking of but I kind of get why you might want to hear someone speak without having to say anything back. Leave it out, Frank, you're not that far gone yet. Texting'd be easier, but Hopper said I should ring.

'Hi,' I go, looking at the piece of paper in front of me. 'I was wondering if you'd want to go for a drink?'

How would she know who I am? Introduce yourself first.

'Hi. This is Frank. You know, the ringworm.'

Wrong. Don't bring that up. I'll have to think of how to get around the whole cure thing if I ever do see her again. I'll tell her straight out. There was a mix-up in the family. I'm not actually the seventh son. That's sounds a bit lame. I'll come up with something better than that.

'It's Frank. From last night. I'm wondering if you'd like to go out with me?'

No, not out with me.

'Go for a drink?' I try, casual-like. Better. I might have to write this down before I do actually call her.

'Go out for a drink?' I say, a bit louder, stronger now.

'Not a chance,' goes this voice behind me.

What the fuck? I swivel around. Lena fills up the doorway. She's a husky-built girl but she walks over to me, dainty as anything, on pointy fur boots with the toes out. Makes her feet look like goats' hooves.

'Where the fuck did you come from?'

She sits down opposite me, crumples her nose up at the mess: the sugar bag and milk carton, the bit of tinfoil I'd squashed up as an ashtray. At the exact same moment, both our eyes lock onto the knife, the one Bernie left on the table

129

last night. She's hardly going to stick me in my own house. She looks at me from under very thin eyebrows, reaches over, and lifts it. Fuck. Her eyes are like pinheads. She must be off whatever she should be on and on something else.

'Where's your mother?'

'It's a bit early to be dropping in on people,' I goes. By the cut of her I reckon she's pulled an all-nighter somewhere. 'You should go home. You'll wake up the house.'

'Who? It's only you. I was sitting on the green earlier, saw the brewery truck pull up.'

As she's saying this, she's using the knife to saw the back off the cornflakes box.

'The Mater took that statue with her,' I goes. 'So it's not here.'

'Why did she do that? To hide it from me?' While she's talking, she's carving away at the cardboard, quare adept at twisting and turning that knife.

'No. Because it's important to her,' I goes. That's all I can think to say. She has me rightly spooked.

She reaches over and takes the tea towel off the rail, uses it to clean the table in front of her. She stands up the cardboard cut-out there. It's an ad from the back of the cornflakes box: a picture of Katie Taylor, the boxer. She's done a right job on it. Now she's shaving tiny strips of cardboard off with the knife to get it more exact.

'You back home for any particular reason?' I says, trying to make it normal. 'For Wolf Night or something?'

She ignores me. Where the middle button of her blouse should be, it's bunched up. I see she's pinned it together from the inside, so you wouldn't notice the missing button. That gives me a bit of comfort, the fact she bothered to do that. I wish Bernie was still here. Even if he arrived down the stairs in a ballgown, he'd be better able to handle her than me.

She puts the knife on the chair beside her, then starts wiggling Katie around, pretending to throw a few jabs. 'Boom boom.'

'Knock it off, Lena. Go home and get some sleep.'

Two swipes of the knife and she stands Katie back up; the hands – well, boxing gloves – are gone. Freaky, the way her stretched-out arms end at her wrists.

'Thing is,' she says. 'I don't know if you're a total fraud. Or a moron. Lies lie on lies.'

'What's the big deal with the statue?' I says. 'You have loads of other stuff.'

'It's not Murt's to give away. It's genuine art, not car boot sale crap.'

The shake's back in the hand. Always a bad sign. Once the hand starts, there's no turning back. Could be on track for a full-scale blow-up.

But instead she takes the knife in her steady hand and pushes the tip of it into her wrist. 'Keep your mitts off my father's business. I know you're trying to weasel your way in.'

'That's not true. I only give him a dig out now and then.'

'I promised the others we could use the d'Emporium.'

The shakes start to slow down as she outlines her grand plans: selling all kinds of shit from tarted-up statues to dried flowers in odd shoes. This all gets mixed in with some paranoid thoughts about who's really running this town, who's pulling the strings. I forget to watch what she's doing with the knife til a drop of blood appears on her wrist.

'What the fuck?'

She lifts it off with the blade, reaches over and sticks it into a bowl of cornflakes. Bernie's leftovers. Stirs it in. My left leg is hopping like mad under the table. I'm holding onto it tight as fuck. If I don't get a grip of the leg, it'll spread.

'Lena, you need to go home, get a bit of kip. Talk to your father.'

She's sawing away at the cardboard again. When she stands the figure back up, there's a slit down Katie's middle. She sticks the knife through from the back so it's pointing straight out the stomach at me. Hang in there, Katie. Olympic gold medal and all that. I concentrate on Katie's face and try and get my head around what's going down.

Of course I could go to the end of the garden right now, dig up the Deadwood. Hand him over. But I have to hold my nerve, do right by him and the Mater.

'Thing is, Lena, my mother really believes that statue has the Da's spirit in it.'

She looks confused; maybe she'd forgotten all about the Deadwood. 'The way people go on about your father,' she says. 'Like his shit didn't smell.'

'He was a decent skin. Took care of a lot of people's troubles.'

She starts laughing at me. 'Now you're the chosen one? Living with your eyes closed, head down. But life's more . . . more . . . more . . .'

'More what?' I goes.

She stands Katie up again. Instead of her eyes are two holes, neatly cut as anything. It does make her face look a lot less determined. 'More like geology,' she says. 'Rocks and sediments.'

Ah here, we're off now.

'Things underneath things. Also things covering up below.'

Stand up, walk out, I'm saying to myself but I'm not moving a muscle. She's using the knife to emphasise her point.

'Your father was the same as any man,' she goes. 'The layers underneath, propping up the patriarchy.'

I notice a picture of a cow on the milk carton. Never copped it before. Farmer standing beside him wearing a flat cap.

Probably not a real farmer, maybe an actor. I need to buy milk. As soon as she's gone, I'm going to walk out of here, get more milk. I haven't a clue what she's on about. 'The fuck're you trying to say?'

She starts going on about her travels around the country, women of Ireland. A change is going to come, kind of stuff. She's rubbing the cut on her wrist, which calms her down a bit. Then she's talking about Wexford and a bath or something.

'Soap and water. Clean heart, clean mind.'

'Whatever.'

'You'll thank me. Cos I'm doing you a favour. If you don't want to talk to Rose, it's your business.'

Did I miss that bit of information in the middle of all the other shite?

'Who's Rose when she's at home?'

'I just said. Your father's cousin when she's at home and away from it, smartarse. I was telling her all about you and your brothers.'

'Telling her what, exactly?'

She says I should talk to her, find out what the truth is about me, my family. When I ask her again what Rose knows, she won't give me a straight answer.

'Find out yourself if you really want to know. I'm not your handmaid.' She's buttoning her jacket, moving slow as you like towards the door. As she passes, she uses the knife to stab the scrap of paper with June's number.

'Seven's the magic number,' she starts singing, like she's on *Sesame Street*. Twirling around, carving numbers in the air with the blade. 'Not eight, no. Seven's the magic number.'

'Why are you so bothered all of a sudden that I'm a seventh son? Is it because of equality or something?'

She looks like she's considering this. 'You're right, there's sons and there's daughters. A girl is only a half-borned yoke. Never thought of seven and a half. Do you think your father knew?'

'Knew what?'

'How many there was?'

'How many what?'

She's lost me again. Unless it's something to do with Bernie but how would she know about him? The knife disappears, gone into some pocket or up her sleeve. I want to say, 'That's not yours,' but nothing comes out.

She flicks the paper with June's number right into the mess in the sink and leaves.

I can't get up. I should get milk for breakfast. Bernie used all the milk for his cornflakes and he didn't even eat them. They're sitting there, ruined. Still milky-looking; you wouldn't know there was blood stirred in.

I pick up the carton and start reading. Mark Hickey – he is a real farmer – three generations of dairy farming behind him; 215 cows in his herd.

I don't know how long I'm looking at Mark and his cow before I think of my phone. Where is it? Jacket probably. My hand is shaking when I take it out. I put the pin number in wrong two times. Three times and I'll be locked out. I can't trust myself to try again so I switch it back off.

Then I remember the Da at the bottom of the garden. I want to dig him out and have him with me in the house. What if she's watching me, waiting for me to make a move?

Eventually I get the phone switched on and ring the Mater. There's people talking in the background and she's shouting. 'Frankie, you alright, son?'

'No, it's Lena. She was here looking for that statue.'

'Can't hear ya.'

'She's out of control.'

'I meant to tell you, Bernie broke it last night. He said use a match, wedge the hot water tap in and turn the other one.'

I'm shouting back at her, 'She was threatening me. In the kitchen.'

I can hear some official announcements in the background.

'It's very noisy, Frank. It's Frankie,' I hear her tell someone. 'I can't hear him. Three sugars.' Then there's a click and the empty sound when someone isn't on the other end of the line. For some reason this fucking does me in.

'Can you hear me, hello? Please,' I go, but it's that echoey silence. I don't want to take the phone away from my ear or hang up. Shit. I try to pull myself together. It rings. Bernie.

'What's up, bro? The Mater said you sounded a bit shook.'

I give him a quick rundown of events. He says, go tell Murt and he'll sort her out.

'She's off her head and she's gunning for me,' I goes.

'Have to go, that's us they're calling.'

'You're not taking this serious.'

'You'll be fine. She's family, remember?' he says.

'Family, right,' I goes. 'Thanks for all the fucking support.'

'Don't be getting freaked out being in the house by yourself. See if Hopper's around,' and he hangs up.

Like I need a babysitter. Thinking of Hopper reminds me of last night, which seems a century ago. And June. Fuck, Lena threw June's phone number into the sink.

I fish it out but it's sopping. The ink has run. Number's gone. Why didn't I put it into my phone last night? Cos I was afraid I'd ring it by mistake. I hold the wet scrap up to the light; see can I remember it. I know it was 087 because that's the same prefix as mine, and there was a 3 and a 4. How many permutations could there be, knowing those two numbers are one hundred per cent in the mix of, what, seven digits? Only five others to work out.

Thinking about numbers is good for my head. But my mind goes blank again; I can't concentrate. First Bernie and Murt, now Lena. Seems like there's secrets in every corner.

Sitting there a bit numb, there's a noise at the back door. I lep right off that seat and leg it into the hall. I have my hands on the front door latch when there's a shout, 'Anybody up in this gaff?'

Hopper.

He sticks his head around the door into the hall. 'What the fuck, Frank?' He puts his arm around my shoulder. 'You're shaking like a leaf. What happened?'

He gets the kettle going, takes a packet of custard creams from the press, and sits down in the very same chair Lena's arse was warming not five minutes before. 'I betcha I know what's wrong with you,' he goes. 'Woman troubles.'

The Penny Drops

It's not like Hopper to be up this early of a Sunday. But he's only on his way home after crashing in Moose's. He thought he'd come over for a bit of breakfast, see how I'm shaping up for a date with June. I'm filling him in on all the shit with Lena.

'Sounds like she's well off the rails,' he goes. 'I thought she was in some place, getting her head sorted out.'

'She finished that and hooked up with some hippy crowd in Mayo. Ballygo-fucking-topia. The load of rubbish she brought home. Art me hole.'

'To be fair, she was fairly talented at drawing. Remember she used to draw them fishes with faces of people.'

I forgot that Hopper went out with Lena when she first joined our class. But she was too way out, even for him. Once she shaved her eyebrows off, it was over.

'Have you checked on your statue?' he goes. 'That's what she came for. You're sure she didn't get it?'

I go over to the kitchen window, look down the garden. I can see a bit of the newspaper sticking out from under the gazebo. Nothing's disturbed.

'The Da's fine.'

That's when Hopper notices the cut-out on the table. He lets out a whistle. 'That's fucking cold. Doing that to Katie. She's quare handy with a knife, though.'

While Hopper toasts a bit of bread, I take a quick shower. Bernie was right; you do need a match to jam the hot water tap. It ends up half-scalding, half-freezing, gets me feeling right sharp. What did Bernie say I should do? Talk to Murt.

When I come back downstairs, I try Murt's number a couple of times but no joy, going straight to voicemail. Hopper suggests we head over to d'Emporium, see what's the go. He needs to check in on his sister's house anyways; switch off some lights, see how the hamsters are doing. I'm not mad keen to run into Lena again, but as he points out, she's hardly going to do any serious damage with us all there.

Locking the back door behind us, there's a bit of me regrets leaving the Deadwood alone. But I'm relieved to be away from the house, out in the open air.

Walking through town on a Sunday morning can be bleak at the best of times, everything shuttered up, stepping over trails of vomit and chip bags blowing up against your shins. At one stage we pass a pair of high-heeled strappy shoes, set together against the kerb, neat as if they were under a bed.

Hopper stops dead. 'Look at that. Sight for sore eyes.'

'The fuck?'

'What do you think of, Frank? First thing comes into your head.'

'Drink?'

'A woman's feet. I think they're Roisín Maher's.'

'Come on, Hopper.'

'Seriously. I noticed them in the queue outside TeeDee's last night; she was in front of me, walking a bit crocked.'

'Like half the queue I'd say.'

We keep going. I'm trying to work out what Lena was getting at. 'What'd ya think she was trying to say about the Da?' I goes.

'No idea.'

'The way she was insinuating, like, he was a fraud or something?'

'I never heard talk of him like that.'

When we get to d'Emporium the first thing I notice is Lucky smashed on the footpath. The main part of his head has rolled down the street, landed up against a drain. At least, it's in one piece from the snout to the ears. The rest is in bits. While I retrieve the noggin, Hopper rings the bell, gives a good knock on the door.

'Maybe yer man Qualter came back for revenge,' I goes.

'Who?'

While I'm gathering up the bits of Lucky, I start to tell Hopper about the set-to at d'Emporium last week. A car pulls up alongside us. Murt. By himself, thankfully.

'How's it going, Frank? Haven't seen you in an age, Hopper.'

I hold up Lucky's head.

He kind of shrugs as he puts the key in the front door, doesn't seem too surprised by the broken dog. 'Come in, come in, though the place is a bit upside down.'

You can sing it. When I get past the shoe counter, I see it's been rightly turned over.

'Story, Murt? Were you broken into?'

'Not really.' He goes on into the kitchen and we follow. It's as bad if not worse. There's broken glass on the floor near the sink. Water or something spilled as well.

'Where's Lena?' I goes.

'Came home in a bit of state and left again,' Murt says, filling up the kettle.

Hopper starts picking broken stuff off the floor and putting it in the bin. The mad statues Lena brought home are lined up on a table in the corner. Looks like they escaped the attack.

Then I cop what's happened here. 'Did she smash up the place?'

'She must've knocked over a few things on her way out.'

Typical Murt, covering for her. I see a sweeping brush in the corner and bring it out front to tidy up Lucky's remains. Don't want the neighbours complaining.

Hopper says he'll head off to throw an eye on Ruth's; be back in twenty.

As I'm getting stuck in, sorting the kitchen with Murt, he tells me what happened. Lena'd a major hissy fit because he won't sell her statues. And because he won't make the Mater give the Deadwood back.

'Seems a small enough yoke to go off on one,' I says. 'Is there something else bothering her?'

'She fixates on something she can't have,' Murt goes. 'Like taking over the business for example. And we're back to square one.'

As he's going around picking things off the floor, he tells me Lena's not the first one in the family to have mental problems. Apparently there was some grand-uncle who lived out his days in an asylum in Dublin. Some aunt who was eccentric to the point of not trusting electricity. Cos of hearing voices in the wires she cut off everything, pulled out all the cables.

'Speaking of family, what's the story with some cousin Rose?'

'Haven't seen her in donkey's years.' He's hanging and re-hanging a picture on the wall.

'Where is she?' I says.

'Ballycalla, her home place. She was nursing abroad, came back years ago to look after her mother. Terrible arthritis in that family. She was a great dancer in her day.'

'Would she know much about my father?'

'Thing is, Frank,' he says, getting all busy putting the tea cloths back up on the rack, 'I find even with the bits and pieces that pass through here, you can rarely say for sure what's true. One son'll say this pipe was the father's favourite; the daughter'll swear blind it ruined every draw of tobacco for him.'

I'm only half-listening; he does go on a bit. There's an old dresser he uses like a filing cabinet, with bills and newspaper cuttings and papers, no crockery. Lena's piked most of the stuff onto the floor. In fairness, Murt is some hoarder. I'm picking up handfuls of papers, stuffing them back in the plate holders.

'He was some go-boy your father. Even as a little lad,' Murt goes.

'I wonder when exactly he knew he had it. The gift. The exactly first time he was sure.'

'All different back then.'

'What d'ya mean?'

'Medicine's come on a long way since. There was very little available then, only all home-made remedies. Religion I suppose played its part.'

Sometimes I haven't a clue what Murt's going on about.

'You, Frank, are not, how can I say, as circumscribed as past generations.'

Another ten minutes, I'm nearly finished, just securing the arm of a chair with gaffer tape, when the phone vibrates. Hopper: *on the way.*

Murt's totally distracted by the whole situation with Lena. She left in a strop with a rucksack full of lavender. She's trying to hitch over to a farmer's market in Portarlington to sell the stuff. I can see he's peppering to go after her, so I say I'll finish up.

Out front, I'm toeing the last of Lucky's splinters to the wall, wondering will Murt bother trying to stick the dog back together, when I hear an engine coming out of nowhere. Screeches up to the footpath. Hopper gunning Ruth's little green car. I don't know did I think Lena was gonna run me down or what, but my heart is thumping. 'What the fuck?'

'Jump in.' He heads off, drives parallel to the river until we reach Slater's Bridge. 'Will we take a spin around?'

'Where?'

'At the top of Killeshin. There's some festival thing on up there.'

It's his funeral if anyone spots him driving Ruth's car. But I have to admit I'm glad not to be going back home just yet.

There's a fair bit of traffic heading up the same direction as us, so we decide to cut off about halfway and park up. There's a field we used to cycle up to when we mitched off. A nice pile of rocks in the corner; if you climb up you're looking down across the whole town. Hopper has a joint rolled already. I get a big hit straight off and climb off the rock onto a nice patch of springy soft moss and lie down. I'm looking directly up at the sky, which is huge if you're flat under it.

Staring at clouds drifting by real high, I focus in on one in particular. It's changing shape at the edges, real gradual, getting longer and thinner.

What did she say, *eight's not the magic number*? Yeah, Lena, so what, it's not. I don't know why she's developed such a set against the Da.

A cricket kicks off with chirping not far from my left ear. Quare difficult yokes to catch hold of, crickets; we used to try and fill a jam jar with them when we were kids.

A girl wouldn't count? Well, there's no girls in our family. Unless she's heard something about Bernie. How could she? No, she wasn't having a dig at Bernie; she never mentioned him. She always preferred Bernie to the rest of us anyways.

Another cricket starts up right near my hand. When I look first, I can't pick it out. Then I see it hanging on to a tall blade of grass. Once you rec it, it's one hundred per cent obvious, real distinct from all the background.

How many he had . . . a girl is only a half . . . Suddenly the penny drops. *How many . . .* I get it. That's why she was going on about eight. She's implying the Da was playing away from home. That he had another kid. And I'm not the seventh son.

'You're gone dead quiet,' Hopper goes.

I don't want to say what I'm thinking, feel like I'm betraying the Da even if it's just in my head. 'I'm listening to the crickets.'

I can't remember which cloud I was watching so I pick another one, concentrate on that.

If there was a son before Lar, or after, that would make eight. I'd be eight. Like she said, eight's not the magic number. In one way it's the kind of bullshit Lena would say to wind me up. But it does explain why the gift's not coming through in me. Nothing to do with Bernie. Bernie. I'm stoned so it takes a minute to sink in. Bernie would be seven then, not me. But if he goes ahead with what's he's saying, if he is on some level not a boy, that's a sort of plus one, minus one situation in the family. Does it work out in my favour in the end?

'Come on, Frank, you'll get something sorted with June.'

'It's not that.'

I wasn't going to tell him, but I need to say some of this out loud. As best I can, I lay out the situation to Hopper, telling him about Bernie, what Murt said. Then this new twist if Lena is saying what I think she is.

'Hang on,' he goes. 'I'm not one hundred per cent clear, but are you telling me you don't have the gift?'

'Probably not.'

'But how did you cure the warts and rashes? And that kid's ringworm last week?'

'Placebo. Just happens. You could do the same if you tried. Nothing special about me.'

After thinking about it for a while he shakes his head. 'Setting the Bernie bit aside, Lena's only winding you up. Even if there was any legs to the story, why would this Rose tell her?'

I'm not thinking clear enough to work it all out. But the minute the notion popped into my head, that the Da might have had another kid, it's got a hold of me. Like I already knew or it fitted into place.

'Their paths crossed in Wexford. She lives in Ballycalla and it came up. But I think she's on to something,' I says.

'I was there once. Got stuck for ages hitching back from Gannagh Strand. Pissing rain in Ballycalla.'

My mind drifts to last night, before all the shenanigans with Lena. Chatting to June at the bar. That was so simple; clean in a way. The last straightforward thing that's happened to me.

'Beautiful beach,' he goes. 'Only about one hour away, tops.'

'What is?'

'Gannagh Strand. I mean, Ballycalla. I'm just thinking, if you wanted to clear up the story regarding your father, we could take a run down. Now that we have the car. Could even head on after for a quick swim and home.'

'I don't know this Rose woman from Adam. Can't just arrive up out of nowhere.'

'Didn't Lena say she wanted you to visit her? I'd say she's hoping you'll show up.'

'That's not what Lena said.'

'Frank, you're in a heap. Sounds like what Rose knows is a bit of this puzzle you can get a handle on. Look at it as a kind of quest, to sort yourself out.'

I don't know what to think. Everybody else is looking after themselves: the Mater and Bernie on their skite to London; even the Da reappearing out of the blue as the Deadwood, all satisfied with himself. What have I got going on: fuck all. No job. The future I thought I had thrown into a heap by my own brother. Finding out my Da never believed in me. Maybe because he was hiding from his own past. Does it make more sense if the Da had another kid why he'd never tell me anything one way or another about the gift? Nothing to do with Bernie. Why not?

'Bit risky, you taking Ruth's car and all.'

'C'mon, Frank. I'm gagging to go somewhere. We've all the time in the world and money in our pockets.'

In my bones I feel there's something in the mix that, I don't know, might change things up. My cloud is after floating over the sun completely, throwing a big dark shadow across our part of hill. Then I remember I was supposed to ring June, but I don't have her number. Even if I did have it, I wouldn't be up for it right now.

'Alright then,' I says. 'May as well go for spin anyways, see how it goes.'

Once I've agreed, Hopper's mad to get moving. If we get stopped by the cops or anything, we're fucked. No insurance or licence or any of that shit. But you only live once. Unless you're the Deadwood; trust him to have an encore.

Back in town, we go our separate ways at the roundabout. He'll pick me up at home in half an hour. He's some cans and a bit of weed left over from last night and I'll bring whatever grub I rustle up at home.

I'm passing along the street again, where the pair of shoes were. Now there's only one, tipped over onto the road. There's something pathetic-looking about it. I don't know why. Maybe because there's no point to one shoe. What did Hopper say this was going to be? An epic journey, like *Lord of the Rings*. From Carlow to Ballycalla and back in one day. Epic, alright.

On the Road

I'm getting my togs and towel from the hot press when I see a cat vaulting onto McDermott's shed, running along the back wall like a bat out of hell. Thinking of the Deadwood under the gazebo, I get a sudden fear that Lena might not have gone to Portarlington at all. She could come sneaking back around once I'm gone. I'd never hear the end of it from the Mater if the Deadwood got lifted on my watch.

Once I've thrown a few things in the rucksack, I go out and wriggle in under where I saw the Mater wriggling out. She hasn't even buried him properly, just stuck a few bits of newspaper and plastic bags around, handful of soil thrown on top. I lob him into my bag, stick a few packets of biscuits and caramel bars in on top. Then I remember the money I got from work, most of it still in the top drawer. May as well bring that too. I tuck it in under the Deadwood. I have a last look around upstairs, the sitting room, and the kitchen. All fine except for the Katie Taylor cut out on the table. It looks wrong, threatening. I pick it up and head out.

Hopper's already waiting in the car, all set to go. I put my rucksack in the boot, notice he has a good bit of gear thrown in. I don't mention to him yet that I decided to bring the Deadwood with me.

'What's all the stuff in the back?' I ask.

'I threw in the tent and a few bedrolls, in case.'

'In case nothing, Hopper. You'd want to leave this car back tonight. Someone'll notice,' I says.

I still have Katie in my hand; I stick her on the dashboard, facing into the road through her empty sockets.

Once we're out of town, I start thinking of the Da having another kid. If it turned out the baby was a girl, bit mad to think we might have a sister, or half-sister or any kind of sister at all. That makes me think of the song Bernie was singing about being my sister. But then she wouldn't have any effect on the seventh son situation.

Could be some kick in the teeth for Lar if it turns out he's not the eldest. Or maybe no skin off his nose, out in Melbourne, living it up. But if that is the case and it makes Bernie the seventh son, how's he going to shoulder the responsibility of producing the next seven sons? Throw a bit of a spanner into his plans.

'Some week, eh?' Hopper goes. 'In a way, getting laid off's given us our ticket to freedom, cash in hand.'

Not sure that's exactly the case.

'Tune in next week,' he goes, 'when Frank's crisis about whether warts is his destiny is resolved. And Billy Whelan's dark secret, revealed. The suspense is killing us.'

Something about my life feels like I'm already a bit suspended. I should be calling June about now. She must think I'm a right arsehole with Hopper getting her number for me and now nothing.

Hopper gives me a dig in the arm. 'Come on, Frankie, cheer up.'

I'm remembering Lena's blood dripping into the cornflakes. I was dead right to take the Deadwood along for the ride. 'That Lena's thrown me right off.'

'Look,' Hopper goes. 'The statue's safe and sound; she'll never go digging up the garden. Let your mother decide what to do about it when she gets back.'

I don't mention that, actually, we have Deadwood riding shotgun with us. Hopper turns the music back up and we get stuck into a bag of prawn crackers. Bit stale. I check the date but they're only out by three weeks.

'Where'd she get the picture of Katie Taylor in the first place?' says Hopper.

'Who?'

'Lena.'

'I told ya, she carved it out of the back of the cornflakes.'

'How old are those cornflakes? The Olympics was ages ago. Sure Katie's gone professional now.'

'Oh yeah. Some pallet fell over in the storeroom. We've about a hundred boxes of cornflakes and Cheerios in the attic. They keep forever. Some of them is well crushed; you're only mixing dust with milk. Saying that, another box'll be all bent but you'd get a decent bowl out of it.'

The countryside is flying past outside. We're going through a part that has a lake and woods around it. You'd start to relax looking out the window for a while. I get a feeling we're heading towards something, like when you're on your way to a party or a match. It's not a bad way to be, different from drifting along, letting things happen or not. We're probably taking twice the time we need, zigzagging around the back roads, but sure, what's the rush? Hopper is full of chat, par for the course. You never get a chance to be thinking about anything for too long before he's off on another run.

'I dropped into that meeting the other night,' he goes. 'About Wolf Night. You know, the council want to change it. Celebration of Lights.'

For a lad who always says he'd give his right arm to leave Carlow, his head is quare caught up in the town's business.

'What's that about?'

'Some historical thing about the switching on of electric lights. They want to downplay the fact we kilt the last wolf in Ireland.'

'What about the scallion eating?'

'That's going ahead, no bother.'

Scallion-eating county champion. Since he was thirteen, Hopper's been gobbing down more scallions than anyone else on an annual basis. You'd be amazed at the respect it gets him; lads in remote corners of the county have been known to stand Hopper a pint on the back of it.

'What'd ya go to that meeting for? Some auld one you're into?'

'Now that you mention it, Colette Aylward was there. You know, from the Credit Union. Separated, two kids.'

'She's fucking ancient. Her youngest is playing on the minor team.'

'Very fit herself. No, I got wind of the word there was going to be a right dingdong. I heard your man Theo Nolan was to be fired from the committee.'

'The hotel Nolans?'

I remember Theo coming into our history class once, giving us a talk on old uniforms and guns. He's mad into all that military stuff. You'd often see him, if there was any historical anniversary, parading around town in an army jacket or wearing a gun belt.

'Is he back on the drink?' I says. 'The Mater said he spent a month on that farm in Tullow, you know, for alcoholics, drug addicts. He was only out a week and got barred from Morrissey's for wearing a bayonet doing his shopping, blind drunk.'

'Think it's more to do with him being some class of a paedophile. He's legged it over to England anyways, so nothing happened.'

'I thought there was only one class. That was into kids.'

'Seemingly there's the sort that gets into it offa the internet, kiddie porn. They can be retrained. And there's another sort it's in their genes, pure born evil.'

'How do you know that?' I says.

'Seen a documentary on one of them lifestyle channels.'

He says it's like getting a vicious pit bull that's been treated inhuman so it's all they know; you have a chance at turning them around. But there's others that's been bred for their fighting temperament. Bred into them for generations. Can't do nothing with them. Impossible to tell which is which by appearance alone. 'I suppose the same is true for people,' he goes.

'What'cha mean?'

'You can't say for sure what's a person's true nature or what they learnt. Like with your healing thing. If it turns out you're seventh in the family or not, maybe it doesn't matter. If you want to keep doing what you're doing, what difference?'

Typical Hopper, make out like everything'll turn out alright in the end. He just doesn't get it.

'Aren't some dogs quare smart though?' I says. 'Seen a programme where they pick the smartest dog and he flies a plane.'

'That's all we fucking need, dogs that can fly planes. Lads like us'll never work again.'

That train of thought is interrupted when Hopper announces he's bursting for a piss and takes a turn off down some dirt track. We both get out and stand over by a low hedge. There's a big stretch of fields, house and sheds in the distance. I start to get this wild tangy smell. Foxes' den maybe.

'Get that smell, Hopper?'

'What?'

'Sharp like.'

'I suppose when you say it,' he goes. 'All I know is I'm starving.' He goes around, opens up the boot, has a root around for biscuits. Next thing he's back holding my bag up in the air. Knew he'd go ballistic when he found the Deadwood. 'What's this doing here?'

'The Mater left me responsible for it. What odds to you?'

'Because it's like it has some weird grip on you,' Hopper goes. 'I thought we left this glorified stumpy jack miles behind.'

'My money's in there too so don't be swinging that bag around.'

He doesn't answer; puts the rucksack down on the ground, steps over a small ditch, and sits up against the grassy verge. He must've found the Jammie Dodgers anyways because he's eating two. He takes a second pair out of the packet and puts that in his gob. Always eats them in pairs. Munches away without offering any to me.

I walk over, take the Deadwood out of the bag. I stand him up on the car bonnet. Handling the wood, looking directly at the lips gouged out, I honest to God feel something, like a vibe between me and him. I've never felt that before, even doing the warts. Maybe that's what the healing is like for him who has the gift. Maybe the Da came back to let me feel this. So I'll know when it's not happening for me.

The sun's reflecting off the metal of the door, kind of making a glow around the bottom of the wood, casting a long, sharp shadow. There's something about it; identical to the Da's silhouette.

'Look at that, Hopper.'

'What?' He's smoking a fag but he looks where I'm indicating the shadow on the ground.

'You have to admit that is fucking uncanny. The shadow, the spit of the Da. The nose. The chin for fuck sake.'

He shakes his head. 'Looks like a million other fellahs that have chins and noses.'

How can he not see it? If the Deadwood grew arms and legs and did Riverdance up and down the fucking road he still wouldn't give me an inch.

'You know,' I says, 'a bit of respect for something you don't understand would be something.'

'I don't like it, Frank. You and your mother. All taken up with this bit of wood. I prefer dealing with things I can see in front of my eyes.'

'Look. I was in a heap this morning. It was a snap decision to bring him. You won't even know he's there.'

He looks at me, then stretches out the packet. 'Have a Jammie Dodger,' he goes. 'Or two.'

We head off, pass a couple of bungalows close together then a sign that says *Welcome to Ballycalla*. Hopper parks up in front of a set of identical half-built houses, given up as a bad idea. They've no windows and only the first three have a roof. Who'd want to live here? It's the middle of nowhere. We get our gear and lock the car.

'Why don't you leave that in the boot?' Hopper goes, nodding over at the Deadwood.

I hitch the rucksack up on my shoulder, 'Nah, it's fine, hardly any weight.'

There's not much chat out of us, humping our bags along. The shine is rapidly coming off this trip for me and we've only just begun. This Rose could be ancient, not operating off the full deck. What's she going to make of me showing up out of the blue? I should've thought this through. We pass up along a road with a post office (closed) and a pub, McArthur's (closed). Not a soul in sight. A sorry excuse of a street on the miserableist day of any week.

Not much further on we land up in front of the Traveller's Rest.

'That's an invitation we can't refuse,' Hopper goes. 'We'll see if we can rouse anyone and find out about this Rose.'

We sit up at the bar. There's a fellah down the end, contemplating life forms at the bottom of his glass; a western is muted on the TV.

The barman is keeping himself busy, rearranging bottles. 'Passing through, boys?' he says as he moves up along. 'What can I get you?'

We order a couple of pints.

As he passes back up again to deliver them, Hopper asks if there's anywhere to get a bite to eat. As soon as he says it, I realise I'm hungry myself.

'Chipper'll be open later,' the barman says. 'Or the Korean place around the back, on Watter Road.'

'Think they're closed today, Charles,' your man sitting at the counter goes without lifting his head. 'Fourth Sunday of the month.'

'Korean?' Hopper says.

'That's right,' the barman says. 'We're all gone mad for kimchi here. Ever tried it, lads?'

'No.'

'Related to cabbage.'

The other fellah starts shaking his head. He's the spit of the barman. 'Not at all,' he goes. 'It's a type of radish.'

'The kimchi, Bob?' the barman says louder, raising his

eyebrows in an exaggerated way. 'More akin to a cabbage, is it not?'

The two fellahs, each side of the counter, neither willing to give an inch, not even glancing in the other's direction. The barman turns back to the cash register, says quietly, 'I'd say he's thinking more of the musaengchae.'

Bob stands up – 'Now you're a mind reader, is it?' – and ambles out to the jacks. When he comes back the barman has another pint set up for him on the counter.

'Is there a woman by the name of Rose living around here?' Hopper asks.

'Rub-a-dub Rose,' Bob says into his pint.

'Alright, Bob, take it easy,' the barman goes. 'Rose Whelan?'

'That's it,' I says. 'She's a cousin.'

'She's on Watter Road. After the Kimchi House.'

'Is that the road we came in on?'

'I doubt it. Everyone thinks the village ends here, but if you follow on around the trees, it splits. Left'll take you out the coast road, and right, the village takes up again.'

'Couldn't pay a man his weight in gold to cut down those trees,' Bob adds.

'She might be at the funeral, though.'

'You mean the removal, Charles,' Bob corrects him. 'She'll have to be back later. Never misses her Sunday–'

'Later might be too late for these boys,' the barman interrupts him, and they're stuck in over what would be late or too late. These two'd pick a fight with their own toenails.

'Are ye on your way to that big shindig?' the barman goes to us, ignoring your man.

'What's that?' Hopper perks up.

'We'd a van come through the other day, looking for directions. Dutch, I think. There'd be all types there.'

'I don't know how they ended up here,' Bob goes. 'Hardly the most direct route from Dublin. Or anywhere.'

'All depends, doesn't it?'

Off again, arguing about the quickest way from A to B.

We finish our pints, pick up our bags, and head for the door. The Deadwood isn't too heavy but I'm wondering now was it a good idea to bring him along, lugging him around random places.

'That sounds like something,' Hopper goes.

'What does?' My mind is fixed on what I might say to this Rose woman. The nearer I'm getting to meeting her, the less clear I am on what's the point.

'That crew that was headed to a party. There's a rave planned for this weekend. Some beach around here, but they didn't know where exactly. Were you not listening?'

We pass Carmine's Chippers (closed). There's a fellah behind the counter wiping down ketchup squeezies with a dishcloth. Hopper reckons we should get a takeaway from the Korean place, if it's open, and bring it with us to the beach. That's after we find Rose.

We take the left at the end of the street. A dense bank of trees rears up sudden and the road splits around it. You'd definitely think you were back in the countryside. We follow along on the right and sure enough, after a few hundred yards, a street starts up again. I spot an old petrol station on the other side of the road. I've a quick gander but the pumps aren't even connected and the shop's deserted; inside is hay bales stacked up against empty shelves. Very bleak turn to this place.

Up a rise is a smaller road with a terrace of houses on each side. *Watter Road* the sign says.

I'm starting to realise I might have made a bad decision, going along with Hopper's notions. I can't believe I was at home this morning with the house to myself and June's number in my hand; now I'm in the middle of nowhere with the Deadwood in a bag and Hopper driving a borrowed car. The closer we're getting, the less I want to meet this Rose. Getting a feeling in the pit of my stomach that this mightn't turn out to be a laugh. Coming here at all is just giving legs to whatever shiteology Lena was going on with.

'Let's skip the Rose thing,' I goes. 'Head straight to the beach.'

'Fuck sake, Frank,' Hopper goes, checking himself out in a window and tidying his hair. 'We're grand. We've loads of time.'

We pass the first few houses on the street, a bit run-down looking. The fourth one has the front converted and a sign, *Kimchi House*, over it. Next door is well kept, painted up blue. That must be it.

'I've nothing to say to her,' I goes. 'It's just stirring up trouble or something.'

'Fine. You keep your trap shut. I'll say I'm you.'

'What?'

'She won't know which of us is which. I'll chat her up, see what Lena was going on about.'

If it means I don't have to do the talking, fair enough. There's a picture in the front window made of out of little stitches that says:

He who dares not grasp the thorn
Should never crave the rose.

Hopper gives me a wink and then gives two sharp rings on the doorbell.

We've Only Just Begun

We'll start out walkin' and learn to run
And yes, we've only just begun

So many roads to choose and I have to hand it to Hopper, I'm glad he's driving us down this one. I don't know am I exerting my influence on Frank or are we just in syncopation? Same tune, just a half-beat off. Whatever, we're heading in the right direction and I'm happy as the day is long.

It's funny for your head to be swarming with an understanding, or more rightly, an acceptance, of everything. Some resting place for my head, given that I'm headless and less all the other bits and pieces. But to grasp the very minutiae of life; for the first time I've a sense what they mean when they talk about the man who sees every fallen sparrow. Not that I've met him, no sight nor sign of him.

For every sparrow that falls, they say; now I'm the *cratúr* and the drop. Every eagle that wheels above us, I'm lifted up too, the wing and the wind. Not as overwhelming as you'd imagine. I feel the spirit of myself everywhere and yet I'm drawn inward and back to the very first ring of the tree stump

I inhabit, the seed in the dark ground that begat me. All is within.

I was never too much of a reader; preferred a radio programme if I was relaxing, loved a hand of cards. A lot of what I picked up was from the books Mossy was forever poring over. His favourite topic was about the wars, First and Second. Not as much interested in our own troubles, but we didn't have any lineage to the struggles of this country. We were part of the great unwashed, who washed once a week. Heads down over a lathe or a sink. Not to say I was unaware of the worth of my labour, I was a union man to the last. Our road crew was renowned in the council; many's the time we battled together for the rights of the working man.

I'm back there now, sitting in my armchair and Mossy trying to tell me about some book, the story of one of Hitler's main men, an architect.

The name eludes me now and here's something to note about the afterlife, or at least my afterlife: forgetting is a different kettle of fish. In life, things you forget still have a hold on your mind; they tug on a thread as if to say, 'Remember me?' You can't, but you can't fully forget. It's a right aggravation. All the memories, they're there in us somewhere, but like a shed with everything piled in, it's impossible to lay your hand on a particular screw or wrench when you need it. Anyhow, it's a different experience now; there's nothing bad attached to forgetting. Can you imagine that? As if the facts you got acquainted with turned into gas and escaped in a balloon. Puff. Gone. The space left behind lets in a different kind of awareness, things you didn't know you could know.

So I'm having a smoke, a cup of tea, and trying to listen to some music programme on the radio, and the fierce face of Mossy explaining it all to me, the concentration camps and so on. There's only a couple of Jewish families living in Carlow, and I don't know too much about their way of life. He's thinking I'd be interested because I work on the roads and yer man was in charge of roads and railway systems. For the Nazis. Eventually I says to him, 'Did he not know his plans was going to send hordes of people to the gas chambers? Was he ever found guilty?'

Mossy gets as frustrated with me. 'It's not that simple, Da. Before Speer officially knew about what was going on, he knew and he didn't know, if you know what I mean.'

Speer. That was your man's name.

I probably laughed at him. I did laugh at him. I'm there laughing at him, except now I'm in the thick of Mossy's frustration as well. I'm the grey cells in his head realising things aren't black and white, and he can't express hisself. I'm inside all that, reaching out to touch life, beyond the edge of it, into the experience. What's the word? Not untouchable . . . intangible. Another new one for me. I like the *tang* in the middle of it. It's bang on for describing the thoughts Mossy was getting his head into. I didn't give the lad a lot of leeway. He was a bit of a philosopher, besides being a quare wild fellah. Even if I couldn't make head nor tail of how he was going at things, I suppose he could have done with a bit of company on the journey. Water under the bridge, as they say.

I feel a bit like that fellah Speer now, with the story that's starting to unravel for me. I'm facing into what I know and don't know. Worse still, facing up to things I did know in my heart but I never let them travel out of that vault. Travelling and unravelling. Seems like I'm to make another journey, though whether it's mine or Frank's, or whether they're one and the same, is hard to make out.

Hard station for him, parked between the knowing and the not knowing. Wasn't like that for me. I knew it, so help me God, when I first laid hands on my own mother's arm. She's taking a dish out of the range and her arm touches off the side. A big red weal comes up. She sits in at the table, her sleeve rolled up to her elbow, a grey-and-blue-striped blouse I can see as vivid, a wet cloth over the burn.

'Show me, Mam,' I says, a child's fascination with pain and damage. I must've only been five or six. I reach out and place my fingers on it to see if it's hot. A burn must be hot as a poker.

'Easy now,' she says. She's wincing as the tips of my fingers rest on the bright red line.

The pain runs through my whole body and back into the earth from whence it came, as natural as passing water. The knowing fills my head, like a road opening up. Mother knows what's happened; she feels the change on her arm.

I wet myself, not through fear, but with the strange naturalness of it all. As she helps me change my shorts, she tells me not to mither myself about this gift. Not to dwell on it either or it could grow into a curse. I'm back there now and I see an expression on her face I'd not noticed the first time. As if something got decided and not in the way she wanted it to go.

What did I know? Youth is a funny thing. Everything is new and rare so it's hard to know what's of importance, what will last. Then you forget what you didn't know. Once you learn to walk, it's as if you never crawled.

Fairly quickly the house was inundated with callers looking for some relief, not just from my father, but from me, the little wonder child. The gift was fully in me and the word was out. It was my mother sorted out the butcher apprenticeship. I don't know what she had to do to get my father to agree to it. I see now she wanted to get me away from it all.

Which brings me back to Frank and what he thinks he needs to learn. If he could only ever know himself as clear and as true as the breath he's taking at this very moment. But sure, hit the road, Jack, there's a journey ahead of us. In the end, the knowledge will settle in him as familiar as yesterday.

I'm plonked here at Frank's feet, fair humming with hope facing Rose's front door. Haven't seen her in years, not since her mother's funeral. I was embarrassed to meet her then because the time before I'd come to her for help . . . about Letty. When she couldn't tell me anything straight off, I felt relief as much as anything. As if I'd made the effort and I had permission now to give up. I think Rose saw that in me, how I wasn't being honest with myself. Sometimes another person can be a mirror for a face of your own you don't want to see.

'He who dares not grasp the rose.' Not me, not this time, not on my last go round.

We'll start out walkin' and learn to run
And yes, we've only just begun

No truer words, Compadre Como.

Kimchi in Ballycalla

An old woman answers the door. Maybe it's the lipstick, or the way she has a big mane of red hair all clipped up, but there's something a bit intimidating about her.

'How can I help you?' she says.

'I'm looking for Rose. Rose Whelan?' Hopper says.

She looks from one to the other of us. 'And you're?'

'I'm Frank Whelan,' he goes, poker face. 'Billy's son. Youngest son. We're cousins, distant.'

'Are we? And you?' she says, looking direct at me.

'Hopper, I mean, Tom McGrath.'

'A friend of mine,' Hopper jumps in. 'We were on the way to Gannagh Strand. My cousin Lena met you recently and she said about dropping in if I was around the area.'

'Did she now? She's an unusual character alright.'

'That's one way of putting it,' I says.

'How did you find the house?' she asks. 'You weren't here before.'

'We dropped into the Traveller's Rest and they pointed us in the right direction,' he goes, giving a full blast of the charm.

She shakes her head at this, 'Those boys, you'd be hard-pressed to tell them apart.'

She must mean the barman and the other fellah. It's then I notice her hands, totally gnarled, the wrist huge and swollen. I seen arthritic limbs before, but these is quare bad.

'An alcoholic and a life-long pioneer. One was always going to be carrying the other,' she goes on. 'Poor Charles with his inner ear, going down into that cellar. Tricky things, families.'

Hopper's nodding away but she's staring at me. I'm looking down to avoid her face. Then, in case she thinks I'm staring at her hands, I look further down at my runners. Hopper's talking again. Telling how he was there once before, hitching back from Gannagh Strand, all this shite. She's looking from one to the other of us. I pick up the rucksack with the Deadwood and then Rose is staring at that as if she can see the Da inside.

'If you're a couple of chancers or clowns,' she goes, 'I don't know which it is.'

'We're not up to anything,' I answer.

'No, but you're a Whelan through and through. The spit of your father,' she says to me. 'I don't know who this other chancer is. Are you in some kind of trouble?'

'No.' She must think I'm a total eejit. 'Because I'm not much for talking, we thought . . . Hopper's more that.'

'Come in. I've visitors due over later, mind.'

She leads us into the front room and tells us to sit. There's loads of furniture, dark, nice-quality teak; strange gewgaws on the sideboards; rugs on top of the carpet. The walls are covered with pictures; a huge curved sword hangs over the fireplace. Murt'd have a field day here. Apart from the woeful whiff I'm picking up off the carpet.

'Which boy are you?'

'Frank,' I says. 'Me and Bernie, the twins.'

'He's the seventh,' Hopper adds.

'So you're Frank. I suppose you're the one who's inherited the gift.'

'Yeah.'

'Or is it a curse?' she goes on.

'It is what it is.' I don't know what more to say so I say nothing.

A big TV in the corner is paused on a cowboy hanging on to a bucking horse for dear life.

'Life before the dish,' she goes. 'Was it worth living?'

A dish? Maybe she's another one mad as a box of frogs; probably why I never heard much about her.

'How's that?' Hopper goes.

'I'm fully connected since last December,' she says. 'Twenty-four-hour westerns. And Al Jazeera.'

The satellite dish, that's what she's on about.

'And the family, Frank?'

I tell a bit of family news; how most of the lads is out in Australia and the Mater is working, and Murt and d'Emporium.

'Lena's like her mother,' Rose says.

I don't really remember Lena's mother so I've nothing to say to that. Hopper sees this as an opening and decides to ask where she met Lena. Rose doesn't seem to want to answer this directly, says something about paths crossing and it all goes silent for a minute. It's now or never.

'It's just that Lena is back in Carlow and we were talking about my da,' I goes. 'She thought you might know a bit of the family history. I'm interested because being the seventh son and all.'

She pauses for a minute as if she's thinking hard about something. 'Lena could put two and two together and get twenty-two so I'm not sure – oh, you're awake.'

165

Before she has another word out, the pouffe in the corner stands up and moves. This enormous matted wig slowly makes its way across the room.

Rose bends down to scratch the furball. 'You've roused Eugene.'

'A fine specimen,' Hopper nods. He involves himself in scratching what I'd have to guess are the ears. Because it's pure dreads, arse to head. The way Hopper's hit it off with the dog seems to have softened Rose.

'Cup of tea now you're here?'

'Tea'd be grand,' Hopper goes.

She unpauses the TV and goes out of the room.

I turn on him. 'Let's head on. A weird vibe here.'

'Hold on.' He's settling himself back into the couch. 'She's sound. Ask her more about your da.'

'I don't think she knows anything. I don't care anyways.'

The smell in the room is getting to me. I bet Eugene sneaks in behind the couch of an evening when Rose is watching TV and has a quiet little piddle before waddling back in front of the fire, acting as if he'd only stretched his paws.

'Watch the ridge, boys.' It's Rose sticking her head in the door. 'Watch the ridge.'

It takes me a second to realise she's talking about the TV. The cowboys are trudging along the valley when the camera pans up to the ridge above them. Sure enough, one tiny silhouette turns into a whole line. She goes over, highers up the sound and stands, glued to the battle, saying nothing. Then as if everything happens by clockwork, the hairball starts to glide towards the door, Rose hands the TV control to me, and they move out in sync. Right as the door closes behind them, the front doorbell rings. Something odd about that.

'What happened there?' I says to Hopper.

He shrugs, picks a book off a shelf.

I can hear another woman's voice. Her visitors must be starting to arrive. More social misery to be heaped upon my head. I wish I was in London, not here. Only for the Mater and Bernie not including me in their travel plans. Better still, I should be getting ready to go out to meet June. Once this day is over, things'll have to change.

'Frank, stop muttering,' Hopper hisses, as the door opens and a tartan shopping trolley is pushed through.

Mrs EB Arrives

The shopping trolley is followed into the room by a tiny old woman, foreign. Her hair is boot-polish-black over lashes that'd cut the eye out of your head. She parks the trolley by the door. Eugene follows, then Rose. Hopper's standing up already.

This small person looks from one to the other of us. She sticks out her hand to Hopper. 'So very good to meet with you. I'm Mrs EB.'

'Likewise. I'm Hopper,' he goes. 'That's cousin Frank over there.'

'Cousin Frank,' she goes, shaking my hand

'Mrs EB is from the Kimchi House,' Rose says.

'The restaurant?' Hopper says.

'You have ever tried Korean food?' Mrs EB asks.

'No,' we both go.

'Everyone delayed tonight, on account of the removal. So sad. Crash.' She folds back the top of her shopping trolley and takes out a load of takeaway boxes. Rose sets up some fiddly kind of metal plate on the sideboard, lighting little candles under it. Mrs EB places the containers on top. The smell would put some mouth on you.

'A feast fit for kings,' Hopper goes. The hungry bastard. We'll never get out of here now.

'You may as well have a bit,' Rose goes, unloading the food. 'My crowd are held up. Massive turnout at the removal.'

Then Mrs EB reaches in and takes out a couple of bottles, the size of naggins but rounded with no labels.

'Chill?' Rose goes.

'Maybe quick freezer,' Mrs EB says. 'New batch from nephew. Little bit special. You must take later with your powder.'

When Rose leaves with the bottles, Mrs EB directs me over to the sideboard for food. It's like an all-you-can-eat buffet. I heap a bit of rice on my plate and then spoon different things on top, none of them anything I've seen before. There's one container hasn't been opened so I leave it alone.

Mrs EB bows her head low, goes out, and Eugene follows her. I sit down, balance the plate on my knee. I try some green veg and a stewy kind of thing. Not bad. Stuck into the grub, I've a chance to gather my thoughts. This could still work out okay. Maybe if we get back late tonight; keep the Deadwood off Lena's radar til the Mater gets back. I could find out June's work number, message her. At least say sorry about today. She's out of my league anyways so that'll be the end of that.

Hopper's digging into the big pile of food he's stacked up. He's got his feet well under the table, as per usual. When Rose comes in, he's asking her about where this yoke came from and what's the story with the sword and how he loves westerns as well. She's chatting about working abroad, Africa and India; right up his alley. Every so often she stops to shout instructions at the cowboys. No sign of Mrs EB.

Rose picks a bottle of green stuff off a bookshelf, not dissimilar to the yokes that came out of the shopping trolley. 'This is Mrs EB's special blend. Does a power of good for my arthritis. Goes down a treat with the kimchi.'

She takes three thimble-sized glasses from a shelf and pours us one each. I'm not sure is this a Korean shot, but we raise our glasses and knock it back. I start to cough. Pure rocket fuel.

She silences the TV, cocks her head to one side like a little bird listening. There's a load of noises coming from upstairs. Water pouring from a tap, the creaks and squeaks of someone twisting and turning in a bath. Mrs EB's hardly nipped in for a wash? I keep my eyes on the TV, with a quick glance over to Hopper. For the moment he's doing the same. Rub-a-dub Rose, isn't that what yer man said in the bar?

'In Korea,' Rose goes, 'they run water over their foreheads to clear the mind. Mrs EB gave me a beautiful hand-made ladle for Christmas. You'd think for all the world it was a giant's soup spoon.'

I presume Hopper, the same as me, is trying not to imagine Mrs EB starkers over our heads, throwing water on herself with an enormous spoon. Even Clint Eastwood and his lonely gun battle can't fully distract me.

'Is there plumbing issues in Mrs EB's own house?' I says.

'She's not taking a bath, Frank,' Hopper goes. 'Did you not hear her saying earlier she was going to wash the dog?'

Rose laughs, refills all our glasses, and we down another green one. 'I can't get him into the bath any more.' She's making no attempt to hide the fact she's listening to the goings on upstairs, smiling away at different noises.

Sweat is starting to trickle down my armpits and my back. I put my plate and empty glass down. 'I might get a drink of water,' I says. 'That's quare spicy stuff.'

'Of course, Frank, you'll find the kitchen at the back. Glasses, second press over.'

Her kitchen is immaculate. I think of the chaos back home. Mainly the Mater and Bernie's mess, left for me to sort out as usual. I chug back a glass of water, fill another one. I'm dying for a smoke, so I try the back door. I wonder what the Deadwood is making of all of this, tucked up in the rucksack beside the couch. Once Eugene doesn't cock a leg over him, he'll be alright.

Outside, I sit down at a low table and spark up. The day's stayed warm and there's a real sweet smell coming off these yellow flowers growing along the wall. She's some back garden, stretching way down and surrounded by trees.

The bathroom window is open; I can still hear the splashing but it's not as embarrassing to listen to by myself. Then Mrs EB starts to sing. Must be some auld Korean ballad, for it sounds quare flat. But you have to hand it to her, she's enjoying herself.

Next thing, this yowling starts up. What the fuck? Mrs EB stops singing and the yowl stops. She's splashing away, then she picks the song up again and the strangled howls chime in. Eugene, the boyo, letting out these heartfelt squalls. Out of tune, but somewhat in time. Despite yourself, you'd be drawn into the whole lunacy of it: Mrs EB singing away; Eugene pouring out his doggie heart. For a minute, I'm enjoying the strangeness of the situation. Then I remember the blood in the cornflakes and why we came here. A feeling spreads across my guts like melting ice. I get up sharpish and walk down the path to shake it off. The garden's all different areas laid out, so if you're in one place you're private from another.

Tucked in behind some tall grasses is a real fancy shed, lovely spruce planks with a high window at the end. I open the door and a blast of heat hits me. Seems like it's not a garden shed at all but a sauna yoke. They have one at the swimming pool, but I've never used it. Stuck my head in once, but I found the whole thing mortifying. Sitting in your togs, getting red and sweaty with a load of strangers? No, I left it at that. Imagine having that in your garden. What kind of set-up have we got ourselves into?

I wander a bit more in behind a few elder trees and find what you'd take to be a little pond. Up close it's pretty deep with steps going down into it. I put my hand in; the water is freezing.

When I go back into the sitting room, Hopper and Rose are sipping away on bigger thimbles, yellowy liquid this time, making no bones about the fact that they're fully listening to the singing upstairs.

'Was he always very sensitive?' Hopper goes. There's something about his voice makes me wonder what the fuck she's giving us.

'It's when Eugene really shows his emotions,' Rose whispers as if they're sharing a secret. 'He's in love with her.'

'Animals and music,' Hopper goes. 'We don't hear much about it all the same.'

What's he on about?

Next thing Rose lifts herself out of her seat. 'I'll put the kettle on.'

The minute she's out of the room I've a chance to talk to Hopper. 'What's the fucking story here?'

'Relax, my man. All is well.'

'There's a sauna in the garden. What are we drinking?'

'Ginseng. Real rare shit. I feel a million dollars. What about you?'

'I want to go.'

'Don't, Frank, don't wreck the buzz,' he goes. 'She knows loads of shit about everything. Now we've got a rapport, you know, we'll get into the family stuff.'

The door opens and in comes the bould Eugene, gliding across to his original position, all fluffed up. Then Mrs EB.

She starts piling the rice on her plate, dolloping sauces on top. When she stops, she gives us the hairy eyeball. 'Very spicy, boys?'

'It's nice,' I go. In fairness, it was better than I expected.

'But spicy?' she insists.

'Not by my reckoning,' Hopper says.

Mrs EB holds up the dish that wasn't on the hot plate. The top is gone off it. She asks if we ate this one. I didn't but Hopper says he had a bit. Trust him to eat the only one that was closed. It must be her favourite or something.

'Oh my goodness,' Mrs EB goes. 'Usually too much hot. Only good for me. Korean people.'

Rose is back with a different bottle opened.

'What's this?' I says.

'This one increases your circulation. Vitality, really.'

'I can feel it already. Miraculous. You could send that to the Vatican, have it canonised,' Hopper goes.

Mrs EB tells us about what we're drinking: Korean red ginseng with ground-up deer antlers. I don't know much about ginseng, but she says there's all different kinds. The wild one is better, very rare. Her nephew in Korea sends it over to her. By a top-secret route. The way she's going on, you'd think they were trafficking cocaine. What I want to ask about is the antlers. Where'd she get them from, the zoo? If you think about it, it's a bit like drinking powdered bone or toenails.

She goes over to her shopping trolley and takes out a red box. 'Take one,' she says, offering the contents to Hopper. Looks like dried-up slices of beef.

He takes one and passes it to me.

'Ginseng, honey, secret ingredient,' she goes. 'One hundred per cent first grade.'

It's fair chewy but not too unpleasant. It does get your system pumping. My heart is racing a bit; the sweat starts rolling.

'How much this box cost?' Mrs EB goes.

'No idea,' says Hopper.

'Guess,' she goes, clapping her hands.

'Twenty quid,' I guess.

'Up up up.'

'Seventy?'

'Up up and away,' Rose goes. Even Eugene shifts his arse with the excitement building.

'Haven't a clue,' I say.

'Two hundred.'

'What?' Hopper asks.

Mrs EB nods seriously. She's taken off her shoes, is using her toes to scratch Eugene's back. He's a bit less whiffy since his bath. But for some reason I'm getting other smells: the fluffy cushions on the sofa, a sharp plastic off the TV, Mrs EB's lemony perfume.

Rose chimes in, 'She cured Eugene of cancer. He owes his life to Mrs EB.'

'Will cure person too with the senses,' says Mrs EB.

'Is that right?' Hopper goes.

'Nearly blind. My eyes returned to me,' she says, opening her eyes as wide as anything. 'Look.'

We all follow her stare across the room. Are we looking at the tiny gap where the strips of wallpaper don't meet?

'I am seventy-eight years old, yes, but I see flies fighting across the room. Doing love together also.'

She seems to be looking at a picture, so I look too, for the flies. Shiny threads are strung from nail to nail and back again to form a sailboat, but no flies fighting.

174

'Not now,' she says. 'Back in my home. Very hot. No flies here. Only on Eugene, maybe.' She squeals at this.

Hopper coughs, his voice dead serious. 'Mrs EB, what about, for argument's sake, the nose? Any impact there?'

'Very interesting.' Mrs EB sits back and stares at Hopper. 'Taste and smell go hand in hand.' She grasps one of her own hands in the other.

I look at Hopper and he's grasping his hands the same way. They both smile at each other, like something major got sorted. Odd and fucking odder.

What Rose Knows

I don't know is it the spicy food or the little shots of whatever you're having yourself, but I feel very alert. I'm tuned
into everything: the kimchi cabbage stuck between my teeth;
the glint off the sword's edge; the speed of the conversation
flying back and forth between Hopper and Mrs EB and
Rose. The only thing is, Rose keeps staring at me like I'm
another of her curious objects. Makes me feel like a fish
out of water.

'What's the go with the sauna in your garden?' I ask her.

'You spotted that. Well, to cut a long story short, I won it.
In the local GAA raffle.'

'That's some prize,' Hopper goes.

'The actual prize was a conservatory. Anyway, when I went
to the showrooms, didn't Mrs EB spot a sauna in the yard.'

'Was ordered by a rich banker,' Mrs EB adds. 'Then he goes
pop. Bust.'

Turns out the place was looking to offload it and it's great
for Rose's arthritis. Once she got that sorted, she decided to
get a cold pool built outside to go along with it. Last year she

got her bathroom done up with a massive tub and some fancy shower.

'Then I suppose it took off,' Rose says.

'What d'ya mean?'

'Rose's Bathhouse. Relaxation time,' goes Mrs EB. 'For ladies only. Tonight they are so late. The removal.'

I'm trying to get my head around this when Mrs EB squeals, 'One hundred per cent excellent,' and points at the TV, just as the baddie in the black Stetson gets his head blown off.

'Hip hip hooray.' She's filling up her plate again, offers Hopper another go of the spicy grub and, naturally, he takes a good dollop of it.

Rose starts to pile up some of the empty containers and I give her a hand carrying stuff out to the kitchen. She sorts some dishes at the sink.

'I never made that cup of tea yet,' she goes, putting the kettle on. 'I'd forget my own head with Mrs EB's brew. Potent.'

There's cake slices under a glass cover on the counter. She must've caught me looking at them for she takes the cover off and puts one on a plate in front of me. It was all talk flowing in the sitting room but it's a bit awkward now, just me and her. She sits down at the table and starts in on a piece of cake herself.

'I suppose you don't have as many coming for the cure as the old days?' she says.

'You sort of have to build it up. Though my father always said desperate people'll try anything.'

'It's no life, depending on other people's misery.'

'It worked out alright for him.'

'I saw it in nursing too, everyone wants a miracle. But you can't sell them a pup. There's a lot to be said for plain human kindness. That's why I love the bathhouse. Something honest about sweat and soap.'

She says that people used always be coming to her for advice, even when she was retired from nursing, but she's found her true calling now. All different kinds of treatment she and Mrs EB offer. I'm not sure what 'treatment' means, but I don't ask. Her favourite thing is letting people have a good soak in the bath.

'Here.' She hands me a drink of water. 'Talking of sweat, that's quite a reaction. Mrs EB is a very gifted herbalist.'

She's right. It's like there's a fire burning inside me, my stomach and organs sending out heatwaves.

'Clearing out all the toxins.' She nods. 'That'll burn off any internal fog.'

A blueish glass yoke hangs from a string at the window. It twirls slowly, catches the light. For a split second it's so bright you can't even look direct at it, then nothing.

'I'll never forget,' she goes. 'The day he had to go home. You know your father lived here with us in this house as a child?'

'Did he?'

She says when my grandmother was sick once, the Da got sent to stay with Rose and her mother. When my grandfather came to bring him home, he hid in the coal shed, had to be dragged out covered in black dust. She says no one would cross my grandfather. 'This whole seventh son business, back then, it was nearly worse than having a vocation.'

'Worse?'

'There was a lot put on him. Someone always watching to see how it would manifest. Your grandfather was a very dominant man.'

I've never heard much talk about the grandfather. He was long gone before I was ever born.

'I've heard he had powerful abilities, alright,' I says. 'Could even read your mind.'

'He thought he could. He'd certainly no *meas* for what went on in the minds of women.'

A phone rings in the hall. Rose gets up and goes out. The glass yoke is still twirling but the sun must have shifted too far to light it up. I put my hand under my T-shirt and feel the sweat drying. I'm cooling down again.

Rose comes back in with another little glass, this one with orangey liquid. 'Try this concoction,' she goes. 'We often have it after the sauna, for cooling down.'

'Are these alcoholic?'

'They're worse,' she says. 'I'm surprised you're not dancing yet.'

I sip the drink, the most pleasant-tasting one so far, like very sweet fruit, peachy. I can't see a way to get the conversation going to ask her about the things I came to find out. Hopper'd be far better at this. Maybe back in the sitting room I could give him the nod to try work the chat around. Then a question pops into my head. 'Was my father ever a butcher or anything like that?'

'Well,' she goes, straightening up and facing me. 'If he ever went down that road it came to nothing, so what odds?'

I ask if she remembers how the cure appeared through the different generations, any stories about all that. Might get her talking about whatever Lena was going on about. She's a bit slow to answer, gets a cloth to clear the cake crumbs off the table. She looks at me real direct and asks if I'm looking for any particular story. I say something vague about stories from when the Da was younger, maybe before he met my mother.

She starts chatting on about who was related to who and different uncles and cousins who emigrated and some priest that ran a hospital out in Africa, some place Rose herself worked in for a while. It's sort of interesting but I'm finding it hard to follow the thread of it all.

'We should be heading,' I goes eventually.

'Billy was a funny little boy. My mother adored him.'

I get up to go. On the way out to the sitting room she puts a hand on my arm. 'The last time your father called here, long time ago, he was on his way to Ballyduff. To cure a greyhound, can you believe? Mammy was confined to her bed at that stage, but he had her laughing away, singing all the old tunes. Downstairs with me in the kitchen, he was different. Agitated. Asking me about a woman. Wasn't a name I recognised.'

'Asking what about her?'

Rose got the impression he'd lost touch with this woman. From County Wexford, maybe some place starting with Glen. Can't really remember. The Da thought Rose might have contacts in hospitals, nursing homes, but she was only back in Ireland a short while. Wasn't really connected in.

'Was he was looking for a nurse?' I ask.

'No, Frank, I didn't get the impression it was a nurse.'

She says, according to my father, the woman seemed to have disappeared into thin air. He was a bit shaky about the details. 'He seemed afraid, he'd hardly look me in the eye when he was asking, and that wasn't like your father.'

Something about the turn the conversation has taken, I wish I was back in the car, heading to the beach.

'I couldn't really get any purchase on the situation,' she goes on. 'I always wondered what transpired. The last time I was talking to him was at my mother's funeral. He gave me a good lift, remembering some of the laughs my mother had with him.'

I finish up the cake and put the plate over by the sink. 'Sounds like him, alright.'

'He said he'd call in again when he was down my way. But sure, then he was gone before his time.'

Well, not one hundred per cent gone, because there's a yoke in your sitting room might have something to say about that. Thinking of the Deadwood makes me a bit antsy again.

I should have known Lena was winding me up, going on as if she was in possession of some facts. If you think about it, all Rose has said is once upon a time my father asked about a woman and it all came to nothing. And we don't even know who she was or why he wanted to find her. Doesn't feel right, digging into his past like this. I'd be better off now to go into the sitting room, get the rucksack, and head on.

'I could get it for you,' she ploughs on. 'I had a rummage around after Lena was here. Found it.'

'Found what?'

'The woman, her name. Isn't that why you're here? Would you like me to get it?'

I know I should say yes but I feel trapped. Damned if I do and damned if I don't. Why did I bring this on myself? She's staring at me, waiting.

'I'm grand. I just need to use your toilet, please,' I says.

It's the second door at the top of the stairs but the first door is wide open, so I have a quick look in. It's fairly steamy and huge; must be the bathroom where Eugene got the beauty treatment. There's a raised platform with loads of big cushions over the other side of the room, might have pipes under it. The bath itself is on legs, a massive old-fashioned one. A whole wall is taken up with shelves with the most lotions and potions I seen anywhere outside of a chemist. Big jars and tall jars, little hand-written labels on them all. Two baskets have towels spilling out of them. This is the fanciest bathroom I've ever seen. Some racket she's got going here.

181

I think I hear someone shifting downstairs, so I leg it into the toilet next door. The only odd yoke there is a crocheted doll sitting up on the cistern. A spare toilet roll is under her pink skirt, fair enough, but her umbrella is upside down, holding a whole pile of toothpicks. Wooden toothpicks. Who uses a toothpick when they're on the loo? How hygienic is that?

I don't want to think about the thing that's pushing its way into my head: *Find out, Frank; you should know whatever Rose knows.* If I had a chance to set the Deadwood in front of me, I could talk it through, get my head straightened out a bit. Suss out what he wants. I'll have a chance later when I get home. We could always come back another time.

When I come back down, I go straight into the sitting room. Hopper and Mrs EB are sitting together on the couch, the two heads nearly touching.

'We should get going now.' I notice the Deadwood isn't where I left him. 'Where's my bag?' I says. Comes out louder than I expected.

'Relax the kaks,' Hopper goes. 'I moved it out of the way, under the table.'

I go get it and notice the top is a bit open. Fucking Eugene sniffing around, probably had a little nibble on the Deadwood when no one was looking.

Rose comes out of the kitchen and I say goodbye, and, yes, I'll tell Murt and the Mater she was asking for them. We say nothing about what she was talking about earlier.

Mrs EB joins her to see us off at the door. Eugene's little head squeezes in between their feet, panting his farewell.

'Billy was a good man,' Rose says. 'He did his best, on every front.'

'All we can do,' Mrs EB chimes in. 'Our best is the best.'

Talk about stating the obvious. That Mrs EB's not dealing off the full deck. Though the way Hopper is nodding back, you'd think he was looking at Yoda crossed with Einstein.

Hopper's Nose

On the way back to the car, Hopper asks me what Rose said about my da when we were in the kitchen.

'Nothing really, more general chat about the family.'

I say she didn't know anything specific about the Da or his past. He shrugs and doesn't pursue it, seems a bit caught up in his own thoughts.

'I'll tell ya one thing,' Hopper says, switching the engine on. 'That kimchi stuff was alright.'

'Was all a bit head the ball.'

'Would've been even madder if that removal hadn't been on. There'd have been a clatter of women, all ages and stages, sweating it out.'

I'm waiting for him to put the car into gear. But he's tapping his hands on the steering wheel, staring ahead. Something's up. 'Remember the auld lads in the pub were talking about the Dutch crowd in the van?'

'No.'

'Turns out, the lads had some session in the Traveller's Rest, but the women had heard about the very exclusive bathhouse run by your self-same cousin. While they were sweating it out, they mentioned the location. Everyone's camping there for the weekend.'

The Deadwood seems to be taking up more room than before in the footwell so I push the seat right back.

'I've got directions,' he goes. 'We could easily get there for tonight.'

'Tonight? We need to get home.'

'For what?'

'The car.'

'Don't worry about the car. Ruth's not due back til Saturday.'

A bit of me imagines the Mater and Bernie getting back, full of theirselves. Now the Rose visit is behind me, I'd be happy to forget about family stuff for a while.

'Maybe your da'd like a trip to the seaside,' he goes. 'Hook him up with a bit of driftwood. C'mon, Frank.'

I wouldn't be Hopper's mate, I suppose, if I didn't half-believe his ideas do work out good sometimes. 'Alright. G'wan, so.'

As the car is purring along, Hopper fills me in on Rose's business. The women used to have a book club going every fourth Sunday. Then one thing led to another and now they have a sauna club instead. It's building up a reputation; women come from all over to Rose's Bathhouse. That's probably how Lena heard about her. A gang of local women are chipping in to put a jacuzzi in the garage. It's causing ructions in the village.

He takes a joint from his pocket, sparks up. I tell him what Rose was saying about my grandfather being a bit of a bollix. He's not that interested.

'You taste that salad at all?' he goes.

'Nah. Too hot for me.'

'That was Mrs EB's special dish, mega-fucking-spicy.'

When she saw Hopper gobbling down a load of it, it got her thinking. She gave him a few different spices and pickled peppers to try.

Then they got talking.

'About what?' I ask.

'She copped it,' goes Hopper.

'What? You've neck for ten heads?' I wait but he's shut right up now. 'What?'

'Thing is, Frank, I can't taste anything, neither good nor bad. The reason for that is cos I've no sense of smell. At all.'

I think about this. 'Nothing?'

'No. Sometimes I think I can, but it's my mind playing tricks on me.'

I'm trying to think why he never said nothing before. Obviously, it hasn't really affected him, socially or anything, cos I didn't hardly notice. It's not a big deal, but I suppose if you hide a thing from people, you must think it's a big deal yourself. About three year ago, turned out my brother Lar hadn't ever learned to read or write. No one knew cos he left school as soon as he could and got working on the sites. Only out in Australia, something must've happened, maybe his kids put it up to him and he started getting lessons again. Can't shut the fucker up now about what he read in a book.

'How long's it going on for?'

'Noticed it more the last few years, but it hasn't been fully operational since I was eleven or twelve.'

'How'd that happen?'

'You can get it from a bang on the head. Or if you're going senile.'

'That explains a lot.'

He thinks it might be cos he'd taken a few knocks from his auld fellah. Or the time we were pissing down Summerhill on the bikes, flew over the handlebars. And that night he fell off the cannon outside the courthouse, was unconscious for a few minutes. 'Remember I was seeing Gwen at the time. She'd done a bit of time with the St John's Ambulance. Kept me walking around. I just wanted to sleep it off.'

'So Mrs EB copped to the whole smelling situation,' I goes. 'And what?'

'She has this powder, put it on a bit of sponge yoke. Got me to rub it around my nose.'

'Powder? That could be any auld shite.'

'It's not, Frank. It works. When I went for a slash afterwards, I could even smell the soap.'

'What was in the powder?'

'Real rare stuff. I smelt meself for the first time in years. Wasn't too bad.'

'I'd've told you if you smelt bad.'

'Would ya, though? It was getting in on me. Washing my hands all the time, showering maybe twice a day.'

Now he's started he can't stop talking about smells and smelling. He asks what's my favourite.

'I don't know, maybe petrol.'

'Or wood?'

'Some woods. Maybe fire.'

He says lime and lemons are the most popular smells. That's universal. They put them in a lot of aftershaves. The only time he wore aftershave he drowned himself in it. Who he was going out with at the time was Dervla Curry. She made a right skit of him. He always carries a bar of soap with him everywhere.

'Jesus, Hopper, I think I've had enough with the washing stories today. Between Rose's Bathhouse and the Mrs EB/ Eugene choir still ringing in my ears. Now you hoarding bars of soap.'

He shuts up then.

Maybe there was something in Mrs EB's little bottles because I do feel more clear-headed than I have for a while, like the body's a bit more fluid or something. The way you'd feel after a long run in the middle of a downpour. Get home, shower, change and you're completely switched on. If she has got a powder version of her drink, what harm can it do Hopper?

I get an urge to take the Deadwood out from the rucksack. Suppose if he can get himself into a log, there's an equal chance he might have escaped out of it. I don't know why, but I have a whiff of him; a general woody smell, bit musty. I smell the colours on him, blue and red, separate from each other, and there's a tarry whiff. Also snow. I don't even know what snow smells like, given that it's frozen water.

A bit of me starts looking forward to the diversion at the beach. Just having a laugh, not wrecking my own head thinking about stuff. While Hopper's singing along to the radio, I have a little chat with the Da. Inside my head.

'Sorry, Da, but when push came to shove and Rose was trying to send me in the direction of this woman, I didn't want it. I know it might have explained the whole seventh son not going exactly right for me. But I don't like imagining another kid out in the world, living parallel to us. Maybe even another family. If I go looking for this woman, it could change the whole future for me. Maybe for better, maybe not. Thing is, I realised when Murt told me that you knew about Bernie, that he was a girl, that it's even worse when the past gets changed. That's the worst and I don't want any more of that. All the secrets you had – this woman, knowing about Bernie, you might even have been a bloody butcher – you can keep on keeping them now. So it's you, me, and Hopper, on a trip to God knows where. That's as good as it gets, Da. Sorry.'

Hopper gives me a dig in the arm. 'Put that statue away, Frank. You're gone in on yourself, muttering again.'

We chug along for another while in silence. It's mostly green hedges outside and the sun still shining. The traffic is light enough. Sunday evening on the back roads of Ireland, fuck all going on. A tractor is waiting to pull out and Hopper slows down to let him go in front of us. Now all that's not going on, is not going on at twenty miles an hour. At least the fields have dropped away to a view of sparkly blue sea.

Before I get a chance to ponder too much, Hopper's off again, asking me how I think the scallion competition will go this year. He never lets me think for too long.

'It's yours, Hopper. One hundred per cent yours.'

He's undisputed champ, putting away buckets of scallions. Never lost except the first year. That was only because we'd nicked a few cans from the festival tent before he started. Hopper fair pebble-dashed the front row.

Some people might think who'd want to be the Carlow county champion scallion eater? Well, nobody, even in Carlow, is probably born wanting it, but you never know what your talent is going to turn out to be. If you're going to be called a scallion eater anyways, you may as well be the best.

'You know they're putting up a bigger prize this year, so it could draw in, I don't know, professionals,' he says.

'Professional scallion eaters?'

'There is lads who do this all over the place; iron stomach stuff, drinking gallons of cooking oil and eating worms. Glass even. One of them could pitch up.'

'I doubt it.'

'I'm glad you're behind me, Frank, and when I get that ball of cash in my little *lámhín*, I'm handing it straight over to you.'

'Get us a pint, is all.'

He shuts up for a minute. Then he takes this little vial from his pocket and holds it up to me.

'Did Mrs EB give that to you?' I ask.

'Doesn't come cheap.'

'You bought it?'

'You heard how much ginseng costs. Top grade. This can actually make dead cells grow back.'

It occurs to me, why didn't he ever ask me to treat his nose, if it's such a big deal? Then he spills what he's been angling around to all this time. He didn't get the nose powder from Mrs EB, he bought it. The bastard's spent all our money on that little vial. Gave her mine as well. Lifted the envelope from my rucksack when I was in Rose's kitchen. Un-fucking-believable.

'She saw you coming,' I says. 'Probably Johnson's Baby Powder, Korean style.'

'It's working already. I'll pay you back, with interest, once I'm in the red again.'

For fuck sake. Flush for the first time in my life and it's gone tits-up already. It appears we've only a couple of quid left between us. We travel on in silence. At one stage a massive stench of silage comes in the window. I hope he's getting a good bang of that shit. I look over, but not a twitch out of him. What a sap. This beach'd want to have the mother of all parties to salvage this sorry fucking episode.

Travelling Down a Lonely Road

If you would open up your heart
And let my love come shining through . . .

I don't know about a choir of heavenly angels, but this
particular version of the afterlife is affording me a personal
jukebox. Every bit of music that ever passed between my ears,
available to me at the drop of a hat, from any direction or
source. One minute it's Roger Miller, *King of the Road,* then I'm
getting a blast of Duane Eddy, heading down forty miles of
bad road.

Right now the lads have some auld hip-hop going strong in
the front of the car, but that's not the only sound I'm picking
up. I'm catching the heartbeat of the two lads and a pinging
noise, the nerves in Frank's hands as he's tap-tap-tapping
away with his fingers on his knee. It's not in time to any music
on the radio; it's beating out the worry tunes in his mind. Each
one of his thoughts, like the striking of a match, sends a
dispatch off down his arms, muscles tensing like elastic bands,
then the clenching and unclenching of the fingers, little
hammers falling, lifting and falling again. You might feel like

you're travelling down a lonely road, Frank, but if you only knew; as Mr C said, open your heart and you'll find me, ready to walk that road with you.

The other sound I can hear, clear as a bell, is the road singing beneath the wheels. It's as if all the years I spent filling in potholes, pouring gravel and rolling out tar, as if the memory of that is being sent back to me through the sounds of the wheels meeting the earth's skin. That's the only way I can explain it.

I remember seeing a programme on television about Aboriginals, the way they'd be able to sing a song to each other about how to get from one side of Australia to the other; different sounds telling of a mountain or a river, where to cross it. Even where the bodies are buried. Couldn't really make head nor tail of it. But now I see there's as many ways of drawing a map as there are people. The kind of travelling I'm doing now is closer to the truth of how we travel, along highways of feeling and desire.

As I said before, this might be my final journey. Like that auld wolf, an animal running his own lines in terms of tracks and trails, nothing to do with maps and borders. Will I feel it when we get close to my final destination, the centre of the story, my story? Or Frank's? Will that be the end?

When I was alive, sometimes I'd be thinking, what will it all add up to once the ticker gives up the ghost? For some men, his work is his mark on the world; if he invented something or wrote a book or put his name to a skyscraper or a bridge. Nothing I left behind has my name attached bar my wife and children.

Yet there'd be times and I'd be going to a dance, off to visit an invalid who was housebound, and I'd be as proud of the surface of the road underneath me as if it were a work of art.

For it was me and the lads who'd cut the verges back that same week, maybe evened out that very stretch over many years. The work was never done in any great haste, it's fair to add, but steady as she goes.

I'd be driving along that road and I'd think to myself, that's how you put your days in and no shame in that. Adding something to every journey made along those highways and byways. Wheels and feet, even the odd hoof or paw, could travel along, thinking about where they're heading, not a bit of notice for the smoothness of the path they're taking. Only when there's a problem and then you'd hear all about it.

I suppose a man's life lingers on in the minds of people; that's the invisible mark you leave. There's many will remember me for the cure and the same again never gave me a second thought the minute they walked out my front door. Whatever it was I had in my hands gave a bit of ease to people. And creatures. I remember doing a job on a horse once that was in a bad way, terrible wind in her stomach. Barrow Lady. Beautiful creature, nervy, would jump her own height again on a good day. Leaving that stable, and she lying down peaceful, I thought to myself, that animal has as much a clue of what happened there as I have. Strange, it made me feel closer to being an animal myself. The way a swallow'd travel halfway across the world and back to the exact same nest under the self-same eaves. It's like there's an instinct for home in us, our own nature being home to each creature. Healing was my instinct for home.

I received something rare from my father. Despite myself, I ended up fulfilling my end in terms of passing it on. But here we are now and I can't tell is it in Frank or what he's to grow into. He's got himself that tied up in knots. Maybe the whole business with Letty and what happened back then is queering the pitch for him. Not to mind Bernie throwing another tuppence worth in.

Wasting my time getting caught up in thoughts of what I left behind and how I'll be remembered. I won't be, not really. Amn't I getting a ringside seat for the final final chapter – what do you call the one after the end? An epilogue. That's it – as the epilogue unfolds. Who wouldn't want it? I was a lucky man when I lived and I'm a lucky man dead, slipping out of the wooden box into the timber itself.

This little wooden prison has freed me in a way I never experienced before. If I could escape it, I'd have to make choices where to go and what to do next. Seems like that's all in Frank's hands now. Tell ya one thing, whatever this whole second-coming jaunt is about, I'm ready to go the way the road takes me.

If you would open up your heart
And let my love come shining through . . .

Oddsey's Bodega

Hopper has us looking out for a blue-and-white painted house that's got a whole collection of gnomes and a grotto in the front garden. Once I spot the Virgin Mary giving us the nod, he takes a sharp left. We turn onto a road that dwindles into a narrow lane with high verges and tall grass; it's only wide enough for going one direction. Further on we end up driving in behind a bank of trees; there's flashes of blue sea coming through. Mad little road you'd never go down. We come to a lay-by with a couple of cars parked up already and Hopper says this is it. Looks a bit quiet to me for the massive crowd he's promised.

There's no direct way down to the beach cos it drops sharpish from where we're parked but Hopper sees a path leading back into the trees. A wooden sign with *Oddsey's Bodega* painted on it points the way. We walk pass a stack of black rubbish bags and crates of empty bottles. Out the other side of the trees we step directly onto this stony beach. First off, no sound system, no lights, no half-naked dancing bodies. Instead you'd think you'd stepped into a secret shanty town. There's a long wooden shack with a corrugated roof sloping down and walls leaning in, all kinds of half-built yokes lying around, a big pointy tent like the Wild West, a washing line with towels. You wouldn't know what's holding what up. Further down I see a shipping container, more tents, and a Portakabin. I can smell a barbeque smoking somewhere.

'We could be on Bondi bloody Beach here,' Hopper goes.

Of course he's trying to pretend this is all turning out as planned, which it's clearly not. And I'm still fucked off with him about the money.

'Give me a break. More like Beirut.'

I can't see anyone hanging around, just the leftovers of some kind of party. Whatever was going on here has already gone on. Hopper heads for the door of the shack and calls in. A voice calls something back out. Inside it's bigger than you'd think and done out like a bar; loads of stuff hanging from the ceiling; driftwood and posters and road signs. It's well kitted-out; even a pool table down the far end, a fellah just racking up.

A fellah sitting behind a counter, untangling some net yoke, introduces himself.

'How's it going, lads? Oddsey's the name.'

We nod, introduce ourselves back. He's a real hippie-looking fellah; long beard and grey hair tied back, maybe a biker vibe with the sleeveless denim jacket and loads of tattoos.

'You found your way here. That's the hardest part.'

'You're the first man I ever met called Oddsey,' Hopper goes.

'Well, they used to call me the Eggman. You never know what's going to stick with you for life, right? Could be a woman, could be a name.'

'Bang on. Anyways, we met some women in Ballycalla,' Hopper goes. 'They said there might be some party here tonight?'

Women? Then I realise he means Mrs EB and Rose.

'Bad timing,' Oddsey goes. 'That was Friday. A crowd from Utrecht. Then another guy arrives straight off the ferry, sets up this incredible firework display all along the shore. Picasso of the sky.'

It was supposed to be a weekend-long party but someone got lifted with a load of pills on their way and a local Garda gave Oddsey the heads up. Most of the crowd headed on to a rave organised by Brazilians outside Ardmore. Once again, we've missed the boat. We've come all this way and it's over already. Typical Hopper getting the wrong end of the stick.

Your man Oddsey says we're welcome to stay and camp but there's a bit of cleaning up to be done on the beach and around the woods. He offers us a couple of home brew ciders and we head outside. The tables there have a clear view out to sea. The waves is crashing down in a powerful manner. Nice view if you're just sitting around.

'You ever feel that someone else is living your life?' I says once we're settled. 'Your real life?'

'What'cha mean?'

'We're too late. The party's over. You've blown all our money before we even got to enjoy it. Now you've agreed to pick up someone else's rubbish so we can camp here? It's like a pathetic country song. It should be—'

'Fuck sake. There's no should be. Enjoy it for what it is.'

Giving there's nothing going on around here, I think we should call it a day and head home tonight. I can tell Hopper's a bit drawn in by the vibe here, but he agrees getting back to Ruth's sooner rather than later is probably for the best.

He heads to the jacks in the Portakabin just as Oddsey's reversing the van down as far as he can. I lift a few bags into the van and stack the crates in after. When I ask Oddsey about the set-up, he tells me he inherited a few acres from an uncle. He started with an old shed and built up his shebeen bit by bit. For whatever reason, nobody in authority is interfering with him. There's a few people who camp long-term and others come and go. He makes a few bob off the drink and everyone's happy.

When I get back, Hopper's scored a couple of chicken legs for us. I get the rucksack with the Deadwood and park it on the bench beside me. Not that I'm trying to make him part of society or anything, but still. It's the kind of place where you could sit a dead cat up, give him a pint and a straw, and no one'd pass any heed. I'm not that hungry after the feed in Rose's, but it's relaxing sitting there chewing on a chicken leg. Once we're fed and watered, Hopper produces a fat joint.

'That's quare strong,' I says, coughing a lung up.

'Someone left a bag of shit behind,' he says. 'Lad at the pool table gave me some.'

'You'd want to take it easy, for driving back.'

But he's changed his mind; now he's all for staying on. He reckons I could still try and find out a bit more about the woman the Da was looking for. Don't know why he's bringing that up, I haven't mentioned it since we left Rose's.

'I'm gone off that idea now,' I says. 'I'll leave well enough alone.'

'You're what?'

He gets rightly stuck in, saying it's typical of me. As soon as I get close to something, I back off. Reverse top fucking speed. I don't know what he's so wound up about. It's not like I was that close to finding out anything. Even if there was anything to what Lena said, I didn't really get much further with Rose.

'If you did a search online for Kielys,' he goes, 'in this county and see if there's any–'

'Who?'

'Kiely. Letty Kiely.'

'Where'd you get that name?'

'When you went up to the jacks in Rose's she told me, if you ever asked, the name of the woman: Letty Kiely.'

'But I didn't fucking ask, did I?'

Then he really gives it welly, all about how I need to get out of my comfort zone, whatever that is; I should try find out for my da's sake; saying maybe I have the gift and if we found a kid, another son, then it'd be easier to accept Bernie being a woman. He's very persuasive.

The Deadwood's still beside me, facing out to sea. I look where he's looking.

'Why don't you ask him what he wants?' Hopper goes.

It could be it's the smoke or the grub or the evening light coming across the water, combination of them all, but I put all my concentration into the Deadwood.

'What'cha think, Da, you want me to find this Letty Kiely woman? Or you could tell me now did ye have a kid? Boy, girl?'

If you listen, you'd think the waves are saying yes when they crash in and no when they drag back out. Then the yes drags back out into the no until it becomes yesno yeshhno jussshdo and it sounds like just do it. I haven't the energy nor the will to argue back with Hopper. Fuck it, we'll stay one night.

'Have you thought at all about how to find her?' he goes, knocking back the cider. 'This fancy lady.'

Something about that phrase reminds me of the way the Mater goes on about Richie Morrissey's bit on the side. Makes it sound low class.

'You know those programmes with families and adoption, all that palaver? The Mater and Bernie is obsessed with them,' I says.

'Go on.'

'They're always checking church records to track people down.'

'She might've got married and changed her name.'

'Yeah.'

I remember seeing women on it who gave up their kids and the whole thing was kept secret. There was often no records, or even false ones. How many churches would you have to check in the whole county? Hundreds probably. Her name rolls around in my head, but it's disconnected, meaningless. Letty. Kiely. Even as Hopper's going on with different notions about what we could do, I feel it's well beyond our grasp. We'd never find her.

'Do you think your mother knew?' Hopper asks.

I hadn't really thought about that. Or how she might feel about it all. That's another complication to deal with if she didn't.

'Haven't a clue.'

I need a slash. Walking across to the jacks, the head is spinning.

Very clean in the Portakabin. Probably cos it's women use it too. Two cubicles. Loads of messages written on the walls. Not the usual shite you get in the lads' jacks. More the kind of weird messages Mossy sends on his postcards home to the Mater. I should put them up in the toilet at home, his postcards. Something to look at. I start thinking of Rose and her bathhouse and all that business. Fancy bathrooms, how are ya. I suppose it makes sense in a way; you do spend a good bit of time there so you may as well make it a bit interesting.

What's this on the door?

Not all those who wonder are lost

200

Or . . . is it wander? Yeah, wander.

Real eyes realise
Real lies

Don't really get that one.

All pain and still no gain

That's for sure.

Imagine if the cure for cancer is
trapped inside the mind of someone who
can't afford an education

Have to think about that for a few minutes. Could you really have something trapped in your mind, waiting to get out? Either it's there or it's not there. Some of the drawings on the walls, fairly artistic. One on the ceiling like the painting of the hand of God reaching out, by your man. But it's an octopus instead of a person reaching back. That's a good one.

'Heal yourself, doctor,' I says out loud. That's what the Da used to say when he'd have a few drinks on him. Maybe he was referring to something else with his 'heal yourself'. Guilty conscience? I'll put that to the Deadwood when I go back out. Should write it on the walls.

Weird-looking hand soap on the sink. Bits of seaweed in it. Making your own soap. Living on a beach. The way some people has chosen to stay off the grid, able to go their own way. There's kind of a herby smell off the soap as well as a sea smell. The whole smell thing and whatever fucking powder Mrs EB gave Hopper. Probably chalk dust, coloured water, but he believes:

201

four hundred quid's worth of believing. Maybe it all comes down to what you believe, what people around you believe. If Bernie always believed what he's only telling me now, could that have been more powerful than what I believed about myself and the gift? I didn't believe in myself strong enough.

The light is very harsh when I step outside; seems like an age since I went into that Portakabin. It takes a minute to adjust my eyes. I'm standing there, trying to remember any of the stuff I read but I'm drawing a blank.

My phone rings. Bernie. 'Where are ya?'

'Out with Hopper. Where are you?'

'Still in London.'

Of course, I forgot about that. 'What're ye up to?'

'Eileen's wrecking my head. Embarrassing bodies up close and personal. Her weeping Jesus leg ulcers.'

'Is the Mater there? Put her on.'

The Mater comes on. She's going on about some park they went to and shops. It's nice to hear her voice. When she draws a breath, I ask her if the Da ever mentioned someone, a friend he lost touch with, in Wexford?

'No. He had relatives in Ballycalla, that was it really. I'm after getting three pairs of shoes from Eileen. She can't fit them since the ankles swelled up.'

'Sounds like it's going well. What about a place called Glensomething?'

'Glenbeigh?'

'Is it Glenbeigh?' I goes, to be sure.

'We went on the jalopies. They weren't putting nappies on horses back then, I can tell you that much. That was our honeymoon, in Kerry.'

She sounds far away, but saying that, she always holds the phone half a mile from her ear in case of cancer.

'What're you asking for?' she goes. 'What're you up to?'

'Nothing. I have to go, I'm running out of juice.'

'Don't be annoyed at me for taking Bernie on a little break.'

'I'm not. See ya.'

I'd say she hasn't a clue.

A woman steps out of the shipping container across the way. Forgot to ask Oddsey what exactly that was. She's walking over towards me. 'Hi, you must be Frank.'

The fuck she knows my name?

'Who are you?' I go.

She's a bit of an accent. 'I'm Mila. Hopper said you guys are going to stay here tonight.'

Fucking Hopper. She totally fits the profile: older, long hair, good-looking. Even in her baggy T-shirt and shorts you can see she's a killer bod. No wonder he was so fucking keen to stay.

'I'll be over in a minute,' she says.

'Grand.'

I go into the shebeen before I go back to the table, get a couple of cans from Oddsey. There's a couple of women racking up the balls at the pool table. Where are these people appearing from?

'What's up?' Hopper goes, when I set the drinks at the table.

'I met your new friend.'

'What'cha mean?'

'The blonde.'

'Mila. She's staying in the container for the summer. It's all fitted out inside.'

'You were in already?'

'No. We were just chatting.'

'That's why you want to stay here.'

'Not just that. I do think it's worth a shot trying to find this Letty Kiely character. And people here, like Oddsey, they've local knowledge. To get us started.'

203

'She's not even Irish.'

'Her friends are. They're all into marine shit, environment. Good-looking too.'

Since the first time he said the name, I can't stop thinking about it. Letty Kiely. First and second name. I can't ever unknow that name now. A name makes it seem more real. Even if Hopper is bullshitting me, just so he can get off with your one, it's got to me. The Da must've had some reason to go to Rose looking for her. Now I have her name, it's on me. Someone must know her. Must be a record somewhere.

When Oddsey comes out, Hopper asks him if, on the off-chance, he's ever come across any Kielys. He's only doing it to appease me.

'Not a name I have any familiarity with.'

He's going to the dump with the load, says to keep a tab on the blackboard inside. Very trusting of him.

The tide has come way in. It's mad because you don't notice it and then all of a sudden it's coming to meet ya.

We sit there for a while, myself and the Deadwood, staring out at the water. You think nothing is going on but if you let your mind drift you notice maybe a particular seagull, the way it keeps wheeling round, out and back. Or the stones click-clacking, and you start to expect a particular rhythm. You're waiting for it.

'Any news from Bernie and the Mater?' Hopper goes.

I tell him they're going to Buckingham Palace tomorrow. And the hospital where Eileen works, which is hardly a tourist attraction.

'I wonder did he ever talk to your mother about it?'

'What?'

'Your father. If he had a kid before he met her. Different back then, though.'

'Don't think she's a clue. I asked her if she ever heard of a place called Glen.'

'Where did you come up with Glen?'

'Rose mentioned a Glensomething.'

'That's another lead, isn't it?'

'What?'

'How many Glensomewhere's could there be? We could find them out, ask around. We've a name and you said a possible butcher connection, remember?'

I'd forgotten that. Bit sketchy but fuck it, I'll think about it tomorrow.

He reaches across, takes the Deadwood, holds him up in front of his own face. 'I love it when a plan comes together,' he goes in a cartoon voice, like it's coming out of the Deadwood.

Not because of Hopper messing, but I'm sure there's a voice from the Deadwood reaching into my head, saying, 'Just do it, Frank.'

Next thing Hopper drains his can, shouts, 'Don't think about it, follow me.'

The mad bastard legs it down to the edge of the water. He strips bollix-naked, fires himself into the waves, his white arse waving goodbye to me. I have a quick look around the beach; there's no witnesses. To hell with it, I follow suit. I just do it.

Ending with a Fish Ballet

I love summer evenings when it's still warm enough to be sitting out late. I'm dressed, warmed up after our swim. The sea was freezing. On impact everything shrivels up, even your fucking eyeballs. Then you get used to it and it's brilliant. Not thinking about things, not working out the odds. Chilled in a way it's hard to get to without a few beers or a smoke.

I stashed my gear in the bodega, but I keep the Deadwood with me under my seat. He might look like barbeque kindling to someone else, but he's worth something to me. Turns out we don't even have to pitch a tent because there's a lean-to room at the back of the bar empty, with pallets and roll-up mattresses.

'You didn't tell the Mater you've requisitioned the Deadwood yet?' Hopper asks.

'No, I didn't get a chance.'

Hopper gives me a look. Then he winks at the Da. 'You're out on parole, Mr Whelan. Best behaviour now. Don't be making our heads spin backward.'

He shuts up then because we hear voices. When I turn

around, I see Mila and two others stepping out of the container. They come over to the table and everyone does the whole introducing thing. They were the ones playing pool earlier: spiky hair is Alice, the other one with curly hair and shades is Tara. Sort of alternative; not the kind of girls we'd be knocking around with at home. Though to be fair to him, Hopper'd get a bit of craic outta anyone.

'You went for a swim, cool,' Mila goes.

'Totally refreshing,' says Hopper. 'It's the business.'

There's a few other people knocking around taking up two tables further down; a group of bikers, Oddsey's vintage. They're cooking up fish and baked potatoes in a fire pit. I give Alice a hand bringing a load of drinks and crisps to our table.

I have to admit the sound of the waves and the peacefulness of the place does get to you after a while. The evening passes chatting and drinking. The sky still has brightness in it, but you can see stars, real faint, here and there. I start thinking about June. I wish she was here. Mad to be even thinking that way given the fact we've only talked three times. Twice about ringworm. But I can't help it. Picturing her at the bar leads me to remembering Lena only that morning, destroying the phone number, going on about the Da.

'Do you have a favourite?' Mila's asking me a question.

'What?'

Somehow the conversation's got around to smells. I'm fairly sure Hopper didn't bring it up. Funny how the exact thing you're trying to avoid comes right at ya.

'Dunno,' I goes. 'Probably chips.'

'You like this?' she goes and gives Hopper the inside of her wrist. They're getting on like a house on fire.

He bends his head right down and inhales deeply. 'Is there such a thing as a lemon rose?' he goes.

Fuck, he's good. Like a blind man who's learned the furniture off by heart, pretending he can see his way around a room.

'No,' she says smiling. 'They should grow that rose.'

I want to say that's wrong because one is a flower and one is a fruit, but I keep my mouth shut. I'm enjoying the music coming from inside the shack: some lad with a guitar and mouth organ playing real bluesy stuff. I'm only half-listening to the conversation before I realise what Hopper's telling them. About his nose not working. Casual-like; makes a bit of joke out of it. They ask him loads of questions. The way they're going on you'd think he'd two false legs or was blinded since birth.

'Close your eyes,' Tara goes to Hopper. She takes this stuff out of her rucksack. It looks like a little sachet of grass, but even across the table I can get the smell, kind of minty. 'You smell this?'

He sniffs it. 'Maybe. Well, not exactly, no.'

They're all processing this information.

'I smell rain before it falls,' Mila says.

'How can you?' I ask.

'Through my senses. I was knowing weather since I was small child.'

Hopper's nodding along, staring at her like she invented the sunshine and rain.

I'm finding it hard to follow the logic of this conversation. 'How can you smell rain?'

'I also can smell different waves. I smell what is coming.'

'When I imagine a smell, it's intense,' says Hopper. 'But I'd prefer to experience the real thing.'

'How are you sure you can't smell?' Tara asks.

'There could be a house on fire right behind me and I wouldn't know.'

Then Hopper's telling them about his magic powder. He even gets the little jar to show them. Right up their alley. Alice starts on about the extinction of animals due to the demand for certain Chinese herbal concoctions. Because of men who want to increase their sexual power. Hopper makes a point of saying he's totally against that. And that Mrs EB swore blind it's natural herbal shit in the powder. He leaves out the part about the pulverised deer antlers.

Alice's more serious than the other two. Red pandas are her thing. She loves them. Some gang in Limerick were caught smuggling rare animal parts recently – livers and noses and shit – and she's gunning for them. That's all me and Hopper need now, for it to turn out Mrs EB is buying her supplies from some heavy-duty criminals.

'No, this is pure ginseng,' Hopper goes. 'Rarest kind, direct from the mountains in Korea.'

'Ginseng's the bomb,' Tara goes. 'Especially for blood pressure.'

'More to do with circulation,' Alice says. 'And the heart.'

Tell ya one thing, those two are as bad as those brothers in that pub for disagreeing with each other.

'Turmeric and ginseng mixed is unbelievable,' Mila goes.

'Turmeric.' Hopper goes all serious, looking into Mila's eyes. 'I'll remember that.'

They're planning some big party for next weekend, and they say we're welcome to come. But Hopper, fair enough he hasn't forgotten himself totally, explains about Wolf Night, how we have to get back for the scallion eating competition. I thought they might be a bit against the whole celebrating the killing of the last wolf, being environmentalists and all that, but they're well taken with the way he describes it. Though Hopper has a way of talking things up that makes it sound like the be-all and end-all of festivals that ever happened. And it is something unique about where we come from and that's something.

The talk and drinks keep flowing but I'm ready to hit the scratcher. The sleeping bags are in the boot of the car. Mila gives me a loan of her torch to find the path through the trees. It's way more powerful than any I ever seen before. Something a spy or a soldier would own with all these features: some kind of UV light and a laser beam. I'd've given my right arm for it as a kid. When I'm a distance away from Oddsey's, I switch it to the thinnest beam and point it straight up at the sky. Rake it over and across, picking out individual stars and aiming it at them. Brilliant.

When I get back, Alice's gone to bed. Mila's got little shot glasses lined up and we all have a drop of this liquor they make where she's from. It's very earthy, like whiskey made out of dirt. Kicks like a mule. We all sit there a bit stunned. Suddenly Mila goes, 'Come on,' and pulls Hopper up by the hand. They're gone.

'Remember I was saying earlier about the spores, the rock pool stuff?' Tara says. 'The armaxzoe?'

'No, I must've been at the jacks.'

She wants to show me some creatures in the pools that you can only see at night. I'm tired but why not? There's half a joint in the ashtray and I pop it into my pocket. While she goes to the jacks, I stash the Deadwood over in the place I'll be sleeping in.

The tide's gone back out a good bit. We get to the water's edge and wander along towards the rocky end of the beach. When I swing the wide beam across the surface of the water, it seems to go on for miles.

'Just cos you're wandering,' I says, 'you're not lost.'

Where the fuck did that come out of?

'You read that in the toilet, Frank.'

'Oh yeah.'

'Hopper told us about you guys getting laid off.'

'Did he?'

When does Hopper have all these conversations with people? Then I wonder if he told them about what I came looking for. Or about the Deadwood.

'What else did he tell ya?'

'Dunno. Just about the job.'

I spark up the joint. It's like a little firefly going back and over and we chat easy enough. We reach the end of the beach, where the low ridges begin before they meet the cliff face. Then she says I've nice energy and reaches out for my hand.

'Look, Tara, I'm kind of involved with . . . it's not that you, you know, but there's a girl . . . we're not exactly dating but . . .'

She's laughing at me. 'I get it,' she goes. 'The whole, into a girl. Not dating.'

'What?'

'Give us the torch, Frank, not your hand. You know I'm queer, right?'

Fuck. How did I miss that? Of course that's why there's no blokes attached, given they're ranging from good-looking to very good-looking. Smart out, college educated.

'All three of ye?' I say.

'No. Alice and I were together, but it's sort of over. Mila is straight, if there is such a thing.'

'Yeah. I get that obviously. Actually, my brother's gay. My twin brother.'

'Identical?'

'Not exactly. We're getting less similar by the day.'

211

Now that I know she's gay it feels different, like we're mates. Not that we weren't. Or were anything else. In fact Tara probably has a few insights about dating girls that lads wouldn't pick up on.

She's heading for a very particular spot. She uses the light to pick out one pool, a fair-sized one. 'Look in there.'

You can see strips of seaweed floating on top like strands of hair. It's dense underneath. I make out loads of shells attached to the sides. She hunkers down right at the edge and I do the same. When she switches the torch to a white-blue beam, shines it into the blackness of the rock pool, these little lights appear. Thousands of them. Darting about, some closer to the surface but others way deeper. It's like looking into the night sky upside down. Then you look closer and they're see-through with a sparkly middle. Sometimes a whole load of them seem to move in one direction, then they scatter. This is the fucking business. We're watching for ages.

'Like a ballet, isn't it?' she goes.

'Dunno.'

I never seen a ballet. But if that's what ballet is, it's fucking mesmerising.

'Must be mad having a twin?' she says.

'Yeah, but we're totally different. Personality-wise, everything. He's very smart, going to college and all.'

She starts telling me about her family. Her grandmother moved in with them a few years back when her mind started to go. She's quare difficult to manage but some of the stuff she gets up to'd have you in stitches. Taking down the curtains and making hideaways under the kitchen table, crocheting scarves the length of the house. She never drank all her life and now she's hit the sherry hard.

'She's always imitating everyone's accent, repeating stuff off the TV,' Tara goes. 'She has it spot on, but it drives my father mad. He's says it's like having a human parrot attached to the TV remote.'

Bernie's brilliant at taking off accents too; he can rip the piss out of anyone he wants. I tell her about this mad shit he used to get up to as a kid. He'd draw pictures on his hands, give them names and act out these plays, with songs and everything, getting his feet to join in. Then he'd paint faces on my hands too. She's laughing her head off hearing about Bernie; making me laugh too.

We go back to saying nothing, watching the little lights dancing in the pool, before we head back up the beach. She goes over to her tent.

'Night, Frank.'

'Night, Tara. Thanks.'

In the lean-to I dust off the mattress. Seeing as Hopper is clearly not going to need his, I pile the second one on top of mine. The Deadwood is tucked away in a corner. I prop him up against the bed, roll out my sleeping bag and climb in. I start telling him about the rock pool and some of the stuff Tara was going on about.

'You know, after your accident I was always doing deals with God. Who I don't even believe in. Some days I'd wish, even if you couldn't walk or even if you were paralysed from the neck down, I just wanted you to be back home again. I know you probably wouldn't've wanted that. Or the Mater. Before I'd go to sleep I'd be saying, please, if he comes back, even if he's in a wheelchair, I'll go to school. Okay, God, not enough? You want more? Even if he can only blink, I'll get up out of bed right now, put on the uniform, and I'll stay in school all day, all week, all year.

Even go to college. Mad the things you'd be thinking about. Now you are back in a way.

'When Tara was talking about her granny, I realised she and me are in the total opposite situation. Her grandmother looks the same, can get around, but her personality is gone, memory is shot to shit. An empty shell. Could you even say she's there? When I was telling Tara about Bernie, about his messing – remember him putting on his hand and feet plays? – I wondered if I had to do a deal, would I choose Bernie staying the same physically but maybe him not feeling he was really there? To be honest, it would save the family a lot of heartache, especially me and the Mater. Or have him change his body, go male to female, but expressing his full personality? I mean, here we are and, even though you're just a piece of wood, I'd swear there's some part of you, the real you, in there. Your spirit or something. And it's way better than not having you here at all. Mad to even think that way, but it's true. Suppose that kind of answers my own question.'

My ear is dead itchy. Must've got bitten outside, or something's having a right chow on it now. The ears are bad enough without one of them taking off on a solo run in terms of swelling up. Wonder how they looked from June's perspective when she saw me in the pub? I start thinking again of June, thinking when I saw her for the first time with the kid in our front room. She changed the air around her, like when you open the curtains and the sunshine makes everything look different, brighter, more hopeful or something. I'm drifting off, slipping into a dream; June's a dolphin with a human face and ears. Her ears grow bigger and bigger. They're wrapped around me and we're floating out to sea, thousands of stars dancing in the water below us.

Mapping Out the Search

When I wake up the next day there's sunshine streaming through a gap in the roof where the corrugated sheets don't quite meet. First thing, I check is the Deadwood alright. He's in the same spot as where I left him last night. When I look at him, I wonder is there nothing here only a lump of wood tarted up like a magic man's totem. Does it be the drink or the smoke or what makes me believe there's more going on? But I keep looking and he does exert a fierce draw on me.

'Some craic last night, Da. Fish ballet.'

He keeps holding on to my gaze, not so much the carved-in eyes but the wood itself, something mesmerising about the whorls and the lines.

'I'm on to you.' I get a twinge in my chest as I say this. Like you'd have after a curry. That's the way Da used to talk to me, not the other way around. I'm parched for a drink of water and dying for a slash. I pull on my runners, leg it over to the jacks.

On my way back, I see someone's cleared away all the bottles and shit from last night. Right up close there's something on our table. What the fuck? Hopper's clothes but empty. His jeans stretched out long, crossed at the ankle, green T-shirt tucked in. *The Hopalong Cassidy Hit Parade* printed across it; definitely his. Seaweed where his head should be. Shells for his feet and hands. Stuff's dripping down through the slats of the table onto the pebbles below. Sticky and thick. Some kind of voodoo sacrificial shit they've done with his body.

Something's moving inside the T-shirt. Shit, it's his heart. Like a science experiment where the frog's heart is still pumping after it's dead. Fuck! It's moving up the T-shirt, towards the neck.

This crab pushes his way out, does a little sideways shuffle into the seaweed hair. I pick it up by its claw and peg it in the general direction of the beach.

Fuck. What if that was Hopper? I should've had a good look at him.

There's two massive pink shells, swirly ones, where Hopper's ears used to be. I put one up to my mouth. 'Hopper,' I says into it, 'what's going on?'

I put it up to my own ear. There's sounds trapped, like waves or breathing. I listen hard and then hear a voice. Getting louder.

'Frank,' it says. 'Frank.'

I look around and see Hopper coming through the scrubby bushes in his togs, escorted by Mila with a snorkel in her hand. She gives his hair a rub with a towel, waves at me, and heads over to the container.

'What'd you think of it, Frank?' Hopper goes, pointing at the shit on the table.

'Fuck is this?' I says.

'Just the girls messing around.'

I tell him what I thought and he breaks his shite laughing. I warn him not to take the piss out of me in front of the others. His night went well by all accounts. So did mine, in a different manner of speaking. He pulls the clothes off the table and heads for a quick shower.

'There's coffee brewing,' he calls back. 'Then we can plan our campaign with a clear head.'

Mila and Tara come over with some kind of cereal and bowls. They clear the drippy stuff off the table: tomato juice spilt earlier. Alice's gone into town; she's working in her Da's insurance company for the summer.

I pour out a bit of cereal. It's the granola. The Mater got a box once, but in the end no one wanted it and we gave it to John Billy McDermott next door for his pigeons. It's definitely something you could see pigeons enjoying. John Billy said there was killings in the loft for a gutful.

Hopper's back. 'Tasty.'

'Home-made,' Tara says.

In fairness, it is tasty; lots of different bits and pieces in it. The milk looks a bit off but apparently it's made from hazelnuts. To my mind that doesn't give it the right to call itself milk.

After breakfast Hopper gets out his little bottle and dabs a tiny bit up his nose. He thinks it's working; says he could smell the soap in the shower. But he isn't able to say what the smell was, exactly. I think he's carrying on; he already knows that soap smells.

Mila and Tara are heading off soon, some whale thing in Cork, another beach.

'We'll see you later?' Mila goes. 'You going to hang out here today?'

Clearly Hopper has given them the impression we're kicking around with no purpose. A good ride and he'd forget his own name. We're leaving today.

217

'Actually, we're trying to find someone,' he goes. 'That's what brought us down here in the first place. Right, Frank?'

I shrug.

'A sort of quest,' he goes on.

I better say something before he completely overeggs it. I explain that my Da had a friend he lost touch with and wanted to see, and I heard from a cousin that the woman might like to hear what happened the Da. It sounds a bit lame.

'Whereabouts does she live?' Tara asks.

I explain I don't exactly know; I think it's Glensomething in terms of the location. A surname of Kiely. Straight away they've their phones out and they're googling and checking out Facebook and all that. As if I hadn't done all that already. Once it's clear there's nothing there, a big conversation starts up about how to trace people and ways of getting at history records I never heard of. Clearly a lot of stuff goes on behind the scenes on those TV programmes.

Tara suggests we start by doing a search of all the places starting with Glen in the county. Then see if any one rings a bell and what records they might have. She gets her phone out and before you know it, she's a list: Glenard; Glenvale; Glenallon; Glencarrig; Glencarlough; and Glenaduagh.

'Six places,' Hopper says. 'At least it not Ballysomething,'

Tara gets a map up on the screen but it's a bit small, so Mila goes over to the container and comes back with a big map of the whole county. Really detailed. She marks in the six; they're spread out from one end to the other. Then she puts a dot on the coastline to show us exactly where we are right now. She's some quare grasp of the layout of the county, for a foreigner.

Tara reckons we'd get to the first one, Glenvale, in about twenty-five minutes, and from there, Glenard's not too far.

'What'll you do when you get there?' she asks. 'Like, I know Glenvale and it's not even a village. It's literally a church and a primary school at a crossroads. I think there's a pub, but I don't even know if that would be open during the day.'

They're looking at me as if I'm some expert. I say nothing.

'I suppose the records might show if a Kiely was baptised in the church,' Tara goes. 'Or buried there.'

'Is she married?' Mila asks. 'Does she have kids?'

'Don't know.'

I can see by the faces on the two women I must be coming across as a bit fucking dim.

'Frank's a very determined customer when he wants to be,' Hopper goes. 'We'll ask around and suss it out.'

Mila says we can hang on to the map if we like, which is sound. They're sorting their stuff off the table and having a bit of a natter between themselves. Hopper and me are getting our gear together.

'Frank, you're into energies, right?' Mila goes.

'What'cha mean?'

'Hopper says you, your family, are healers.'

Just when my chances of ever being a healer have all but slipped through my fingers, Hopper's using it to wangle his way in with Mila and the girls. Unreal.

'There is a family thing, alright,' I says.

'I've a talisman. It's got amazing energy. It might help direct you. What do you think?'

More wack-fucking-jobbery, is what I think. Hopper is nodding along like this is how he decides what colour jocks he'll pull on in the morning. I'm all for packing this in now and moving on. But something is holding me back.

'I've got this thing too,' Tara goes. 'I found it at a dig, not far from here.'

'Sounds good,' Hopper says, looking at me.

Here we go, pissing away another hour so he can cement his credentials with Mila. She spreads the map out on the table, uses a few pebbles to hold the corners down as a breeze is rising. Tara gets this yoke out from her bag. I have a closer look. An antler or a ram's horn, about half a foot long, curved, the edge cut straight across. I seen an exact one of these before, last Friday in Murt's.

'Viking, isn't it?' I goes.

'Yeah,' she says, looking a bit surprised I know.

Mila produces a shell about as big as your hand. Dark coloured, it'd remind you of an old roof tile that's seen all kinds of weather and hasn't been scraped in years.

'What's that?' Hopper goes.

'It's a clam shell.'

She says they've dated it and it lived for approximately four hundred years. Possibly more. Lived through wars and storms and generations of humans born and dead. Now it's ended up in a converted shipping container with a bunch of hippies. You never know how things'll turn out.

'The clam's not still in it?' Hopper says.

'No.' She gives him a squeeze on the arm. 'Keep taking your powder. You will not mistake the smell of rotting shellfish.'

Mad to think of it spending hundreds of years alive. When it was born, she says, Henry the Eighth might have been king and explorers were going to America for the first time. Must be dead interesting to study shit like that.

'Frank,' Hopper is saying, 'Mila is asking you something.'

'Do you have anything belonging to the person you are seeking you could put on the map?'

I'm shaking my head no, but Hopper is giving me the hairy eyeball.

'Deadwood?' he goes.

'What?' I no more want to subject myself or the Da to the ridicule of this shower. I could fucking kill him. They're all staring at me. So first, I explain a bit about the Deadwood, broad strokes. I imply it's the Mater who's convinced the statue has some connection to my father's spirit. I'm just minding it for her while she's away.

I take him out of the rucksack, put him up on the table.

Mila handles him real careful, putting her hand around the neck. Then she holds it up directly in front of her face. 'There is restless energy.'

'How come your mother doesn't keep it with her?' Tara goes.

'Okay, let's give it a lash,' Hopper says, moving things on.

I don't know how long we sit there, all four of us, staring at the map in silence. Staring at the three objects plonked on the map: the pokey horn, Deadwood Da, and the clam shell. I'm not great chatting to people but it's even worse when nobody is saying fuck all.

Mila has her eyes closed. Tara had at the start, but she opened them and kept staring at the map after that. Hopper, eyes closed, hands palm down on the map, looks as relaxed as if he was at this malarkey regular. He might even be having a sneaky kip.

After a while, Mila lifts her head. 'Anything?'

Me and Hopper shake our heads.

'I thought I was drawn to Glenallon at the start,' Tara goes. 'But I know a bloke from there so that could be it.'

'What about you, Mila?' Hopper asks.

She puts her hand on the shell. 'It's so weird. I'm getting a very strong sound.' She's speaking real quiet, so we all have to lean in a bit. 'Like a wave or a child's call. Glen kchh Glen kcch.'

'No offence,' I says, 'but we kind of had Glen already. Though the kcch bit is quare useful.'

Hopper has to jump to her defence. 'Easy, Frank. I felt something too, energy-wise.'

This is getting pathetic. I take the Deadwood off, put him in the rucksack. 'Fuck sake, Hopper, you no more believe in this stuff than the man in the moon.'

'That's rich coming from you. Seeing as it was you thought I'd been magically turned into a crab this morning.'

'What?' Mila and Tara say together, turning to stare at me.

I can't fucking believe he's bringing that up in front of them. I was wrecked this morning, hungover and not thinking straight.

'Well, I hope there isn't a hamster massacre when you get home,' I goes. 'You're not that sensitive, if people actually knew.'

'What the fuck?' Hopper says.

I don't even know myself where I was going with that but he's a right prick to rip the piss out of me like that.

'Look, we'd be as well to head on,' he says. 'See what turns up.'

They put their stuff away. Everyone is a bit quiet. Hopper walks them over to the container. When he comes back there's a bit of coolness between us. We pack up our gear and he says he'll head to the nearest place, Glenvale.

As we drive back up the grassy lane away from the beach, the sun is bleeding in the windows. Could be bucketing rain for all I care. Maybe it's the effect of the late night and coming down off whatever the fuck was in Mrs EB's little bottles, but there's a knot growing in my stomach. I know I spoke out of order and I've fucked Hopper right off. My ear is itchy as anything. Probably got fleas from that mattress.

Hopper's whistling away. 'Fuck sake, Frank, you're as miserable as a wet Tuesday.'

'I don't know what the fuck I was saying. About the hamsters in Ruth's house. Popped into my head.'

'Forget it. I told them you've a phobia about small animals. Guinea pigs, hamsters. Can't even look at them on a screen without heaving.'

'Fuck off.'

'I shouldn't have stuck your statue in the thick of it,' he goes. 'I know you think that map thing was bockety auld shite. But I wanted them to think we were more than two regular joes.'

When I switch my phone on there's a couple of missed calls from the Mater and Bernie. Reading through the texts, she wants to let me know she's staying an extra night. Bernie says Eileen has got something lined up in the hospital. Whatever that means.

An extra night before I have to get myself home and the Deadwood back under the gazebo. Maybe it's meant to be, give me a chance to get few things sorted by the time they get back. Who am I kidding? I'm the last person the Da'd choose to settle his affairs.

Hopper's singing away, his elbow out the window like he's in a film about himself. I light up and enjoy the first drag of the day. Just when I stick the fag out the window to tip the ash, Hopper swerves to avoid something. I drop the smoke but my hand catches in a branch. When I pull it back in, it's bleeding a bit.

'Jesus, Frank, I'm sorry. Crater in the middle of the road.'

'It's grand.'

I give it a wipe with a tissue; it's only scratched. I've a good look at my hands. My raggedy fingernails, chunk gone off the top of my left thumb, new scrapes across the knuckles. The man with the hands, alright. Sorry-looking specimens by any stretch.

The First Glen

I have the big map on my lap and we're heading inland. The odd tractor and car passes us, not much going on. Why there's so many bungalows in the countryside I don't know. I could ask Hopper; he's something to say about everything. Mila suits him. Better than some of the ones he's been into lately, like Granny Grim and her knitted bootees.

A couple more messages from Bernie; photo of himself and the Mater outside big gates, Buckingham Palace. Then Eileen and the Mater outside a hospital. I message him, say me and Hopper are camping in Wexford. Thought he'd get back to me, but nothing. Must be busy.

Hopper starts sniffing, drawing in real deep breaths through his nose.

'What're ya at?'

'For no reason I sometimes get hit by these smells, no matter what way I turn my head — like being inside a cloud.'

'But it's not real?'

'No. This one is the Three Kings.'

'What?'

'That's what I call it. *We Three Kings of Orient Are*. Precious oils, you know, myrrh and the other ones.'

'Fuck are you going on about?'

'When I was small, this aunt was home from the missions. Sister Bernadette. She and the mother were in the kitchen going on about corpses. They'd just buried a great-uncle who had some kind of condition, all swollen up and purple in the coffin.'

'You've lost me.'

'Hold up, Frank. That led them to discussing the oils for embalming dead bodies. Where the aunt was in Africa, they'd bleed this particular tree for the resin. It'd be dark yellowy lumps. Myrrh.'

'What's that to do with the price of eggs?'

'Dunno. All mixed up in my head; what I imagine that smells like. I can't tell which half of the shit in my head I've heard or which half I've made up.'

'It's there all the time, the smell?'

'No. I've this other one, shocking bad smell gets in on me regular. Call it the curse of the cabbage.'

'Weird.'

'I thought if I lived for another hundred year, I'd never smell one true thing again. Not a roast chicken, a woman, the sea nor nothing.'

I take a quick look over at him. I hadn't really given the smell thing much thought other than taking the piss out of him. 'Never say never, Hopper.'

'You know it. Now this powder is my ticket out.'

'Crisps?'

'Nah. Give us an extra strong, will ya?'

I flip open the glove box and have a root around. Maybe cos he's going on about it, everything smells sharper to me.

Whiff of the engine and grass coming in the window. I can even smell the heat. The mint in Hopper's mouth cuts across them all, as fresh as anything. I cup my two hands over my mouth and nose.

'The fuck're you doing?' Hopper goes.

'Nothing,' I says, rubbing my face, pretending that's what I was going to do. But I was smelling my own skin. Though I'm not too sweaty, I smell human.

'Don't be getting all in on yourself,' he goes. 'We're arriving into Glenvale.'

Sure enough, one pub (closed), then further down opposite a school is a little church. Hopper pulls in alongside it, in front of the graveyard. Just past that is a football pitch, and then back to green fields. It's all going on around here.

'Do they keep church records in the church itself?' Hopper goes.

'Dunno. I'll have a look in.'

'I'll check out the headstones. Never know, could hit the jackpot.' He sparks up and goes through the pedestrian gate into the graveyard.

There's a porch with two doors off it leading into the church. I try both but they're locked. The noticeboard's jammers: the lottery winners, no Kiely's there; trip to Medjugorje, led by the very experienced Fr Matthew Walsh (led over fifty tours), contact Turner Tours to book a place; volunteers needed for the cemetery Mass, ring parish office; rota for Mass servers and readers. I scan the list of names, no Kielys there either. Plenty of Reillys and Cannings, a Simon Eto and Rosemarie Eto and Precious Eto. Imagine travelling half the way across the world and ending up here. Fuck. If I emigrated to Africa, I wouldn't be thrilled to end up in the arse end of nowhere. Though Precious Eto is probably leading out the Glenvale team in the club championships. I get a sudden flash of June and the camogie. Wouldn't mind seeing her play. I put the number of the parish office into my phone and go back out to find Hopper.

'Any luck?' he says, vaulting over the low wall between the church and the graveyard.

'No, locked up. But there's a number. I'll give them a call.'

We sit on the wall at the front; the moss on it is lovely and warm. Hopper gets a couple of Cokes from the car. A bell rings out from the school and a load of kids come screaming out into the playground. One bunch of lads go straight over to the grass and set up two goals with their jumpers. Some smaller kids are making a camp under the trees. The teachers are chatting away beside the basketball hoop.

'Remember the buzz, getting out at break?' Hopper goes. 'Running around like mad yokes before you'd to park your arse for another two hours back behind a desk?'

'Not really,' I says, punching in the number of the parish office. It's ringing and ringing. Someone answers it, says 'Hello' and then it breaks up. I try again.

Next thing Hopper's pulling my arm.

'What?'

He points. One of the teachers is heading through the kids in our direction. She's pointing something at us.

'What've we done now?' Hopper goes.

'She looks like a right auld battle axe. Let's get the fuck outta here.'

'They'll definitely nail us as a couple of paedos then. If she takes the car reg we're fucked. Sit tight.'

Your one is not too fast on the pegs. She summons us across the road in a real teachery way. 'I was watching ye.'

Fuck. Hopper's right.

'We're looking for the priest.'

She has a phone in her hand and she attacks a few buttons with her index finger. Next thing my phone rings.

I answer it. 'Hello?'

'Hello.' The teacher is helloing into her phone. What the fuck?

'You rang this number,' she says into her phone.

This is mad. I hang up and say directly to her, 'I rang the parish office.'

'That's me,' she goes. 'I'm the school secretary and the parish secretary. What were you looking for? You're not the band, are ye?'

'No, I was looking for parish records.'

She's clearly disappointed. A few of the kids have wandered across the grass, standing close enough to hear what's going on, far enough away to make a break for it.

'I thought it was the wedding band. We're having a choir rehearsal this afternoon. They're using local children, which is lovely.'

Without turning around she barks out, 'Emer McDonnell, if you have been told once, you have been told more than once, you are to sit out the *sos mór*. Or you will be making a very direct visit to Mrs McHugh's office.'

Emer McDonnell, one of those twelve-year-olds who looks like she might be taking a direct visit to sixteen any day now, turns on her heel and drifts off, her entourage trailing behind her.

'We've had a lot of interest since Jenny went public last week. I knew for months obviously.'

'Excuse me?'

'Jenny Deane. The newsreader. She's marrying that footballer. The Belgian, from the shampoo ad. Her parents are originally from Cork, but a great-aunt was very connected to our parish.

They're coming here for the service and having the reception in Wobourne House.'

'Isn't that something?' Hopper goes. 'Not dissimilar to Frank here. He's trying to track down an old grand-aunt who might be from the parish. Kiely, Letty Kiely.'

'I've never heard that name around here.'

A piercing whistle rips across the yard. Kids collect up their gear, line up at the school door.

'That's why we wanted to look at church records,' I says.

'But sure you don't need access to the church for that. We've it all digitalised. From 1900 to 1985 so far. Births, deaths, the works.'

'So we could look it up on the phone, even?'

'No. Unless you've a library card. Otherwise you'd have to go in. Hold on.' She bustles back across the grass towards the school.

'This is dead handy.' Hopper winks at me.

She comes back quick enough with a leaflet outlining the Glenvale Historical Records Project. They've all kinds of yokes put online. Church records, maps, GAA teams going back to 1942.

'I was on the committee myself,' she says. 'Rural Redevelopment Heritage Working Group.'

'Sound as a pound,' Hopper goes. 'You have the place in great shape anyway for the visitors.'

'We're very lucky. The aunt's house is dead on the border of two parishes. She always attended Mass here, but there's another branch of the family buried in Kinlasha. Did you visit Kinlasha church?'

'No.'

'Father Kirk is very active with the musicals. *Fiddler on the Roof*. All into the mindfulness. But he had the pulpit and the font removed when they redecorated. We've kept it simple here.'

'Sometimes simple is yer only man,' Hopper goes.

'We've been asked not to take photos on the day.'

'Fair enough,' I goes, keen to get away now we've got what we came for. I can see your woman would happily spend all day hanging over the wall, gossiping.

'No photos at all?' Hopper says.

'We could be offered unknown sums by the paparazzi.'

'Right, so,' I says, heading over to the car. Hopper follows. Mrs Secretary General heads back to school. 'Take it easy on the roads, boys. *Slán.*'

Back in the car, I says, 'Should we go to a library or something and check this out?'

'Or we could head on to the next Glen and knock that off our list?' Hopper goes. 'It's only about half an hour away. Then see about a library.'

I know the whole thing is a bit of a wild goose chase, but it beats sitting at home, killing time. And Hopper is all for it. It takes us a few minutes to work out the best way to the next Glen, Glenard. I'm getting into this now; if we get there quick, we could maybe get a third one done this afternoon. But Hopper's still a bit wary of going on the main roads, so it's the back roads again and I'm to try and direct him with the map.

I'm peckish so have a root around in the back of the car to see what we have in the way of supplies. A pack of chocolate chip cookies and a bag of Doritos. As we're driving along there's this fellah on the radio talking about how he became a millionaire. I'm only half-listening.

'D'ya hear that, Frank? One of the richest men in Ireland.'

'What's he on about, shampoo?'

'Hair restorer. If you're going bald.'

'I'll tell ya one thing, that's a load of shite. Always bald lads coming to the Da. Especially at night when they thought nobody'd notice. Or slippin' in beside him at a match. One of the few things he'd say is impossible, getting hair to grow back.'

'Well, I hate to best yer auld fellah with science, but it's not impossible.'

I'm telling him about this time as a kid I snuck into the front room to watch the Da working on a pure cue ball. Only a few wisps stretching from one tiny flat ear to the other. I thought the fellah'd brought his little dog along. It was on the chair so I gave it a stroke. Fucking rug. The deadest feeling. Never forgot the sensation.

'I'd bet I know exactly who you mean,' Hopper goes. 'Christy Conway?'

'Bang on.'

'They say he gets the wigs from Lacey the undertaker. He's a set of teeth wasn't fitted for his gob either. Wears women's tights.'

Hopper's recounting some encounter he had with Christy in the women's underwear section in Shaws when his phone rings.

'Hello,' he says. 'Alice who? Oh yeah, Alice. Frank's here beside me. I'll put him on now.' He covers the phone and winks. 'Alice, from the beach.'

'You mean Tara?'

'No, the other one. They're throwing themselves at you.'

I take the phone. 'Hello?'

'Hiya. Tara said you were looking for some place called Glen.'

'Yeah. We've been to Glenvale and we're heading to Glenard now.'

'It was a bit slow in the office this morning and I was talking to my mother. She knows loads of stuff cos her family's from here. She said there used to be this place called The Glen. Like ages ago.'

'The Glen what?'

'Just The Glen. Near Ardan, but really remote in the countryside. It wasn't official.'

'How d'ya mean?'

'Not a regular mother and baby home. It's closed down years ago. Was run by a sister and brother. Very secretive. "For different circumstances," that's what she said. Maybe if the family had money, or depending who was involved.'

'Right.'

She tells me her mother heard about it again recently at a talk by a local woman who's all up on this stuff. It was sort of notorious in the area and spooky. She'll text me contact details for the history woman. As I'm calling out my number, one part of my brain's computing what she's saying and the meaning of it, in terms of the Da. Another part is trying to stay on the old track. Where the Da married my mother and had seven sons and whatever happened before that was of no real consequence. Wasn't real like our life. Isn't real at all.

When I finish the call, Hopper's gagging to know what she wanted, why I gave her my number.

'Some other Glen place they came up with,' I goes.

'Grand, mark it down as number seven. Hopefully we'll have the thing sorted before we get that far down the list.'

'Yeah.'

He goes back to talking about baldness and hair. Although I'm half-answering him, the real conversation I'm having is with Deadwood in the back. I felt we were on the same track before now, but something else is rising in me, something going the opposite direction from the Deadwood, from Da. I suppose I was thinking I might find some old flame of the Da's, maybe find out there was a kid who's grown up now and everyone's life went on, happy out. That's not even true. I didn't think of them as living, breathing people. It was more about myself, what it would mean for me. Not what could've happened in other people's lives.

'Do you hear that, Deadwood, a mother and baby home? They're all over the news. I even watched a film with the Mater about a woman, and her baby was sent to America and then he was gay and he died before she was able to track him down. They were using the women as free labour in those places, selling babies off and shit. What the fuck? Would you have left someone in a place like that? What did you believe was going on? Just do it, you used to say. But what is it, exactly, that you did?'

I Believe

. . . for every drop of rain that falls, a flower grows . . .

'What is it exactly that you did?' Fair question, Frank. I
suppose if I could give you a general answer, I'd have to say I
did some things I knew for sure was right, some things I knew
one hundred per cent was wrong, and mostly I lived in the
in-between. Beliefs, that's an even trickier one. But whatever
state I'm in now, it's all washed away; the shame of my
weaker moments and the pride of my achievements. They all
feel as neutral as a pint of milk. I'd give the same welcome to
my mistakes as anything else.

Anyways, it's often a mistake can set you on the path to
where you should have been heading in the first place. I know
Frank's annoyed with me now, thinks this whole trip is gone
sour, but I still maintain the only thing to do is to try, even if
you haven't a clue how things'll turn out. That's what I'd tell
him. As the far as the healing went, the ones that come good
were as mysterious to me as them that didn't. That's the trick,
to be able to live with whatever way the cards fall. You could
straighten out some fellah's knee, have him walk tall for the

first time ever. He could step out the front door, walk across the road, and be knocked down. Stone dead. Been known to happen.

I often wondered the same about the Brownshill Dolmen, out the Hacketstown Road. The lads that hauled them stones into that particular field and propped them up, they'd have had no sense they'd gone a bit beyond other dolmen makers, would they? As far as I'm aware, they weren't travelling around the country specialising in this particular aspect of monument building. Local job by local boyos. Did they think to themselves, come here, lads, we'll go big on this one? Or was it random, did they just happen on the biggest top stone already lying in the field and heave it up? They might even have been considering a bigger job, maybe even looked at a bigger stone. But it was beyond them. They lived and died not knowing they had created something special. All in a day's work for them, no more than them slaves in Egypt.

Could've been the same scenario with the pyramids. Maybe the gaffer wasn't on top of his game, got the plumb lines a bit off. Next thing you know the walls are coming in to meet each other. The pharaoh has a look and says, feck it; we'll go for the Toblerone instead of the four walls and ceiling job.

Here's the thing. Say you're only one of the worker ants left finishing the pyramid; the last labourers after - what is it? Fifty, one hundred years? You're fixing in the blocks at the top, do your bit, head back down the scaffolding, get your arse whipped for your efforts. Onto the next job, maybe the first paw of the sphinx, or digging out a dam across the Nile. Or maybe you're left behind to sort out the snag list. Probably no end to a construction job like that. By the time the lads at the top had smoothed off the last trowel of plaster, satisfied themselves with the effect they'd achieved, there was probably

236

another crew starting repairs at the bottom: a badly hung door that won't close right, a leak over there, crooked coving.

No photographs back then. So to realise the magnitude of the whole operation, you'd have to remember how long it used to take you to carry a hod of bricks to the top, or haul a bucket of water. But you'd have no sense of its place in history and no place in history for you.

I can see one of the Carlow lads now, a quare hairy fellah, sitting at his fire on a beautiful summer evening, the same moon rising as the very one is in the sky tonight, two thousand years on. He's sitting there, chewing on a bit of meat, dry and warm and his little brood asleep around the hearth, dogs and children and women all tangled up together, and he can see the silhouette rising up in the distance. The flat capstone, stout legs holding it up, the stone door.

He wasn't the only one who built it, but he knows it was his shoulder heaved against it, his sweat marks left on the underside of that hunk of rock. Maybe he dreamed up the whole thing. Found the materials for the job, chose the burial site, rounded up the lads.

Course, you have to consider the fact that people stopped building dolmens. That's the other side of the coin. My point is, if people had kept on with that sort of craic, putting one massive stone balancing on top of a few smaller ones, eventually they'd have had better tools, the equipment to go bigger and bigger. Quarry an even immenser capstone. Mechanical ways'd take over; a crane'd easily lift and put it together in a day.

They stopped. Maybe Carlow wasn't the last one built, but times change. Before you know it, you're the tail end, last stop. That fellah sitting there at his fire, looking over at the black outline of that dolmen, might have been imagining his son

237

doing the same thing when it was time to lay another set of bones in the ground, marking off another grave with something similar, and his son's son doing the same. Not that he'd be remembered in such a fashion, only the chief of chiefs and his ilk would lie there.

Or maybe in those days, there wasn't as much time to pretend you knew anything about the future. Life needed attention: get fed, fend off wild animals, stay warm. Still, though, when you look at the massive effort them lads put into making a yoke like that, you think mankind, even back in the day, was always stretching his auld bag of bones, trying to touch something beyond himself.

I feel that man's death coming on. Maybe he feels it himself that night, looking at the white monster that occupies the sky, robs the daylight for itself and then relinquishes it agin. Relinquish, that's a good one. Relinquish and extinguish.

In case you can't picture the dolmen I'm talking about, its arse end is planted firmly in the ground. That didn't happen today or yesterday. The capstone is balanced on the three boulders beneath, but tipped over in a way that it's half-resting on a littler stone. Brings me back to prehistoric Carlow man. Sitting there. Looking across and his eye drawn agin and agin to the fecking capstone, like a duck that's dipped its head in the water and its arse pointing westward. That capstone, after all their pulling and pushing and smoothing off, was too hard to handle. He's looking over at a construction not pleasing to him, untidy-looking job. Bit of a let-down and it pains him, thinking of the bodies buried there and that was the best they could do. If he only knew; there's experts from Canada to Norway and beyond who come here specially and solely to have a gawk. To wonder at your handiwork. Fair dues, lad. Any mistakes have long been absolved; what's left is a mystery and a marvel. I can see it all around me; the affinity of the ups and downs, the give-and-take, here's the word for it now, the reciprocity underneath it all. Accepting it all equally, your misfortune and your fate, is a fairly sound foundation to be getting on with.

. . . for every drop of rain that falls, a flower grows . . .

To the Power Of

We're still heading toward the next Glen, Glenard, although I know it's pointless. What Alice said on the phone about this place The Glen, that must be the one. I don't say nothing to Hopper cos I don't know what to say. And ever since I told him the Mater and Bernie aren't coming home for another night, he's pushing for us to stay on at Oddsey's. He's trying to make out it's for my sake, to do more searching, but clearly it's about him and Mila. I don't think he gives a shit one way or another how this all shakes down for me. Now she's texted him and he wants to skip going to the next Glen place, head off to some beach to see seals.

'Come with us, Frank.'

'No.'

'Or I'll drop you off at a library. That might be worth a shot, now you have the leaflet from your woman.'

Ever since Alice's call, I realise even a fool would have seen that digging into any bit of family history that's hidden . . . well, it's probably hidden for a reason.

'We should go home today.'

'What about the search? Seventh son and all that?'

'Forget about it.'

'How can I forget about it,' he goes, 'with you going on about it for fucking years?'

'That's not true.'

'All I ever hear is you going on like an auld one about whether you have the gift and if you'll fit into your Da's shoes and–'

'I never talk about it.'

'Once you get a skinful into ya, you never stop. GBH of the fucking ears for whosoever is in the vicinity.'

What the fuck's he on about? Always exaggerating, make a laugh out of everything.

'Fuck you, Hopper. Mila's just using you til something better comes along. She's way out of your class.'

'Rich coming from you. You're getting so bad you couldn't pull a fucking turnip. Don't think I haven't noticed,' he goes on. 'That's why I had to set you up with June. Nobody gives a fiddler's fuck if you can cure a dose of the clap. They could make you president of the Padre fucking Pio society and you still wake up as Frank Whelan.'

I can't believe Hopper's decided to have a go at me, on top of everything else.

'Drop me near the town,' I says. 'I want a bit of time to myself.'

At the next junction he takes the road left to Rosbay, away from Glenard. Silence for a change because usually he can't shut up for two minutes. We part ways on the outskirts of the town. I get the rucksack from the back seat, close the door.

First chipper I pass, Aldos, I go in, get a milkshake. I ask the girl behind the counter where the library is. She looks at me like I've two heads.

'Right next door,' she goes, snarky out.

I ignore the attitude oozing across the counter. The minute I go out, I see that I walked past two big windows with shelves of books in them.

Maybe cos the weather is so good there's hardly anyone inside except for a few sad cases who probably use it as their personal sitting room. I reckoned libraries were real gloomy places but this one is more like a cafe with books, but without the coffee or grub. They've loads of computers and nice chairs, even a PlayStation. I ask the fellah behind the desk about using the computer and he gives me a code. He asks if I'm looking for anything in particular. I reckon if they have all these parish records up, they might have some history thing about this place, The Glen. Not that I want to get into that with him. I show him the leaflet for the Glenvale Parish Records and he gets all chatty, explains how to pull up those files.

I sit up at a desk, log in, follow the directions on the leaflet, and get the parish records. I put in the name Kiely. I know it's pointless, but I want to be doing something. All the time, it's in the back of my head, The Glen, home for pregnant women. The Da got some young one up the duff, legged it, left her there. I'm getting annoyed thinking about it. The rucksack is at my feet under the table and I give the Deadwood a good kick. I should've given you back to Lena with her little paring knife. She'd've peeled you quick as all get out. That'd be your eternity. Now my toe is stinging. Fuck ya.

I'm staring at the screen doing nothing. Your man comes out from behind the counter, wheels himself over to me. How did I not notice the wheelchair before?

'You alright there?' he goes.

'Yeah.'

'Any luck?'

'Not in these records, no.'

'Have you any other details?' he says.

I suppose I'm here now, I may as well ask. 'Well,' I goes. 'There might be a place called The Glen?'

'Where is that?'

When I tell him it was a house for pregnant women, I see the light bulb go on.

'Hang on,' he goes and wheels himself up beside me. He's some fucking flyer on the keyboard. He has loads of pages open before you can say jack shit.

'There was a few newspaper articles about it recently.' He points out a few pages. 'Anniversary of the hurricane.'

'A hurricane?'

'Back in '71. People forget how extreme the weather can be, even without climate change. The main building was destroyed. But it had been unoccupied for years. There's a local historian well up on it: Evelyn Sayers.'

The same name Alice gave me.

He writes down the name and an address on a bit of paper. 'I'm adopted too,' yer man goes. 'Not from The Glen though. That was a very particular set-up. Privately run.'

'I'm not adopted meself,' I go, real quick. 'Just checking out information. For a relation.'

Someone calls him over from the desk and he wheels off. I wonder did they adopt him in the wheelchair? Did he have an accident afterwards? That's a lot of bad luck for one person.

Looking at the computer screen, there's a photo of a grim-looking house standing alone with big trees all around it.

Why would the Da have left her in The Glen and skedaddled off to live happy ever after?

I remember he had great time for us as kids, other people's kids too, kicking a ball on the green, fixing up a bike. But who knows anyone's true nature? What did he ever think looking at me? Wondering was I his seventh kid, but knowing I was probably eighth. And it might be Bernie was the one. No wonder we're all fucked up. My stomach is seizing up, probably that fucking granola from earlier. I need to walk it off.

I take a stroll along what might be the main street. The town's not dissimilar to Carlow; a lot of the same shops. A bit livelier, not as many fronts boarded up. The main square is well kept, big barrels of flowers and a statue of some local hero with a pike and a dog. Heroes with pikes and dogs all over this country, everyone clinging on to their own bit of glory.

I turn up an alley not even wide enough for one car. There's Nikita's Beauty Salon and O'Dea's Locksmiths. Coming out the other end, I spot a pub facing me, McIlhatton's. Wouldn't mind a dark pub and a quiet corner of my own.

Heading across, I notice the street sign, Pound Street. I take out the bit of paper. Same address. I walk about halfway down and see a sign beside number 19:

Bell One   *Sharkey and Co. Insurance*
Bell Two   *Samuel Kirby's Camera and Watch Repairs*
Bell Three   *Local History Project*

I should skip this now; go for a pint, sit tight. But I ring the bell. Nothing. Give the door a little shove and I'm straight into a shabby hallway. A sideboard is covered with a load of flyers and an ornate mirror, all bevelled around the edges with peacocks and ivy. Something about walking past a mirror forces you to look at yourself. I could do with a shower and a shave. I run my fingers through the hair before heading up the narrow stairs. First floor, just one door with a logo for Sharkey Insurance; the next floor up, a toilet and a door into what must be the camera and watch repair workshop. Who gets a watch repaired any more? Who even has a watch only drug dealers or footballers? Through a glass panel there's two men sitting at a long workbench with loads of shit in front of them. They've their backs to me.

One says to the other, 'Would you say she had or she hadn't?'

I slow down but I only catch the end of the answer: '. . . for all that, you have to be able to tell the difference. Your life could depend on it.'

Probably not discussing watches or cameras. I'm tempted to just stand there and watch them fiddle with cogs and say things that have nothing to do with me. One starts to pull his chair back slowly. No time to think what she might have had or hadn't and whose life could be depending on it. I shift my arse up the next stairs. At the last step I'm looking at a door with *Local History Project* written on it. There's a poster on the outside, a woman with her sleeves rolled up and a slogan that says *We Can Do It*. Before I even have a chance to knock, the door opens.

'Can I help you?' a woman says.

'I'm looking for Evelyn Sayers.'

'That's me.'

She opens the door wider into a small attic room with the ceiling real sloped. There's a Velux window wide open. You'd need it because all the heat from the day has risen up the building and gathered here in the eaves. The place is heaped full of folders and papers and a couple of computers. Like a detective agency from an old film.

'We're not always here, you know,' she goes.

'I came across the sign by accident. I meant to ring to check first.'

'I didn't catch a name.'

'Frank. Frank Whelan. The lad in the library gave me your name. You know the fellah with the . . .'

'Who?'

'With the darkish hair. Youngish. No beard.'

She doesn't pick up who I mean.

'Anyways he works in the library, and he said you might be able to help me.'

'I can try but there's more people I can't help than can.'

'It's to do with this place called The Glen.'

She clears an armful of folders off a chair onto the floor. I go and sit down and give her the gist of the story. As I'm talking, she's asking questions and digging out files. She says for every one story that's clear there's another hundred we'll never really know. At the start I feel like I'm dobbing the father in. She probably hates men like him who caused all this shit. But as it goes on, I let that go, partly because she doesn't seem to be going down that road and partly because I'm getting drawn in by what she's saying.

An hour later I'm sitting in McIlhatton's, sculling back a second pint, trying to make sense of the bits and pieces knocking up against each other in my head. It was like when I started in the mill, where they tell you everything you need to know. It all makes sense to them but once they're gone, you haven't a clue how to switch on the machine or what RA stands for or where they keep the keys for the shed. Even though she was trying to keep it simple for me, she kept getting carried away with all she knows.

I was quare parched when I got out, knocked back the first pint in three mouthfuls. I check my phone, a few messages: one from the Mater, just how are ya kind of thing; one from Hopper to say what am I up to and he's going to be swinging back around fiveish. Clock behind the bar says 4.35. That gives me a bit of time to get my head together. I take out the notebook Evelyn gave me to write down stuff. I didn't even have a pen.

All the facts is like a swarm of bees buzzing around. The queen bee, at the centre sitting tight, is the fact that Evelyn had a photocopy of a ledger that said Letty Kiely was put in The Glen aged approximately fourteen. She said this was from the records of a Dr Williams. He's a character crops up regular in her files. Him and a priest, Fr Benedict. Judge and jury for women around here. That Dr Williams was working out of the mental home. Looks like Letty was in The Glen for two and half years before being sent on to the County Mental Home. Evelyn was a bit surprised by how long she was in The Glen, unless they kept her on as a servant. Usually once the baby was out, they moved them on. That's only some of the facts, as she kept saying.

She was going on about what was fact and supposition. Then patterns of truth, which was a bit different again. But what's missing is other facts. For one thing, there's no record of a baby. Boy, girl, or the Invisible fucking Man. Evelyn thought that was a bit odd, although there's all kinds of skulduggery regarding record keeping that she comes up against. But that Dr Williams was very thorough in keeping his ledger of births and deaths. Must have given him personal satisfaction, something to present at the pearly gates, Evelyn said. Or maybe insurance against powerful people.

The Glen had a particular reputation. Remote place, out of the way. The sister and brother who owned it were related to the Fr Benedict that ran the show in them days. It had a reputation for all kinds of shit. She knows of at least one exorcism there. Mad shit. Also most of the women ended up going from there to a ward in the mental hospital. Some even came from the hospital to The Glen, gave birth, and were sent back. One woman, not Letty, was there three times, twice from the hospital.

One reason it was hard to concentrate on everything she was saying was because I couldn't get over the fact that my father knocked up a fourteen-year-old. Like, it's very fucking young, even for back then. And that was the end of the road for her. Into this Glen house, then bounced over to the funny farm for the remainder of her days. Probably buried in some pauper's grave. Evelyn rang some friend of hers, another one who's all up on the history and knows the mental hospital stuff. She emailed her back before I left. That's how she knew Letty was admitted, but she kind of disappears then. To make it more complicated, the hospital's closed now, turned into offices and clinics.

'The Glen is just a pile of rubble,' she said. 'The roof came off in a storm. Actually a small hurricane.'

'That's what your man said in the library. My mother always said her wedding day was destroyed on account of a freak hurricane. Probably same one.'

'Some around here believed it was retribution for what went on.'

'How'dya mean?'

'All that evil that was visited on the powerless, women and children, has to go somewhere, I suppose.'

On the bar stool beside me I've the rucksack with the Deadwood propped up. It's like we're both on this journey waiting for something to happen. The difference now is we mightn't be waiting for the same thing any more.

'What kind of man were ya?' I say under my breath, but I don't even want to be talking to him.

My head is gone back inside itself, sifting through the odds and ends of information and history she gave me. I thought once I found out, that'd be it. I'd know what there was to know. But I didn't find out about the kid, boy or girl. It doesn't feel like I got to the end of things; or I got there, but there is no there exactly. Listening to Evelyn talk, all the questions about the seventh son stuff and the cure shrank away inside me. Doesn't feel like this trip has anything to do with my inheriting the gift and all that any more. I half-wish Bernie was sitting beside me, sucking on some mad cocktail and giving a bit of perspective on it all.

I nearly spill half my pint when my phone starts ringing. Hopper. I never answered his text.

'Frank, where are ya?'

'Just around the town.'

'I was talking to Alice. She was wondering how we got on with some place called The Glen. Some home.'

'Yeah, well that's it.'

'No wonder you were like a cut cat earlier. Are you there?'

'No, I'm in a pub. McIlhatton's.'

'I'll drive in.'

'Thought you didn't want to take the car into town.'

'Oh yeah,' he goes. 'Meet ya where I dropped you off. Be there in twenty.'

'Who's with ya?'

'I'm on me own.'

I drain the glass, put the notebook in the rucksack on top of the Deadwood, and head out into the street. Might be easier to make sense of this with Hopper than trying to puzzle it out inside my own head, which is like a multiplication factory. Every thought that pops up gets magnified. Those numbers, what do you call them, exponential; to the power of. Two to the power of fifty is way more than a hundred. Even as I'm walking back to meet Hopper, it's happening: every two bees swarming inside my head is to the power of more and more. Each angle I think of: the Da's carry-on; what about the Mater, did she ever know; Letty's life; no records of a kid, probably given away, if it even saw the light of day, or buried in the middle of nowhere. How one little action sets off all these other things that carry on and spread out and grow.

To the power of. To the power of.

I must've walked right past Hopper because he grabs me from behind.

'Freeze,' he says, pushing an ice pop against my neck, breaking his shite laughing.

'Fuck off.'

The car is parked around the corner. With that we're away, windows down, demolishing a couple of choc-ices.

Collecting Mussels

I'm telling Hopper as much as I can remember from what Evelyn told me. Half the questions he's asking me, I don't even know the answers myself.

At some stage I ask, 'Where are we going?'

'Get a bit of grub.'

I'm not hungry but he wants to go to some village that's famous for its curry sauce, though I'm not into curry sauce. He's like a local now, flying up and down little side roads.

'How's Mila?'

'Asking for ya. Anyways, go on.'

After a while, he interrupts and says it back to me, clearer: 'So what you're saying, she was put into this home for pregnant girls. Ended up in the mental hospital. She must've had a kid. Fifty-fifty chance of it being a boy. Chances are that kid was adopted off somewhere, even as far as America.'

'Yeah, I suppose, or it might've died.'

'No records anywhere. This Glen place is gone, the women are all dead and gone, and this Evelyn has no more leads for you regarding Letty Kiely. No idea where she's buried or nothing?'

'No. Complete dead end. In fact The Glen place was that bad, some local women went out and torched what was left of the ruins a few years ago.'

Hopper has a long drag on his fag, digesting all the facts. 'Jesus, if she wasn't a head case at the get-go, she must've turned into one. You did your best, but maybe it's time to give up.'

He's probably right. That Evelyn's been researching this stuff for years, and that's all she could dig up.

When we get to the curry village, he pulls up at the chip van. I stay put in the car, thinking about what's left in this for me. I can't pretend things that have been said aren't stuck in my head. I knew the Da wasn't perfect, by any manner or means, but he treated the Mater like a queen. Never gave up on any of us, even Mossy with his mad ideas and Bernie who was a bit different from the start. Was he a coward under the surface the whole of his life?

Hopper comes out with two steaming bags of chips and a big side of battered cod.

'Famous,' he goes. 'All across the sunny south-east.'

'Which is mine?'

'There, yours are vinegared.'

He drives off, turns in to a lane, dips down toward the sea. We're fair bouncing along until we come out at an old pier with two small boats tied up. The tide is out and there's loads of birds working over the rocks, lifting the seaweed, filling their beaks with, I don't know, little insects or crabs.

Hopper parks up and we get out. The way the fields rise up means you can't even see the road. A single bungalow is off up to our left; I can see shed roofs beyond it. Apart from that, you're looking at sea and the coastline. Patches of these red flowers are everywhere, standing tall, bright as anything.

They must've stopped using this pier years ago; the back wall of it has collapsed down and crumbled into the sea. There's a few lobster pots and tangled-up nets lying around. Close up you can see one boat is falling to bits, but the other one, low in the water has been kept up nice. Fresh coat of white paint, the name *Mary Ellen Carter* standing out real sharp in blue.

We sit on a stack of red crates. Hopper takes two bottles of Coke out of his pockets. Nice one. We don't talk for a few minutes. Hate to admit it but these chips are way better than Fast Dan's. A big seagull keeps shifting itself towards us and then backing off again.

'There's always one, isn't there?' Hopper goes. 'Looking for the easy mark.'

Eventually it fucks off, joins the others on the rocks doing an honest day's work.

'What'll I tell the Mater?' I say, wiping my hands on my jeans, crumpling up the chip bag. 'She'll be gutted.'

'Say nothing, Frank.'

'Why shouldn't I? Shouldn't be just me carrying the burden.'

'What burden?'

'Knowing stuff. About the Da. What he left behind him.'

As I'm saying this, I realise I've left the Deadwood back in the car. Is this the first time since we set off that you're not at my side, Da? No, that's right, you missed the fish ballet.

But it's more than the distance from here to the car has come between me and him now. In fact, I'm looking forward to giving him back to the Mater, and if she has to return him to Lena, so be it. See how he likes being passed from here to there for the rest of his life. Or death, or whatever fucking limbo he's got himself into.

'Say you had found this kid?' Hopper goes. 'You use it to, I don't know, manipulate things one way or another for yourself. How's that going to work for your mother? The brothers? To think your Da was the cause of this kind of misery? Say nothing.'

'Well, for one thing, they're going to need to know why I'm not giving people the cure any more.'

'You're missing the point. Forget the poxy cure for a minute. I'm talking about important stuff. Like your family. The way you all have each other's back. That's not how it is for everyone.'

'How d'ya mean?'

'For example, me. I wasn't handed shit to start with. Other people was always deciding I'm this or I'm that. I'll turn out bad like the auld lad or mad like the mother. At home, school, even people I barely know in town, dictating how it's going to be for me. Minds made up already. I decided, fuck that, I'm backing meself. Once I copped to that, anything was possible. Even having a shot with someone as smart as Mila. If I blow it, fuck it, I wasn't going nowhere in the first place.'

He's right about his family. His da was rough as a bear's arse, then he hightailed it to England with a young one from Borris and a load of charges trailing after him. Mrs McGrath is a walking corpse, strung out on sleeping tablets and Valium. Apparently, half the women in town were like that at one stage, except she went under and never surfaced.

'Whatever I try, I want to go big,' he goes. 'I have to. You don't, and it can be a pain in the hole. Chasing your own tail like a dog.'

'When did you turn into Jeremy Kyle?'

'Remember the nurse used to come to the school? For the nit treatments?'

'Hells Bells.'

'That's the one; Helen Myers and her three-wheeled bike.'

'Massive bezungas. What about her?' I goes.

Apparently, she used to be always coming over to his house after his auld lad left, asking loads of questions, trying to catch him and Ruth out. They were all but raising themselves. They never let on about the mother who was asleep half the time, packing to leave the other half.

'Packing what?'

'Always packing a suitcase. When the auld lad was still throwing his weight around, me and Ruth'd be thrilled to see the case coming out. Thought we were leaving with the mother for good. She'd talk a good game back then, but she never did leave, not even once. After he was gone, she kept doing it. Addicted to it. Could be ten times a day.'

'Packing a suitcase? To go where?'

'Nowhere. I was terrified she'd leave me behind. Then I copped she was only packing mad shit.'

'Like what?'

'A fucking teapot, all her shoes. A trowel, toilet paper. You'd be looking for something and you'd find it under a bed in a suitcase. Forgotten about. Biscuits gone mouldy. Rotten meat bleeding into socks.'

'Fucking hell,' I says. 'She should've got a job on the checkout.'

'Wouldn't have been able to keep her eyes open. When Ruth split her head that Christmas, it was the auld lad did it. That's when he legged it for good. The ambulance man told my mother to pack up a few things for the hospital, for Ruth, but she couldn't. After all the years of fucking packing, she was opening drawers and closing them. It went on and on. In the end they left. I had to put a bag together, hitched over to the hospital.'

He never said before it was like that. Even when things seemed a bit off, he always made a laugh out of it. I suppose we never spent much time in his house; he was always hanging

out at ours. One more mouth to feed is hardly going to
bankrupt us, the Da used to say.

Hopper walks off down the pier to stuff the empty bottles
and bags into a plastic barrel. You'd have to say the Mater's the
opposite of Hopper's ma. She'd go anywhere at the drop of a
hat, up for any bit of action. Always seeing the possibilities of
life in everything. I know my head often gets itself wrapped
around negative shit that doesn't do me any favours. Hopper's
right, the family do have my back. Whether I have the cure or
not, they'll still see me as me. At the end of the day, the lads'd
give me the shirt off their back if I needed it. Especially Bernie.

I notice Hopper taking off his shoes, climbing down a ladder
from the pier onto seaweedy rocks.

'What the fuck are you up to?'

Next thing, he has his T-shirt whipped off. He's not going
to fucking strip again and swim out, is he? Definitely not
joining him this time. Probably freezing. But he's bent over,
searching for stuff.

I go over to the edge. 'What are you at?'

'Dinner.' He's filling the T-shirt up with shells.

'That T-shirt'll reek.'

'Fuck sake, Frank. Relax. Fresh mussels. We'll cook them
back at Oddsey's.'

I walk to the end of the pier and look out to the sea. There's
something on the horizon, could be an island or a ship maybe.
I've no idea where we are. Standing here, focusing on this
faraway yoke, it could be anything, and all the water from here
to there, sparkling and breaking with the white tops of the
waves. A few gulls pass by, not hardly flying, just drifting on
air currents. Gets simple for a minute.

'Frank, gis a hand.'

I turn around. Hopper has made his way along the shoreline.

He's used one of the old bits of net to wrap up the shells, hands it up to me. Back at the car, we throw them in the boot. I never ate a mussel before, so I'm not sure about this. But he seems convinced they're fit for human consumption.

'How do you cook them?' I ask.

'Maybe barbeque. See what way the lads prefer them.'

He hasn't a clue either. Fair fucks to him, though, he'll give anything a go. Then on the way back I start to wonder how does he even know if they are mussels? We'll find out soon enough.

It's pretty quiet at Oddsey's. Hopper presents his stash of shell-fish to Mila. It'd remind you of our old cat Snowy dropping dead mice at the Mater's feet.

They're all going for a swim, but I'm not interested. Oddsey says he'll cook the mussels if I clean them. I haven't a clue, so he sets me up with a bucket of cold water, tells me to throw away any ones that are open, that seems to be the main thing, and pull the hairy bits off the rest.

He's blaring out some mad music. Calypso. I look at the album cover, *Sparrow at the Hilton* by the Mighty Sparrow. You could say this whole set-up is Oddsey's Hilton: he gets to run the show his way; home-made cider and fish direct from the sea; sunsets and swimming. Not bad.

He's some record collection; hundreds of them stacked in beer crates by the wall. Mostly old stuff and a good few psychedelic-looking covers. I wouldn't say he listens to anything past the seventies. A few of the singers are ones the Da would've had, Aretha Franklin, the Beatles, Van Morrison. He even has a Perry Como, the one with the Italian songs. The Da'd pretend he knew Italian, singing along.

Oddsey comes over to see what album I've taken out.

'That's a good one,' he goes. 'Smooth as velvet.'

'One of my father's favourites. I think he had a leaning towards him because of the seventh son thing.'

'What's that?' Oddsey asks me.

I explain to him about how Perry Como was a seventh son, same as my da, and me, and how my father always felt he brought a special quality to his singing because of that.

'I knew he was a barber, but this I did not know.'

Once the Mighty Sparrow has finished singing about some woman called Sandra, Oddsey puts on Perry and blasts it out. Hearing that first song about the Mediterranean Sea makes me feel like I'm only three foot tall, back in our front room.

The mussels go down a treat. You only have to boil them for a few minutes, dead simple. By nineish there's a crowd after arriving, celebrating some birthday. Oddsey's done a load of barbequed chicken; someone brought a cake. Cases of home brew and loads of blow doing the rounds. Myself and Hopper and the three girls are at one table. They've all been filled in on The Glen, want to know how I got on, what Evelyn had to say. Everyone has some horror story about how women were treated in the old days. Nobody is saying it, but I know they're wondering about the father, reassessing what kind of man he was. Probably having a second look at me too. They're not asking for the Deadwood to add his energy to the mix now. And I'm not offering.

Late on, we're listening to this fellah playing some fancy guitar when Mila says out of the blue, 'It is also challenging to think about the fathers of all these infants.'

Hopper shoots her a look.

Probably cos Mila's foreign she's a bit more direct. 'For some of the men,' she goes on, 'they also suffered a loss.'

'Yeah, but they didn't get locked up.' Alice, clear as anything and loud. 'Not like the women. Made to feel lower than shit on your shoe. A lot of the women weren't even, you know . . . They were just abused, raped. Fucking pricks walked away, got on with their lives and families. As if nothing happened.'

I feel sick to my stomach.

Hopper stands up, lifts a few empties from the table. 'Gis a hand clearing here, Frank, will ya? See can I get Oddsey to cough up some of this special shit I've been hearing about. Seaweed-flavoured champagne or some such.'

I pick up a few cans and follow him in. 'Think I'm going to hit the hay early,' I goes.

'Don't mind what they're saying,' Hopper goes. 'No one knows what goes on between two people. You'll never know what your father did or didn't do. But you know he was a decent enough skin. He always was to me. That's more I can say about my auld fellah.'

'Not so sure now.'

'Why think the worst?'

'I wish I was home. Leave the Deadwood back where I got him. Everything back to normal.'

'First thing tomorrow we'll head.'

'Yeah. Anyways, have a good night.'

I pile the mattresses up on top of each other and roll out my sleeping bag. The Deadwood is in the rucksack beside me, but I don't take him out. There's loads of different sounds: someone still picking out chords on the guitar, not adding up to any one song; talking; bursts of laughing every so often. It sounds like good craic out there, but thanks to the Da I'm not part of it. Someone starts up on a mouth organ, an old tune. I'm trying to recognise it cos he's playing it different to usual, drawing the notes out real long. Behind it all you can hear the waves. At home it'd be the occasional car going by, later on a crowd coming back from the pub, maybe the bin lorry early morning. Mad that I'm close enough to be able to hear the sea as I'm going to sleep.

Eventually the other noises fade and it's just the waves. It's nice, but you could get lonesome or something. Being from a big family, and a twin, you get used to people around, always stuff going on. Bernie's dramatics livens things up and the Mater with her tea leaves and her gossiping with Cissy. Even Murt and his antique yokes. With all the shit that's gone down today, I feel that alone. I reach in under the top of the rucksack. I'm annoyed at him and yet, fuck it, as Hopper said, he was a decent skin at the same time.

Rubbing my hand across the top of the Deadwood, I think I feel something; some kind of hum, like music, going up my arm. Don't feel like having a conversation tonight. Too tired anyways. *Put it in your pocket* . . . that's the song your man was playing . . . *save it for a rainy day*. What's the name of it again? The waves kind of tune into it, rainy day, catcha, rainy day, catcha, and then I'm fading, *never let it fade away*, down into a black tunnel . . . fade away. 'Night, Da.'

Catch a Falling Star

Catch a falling star and put it in your pocket,
Save it for a rainy day

The sounds coming up from the beach send me spinning back to a night in the next-door neighbours', McDermott's. That was a great house for music and storytelling.

This fellah's come up from Wexford, a bird man the same as John Billy McDermott. He's bought a couple of peacock chicks from some farmhouse near Duckett's Grove that afternoon. They look like a couple of miniature turkeys, nestled in a cardboard box near the fire. Every so often they call out, the most piercing sound. Ger Murphy is the man's name, and he's well-renowned for his abilities on the mouth organ and the Jew's harp, and there's not many can pull a jig or reel out of that. We're in John Billy's kitchen. The end of the night, the stories doing the rounds getting more and more peculiar.

John Billy is a bird fancier in the extreme: breeding racing pigeons and budgies and other songbirds. Even kept a swan in his back garden at one stage; vicious, terrorised the local cats. You could be sure he'd top any story with one that involves a feathered creature of some sort. He's sitting back in his chair and he's telling us about a woman who felt a kinship with one particular egg she collected from the hen house a nice Sunday morning. Whatever it was about that egg, she wouldn't even to go to Mass that day, she was so taken with it. She kept it with her day and night until it hatched. Lo and behold, from day one it was clear from the bird's demeanour that it was possessed by a devil of some sort, for it had the clearest bluest eyes, as innocent and lethal as a baby. The wife was in thrall to it and took against her husband. Nothing would do her only to have a child with the same eyes. No doubt where this story was heading, trouble all around.

Murphy interrupted there. He wanted to get another round of dancing and drinks going but his twanging away on the little metal reeds wasn't enough to turn our attention from the chicken that was now entrenched in the marital bed, leading the husband and wife a merry dance. Some joking and messing going on that night about cocks and hens. I can feel it again, the warmth not just of the little fire in the grate, but of company and life being lived as only people can; playing and joking and listening and laughing.

So Murphy puts down his mouth organ and comes up with a story to best John Billy's, about the most mysterious and frightening pregnancy ever, down his end of the country.

A young girl, simple, good-looking. All started off normal enough, bar the fact there was no father to be found, and that wasn't too unusual either, until nine months passed. Her belly had swollen and now it held fast. Ten, eleven months, a year; not a sign of anything emerging into the light of day, and still growing. People even claimed they felt the yoke inside move when they placed their hands on her stomach. Not so much a kick, but a tremor you could pick up on. But as the time passed, there was less and less wanted to touch her for fear of what was only inches away, only separated from their hand span by a few layers of human tissue. In the end, the village rose up against her, her family. They had her sent away to one of those homes for girls like that, but the belly held firm, kept swelling up. Went on for years; two, maybe three.

That Ger Murphy had a way of dragging a *scéal* out, enjoying his day in the sun, til you'd be hanging for the finale: what did it look like when it was delivered? Half-human, half-creature? Did it devour the woman or haunt the town? But his story petered out, fell completely flat at the end. Seems like the pregnancy wasn't a real one at all. Just an unusual medical phenomenon where the body creates a ghost of itself inside its own womb. Only mimicry. Someone asked why that would happen, but Ger didn't know. Tell the truth, at that stage of the night we weren't interested so much in the why of the stories. It was all about what happened, and then what happened next.

The talk moves back around to a discussion of a new factory being planned for the edge of town. Five Germans had arrived, scouting out the site. What they apparently wanted for their breakfast in the hotel was cheese. But once they discovered porridge, they couldn't get enough of it.

Your man Murphy, he's fair put out by the way he's lost his audience to a discussion of porridge and the strangest ways people do go about cooking it.

'Wait,' he goes, 'I wasn't finished, there's more to it. In the end, they forced her to give birth but nothing was born. Years later, a hurricane was twisting its way across the country. Such a thing never seen before or again. You'll all remember that, surely? Where did it end its journey of death and destruction? Only at the very building that woman was confined in. Kilt stone dead a number of innocent people. Destroyed the village. People in those parts are convinced it was her phantom child returned, searching for its mother. And revenge. Anytime the weather forecasts predict gale force winds and rising slowly, there's many a person who's shivering in their bed in that corner of civilisation, thinking they might be the next one to have the wrath of the wind brought down on their heads.'

I try putting the story out of my mind because I haven't much time for Murphy and his notions and his fancy clothes. He's a right peacock himself; the purple polka dot cravat round his neck lifting and settling with the tunes flying out of him and the hand-tooled leather boots tapping away.

I seen him later having a slash in the back yard. He takes the cravat off to wipe sweat from his forehead and there's a big protuberance on the side of his neck. The disguises we wear, and in the end, drawing attention to that we're trying to hide.

Yet I'm disturbed in myself for there was one detail in his telling that gave me a quare gunk. He said this woman, she loved meat. Unlike most women who'd be heaving at the sight of raw meat in that condition, her want for it grew along with her belly. It was another reason people were afraid of what was going on. What kind of creature was living like a parasite inside her and devouring every kind of flesh it could get its hands on?

I can't shake off the feeling I'm hearing something, but it's a shout from a distance and you can't make out the words.

You see, no one I ever met was fonder of meat than Letty.

Now all these years later, I've a chance to divide the feeling I had for Letty and the shame that grew in me after. The truth lies somewhere between facts and the feelings. There was a truth in what I felt that I couldn't grasp in my head. Can you call something love if it's only brief, especially after you've spent a lifetime with someone else? Enduring love, dormant like some kind of exotic flower you see on the television, underground for years and then out of nowhere it blossoms. I heard tell of a seed that can sit tight that long: twenty, thirty, even fifty winters, not responding to the lengthening of the days or the warmth creeping back into the earth until it senses the time is right to make a go of it. Puts on a massive show for a few days, all bright colours and exotic perfumes. Then curtains for another couple of decades. What kind of clock is our life biddable to? What are we capable of? Tick, tock, the steady pulse, hours, days, months, and yet . . . I seen a man in such pain, he'd age five years in front of your eyes. Against that, I'd look at the Mater and she was still the laughing girl I met and married. Same sparkle in her eye, same toss of the head, like the first hour between us hadn't even passed.

I loved her. But I never told her about Letty. I thought she'd always be measuring me against it, or maybe measuring herself against another. Elevating or putting herself down, I don't know which'd be worse.

Holding my whisht all these years; now the judging and second-guessing is gone out of it. I'm suspended in the middle of every happening and every truth of my being, upside down and inside out.

Going over and over what did go on between myself and Letty took on a hypnotic quality in my head. All the looks we'd exchanged in that mirror hanging in Sweeney's Butchers, with the Mona Lisa Cow joining in. That's the name we gave to the diagram of the cow. Letty loved the poster, all the cuts of meat sectioned out with broken lines and labels. She mightn't have been much schooled, but she knew more about meat than any man there.

265

A powerful thing happened, whatever way the light fell between us, whatever way that auld mirror, like a fairground attraction, twisted and turned it around.

Mirror, mirror on the wall, she was the fairest of them all.

A few kisses exchanged behind the back shed and it went no further. Unless the force of desire and wishing can outplay your actions. If that was the case, we'd all be in some state. Before anyone thinks I'm casting myself and herself as a type of Joseph and Mary, the virgin birth and all that jazz, no, that's not it. I just knew the truth was that we'd done nothing to cause Letty to fall pregnant. But my father believed otherwise, and he barracked me day and night til I thought I'd go mad. I hardly knew what to believe in the end. The way everyone said nothing about her; saying nothing tells its own tale. Everybody knows and nobody says nothing. Irish ways and Irish laws, how are ya?

Even when I was old enough to set my own course, to my shame I never did. No need for dissembling or lies now. No need to dress myself up in any clothes of dignity, for even shame confers a certain . . . I don't know what the word is. You'd nearly need a top philosopher here for this kind of territory. I grew away from my own feelings, and as time passed, life went on, gathered a bit of momentum. It was as if I went for a ride in a hot-air balloon and Letty was down below in a field. I was lifted up higher and higher, til she was only a speck, then nothing at all.

I held certain moments in my pocket the way we all do. I'm inside the first kiss we exchanged. I was young, on the cusp of becoming myself, on the cusp of knowing myself. Knowing I had a special power inside me, getting a sense there was forces I'd never fully understand.

That's part of living your life; you bank the moments into an invisible account in your noggin. That kiss was one of them. It deserved to shine strong, but I lost it through shame. I know full sure what I lost was nothing compared to what befell Letty. That's not to say the Mater wasn't the one for me. But I lost a bit of meself not owning all of what went before.

Letty took me out of myself, out of time itself. Eternal moments. Keep them close, polish off the wherefore and the why. You'll need them for the rainy days. Hope she kept a few too, carried them in her pocket with her wherever she went.

Catch a falling star and put it in your pocket
Save it for a rainy day

Paying Respects

When I get up in the morning, the place looks fair bedraggled. There's a woeful snoring coming from somewhere. I check it out and find a room behind the bar I hadn't noticed before. It's all decked out: sheepskins and old rugs covering the floor, huge paintings on the walls of tropical islands and hula-hula girls. Oddsey's stretched out in a massive bed, very comfortable looking.

Outside, someone's pitched a new tent near the fire pit. I suppose that's the kind of place this is, the next crowd drifting in already; when we leave, we'll be soon forgotten. I'm heading over for a slash when I meet Hopper coming out of Mila's container.

'Alright, Frank?'

'Right, Hopper.'

'I'm heading down for a swim. You interested?'

'Not really. Looks a bit cold.'

'Still want to head back today?'

'Yeah.'

'Right, so.'

He heads down to the water and, true to form, strips off everything and dives headfirst into the waves.

Fuck it. What am I doing sitting here? I need to stop thinking and get on with things. I get changed into my togs and head down. When I walk in, the coldness bites into my feet and legs. Hopper swims over, then throws his whole body on top of me so I'm completely submerged. We have a good mess shooting in and out of the waves. After he gets out, I float on my back for a couple of minutes. I feel good in myself, like I've more lightness in my whole body. I swim out and dive down as deep as I can go. When I shoot back up, my lungs are bursting. I break through the surface and nearly gulp down the whole sky. I'm buzzing heading back up the beach.

There's a pot of coffee on the go. Hopper opts for that while I brew up a mug of tea. When I go out, he's sitting at what I now consider to be our table, staring at the sea. Once we've drained the mugs, we get going. It's not like we've much to pack up and there's hardly anyone around. Tara left earlier this morning; I'd've liked to say goodbye to her. Alice is gone to work. While Hopper is off with Mila saying their goodbyes, I'm hanging with Oddsey. He starts his day chilling with a pipe and a mug of funny-smelling tea.

'Thanks for letting us kip here and all,' I says.

'Go easy, my friend. As the Mighty Sparrow would say, *only a fool breaks his own heart.*'

'Could be something in that.'

'I was reading up some biographical material last night. On your main man, Perry Como. Passed away on the very same day I was celebrating my fiftieth birthday. Small world?'

'I suppose so.'

'That seventh son vibe, that was just a myth that grew up around him.'

'No, I don't think so.'

'He was a barber, alright. A singing barber. His voice could heal a broken heart, but he had a raft of brothers and sisters. Seven and the rest.'

That can't be right. Oddsey gives me a bottle of his seaweed champagne to take with us and I head off up to the car.

Mila is well into Hopper, the way she's holding his hand walking up through the scrubby bushes, then wearing the face off him at the car. Just my luck things got fucked up with June before I even had a chance to see how it'd go. I'm still feeling a bit odd after last night, so I sit in the car, tidy up a few wrappers and empty bottles. Weird what Oddsey just said about Perry Como. Typical stoner getting it all arseways.

When Hopper gets in, Mila calls in to me, 'Take care, Frank, hope you find closure. Love you, Hopser.'

'What's that about?' I goes to Hopper as he's reversing out.

'Well, the Hopser thing is—'

'Not that. I mean the "closure" thing?'

'Relax the fucking kaks, it's nothing. I'm starvin' Marvin. Mila gave me a bag of that granola, but my stomach is crying out for a layer of fat.'

'Might need to get some petrol too.'

He heads for a garage we passed coming out of town the other day. While he fills up, I get a couple of sausage rolls. The girl overdoes them in the microwave; tastes like leather wrapped in cardboard.

I notice a woman trying to put air in her tyres, making a bags of it. Usually Hopper'd give a dig out – she's his type too: older, good-looking. But he must be distracted; sits there horsing into his sausage roll. Once we're both finished, he takes off, slowing down at the bin outside the shop to peg the rubbish in. He misses by a mile, has to get out and put it in because your one is giving us daggers through the glass hatch.

Once we get out the road, I go straight to googling Perry Como. Right enough, it says he wasn't the seventh son. Was just something people started to believe because he kept saying it. I don't know why but I'm more gutted about this than most anything else that's happened on this trip.

Is that the big reveal, Da? Did you come back just to let me know you bumped into the Maestro and you don't have as much in common as you thought? Bit of a let-down, isn't it, when you think one thing about a person and it turns out quite different? Well, welcome to the club.

'Alright,' Hopper says, as he's driving along, 'here's the thing. I know you're pissed off about the whole shit that went on with yer Da and you're done with it. But the old mental hospital is very nearby. Do you want to have a look?'

'What're you shiteing on about? There's no point.'

'You're right, Frank. There's no particular point. Except to see where she was.'

My mouth is killing me from the sausage meat. When I run my tongue over it, I feel a blister coming up already. My eyes are stinging. I don't know did I sleep really well last night or did I not hardly sleep at all. For some reason, the whole Perry Como thing has really fucking got to me.

'To be honest, I don't care about seeing it.'

'Might be good for closure.'

'Says who, your girlfriend?'

'Look, you'll never be back here again and it's sort of on the way towards home.'

What's he know about closure? I close my eyes and say nothing.

He must've got very good directions because, before you know it, he goes 'That's it,' and I see there's a sign for St Clare's Hospital.

'I never said yes.'

'Well, we're here now.'

When he turns in, the road continues on through a whole complex of buildings. The biggest one to our right must've been the main hospital. There's signs for an Ophthalmic Clinic, St Brigid's Day Centre, the mortuary, and laboratories. It's a sad collection of sinister buildings and tired-looking prefabs. Hopper turns in and parks up at the back.

'What're you stopping for?' I goes. 'I've seen it now.'

'We've come this far.' He gets out.

'What's this about, Hopper?'

'Look,' he goes. 'Maybe it's a pile of shite, but Mila thought you should be here.'

'Here? Why? So I could feel more crap than I already do?'

'No way. Pay respects, you know. You don't know where she's buried so maybe this is as close as you'll get.'

This is him all over. Throws himself into whatever's going on around him, shallow as a fucking puddle.

'Pay respects at the bughouse?' I says. 'What you wouldn't do to get your leg over isn't worth talking about.'

'That's a bit fucking rough. People who lived here, not like it was all by choice. You know, if I wasn't at home with the mother, she'd probably end up in a place like this.'

He's walking off across the tarmac, turning in behind a derelict two-storey building. Fuck this for a game of soldiers. I throw the rucksack with the Deadwood on my back. At the end of the building we come to what must have been a playing field. Although it still has the shape and size of a pitch, there's no lines marked, no goalposts. It's just a nothing space. The grass has recently been cut and you can see by the piles it was fairly long. There's a bench at the side where Hopper sits down and takes out his fags. We both sit there, smoking. There's a kind of avenue of trees on our right and, although you wouldn't think there was a breeze, they're so tall the tops of them are swaying over and back.

'You think I'm a fucking idiot to go along with her ideas?' Hopper goes.

'Abso-fuckin-lutely.'

'And I'm an idiot for spending my spons on the nose powder.'

'I couldn't give a shite about your spons. Mine. My cash, Hopper.'

He takes a last drag and flicks his fag off to the left.

The two of us sit back. It's some beautiful day. I wonder if the weather makes a big difference when you're in a nuthouse? Must've been a total headwreck to be locked in, waking up in the winter, rain streaming down the windows and the darkness outside. Watch all the seasons from inside and then see them all come around again and again and again. Hopper and me, we can sit here, have a smoke, free to walk away. I suppose it's not the worst idea for me to see the place.

'I never copped your mother was in that bad a way. She's lucky to have ya. I'm glad you're—'

Before I get a chance to go on, a voice pipes up from behind us. 'You're smoking here.'

This lad comes around, a white coat like a chemist, carrying a bag stuffed with files and sheets of paper.

'Yeah,' Hopper says. 'Just having a break.'

'Only, the thing is,' your man goes, 'there's an oil tank a few metres from where you're sitting.'

We both look around to where he's indicating. The path behind us splits in three ways; signs pointing in the direction of *Blood Testing*, *Highgrove Unit*, and the *Optical Centre*. No sign of a tank.

I stub out my fag. 'Sorry, didn't know.' Even as I'm saying this, I notice the ground is scattered with butts, so we're not the first by a long shot.

'You could pick up an awful cold around this pitch. That's why they gave it up.'

'What?'

'Hockey. Do you ever watch the hockey?' he says. He's very clean-shaven, tanned skin, and the neatest grey curls on his head. Looks like a child but turned old.

'No,' we both answer him. He puts down his bag and faces the field. Maybe this is his bench for a sneaky fag.

'There'd be games on there every weekend, training during the week.'

'Always took hockey as a Protestant game,' said Hopper. 'More up north.'

That's one thing you can say for Hopper. Throw that man a conversational bone and he'll fucking chew it. I honest to God can't think of one thing to say about hockey.

'Quare hot,' I says.

'That's the summer,' your man says back.

A couple of figures emerge from the prefab across the grass, wearing the same white lab coats.

'They're off now,' he says, waving over to the others. They mustn't have noticed him because no one waves back.

He's still standing, looking at us. 'I dropped a packet of cigarettes here. Did you see them?'

Hopper's packet of fags is on the bench between us.

'No,' I says, real quick.

'No,' Hopper goes. 'Do you want one of mine?'

'What kind?'

'Marlboros.'

'Not Marlboro Light?'

'No.'

'That's the very same as the packet I left earlier.'

This is the point in the conversation where I'd be telling him to take a fucking hike. Puffed up little popinjay.

But no, Hopper picks up his pack, a good six, seven fags left in it. 'Sure, hang on to these.'

Your man smiles a big wide empty grin. He takes one out and sits the pack in the breast pocket of his lab coat, with all his pens lined up. He leans forward to get a light. 'They couldn't get a team together now, for love nor money.'

'There seems to be enough people working here,' Hopper says.

'They're scattered.' He laughs, sort of shifty, and says the word again, 'Scattered. I painted the lines on that pitch, many's the time. You have to walk a straight line to do that job, Mr Scarfe used to say.'

We all sit there staring at the place where there used to be white lines on the grass.

'Are you waiting for someone?' he asks, looking over at the car park.

I can see a woman looking around as if she's lost something. 'No,' I goes.

'They've put a new gate at the end of the Serpentine, to the cottages.' He points over at the avenue of trees. 'But you can't get out to Tesco's that way. You have to use the main gate. I tell people all the time.'

'We'll give Tesco's a miss,' Hopper goes.

'A woman came to measure it and she said they walked a couple of marathons a week.'

'Who?'

'Them that lived here. Up and down the Serpentine. To the wall and back.'

'Is that right?'

'The first marathon took place before they planted those trees. In Greece.'

'Athens and the Olympics,' says Hopper, as if your man has a twitter of wit.

'How long are you working here?' I ask.

'Well,' he goes, sucking the life out of the fag, 'I was here before anyone there,' indicating a building I hadn't noticed before, past the prefabs. 'The bingo's on now and sometimes Siobhan does stained glass.'

I suddenly cop; this fellah is no more a doctor or a chemist than I am. I look over at Hopper and realise he knew all along. Must be an ex-patient, someone who got left behind.

'What about the crowd that lived here?' Hopper goes.

'Very few left, of that era and ilk.'

'Where did the last ones go?'

'In the cottages. They were decanted.'

I don't know what he means. I never came across that word before, decanted. I'd say he loves spouting out words; probably doesn't even understand them himself.

'You remember any of them?' Hopper goes. 'You might remember treating a patient that went by the name of Letty Kiely.'

I see where this is going.

'Decanted,' he goes again, thrilled with himself now that Hopper's pretending he's a doctor. He smoked the first fag as quick as a condemned man, chains the next one off it. 'The nuns have the first cottage and then there's St Catherine's for the women. I can't go into the main building any more but I know where the fire exit is at the back of the kitchens.'

'So maybe someone in St Catherine's might have known her?' Hopper goes.

Your man's agitated now, speeding up the drags of the fag. 'Be careful of the oil tank.'

He's making to go but he's still here, hopping like a scalded cat looking over at the woman. Now she's staring back at us.

'Is someone looking for you?' I goes.

'I think I left a packet of cigarettes on this bench,' he says to me. 'And my lighter.'

'In your pocket,' Hopper says.

A soon as we get up to move off, your man is down like a shot and has our butts collected and stashed in his bag. He waves at the woman and heads her way. Hopper strolls across the pitch, cuts up into the walkway between the two lines of trees. We're at the wall. It's high; you wouldn't climb over that in a hurry. Hopper spots the gate your man was going on about. Of course he goes through and I follow. Facing us is a little terrace of houses with nameplates: *St Mary's*, *St Andrew's*, *St Catherine's*. I'm turning to go back.

Hopper puts up the hand and goes, 'Maybe someone remembers Letty. You should see if you can get any suss.'

'I'm not bothered. Let's go.'

'C'mon.' With that, he runs up to the door of St Catherine's, presses the fuck out of the bell.

'I've a good feeling,' he shouts, running away. 'I'll wait for you in the car.'

'Fuck ya, Hopper.'

As he legs it through the gate back into the hospital grounds, the door is opening.

Our Happy Place

When we were kids doing knick knocks, I'd always be the last; Bernie and Hopper gone like the clappers and me still standing like an eejit at the door. Here we go again.

A grey head peers out. 'Can I help you?'

'Sorry, didn't mean to bother you. I was looking for someone who might know someone.'

'We're expecting the chiropodist.'

'That's not me.'

'Maria's on maternity and a man came the last time. I thought you might be the man.'

Before the door opened, I was nervous. But there's just a bunch of old dazzies living here, probably glad of any inter-ruption to the routine.

'There was this woman who used to live in the hospital.'

'I lived there,' she goes, perking up. 'I'm the only one who still remembers Mrs Jakes. Scottish. She'd put the sheets out on the grass to dry and Sister Margaret thought they'd be ruined, but they weren't. Her and her fancy hat. There's not many remember that hat.'

As she's chatting on, I look past her into the hallway. It's ordinary enough, except for a gate at the bottom of the stairs and a stairlift. A few notices pinned to the wall look official, maybe sign-in sheets. The door at the end of the hall is open; I can see a bit of a kitchen. Voices are coming from somewhere.

'If you step in, I'll get Marcus for you.' She indicates a chair for me to sit on, one of those toilet chairs with a hole in the middle.

I give it a miss.

The place is like a sauna; the radiators must be going full blast. Yet your woman has layers on: shirts, cardigans, and a scarf over them all.

'What are you collecting for?' she asks.

'No. You were getting Marcus for me.'

'For what purpose shall I say?'

'It's about a woman from the old hospital. Letty Kiely.'

She straightens up. 'I am she.'

'What?'

'I am she. Letty Kiely.'

Fuck. I am she. She's alive. This is her. Mad as a box of frogs but alive and kicking.

'My niece won't get the picture printed out,' she goes, lowering her head.

Niece? She must have family as well.

'You might help me out and I could return the favour.'

'How's that?' I says.

'You could get a copy from the newspaper.'

I don't know what to say. She looks so old. Any of the questions in my head disappear. She takes a massive rag from her pocket and blows her nose, then rubs it hard.

'You're Letty Kiely?' I go again.

'I am, I am,' she says. 'I have the address of the department for the photograph section. It's written in my notebook, in my room.' She covers most of her face with the rag, peeps out at me across the top. Might be a tea towel, not a hanky.

'Where's Marcus?' I say. I wish this Marcus, whoever he is, would get up off his arse, come give me a dig out.

'You know Marcus?'

This is going nowhere fast. She presses something on the stairgate and lets herself up. I wait. She's not the full shilling. I hope she was in better nick when the Da knew her. I head towards the voices. I'll need someone to help get any sense out of her.

The first door I come to has a sign that says *Sitting Room* and under that a sign, *This Is Our Happy Place*, and then another one, *DO NOT TAKE THE REMOTE OUT OF THIS ROOM.*

A man is speaking loudly, 'No, Patricia, let's see. Oh my goodness, looks like your ship has come in. But beware of strangers bearing gifts. What about you, Doreen? When are you? I'm remembering, Capricorn, stubborn as goats. Sunshiney days ahead. Get ready for a big trip.'

Fuck is he on about? A big trip to the cemetery, that'll be the next big trip for this lot if Letty is anything to go by.

'Puffa, you're nodding at me, you agree . . .'

When I go into the sitting room, I'm facing the back of a big man in some class of a blue uniform. He's sitting at the table reading out the horoscopes from *The Sun* to two women. The one facing me is tiny, propped up by a tray fixed across the arms of her wheelchair. The other one is asleep, her wig sliding down the side of her pink head, mouth wide open. A big screen in the corner is on low, one of the cookery shows in full swing. I do that fake cough thing and Marcus turns around. I'd say he's from India or somewhere.

'Oh, hello,' he says. 'How did you let yourself in?'

'She opened the door for me. Letty.'

'Bold, bold girl. Not supposed to do that. You are the new chiropodist?'

'No, it was Letty I was actually looking for, but I didn't think . . .'

'Who is Letty?'

'She opened the front door.'

'You mean Bernadette.'

'She said her name was Letty.'

'She's annoyed because we are taking a break from the snooker.'

'Snooker?'

'On TV. Did she go out?'

'No, she went upstairs.'

'She is telling tales, but that's Bernadette. Maybe you are looking for the day centre?'

Of course it's not her. Why did I fall for that so quick? I'm quare disappointed. Even if she was mad as a wobbly brush, I wanted . . . well, I don't know what I wanted.

'Me, me,' a little voice comes from behind the door. I hadn't twigged the room is kind of L-shaped. Another old woman is sitting in the short leg of the room stretching behind the door. She's the head down, polishing a spoon with a shammy, real careful. 'Me, me,' she says again.

'Don't worry, Puffa,' Marcus goes. 'I'm getting the tea now.'

She must've been saying tea, not me. You'd want to be up early for this crowd.

'Goodbye,' the little cleaning woman goes. 'Goodbye.'

'She means hello,' Marcus says. 'Her speech is back to front.'

'Goodbye, William,' she goes again, waving her spoon at me. I feel a bit breathless all of a sudden. The rucksack is turning into a deadweight, the Deadwood sucking the air outta me. Maybe he got a gunk as well, with it not turning out to be Letty at the front door.

'You alright, man?' Marcus asks.

'Yeah,' I say.

'What unit were you looking for?'

I mumble on a bit about this history woman I was talking to and the history stuff she was saying.

'Yes?' He's looking puzzled. I know I'm not making sense. But something keeps pushing on.

'She's researching records, this woman Evelyn Sayers.'

'Yes, of course,' he goes, relaxed now. 'Evelyn. She comes to visit our ladies. Very kind person. Talking to them about the old days.'

'Yeah. I'm doing research too.'

'She mentioned a student. Was it today you are coming for the visit?'

I don't even blink. 'More or less, if it suits, yeah. To talk about some old stuff. The local history thing.'

He goes on to tell me about how they moved the women here out of the main building when it closed down, about fifteen years ago. The last residents. They wanted to stay together.

'Even when they can have one bedroom each, Bernadette and Patricia, we had to put their beds in the same room.'

'You get used to things, I suppose,' I says.

He goes over to the bookshelf, gets a book, and gives me a pen. 'Sign in, please.'

Visitors Book. The only two other signatures for this week are an electrician and the Sky TV guy. I don't know what to write in the column for *Organisation*. I don't want to out and out lie, so I scribble the name of the sawmill, Daly's. Fairly lame, I know, but fuck it, there's a lot going on.

'Usually we are two here, but my colleague Ann has taken Claire Barrett out for an eye test,' Marcus says. 'It was not on the calendar. You could talk to Bernadette when she comes down. Or when we finish *Deal or No Deal,* Patricia is also a great teller of tales.'

He's going to make tea, offers me a cup.

'William,' a voice goes from behind me. The spoon cleaner is right there, waving a shiny dessert spoon at me.

'No, I'm Frank.'

She takes hold of my hand. Her own hand is no more than a heap of matchsticks in a paper bag.

'Don't worry, Puffa, tea's coming,' Marcus goes. He goes out to the kitchen and indicates I should follow. She keeps a tight hold of my hand and comes too. She shuffles over to the kitchen table and sits down. She's still hanging on to me, so I have to bend down, sit in beside her.

'Goodbye, amen,' she says, looking at me.

'Puffa can be confused with her words,' Marcus says. 'She had a stroke before, and a little bit dementia, but always in a good humour. A smile for everyone. Did you say you're William?'

'No. Frank. Though my father's name is William. Was. But everyone called him Billy.' Then I cop it; she called me William. Billy Whelan. She thinks I'm my own da. 'Are you Letty?' I says to her.

'No,' Marcus says. 'That's Puffa Kelly.'

Like a ton of bricks landing bang on my head, I'm sure of it; this is her. 'Letty Kiely?'

She smiles and squeezes my hand. The knowing of it goes from her little hand to my head.

'You knew Billy Whelan?' I goes.

She smiles, squeezes my hand.

'Why's she called Puffa?'

'Maybe she was big smoker,' Marcus says. 'You know, always with the cigarettes. No smoking now. You like big cigars?' he goes to her. 'Like Fidel? Puff puff.'

'You were called Letty Kiely before?' I ask her.

She smiles at me and squeezes my hand.

'Might be better to interview one of the others,' Marcus goes. 'Puffa has stories but I'm not sure how true.' He puts the kettle on, says he'll be right back, has to get Bernadette down or she'll be under a duvet, curtains drawn, and walking the floors all night. He takes the spoon from Puffa and gives her a small sponge. 'Always cleaning,' he says. 'If you don't give her something, she'll use her sleeve, her hand. Until it is red.'

Sure enough, she starts to wipe the table in front of her, round and round in circles.

'William, come and go,' Letty says.

This is a head wreck. Maybe she's gone back into the time before things turned to shit. I'll go along with that. At least she's not angry.

The phone goes off in my pocket.

It's Hopper. 'Any luck?'

'Yeah. Sort of.'

'Do they know anything?'

'I think I found her,' I whisper.

'Where?'

'Living here.'

'Jesus Christ nailed to a fucking cross.'

'She thinks I'm him. My father. Give us a few minutes.'

'No worries.'

Letty is rubbing away at some stain on the oilcloth only she can see. I'm quare stuck for what to say. She's still holding my hand, which is weird but okay at the same time. She's smiling. It's kind of hypnotic, sitting there and her wiping, slowing down over particular areas she thinks needs an extra going-over, then back again. She's polishing more than cleaning, though I know you can't really polish a tablecloth.

'Goodbye, goodbye, William,' she says a few times and squeezes my hand, but I think she means hello. She's dead calm. Not like lying Bernadette who pokes her head in.

'*Deal or No Deal* is over in five minutes, Puffa,' she says. 'Marcus says we can watch the snooker until the final's over.'

'I think this is Letty Kiely,' I says. 'Do you know if that was her name in the hospital?'

'I know who's who,' Bernadette snaps and out she goes.

No sign of Marcus coming back to make the tea, so I find a couple of mugs and tea bags. Letty's keeping a close eye on me, only looking away when Marcus comes in.

'Sorry about the tea,' he says. 'I see you're okay. How is the research going?'

'Yeah, bits and pieces,' I say.

'We're in the TV room if you need anything. You okay, Puffa, chatting, chatting?'

'No, no,' she says, and he leaves.

'Sugar, milk?' I ask her.

'No, no,' she says but her head is nodding yes.

I'm getting the hang of it now, so I say sugar and she nods yes, says no. Milk? Nods yes, says no.

I put in a spoon of sugar and a drop of milk. Something about sitting at a kitchen table drinking tea makes me think of home, gives me an idea. I get the Deadwood from the rucksack and put it up on the table in front of her.

She looks at him and her hand goes all jiggly. She reaches towards him. When I move him closer, she starts to peck at him with her fingers like a bird's beak.

First I think, I don't know, maybe she's attacking him. Then I cop; it's the same thing she was doing before, on the table-cloth, trying to polish it. I go over to the counter, open a few drawers til I get a clean dishcloth. I give it to her and she settles into it, starting on the top of his head, rubbing over and back, over and back. She's totally fixed on the Deadwood now, not me. That's when she starts talking, strings of words pouring out, like she's clearing them out of the very grain and the grooves.

She's listing things like you'd learned them off by heart, maybe prayers. Then bursts of songs, some I recognise. She seems happy as Larry and not really needing me to do anything except be there. My head is flipping around; her thinking I'm him, the fact she's here at all and not dead; what kind of life she's had, locked up all that time; then her reaction to the Deadwood. Maybe she thinks he's come back for her at last. Maybe he has.

It's like everything's turned the other way round. I wanted answers from her, see what it all meant for me, but I'm only a little sliver of her story. She's the one who should get to tell the story. To the Da. Even if she doesn't know I'm me and not the Da.

Marcus must have some situation in the toilet to deal with; I can hear a woman's voice shouting, 'My soap. Was not lemon. My soap, my soap.'

Bernadette's back to report on the snooker, but Puffa's not having a bar of it. She keeps on singing and talking, laughing away.

I'm even writing down a few things in the notebook. They're not exactly sentences, more jumbles of words like, 'To judge the living and the dead . . . kingdom from valensha to eris head to fare head.' Mad shit. Eventually I can't concentrate any more.

Marcus comes back in. 'What a funny little statue,' he says.

'Just an auld family yoke,' I says. I lift the Deadwood off the table to put it in the rucksack. But Letty reaches over and takes a hold of it. She's not strong or anything but you don't want to be getting stuck into it with an old woman. I leave her hang onto it.

'She's getting tired,' Marcus says. 'Tea-time soon.'

'Tulip,' she goes. 'Leave tulip.'

'She wants something,' Marcus says. 'From her room.'

Don't know how he worked that out, but he must be right cos Letty goes, 'No, no.'

She pulls on my sleeve. So, with herself toddling along, the Deadwood tucked up under her oxter, me and Marcus trailing behind, we head to the back of the house. There's pictures of flowers on every door and the names written in big letters; *Sweet William*, *Snowdrop*, and *Daffodil*.

When we get to Letty's room, *Tulip*, it's small as anything and plain. I'm still hoping for something, maybe a photo or letter that might clarify the kid and the Da situation. Back in the kitchen, when I asked had she ever any children, she started going on about the weather. Every time I'd try and move the conversation around, she'd get going more furiously with the cleaning, and turn in on herself. So I just listened, going more with the tones than the actual meaning. Anyways, I think she was more chatting to the Deadwood than me.

She places the Deadwood down carefully on her dressing table. There's only a hairbrush and a water glass on it, a few brown clips and a radio. At the back, a freestanding mirror with an oak frame. She might think the polishing has given her some class of ownership rights over the Deadwood. Hopefully Marcus'll sort it out if there's a shakedown.

The walls are bare except for some mad poster of a cow stuck up over the bed, like you'd see in a butcher's shop but real faded, and a holy picture of Jesus on the other wall. The kind of picture where he's holding his heart in his hand – not what you want to be looking at going to sleep. I'd definitely focus on the cow. Kind of an odd smell in the room too. In fairness there's a smell everywhere: cleaning products, medicinal shit, and old people all mixed together. Extra bit of tang to this room, though, animal or something. Marcus makes a face, opens the window to let air in.

Letty gives a nod to the cow before she goes over to the wardrobe, roots around on the shelves. Maybe she has some papers or photos she wants to show me. Inside my head, something's trying to make a connection with something else, the way one thing reminds you of another. Because that's the kind of diagram you'd have in an old butcher's shop and Eithne said something about my Da being a butcher.

From where I'm standing, bang in the middle of the room, the cow's eyes are watching me; then I look across and the Jesus is doing the same, giving me the hairy eyeball. But if I tilt my head back it looks like they're staring each other down in a Mexican standoff. No matter what way I go, Jesus is looking at me, but also keeping his eye on the cow. The cow, as cool as you like, is giving it back in spades. I'm turning my head this way and that, trying to see how they're doing it.

I catch my reflection in the dressing table mirror.

Whatever way the mirror's angled, their eyes – Jesus and the cow – are locked directly on my own. *Clear the way*, the Deadwood says, sitting dead centre in it all. *I'm coming through.* I feel time sliding out from under me. My ears are pinging; head is spinning. Fuck. Something going down with the eyes; the Jesus eyes, the cow's, my own, the Da. The vibes are going from one to the other and somehow my da, Billy Whelan, is drawing all the looks back into himself. I pick the Deadwood up. It's the same heft as before but completely changed. Maybe Letty's rubbing and polishing took a layer offa him. Holding it, I feel light-headed. Not just my head, this feeling's going throughout my whole body. When I look down at my hands and my runners, I'm exactly the same, except it's like my skin is an outside suit. The suit is only holding all the cells, all the molecules of me together and they're all mixed up with the cells of the Da through the Deadwood. He's in me but I'm more particularly me than before. And at the same time I'm more everything around me.

I must've made a sound because Marcus looks at me. 'You alright, man?'

'Yeah, no worries,' I says, putting the Deadwood down.

'I think maybe, Puffa, there is a stash here somewhere?' he says to her. Then to me. 'She likes to keep little bits of meat. Right, Puffa?'

'Maybe she's hungry,' I says, seeing the guilty look on her face when she turns around. I'm still reeling from the eye thing. When I look at them all now it's just a regular bleeding Jesus and a butcher's cow poster and the Deadwood.

'It's raw meat,' Marcus says. 'She takes a rasher from the fridge. The smell; you feel nauseous?'

'A bit,' I says.

'Okay, today we do a clear out, Puffa. Search and destroy.'

Puffa nods yes.

'You say yes,' he says, laughing. 'That means you help me this evening.'

Bit smart-arsed of him because it's clear she means no.

When she's finished rooting in the wardrobe she comes over, sits on the side of the bed. All she's got in her hand is a cardigan. No pictures or papers. She takes my hand and holds it.

'Goodbye, goodbye again,' she says. Then she stands up real

slow, goes to the dressing table. She switches on her radio and picks up the Deadwood.

'No, no.' Marcus goes over to her. 'This belongs to the young man.'

'Yes, yes,' she says, sitting back on the bed with the Deadwood, using her hanky to start polishing it. She's working away, humming along to the radio; some corny old song about being sixteen and in love. One of the Da's favourites.

'You must let go now,' Marcus says to her.

Then it hits me. What am I doing? I'm the one who should let go here.

'For you,' I says to her. 'He's yours, for keeps.'

'No, no,' she goes.

Marcus looks at me. 'You're sure?'

I nod yes. 'I had it with me to get rid of anyways. So it's hers if she wants it.'

Fair enough, the Deadwood's not exactly mine to give away and I'll have Lena and the Mater to answer to back home. But Letty's probably got a lifetime of stories to tell the Da; maybe even tell him what happened to their kid, if there ever was one. She has nothing. No two ways about it, she needs him more than anyone else.

'Goodbye, William,' she says to it.

'Goodbye, Puffa.' I pat her on her sleeve. 'I mean Letty. Goodbye, Da.'

I give her hand a squeeze and she squeezes back. I'm leaving with a clatter of words in my head; saint this and saint that, cold fronts coming in and the wind force, Brasso and Omo. Stuff that makes sense inside her head but comes out of her mouth back to front and broken up. I knuckle the Deadwood across the noggin. Solid out. It's still the Deadwood but it's not the Da, not for me any more.

On the way out, Bernadette appears again. 'The butcher boy. Puffa waited for you.'

'What?'

'Everyone is looking for the babies now,' she goes. 'The near-misses Mrs. She held fast but it escaped from her.'

'Did they take her baby away?'

'Puff of wind; up, up and away.'

'Did she have a baby?'

'Not a baby baby.' She turns on her heel and heads up the stairs. 'It's not only make-believe either.'

As soon as the door closes behind me, I think I should've probably given Letty a hug or something, what with her thinking I was some version of the Da.

Once I'm through the gate, I spark up. What did your man call the path between the trees? The Serpentine, something to do with a snake? It's a bit twisty, alright. Like everything around here. Twists and turns, but in the end, it's just a longer way of going from nowhere to nowhere.

When You Were Sweet

When first I saw the love light in your eyes
I thought the world held naught but love for me

The gravelled pipes of Finbar Furey, the pain of recollection
furrowing his brow, singing sweet sixteen. The curse of the
Irish, the weight of memory and history. I'm propped up here
on the dressing table beside Letty's little radio and it's
broadcasting that song, a special request for Liam and Emer
Broderick, celebrating their sixtieth wedding anniversary today.

I love you as I loved you, when you were sweet

You'll not find it such a regretful song when Perry wraps his
larynx around the notes. They say he's only a crooner and
what of it? He makes you hear it a different way. *I love you as
I loved you*: he means it goes on and on, the love is as alive
now as it was then; timeless, like myself. There's something to
be said for a voice that can capture the softer aspects of life,
the dreaminess and drag of a long afternoon, be it penned in
behind a desk or a workbench, your finger running over a knot
of wood or the line on a page, the thrum of a wasp creeping
to the top of a glass pane. It draws you out of yourself. A

place beyond your reckoning. The way those moments go on and on and you're in them.

I'm going on and on, droning away like a saw, voicing the refrain that has caught me. We sang that song together, Letty and me, though she'd not reached sweet sixteen yet. Many times over the years, I'd walk past a butcher's window, trays of lamb chops or red, raw steaks laid out, and I'd think of her. Letty loved meat, raw meat; loved being around it. That's why her mother got her into Sweeney's Butchers, sweeping up sawdust and polishing the glass. Pure sweetness, not a crease on her face to say she was giving a care about anything, only joy.

Every few sentences I string together now, I mean to start down a road. But more times than not they dissolve like an Alka-Seltzer in a glass of water. Is that why all these highfalutin words are floating into my vocabulary, giving me more latitude with the language to express myself? It's now or never, as the man said.

I want to set it out straight, but any particular word can send me off in a spiral. Similar feeling to when you were a child, spinning. Spin yourself around til you fall down; pick yourself up and whirl til you drop and the world is still spinning round you. Two of you go hell for leather, hands crossed til someone lets go and you're still spinning, going backwards when the head is going forward. You've left yourself behind over and over before you come good again. Using clever words to make sense is the spin away from the centre.

Every day, as soon as we walked through the doors of Sweeney's, we were subject to a strange kind of tyranny. On the back wall of his shop, James Sweeney installed a mirror that doubled as a notice board; betting slips and invoices and other scraps are jammed in around the rim. No butcher can pass it without adjusting his apron or smoothing back his hair with his wrist. If he worked on a farm or down the mines, a man's own face might not cross his mind all day long, but the mirror's like an eye that changes the character of the place; each butcher going about his business, catching glimpses of his reflection, meeting the eyes of customers in the mirror watching him watch himself. Pinned to the tiles over the chopping block is that picture of the cow. Each section of its body separated from the next with a broken line and a label, the title of that cut. The cow is side-on, but the head faces out directly, its eyes following the customers' movements. The eyes of the cow watch men watching themselves.

Sometimes there's a, what you might call, complicity between meself, Letty, and that cow. Mona Lisa we called her. Maybe because of where she's pinned, up above the mirror, but it's the only set of eyes that isn't looking at itself and looking back at ya twice. It's strange the comfort you'd get from a thing like that without fully knowing why; the way some people feels about a picture of Jesus holding out his bleeding heart, his mournful eyes following you around a room.

There's all kinds of vanity. Sweeney's shop mirror is one kind. But a worse kind is using people as your mirror, looking at them and seeing your reflection. That's what James Sweeney made Letty's life into, a hall of mirrors where he grew bigger, taller. Once he tied pig's trotters to the end of her sleeves and had her walk around the shop. Mocking her, setting impossible chores, anything to get a laugh out of the other lads. Can't be doing that to people and not expect something to come of it. There's some does that with their children too. My father tried to do it to me, squeezing me into the shape of a perfect him.

Between Sweeney going on at her and the way other people treated Letty as some class of lesser being because she was different, something did come of it all. Not a flesh and blood child the way my other seven were. But I'm closing in on the truth of it now. She grew it inside her, in defiance of them all. A sigh, the air, the wind, the story of a hurricane.

Sweeney's Butchers disappears and I'm back in the room with Letty. She's rubbing and rubbing the top of my wooden noggin, caressing the truth out of it. Between her polishing and the murmur of words she's muttering, she takes me to the moments she needs me to see, to be.

She's in a small room at the back of the old house at The Glen. One window in the far wall lets in some bright autumn morning light. There's a tree outside it, one branch knocking up against the glass; a careless kind of sound, letting you know the wind and the world will carry on regardless. Regardless of the machinations and monkey business going on inside these walls.

The powers that be have had enough of Letty and her constant state of pregnancy. They're determined to bring the whole thing to an end, get her body back under their control. 'The longest-running show in town,' Dr Williams says to Fr Benedict, 'must come to an end.'

Whatever poison he forces into her, it's only minutes before cramps roil through her stomach and her whole body is racked with nausea and pain. Eventually a final dribble of vomit leaks out the side of her mouth and with that she feels it: a tiny rush, a silent whoosh into being. Nothing visible, but I catch it the same way she does. Air, a tiny puff of air. She lets out a sigh of relief. Lying still as death on the bed, the breath returns to normal. They leave her alone to pull herself together. Just as they expected, what issued from her is the full sum of nothing to the eyes that feasted on the spectacle of her efforts. Right in one way, but they are so wrong to think that was the end of it. That was only the beginning.

She's soiled herself; she'll have to rinse out the sheets before she's brought down to Fr Benedict's room to make her confession. Even a phantom pregnancy – that's the medical term Dr Williams put on it – is enough to mark you out as a body with wants and willpower brewing away, that won't be denied one way or another.

Shaky, she's walking to the laundry room with the sack of bed linen. Even when she stops at the nearest sink, a voice calls out, 'Use the tap outside.' Another few steps out in the cold. But when she sees her face reflected in a metal sluice bucket, she clocks a change. She has company; something's watching her watch herself. Her face stretching around the curve of that bucket smiles a welcome, blows a kiss into the air. Something has escaped their mockery and slipped out to join the free air. True, but she won't ever hold a child, no more than you can cradle a gentle breeze or swaddle a howling storm, but she knows what she knows. The knowing of it settles inside her.

Nothing'll do her from that day on only to walk the Serpentine every chance she gets. She walks a thousand marathons and more, up and down that avenue of trees, turn at the boundary wall and back again. She's there now and the wind is strong enough to snap a branch down on top of her head. A gust lifts an inside-out umbrella over the end wall and carries it into the maw of an oak tree. The bright colours of the material and the power of the gust fills her with joy, even as her light frame is buffeted this way and that. She's developed this little habit of filling her cheeks up and blowing out. She does it now over and over til she's light-headed.

Light-headed and light, for just a few moments, as if this wind and all wind, and all breezes and storms and hurricanes, are a part of her, will pass through her without harming a hair on her head.

That's why they took her name away. Nicknamed her Puffa.

So a bit of her story and my story and the wind. The very day I married the Mater, fixing my tie in the kitchen, the radio on – 'Four people have died as a result of the hurricane, a widow, her two daughters and granddaughter, after a tree fell on their car . . . fifteen people injured, one seriously' – something in me knew, the way you know without knowing. And now I know, Letty birthed a phantom child. Wind, a comfort to her but at the same time filled with an impossible rage. There you have it: silence people, staunch them, that's one way to cultivate trouble. I seen it with many a sickness, people bottling things up. Doesn't do a body any good.

Of all the times to return to, here I am where the knowing and the unknowable meet. Letty and myself and her child. Our child as she conceived it. Wind. Maybe only as insubstantial as the air we breathe. But in saying that, it's free, free and always and everywhere.

And even though we drifted far apart,
I never dream but what I dream of thee

Walking the Serpentine

The sun is streaming through the trees like one of those religious posters they used to have up along the corridor in the school. Trying to get you to think about God without admitting it. I step off the path, nearly tripping over a massive root. There's a nice flat patch behind the tree so I sit down for a minute. Then I lie down. Looking up into the branches is relaxing; would nearly hypnotise you.

When you watch a movie, they always finish up with a clear-cut end. Even if the hero dies, he's giving up his life for important stuff. It makes sense. One thing leads to another until it comes to an end; that's the way stories work. This is shit compared to those. In a way I've got more than I bargained for, but I feel like I know less than when I started. I always thought history was facts that were there if you were interested enough to go looking for them. But Letty's whole life is invisible, just all rubbed away. I'll never know if she had a kid. I'll never know where the Da stood regarding the whole situation. Now I'm going to have to get on with it regardless.

One bit of Letty floats across my mind, gets mixed up with another. The way she got everything back to front; maybe when she said sister, she meant brother? Or she could have been talking about some nuns. She'd be reciting lists of flowers and prayers, singing bits of songs. Deepening her voice, 'I'll mince the lot of ye.' She'd look at the Deadwood and sing out cuts of meat in a funny voice: chuck and blade, silverside, ribeye, goose skirt. Must be from the old poster on her wall.

The mirror and the eyes; and the way the Deadwood seemed to change without actually changing; and the way I was changing alongside him. The most mysterious moment of my whole life took place in that room. It's neither good nor bad, just strange out. Whatever it was it took something off me, like a load I didn't even know I was carrying. Haven't a fucking clue what it means, what it was, but it happened. To me.

It was some hard call to make, leaving the Deadwood behind. I start to calculate how many branches there might be above me, counting one section then multiplying it up, taking into account how much smaller they get as they go higher. How many more rings and branches does each year add to a tree? Circles of tree calculations are getting wider and wider round me.

I close my eyes again, lean up against the trunk.

'G'wan, ya fucking tree hugger,' a voice interrupts.

'Fuck sake, Hopper. I'm just sitting here.'

'Quare wild tree you picked. D'ya see all the stuff caught up on the other side?'

'What?' I get up and walk around.

He's right, there's loads trapped in the branches. Probably need a cherry picker to get at it. We're staring up at a variety of yokes: definitely a football, a scarf, some long red stringy thing, what looks like a plastic bucket. A funny-shaped stick with blue tape on it, hockey stick maybe? Someone must've thrown it up to get something else down. Throwing up one thing to get another and then that thing gets stuck. Could go on forever.

'What's the story?' Hopper goes.

'Found her. They call her Puffa Kelly, but I'm sure it's her, alright. Letty Kiely.'

'That's unbelievable. You found Puffa. No way I thought that was going to happen.'

I don't want him to be calling her Puffa. It grigs me she's lost her name as well as everything else.

'Any news of the kid?' he asks.

'Not exactly.'

'Listen, we need to shift our arse. There's a very enthusiastic security guard doing the rounds.'

'Could be another wack job in a costume.'

'World's full of them.'

I put the rucksack on my back, quare light now without the Deadwood, and we head over to the car park.

'Want to hang around for another night?' Hopper goes.

'Nah.' I'm ready to head home.

Hopper tones down the usual shite talk when he's driving, leaves me to my own devices. He pulls in at a field to take a piss and we stand there, one at each gatepost, sharp green fields stretching on and on to these bluey mountains way off.

'Must've been full on,' he goes. 'Especially if yer one thought you were your own father.'

'Quarest thing ever,' I says, as a cow and a pair of calves amble over.

'And you're positive your da was the one landed her in there?'

'Not really positive of anything.' I pull up a big wad of grass and offer it to the smallest calf through the bars of the gate.

He rolls his lip back, Elvis-style, as he's twisting it out of my hand. 'For one thing, she talks backward. When she said hello it was goodbye. She had a stroke. Probably wasn't in the best of nick even before that.'

'Did she say what happened to the kid?'

'I've this feeling in my gut there isn't a kid out there. I don't know why. I know it doesn't make sense she'd be sent to The Glen if she wasn't pregnant. But, no, she couldn't say. I'm never going to know for sure, one way or the other.'

'That's life, isn't it? I mean, one day they say eggs'll kill ya and the next day, have two for breakfast. Even the planets. There's nine, then they downgrade one and there's eight.'

'This is different.'

He has his little vial of powder out, sniffing it goodo. 'What's she like?' he goes.

'Old. Nice, gentle. Her bedroom was the worst. Nothing in it, nothing personal. She could be dead tomorrow and they'd change the sheets and move the next one in.'

'Bit bleak, alright,' he goes. 'So what are your chances of graduating from the warts division to the premier league of, I don't know what, baldyness?'

'It's not about that.'

The calf nearest the gate turns his back to us, lifts his tail to squirt out a load of piss. Then he drops a fresh turd.

Once the stench hits me, I reckon it's our signal to vamoose. It's not til we're back on the main road that I cop it.

'You didn't smell that pile of shite back there, did you? What's the story with the powder?'

'I think I did, alright. Whether Mrs EB's stuff done its magic, or my mind's playing tricks on me, it's working. Thing is, the good smells are coming back more strong. Tell ya one thing, I'm going home with the peachy smell of Mila, the—'

'Leave it out.'

We knock off the last few snacks, chat about ordinary shit. When we get to the outskirts of Carlow, it's about seven in the evening.

'You want me to drop you off first or what?' Hopper goes.

I'm after getting a text from the Mater to say she's in Dublin airport waiting for the bus to come down. 'Come in for a bit if you want,' I says.

'Sound.'

The empty rucksack is at my feet.

'The Deadwood's gone.'

'What d'ya mean?' Hopper's noticing how flat the bag is for the first time.

'When I was with Letty, she was polishing him away. That's what she does all the time, and it was like he was fading out. I left it there. With her.'

'What? You mother'll string you up.'

'She needs him more than the Mater. Or me.'

'Big move. You're some go-boy.'

When we pull in at the back, John Billy McDermott from next door is out, letting his pigeons off for their evening run. Bernie said he sees him come out of the loft some mornings dead early. He reckons he's taken to sleeping there since the wife died.

He gives us a wave. 'That's some colourful jalopy you've got there.'

'She's a beast, alright,' Hopper calls out.

'Every day is yours to win, lads. Enjoy it while you're young.'

Always Something New

I forgot what a mess I left the house in, especially the kitchen. Hopper nips out to get some milk, a few slices of ham. First off, I put the kettle on for a cup of tea and a rinse of the dishes. When I turn the tap, it does that thing where it spits out twice before going full flow. It's good to be home.

I scout around the presses to see if there's anything stashed and find a mini Christmas pudding on the top shelf. Last February, the Mater got a whole load of puddings. We were eating them morning, noon, and night. Sell-by date well past now, but they've enough preservatives to get them through a nuclear war intact.

All the grub she stocked up on last Christmas, thinking some of the lads'd be home for the holidays and they never made it. Lar got a contract in the mines in Tasmania: the money was too good. But Pat told me Lar's run into some visa trouble, and if he leaves he mightn't get back in. Pat's ex and kids wanted to go back home to Thailand, so he went there instead. Haven't seen them now in over three year.

At least Murt came over for Christmas dinner. It would've been a pathetic day, only Bernie made a few cocktails and the

Mater was flying by the end of the night. She put on all the Da's favourite records. We were belting out the classics, *Blue Christmas, Love Makes the World go Round, Till the End of Time.* Corny old shite, but good craic all the same.

There's a noise at the back door.

'Just me,' Hopper goes.

The first load of toast pops out.

'Nothing like the smell of batch bread toast,' I say.

We load up the slices with ham and cheese and larrupings of ketchup. Hopper mixes his with brown sauce, but I can't be doing with that. Why does he bother if he can't taste anything?

Looking at him laying into the grub, I wonder what did he think would happen if I tracked down Letty or found out about a kid; another son? I've never asked him straight out if he ever believed I had the gift. He wouldn't answer anyways; he'd laugh it off. I'm no fool; I know how he operates.

'I know well why you were so dead set on me searching for Letty,' I says. 'Going to Rose's was just an excuse to go somewhere. You were all set to blow our money one way or another.'

He downs a good draught of tea before he answers. 'I knew the family history'd get us out of here. Even if we only started off in Ballycalla, the arse end of nowhere, we could take it from there. Was a laugh, though, wasn't it?'

He starts imitating Eugene howling his dog heart out. It was a laugh, alright. Although finding Letty was bit a rough, giving her the Deadwood was worth it.

'So you're either a six and a half,' Hopper goes, sticking on more toast, 'or a seven and a half son.'

'Not an actual seven?' I says.

'It's as close as.'

Hadn't really thought of it like that. I put the mini pudding in the microwave.

'You're a bit of an inbetweener,' Hopper goes, wiping his mouth. 'Bernie's some class of an inbetweener. Could be a twin thing, not being all of one thing or another.'

'You want a bit of Christmas pudding?' I says to shut him up.

'Wouldn't mind. Though it can be quare dry without the custard. What are you going to say to the mother?' he asks.

I've been avoiding that question myself. I still haven't got it straight in my head the best way to approach it. 'I'll see what her form's like when they get back.'

I get a carton of custard from the press and give it a spin in the microwave with the pudding. 'Custard's ready,' I says, and Hopper gets a couple of bowls and spoons from the drawer.

'Is someone making custard?' a voice calls out.

'Mrs Whelan.' Hopper rises up from his seat. 'You're home sweet home. Looks like travelling agrees with you.'

I don't know if it agreed with her, but it's dumped some class of a flower arrangement on the side of her head. She puts down a rake of bags.

'Come here to me, son,' she goes, opening out her arms.

I give her a hug. 'Where's Bernie?'

'I'm parched,' she says. 'I can't say a word til I've a proper cup of tea in me. They had the heating going full blast on that bus. The driver must be trying to bankrupt Bus Éireann.'

'I'll head.' Hopper winks at me. 'Don't stay up too late chatting. See you at the main stage tomorrow.'

I'd forgotten all about the scallion eating; it's on tomorrow night.

'Good luck,' the Mater goes. 'I'll keep an eye out for you. I should be finished with the wolf choir by then.'

'Thanks, Mrs Whelan. Night.'

She goes upstairs with a few of her bags and I get the kettle going again. When she comes back down, I'm expecting her to ask for the Deadwood straight off. But, first thing, she tells me Bernie's staying on in Eileen's. He's got a job in her hospital. As a cleaner.

'As a cleaner? What about college?'

'It's a summer job, though he could be made permanent.'

He doesn't hardly know Aunty Eileen and he never said he wanted to go to London, ever. The Mater's full of her own stories; she asks me next to nothing about what I got up to. I'm not listening to her, thinking about what the summer'll be like here: no job and Bernie gone too. I can tell by the way she's going on, he mustn't've got around to having the conversation with her.

'How was Bernie's form?' I ask.

She says he was a bit up and down, all chat one minute and clamming up the next. She thinks he has a secret.

'Oh yeah, like what?' I goes.

A new boyfriend is her best guess and he's being a bit quiet about it because she reckons he's an older man. I say nothing; not really for me to get into.

Then out of the blue she goes, 'Did you take the statue back into the house or leave it outside?'

'I took him in,' I goes.

'No more trouble from Lena? She has poor Murt mithered.'

'She has, alright.'

'Where is it then?'

'I'll get it.' I want to say the words, *he's not here. I gave him away.* But I'm not saying them. I stand up and I'm going to say it straight out. Instead I walk out of the kitchen into the hall. I start going up the stairs. I hear her get up, the click of the fridge door opening. The clunk of the door closing again and the motor's hum starting up. I get to the landing, stand there. The house is dead quiet except for the kettle boiling again, the Mater singing to herself. I turn and walk back down.

She looks up, sees my hands are empty. The man with the empty hands.

'I said it to Eileen this morning,' she goes, 'I knew you were up to something.'

'He's not here.'

The kettle reaches the boil; never realised how loud it is. She was after taking some clothes out of her bag; new gear she got, it's on the table. Must have been going to show me. Or the Deadwood. She's holding this striped-orange cardigan in her hands, rubbing the buttons, nearly working the colour off.

I lift the teapot up. I can't look direct at her. Her head is moving like she's trying to make out a puzzle. I brew another pot of tea, put the plug in the sink, pour the rest of the kettle over the bowls and plates. I put the tea on the table, but I don't sit down myself. Can't face across from her.

'Was it Lena?' she goes. 'She bullied you from day one. That time she covered you with dye, in the art class. Your neck and ears, even your runners, was purple. Ruined.'

'No.'

'Well, that's something at least. You couldn't trust what she'd do with it.'

I turn back to the sink, squirt in the washing-up liquid. Mad how it changes into bubbles when you turn the tap on real hard. A big head of froth shoots up, every bubble splitting into loads of smaller ones. When I start scrubbing the first mug, a few words come into my head.

'I don't know how to say this. I think he, the Da, didn't come back for you, or me. Or not just for us. No more than when he was alive, there's others that need him.'

'How'd you come by that notion?' she says.

'Anyways, he's not here right now.'

'Right now?'

'Nor won't be again. Look,' I goes, rinsing a mug under the tap, turning it upside down on the draining board, 'I had to make a decision. I don't exactly understand it, but I stand by what I did.'

As I start on the next bowl it's getting a bit clearer in my head. Not all of what happened between me and Letty and the Deadwood. But it's clear that I did right. Right by myself, the Da. But more so by Letty. Even if it looks wrong against the Mater.

'I knew from the get-go,' she goes with the dramatic flourish of her head that means she's coming back to herself. 'At least I was ready this time, knew it wouldn't last forever.'

She's not going ballistic.

'So where exactly is it?'

Shit. Hadn't really thought this through. If I say anything, the whole story'll have to come out. Whatever idea I had of telling her about Letty is gone. I'll never tell her. She either knows already or she doesn't, and anyways, what's to tell? I can't say for definite what went down. No one can, only the Da and Letty, and that boat has long sailed.

'You'll have to trust me. He's where he should be now.'

She pinches up her mouth like this could go either way. She takes a good sip of tea, then shrugs. And she's off again talking about the holiday. The thing I was dreading is over. Just like that.

At some stage we decide to move into the sitting room with the bottle of seaweed champagne. She's picking things off her shelves – pots and ornaments, the glass animals – giving them a twist or a touch.

'Is Bernie alright?' I ask.

'He's good. Though I'd miss him if he stayed over there.'

'It'd be quare quiet here.'

'That reminds me. Do you still have that rocket? Made out of the Lego bricks.'

'The Millennium Falcon? Yeah, it's in the attic. Why?'

'Eileen's grandson. Lovely little fellah, real Englishy. Mad into all that, and I said I'll send it over.'

'But it's mine.'

'Was it not yours and Bernie's?'

'No, I swapped him my walkie-talkies for his half. I might want to sell that on DoneDeal.'

'One minute you're all "I'm making the decisions" and "trust me" and then you have a puss on you about your auld toys.'

I say nothing. She's right in a way. That's not what's really annoying me anyways. Seems like after everything that's happened in the last few days, nothing's changed for me. Bernie's managed to get himself set up in a London job and all, and I'm still here. No better off than when I set off last Sunday.

'I don't know will I ever have it,' I says.

'Your Lego?' she goes.

'No, the gift.'

'Why don't you stop getting in your own way and enjoy what you have. Murt was only saying the other day about how talented you are with your hands.'

'What was he saying?'

'He's getting on. He could do with a dig out.'

'What about Lena?'

'She's not at the races. He'll make sure she's looked after, but he'd never risk it, letting her loose on a pair of wedding shoes. Cutting keys, you have to have the right temperament.'

'Temperament?'

'You could come under pressure from the wrong types. Criminal. Whatever about the future of keys, there'll always be a call for shoes. Which reminds me, I've three new pair.'

'So you said.'

She asks me to bring her black bag with the shoes in from the hall. And the biscuits in the red bag. It's still grigging me, so I say it.

'You know the thing that gets me, Ma, is not even whether I do or don't have the gift. But I'll never know did the Da think I had it. Cos he's . . . you know. So I'll never know.'

'He loved you, Frank, not any of that palaver about the gift. He never wanted to see you burdened the way he was.'

'What d'ya mean?'

'His father was very harsh on him. Billy vowed he'd never put that on any son of his. Then imagine, the first twins in living memory, from either side of the family.'

Nobody has a good word to say about the grandfather, how he treated the Da. The thing Rose said about my father hiding in the coal shed; that's been at the back of my head the whole time. He must've had some fear of him.

I'm digging into the biscuits and she's parading around in her new ankle boots. I can't get a fix on what she's trying to say. I suppose it is a bit unusual, twins, but there's a few sets around the town. The shoemakers, Fonsie and Alf, identical. The Kavanaghs . . . the who else?

If the Da already had a kid out there somewhere, maybe he was . . . numbers start to add up and subtract in my head. If you add in an extra kid . . . but if there wasn't one? Not to mind if I add Bernie in, then subtract him out again, and if I take what Hopper said on board I'm getting into fractions of sons.

Then I remember back to the room, Letty's bedroom, and that feeling of being the lightest version of me. As if I was nothing except air, one breath. Suppose that's the only difference between life and death if you think about it.

The Mater is tapping me on the head. 'Look at these, Frank. They're as comfortable, even with the bit of heel. I think I'll wear them tomorrow night.'

'Yeah.'

She's putting some shawl thing around her shoulders, all bright colours and fringes and tassels. She got it at some big outdoor market with hundreds of stalls.

'You weren't going to have me, were you?' It comes out of nowhere.

'What are you on about?' she says, still admiring herself.

'You were only going to have six. Kids. Sons. Not me. He didn't want a seventh. He wouldn't give his father the satisfaction.'

'To be honest, the left one is crucifying me,' she goes, sitting down on the couch. 'I might pass these on to Cissy.' She bends down, starts unzipping the boots. 'That's a very low thing to think of your father. If you knew what your grandfather was like, you'd know why your father didn't want it to keep going on. We didn't. It was too much. When I met him first, he was carrying the traces heavy on his shoulders. The very day of our wedding he got a notion into his head he brought a big storm down on us. A curse from someone he did wrong by. Maybe even his father.'

This shuts me up for a minute. Some quare coincidence that I've heard about this self-same hurricane twice in as many days. But my mind pulls me directly back to the thing I know now is somehow true. 'Ye never wanted me.'

'No, Frank. You're going down a wrong road there. We never wanted a son hitched to the number seven day in, day out. But that was nothing to do with you, Francis Whelan, because we knew nothing about you. We didn't even know you existed. I'd no time for doctors' appointments, five boys under my feet here. When out you popped behind Bernie, it was a miracle. Your father took it as a sign.'

'Sign of what?'

'Sign that no one can make life run its course through their choosing. In a way, you gave him freedom. As far as we were concerned, yourself and Bernie were the best gift we could've asked for.'

It's like he's back in this very room and we're kids again: the Da, waltzing around with Bernie in his arms, and me standing on the table conducting the music from the record player; the Da bowing to me when the tune finishes. Then picking me up, holding one of us in each arm, swinging us around.

'He loved every last bone in your body,' she goes.

She's opened another packet of biscuits. 'Try this one, Frank,' she goes. 'It's something else.'

Right from the first bite, I can tell they've hit on something original here.

'There's always something new, isn't there?' the Mater goes. 'That's one thing I have to hand to Richie Morrissey, he's not afraid to try a new line. Imelda said, who's going to buy this granola, you'd only get a couple of bowls out of a packet?'

'Some granola's alright. The home-made kind anyways.'

'Flying offa the shelves now. He's a way of knowing what people want before they even know it themselves.'

'There's a lovely crunch to these biscuits.'

I sit there listening to all she's telling me about herself and Bernie going to see Buckingham Palace, and if the Queen was standing in her hall for some reason, the distance from the main gate, where they were standing, to her door, is only the length of our road. And Eileen's electronic devices for everything: a robot mop, and fitness yokes, and a popcorn maker, and some type of smart bone for her dog. I'm trying to picture Eileen at her hula-hoop class. That's her passion. The Da'd get a good laugh out of that.

'What's in this again?' I goes.

'Pecan, caramel, and you know what the big thing is now?'

'What?'

'What you're tasting. Sea salt. Who'd have credited it? It's in everything. They'd nearly put it in your tea.'

'Works, though, doesn't it?'

'That's for sure,' she goes, wetting her finger to gather the crumbs up off her lap. 'You never know what's going to work, but God created sea salt for a reason. I'm done in. I may hit the hay.'

As she's passing me, I ask how come she's not bulling about me giving the Deadwood away.

She stops, leans in against the back of my chair. 'When he passed the first time, for months after, I was plagued by what I wanted to tell him.'

'Were there not questions you wanted to ask?' I ask.

'No. No big secrets between your father and me. Neither of us perfect. But we did our best. He was himself and I was able to be myself. *Sin é.*'

I sink down into the armchair. If she's no regrets, fair enough.

'When this statue turned up, I saw something, maybe I wanted to. That first evening I told him everything I could think of.'

'Right.'

'But I was torn; something wasn't sitting easy with me. The next morning at work, I was on the freezer section, though Imelda was rostered. She finagled her way out of it, because of her eczema. You know I hate the big gloves, and I was giving out in my head and was imagining telling Billy. When I came home, I brought him up to the room with me, put him up on the dressing table.'

She stops, shakes her head like she's trying to shake something loose. 'I've experienced a lot of things, Frank, beyond the ordinary, but this was so strange. I put him up on the dressing table. I was talking. Next thing I looked into the mirror and he, the statue, was looking into it, and our eyes met. Jesus Christ, I thought it was your father smiling at me. I couldn't stop looking. I was crying, Frank. I thought he winked. I can't explain it, but he was gone. I looked back at him, not the reflection. No. Nothing. I kept talking, but I knew I was only talking to myself.'

She's saying nothing now, just staring off as if he's there looking back at her. I want to say something, give her a bit of comfort. But if I tell her about Letty's room and the mirror and the eyes, I'll have to go the whole hog with what's happened.

'Why did you keep letting on to me his spirit or whatever was in it? Hiding him under the gazebo?'

'Well, I had no intention of letting that little madam Lena have her way. Honest to God, Frank, I fully felt he was there that first night in Murt's. Then I didn't know, did it change or did I.'

She thought with herself and Bernie leaving the country, it'd be good company for me. Maybe it was her believing convinced me. I don't know do I feel more foolish now or more certain I was right. But I felt something, a connection beyond imagining. He was there. He led me back to Letty so at least she wouldn't be as lonesome.

She gives a rub to the top of my noggin. 'You don't need tea leaves or a statue to have a chat with your father. Coming down on the bus, I was only telling him about Barry Dowling last week, giving out about the potatoes travelling from Israel to Carlow, the usual palaver. Eileen's hula-hooping. He'll always be around, one way or another.'

Once she heads upstairs, I go back into the kitchen for a drink of water. It can be nice here at night when everyone's gone to bed. It's like the table and chairs are nearly smiling at you, saying 'why don't you come in, rest up a while?' There's real silvery light coming in over the sink. Sure enough through the window I catch sight of a full moon. The draining board's like a sheet of ice with the few upturned mugs I rinsed earlier, waiting for the lift at breakfast and the next hot drop of tea. I sit in at the table for a minute. Some quare yokes are lying around; the Mater must've taken them out of her bag. A fridge magnet of a red bus and a Paddington Bear. He looks right ominous, the moonlight sharpening the edges of his hat.

I take a hold of the little bear. For a split second I see his hands gripping the furry paws; hands scraped across the knuckles, deep grooves from a life working at a hard graft job. Ordinary-looking but special. The Da's hands, steady out.

Wolf Night

Even though I wake late enough the next morning, I can still hear the Mater snoring away. I take my cup of tea and a smoke into the garden, head down to sit in the gazebo. Although Bernie'd often be out all night, or left the house before I'd get up, it feels different now I know he's gone. Sounds like they had the craic in London.

Maybe I'll take a trip over when I get my money back off of Hopper. I wouldn't mind seeing Bernie, face to face. Wonder what he'd make of it all: the Deadwood and Letty, Oddsey's place, Rose and Mrs EB and their shenanigans with the bathhouse. That rock pool with the fish lit up, pure wild stuff you couldn't make up.

I'm looking up at Bernie's bedroom window and I'm not half as annoyed with him as I was. When you think of what Tara was saying that night about watching her grandmother disappear bit by bit, mentally, even though her body's still there; she was fading out the way the night comes in. One thing I would've always said about Bernie, he's himself and you know what you're getting. I know now that's not a hundred per cent accurate, but I suppose he'll become more himself, in a weird way. More true or something. Maybe I'm getting more and more like myself too, whatever that looks like.

I can hear the Mater calling for me inside. She's puttering around the kitchen, laying out bits of grey furry material across the table. 'You're up already,' she goes. 'I'm after getting an emergency call from Cissy.'

Some parent is after having a fit because they used real rabbit skins on the choir costumes. Only the collars and ears, mind, but they have to switch to fun fur.

'Two of them is vegans.'

'The kids?' I goes. 'What age are they?'

'Too young for that carry-on.'

I pick up a key ring off the table, a rabbit's foot.

'Paddy Curran gave me a couple of them, along with the skins,' she goes. 'Cissy was going to give them out as prizes. For the best behaved. That's gone by the wayside now. I may pick up some lollipops later.'

There's a nice feel to the foot, fur tapering down to the nail. I stick it in my pocket.

'What are you up to for the day?' she goes.

'Nothing much. Head in around five. They're putting the scallions on early this year.'

'That's probably because of the lights.'

'What's that about?'

'What's going to happen is once it gets dark, they're going to have every light extinguished all down Barrack Street and Tullow Street, even the shops windows, signs, everything, and then a celebrity is going to turn a big switch and these old-fashioned lights will come on.'

'What celebrity?'

'Is it that hat designer Laurence Connell? They were going to do a whole show, Parnell's speech and the whole shebang, but that's gone by the wayside.'

'Who's Parnell?'

'Charles Stewart. He was the original one brought electricity to Carlow. The Great Electrifier. But the money got used up on the trees.'

'Trees?'

'That whole row of trees from the Cattle Mart up to Glitz and Bitz had to be cut down. Dutch tree disease.'

'You'd think they'd be insured for that kind of thing.'

'Anyway I'm off,' she says, packing up her sewing bag. 'See you later, son,' and she's gone out the back door.

So I've the house to myself again. I go into the sitting room and see what's on the box. Nothing much, as per usual. When I'm emptying out my rucksack, I find the Katie Taylor cut-out stuck in the front pocket. Have a hard look into her eye sockets, give her a wink she can't return, before I put my lighter to her leg and peg her into the fireplace. A whoosh of flame, paper curls up, then a leaf of white ash drifts across the grate. That's the end of that.

Around two o'clock, I lay into a box of fish fingers and oven chips. The day is feeling long drawn out. If this is how it's going to be without a job and Bernie away, maybe I will see if Murt has anything going for me, workwise.

I get a message from Hopper checking to see everything went okay last night with the Mater. He left the car back and gave it a good clean out; the hamster delivered eight babies, all uneaten.

Two missed calls from Bernie. I get a can of Coke from the fridge and settle into an armchair to give him a ring.

Straight off, he's telling me about his job at the hospital and some supervisor he has who fancies him, some Spanish lad. He was showing Bernie how to clean the toilets and sinks and all that; they take it real serious, not just a quick wipe and off you go. He really went into detail, dragging it out, as if Irish people never did a lick of cleaning in their lives.

'Are you thinking of staying?' I ask.

'Nah. I've brought hardly any gear with me. Want to go back to college. I'm going to get a bit of cash together first.'

I'm relieved he's coming back. He's going on about this club he's going to next weekend. Some friends of his from Kilkenny are over for the summer; he might move in with them.

'What did the Mater say when you told her?' I goes.

'What?'

'You didn't tell her, did ya?'

He starts going on about not getting a chance to talk to her properly on her own; how he didn't want to upset her on holidays.

'Not having a chance to talk to her? You've just spent four days only the two of you together.'

'What if she doesn't want to be around me? It happens, you know.'

'That's bullshit.'

If he turned inside out, the Mater'd still want him around. Probably put him up on her shelves and talk to him every day. It's not like Bernie to be behind the door with this kind of thing; when he came out, he practically took a full-page ad in the *Nationalist*.

'Eventually you'll have to say something,' I says. 'At the end of the day, better to get it over sooner.'

'You don't get it, Frank. I seen her reaction to trans people on TV, like they're a joke or something.'

You'd never think he'd give a shit what anybody thinks.

'Seriously? That's just pure ignorance, Bernie. Everyone laughs at things without thinking. She's not really thinking, that's all.'

He's real quiet on the other end, like he's waiting for me to say something. I don't know what. Like, it's obvious to the world and his mother that the Mater is totally mad about Bernie.

'You're not those other people, Bernie. You're family, no matter what happens.'

He goes around the houses a bit before he says what's stuck in his head. Turns out, years ago when he told the Da, he thought that the Da'd tell her. When that didn't happen, Bernie took it as a sign she wasn't going to be happy about it. That's why the Da was avoiding it. Then the accident happened and for some reason he couldn't do it himself. He got stuck. We all got a bit stuck. He's not making sense. I tell him the conversation I had with Murt, how the Da was waiting til he felt Bernie was ready to tell the Mater himself. Then he was gone.

'We've got over worse,' I say. 'It's not like you're dying.'

'Actually, I thought I was going to die yesterday. Couldn't believe they put me on the floor polisher first thing in the morning.' He's back to himself, telling me about this bar he went to from work with jugs of real cheap cocktails. Dying the next day.

'You know I was only messing with you,' he goes.

'What?'

'Saying about you not having the gift and all that.'

'I'm not that bothered.'

Now that I think about it, I'm not. Maybe any ordinary Joe could cure warts and rashes if they put their mind to it, but how many is going to bother trying? And I'm starting to kind of get some of the things the Da used to say. Like the whole trick is just having the nerve to hang in there with someone and their problem. Obviously, I'm not going to do that if a fellah comes in with a massive tumour on the side of his head. But there is five different kinds of ringworm at least and warts can be very draining on a person if they get out of control.

'You're easier to wind up than a clock,' he says.

'Heading into town later. Wolf Night.'

'I know. First one I've ever missed.'

'It's not all that anyways.'

'Send me a clip of the wolf call. That's the bit I love. Catch you later, bro.'

'You too, bro. I mean . . .'

'It's fine.'

'Got your back.'

This time I mean it.

When we were growing up, Wolf Night wasn't as big a thing. There'd be a pageant near the bandstand where they'd act out the hunting and killing of the last wolf in Ireland. Then it got bigger and they started closing off the main street and having this chase around and it'd end with a party in the middle of town. Now they've started adding in different things to make it more of a festival. All the pubs get decorated, have bands in. There's animal fancy dress, fireworks, céilí dancing, and the scallion eating.

If you think about it, though, the last wolf couldn't have known he was the last one. So this whole thing where the choir and the town sings the big happy wolf chorus as if the wolf is celebrating doesn't make a lick of sense. Why would the wolf be celebrating the dawn of a wolf-free Ireland? Or crying about his last night on earth when he wouldn't actually know? It's impossible to know the beginning or the end, especially if you're it.

Heading into town, every place has some kind of decorations up and the streets are hopping. There's loads of stalls along the river with food and all kinds of gewgaws and there's carnival rides set up behind the square.

I spot Lena and a group of oddbods standing behind a table with loads of her shit on it; at least the Deadwood was spared that. I duck into the front porch of Waxy's to avoid her. Murt must've persuaded her to keep her crap out of his front window. Small mercies.

I'm meeting Hopper and the lads in the beer tent at Castle Hill. Of course he's wearing one of those flashing pink wolf collars and ears they're giving out. He's in full swing, telling them all about Oddsey's Bodega and Mila.

'How's it going?' I says.

'Alright.' He's buzzing because he just heard. As part of the prize this year, the brewery's going to be running scallion eating challenges in their beer tents at all the music festivals and the winner'll travel around with them. Free passes to everything.

'Think about it, Frank. You can be my corner man. I texted Mila. She's already got tickets for Live at the Dive in Bairdstown. This summer's going to be epic.'

Trust Hopper to get us sorted for a good time, even without cash or jobs. Nice one.

We've time for a couple of beers before we head over. On the stage there's two buckets of scallions waiting. Regular strength. Some fellah in Clonegal's been cultivating extra strong ones for the final.

We spot the Mater and Cissy Agar herding a group of little wolf children down the street. She gives Hopper a big thumbs up. Loads of people are coming up wishing him luck, doing wolf calls. He's a very popular winner. Last year this lad from Tullow turned up who'd won some iron stomach competition in college in Dublin. Wasn't even through a quarter of his bucket by the time Hopper was picking the last scallion out of his choppers.

Me and the boys get a good spot up near the front.

Then Harry Morrissey comes out and announces that the 2017 finals will begin: 'After scouring the pubs and bars of the county, we've narrowed it down to the final four.'

'That's all that entered, you lying dog,' Moose shouts up.

Harry ignores him, 'So two v two for the first rounds, grand finale at eight o'clock. The scallions are sponsored by Morrissey's Supermarket. The prize is two hundred and fifty quid, a crate of Scalaters, and free passes to all the major music festivals. Representing your county and our beer. You know the rules, lads: bucket of scallions, washed and trimmed, first one to get them all down.'

With that, Hopper and this real tall young fellah steps up to the table. Never seen him before. Red curly hair and a long nose that nearly goes down over his lip. He's like a big orange ice pop.

'Contestants are allowed one pint of beer and as much water as they need. Beer this year is Scalaters IPA.' Harry lands the two shiny buckets on the table, green stalks sticking out the top. He tips a pile out onto each plate. 'Hopper McGrath, last year's champion, on the left, and Podge McQuaid all the way from Hacketstown on the right. Ready, set, go. If you're going to heave, there's kitchen paper and a basin at your feet.'

It's always mad watching the way Hopper can gobble through them. He takes a swig of the beer and then sets to work. The other lad is using a knife to cut the scallions into smaller bits and putting them in his mouth a few at a time. He'd want to pick up the pace to avoid total annihilation. Hopper powers through the first handful.

The crowd's filled out now and your man Podge's mates are right beside us, shouting him on. 'G'wan Podge, get stuck in.'

Hopper's stopping, gulps down half the beer. His face is reddening and he's belching something woeful. Odd.

'Alright, Hopper,' I shouts up. He shakes his head as if to clear it, takes a swig of the water, and starts on the next handful. His eyes are gone watery. He's chewing real slow, then he pulls a few stalks out of his mouth, half-eaten. What's he playing at? I look up the other end of the table. Yer man is still at it, little platefuls, cutting them into bits and placing them in his mouth real delicate.

Hopper's struggling. Something's wrong. He keeps gulping and he's hardly made any inroads on his pile. The crowd think he's messing, toying with your man.

'Get it into you, Hopper,' I shout up. 'Pick it up.'

'Have a lash of beer,' Moose shouts up. Then he turns to me. 'What the fuck gives? I've fifty quid on him to beat last year's time.'

He's all but stopped and the other fellah has only one bunch left. Before he starts them, he looks across at Hopper. He doesn't smile, the little prick, but he relaxes. He eats the last handful as if it's a plate of chips or something. Hopper's still trying, using his hand to push green back into his mouth, but he can't swallow.

Once McQuaid has the plate cleared, he has a big draught

of Scalaters and looks for Harry to call it. I'm looking at Harry too. He's hanging back to the side but there's no way around it.

He rings the bell on the end of the table. 'The winner, Podge McQuaid.'

I see Hopper reach down, pull a few sheets off the kitchen paper, and spit out the contents of his mouth. He shakes your man's hand, shakes Harry's, and jumps off the back of the stage real quick.

They start cleaning up and setting up for the next two contestants. I thought I'd be watching to see which one was going to be up against Hopper, but that's not the case now. Moose and the lads head back up to the beer tent. I go around to see what happened with Hopper.

'What the fuck, Hopper?'

'That stupid fucking powder.'

'What are you on about?'

'My nose. I can't do it.'

He's gutted. Then I cop it. Of course. Because he couldn't smell, he couldn't taste. That's why he was able to eat anything: spicy curries, raw onions, buckets of scallions.

'You know what a gobful of scallions tastes like now?'

He nods, miserable as sin. 'First time ever.'

I don't know what to say. So we wander over to the carnival rides, saying nothing. I want to have a go on the waltzers. But Hopper is still quare shook after the scallions and wants to get a pint. He says his mouth is burning, but I think he just wants to be on his own.

I feel like Billy-no-mates, lining up for the waltzers by myself. I can hear a band starting up on the main stage by the old post office. Sounds good. I drop out of the queue and head over.

It's jammers in the square; I hang at the back of the crowd. You wouldn't think the band is just a bunch of school kids; the lead singer sounds like he smokes forty a day. Good view, except I keep getting a poke at the side of my knee. I look down and it's the ringworm kid. He's wearing the full wolf gear and using a toy arrow to give me a dig.

'Take it easy,' I go.

'You take it easy, Harry fucking Potter,' he goes, face like thunder on him.

Next thing June comes up behind him and gets hold of the weapon. 'C'mon Conor,' she goes. 'Don't make it worse for yourself.'

He lets go reluctantly, hanging onto the bow.

'He was only messing.'

'Oh, it's you,' she says. 'Hi.'

'How's it going?'

The band's finishing up and I can see the kids' choir at the side of the stage, getting ready to go on.

'Better get moving,' I says to the kid.

He gives me the stink eye and starts sticking the bow into his foot. Only plastic so it should be broken in about two minutes, no major damage done. While he's stabbing himself, June tells me that at the final rehearsal Conor thought some girls were laughing at him and decked one of them. So he's missed his big chance to get up in front of the town in fake fur and howl like a wolf with fifty other kids. And he's got June all to himself for the evening. Sounds like he has it sussed to me.

I take the rabbit foot key ring out of my pocket. 'Here.'

'What's that?'

'Rabbit's foot.'

He reaches out to touch it. 'For real?'

'Yeah, hundred per cent. My mother made the costumes. Did it all on the kitchen table. Cut their feet and the heads off, peeled the skin offa their bodies like a grape.'

He's impressed.

'You know it's supposed to bring good luck,' June says.

'Not for the rabbit,' I goes, then wish I could shut up saying shit. But I can't. If I don't keep talking, she might leave. 'How come you're here at the weekend?' I say.

'Stayed around for the festival, heard so much about it. And I've a match Sunday.'

'Oh yeah, the camogie.'

'How'd you know? You psychic as well?'

'No. I mean you said.' Then I realise she didn't; it was Hopper told me. I'm going to come across stalkerish.

'Did I?' she goes. 'It's actually against Naomh Bríd. That's your local team in case you don't know.'

'Know them well. That'll be a good one.'

We stand for a minute, watching the kids get lined up on stage. I see the Mater and Cissy running some last-minute repairs.

The kid is well taken with the rabbit foot, attaching it to his belt loop, taking it off again. I catch him rubbing it against his cheek. When he sees me looking, he crosses his eyes. Then I spot Hopper ambling towards us looking miserable.

He stands in beside me. 'The stomach's well off,' he goes, before he notices June. He straightens up. 'How's it going?'

'Good,' she says.

'Glad we caught up with ya,' he goes. 'Because I got wasted last Friday and, to be honest, I lost that bit of paper you gave me.'

'Did you?' she goes.

'With your number for Frank. Did he mention there's a twenty-first in Waxy's tomorrow night if you're around? Or any of your friends?'

'No, he didn't mention it.' She's laughing at him. 'Are you his social secretary?'

'He could do with one, let me tell ya.'

The kid is getting restless, pushing into the people in front of us.

'We better go,' she goes. 'See you tomorrow?'

'Definitely,' I goes.

Once they're gone, the shoulders slump on Hopper again. He wants to get skulled and fair enough. We go for a pint in Waxy's. I spot the big hairy fellah from June's work at the bar. He waves over and I feel I have to give him a nod back. Now he's picking up his pint and coming across to join us. Don't think Hopper's in the mood for company.

'Alright,' he goes.

'How's it going?'

'Good. Getting the stomach lined before the final, eh?' he goes to Hopper.

'How d'ya mean?'

'I'm your competition, mate. This scallion eating's gone international. Ireland versus the Aussies.'

Hopper's dead quiet for once so I step in. 'He's not in the final. You must be mixed up. It's the other fellah, the redhead.'

'Didn't the beer boys find you?'

'For what?'

'You're back in. You have to be over eighteen − for the festival circuit, promoting the beer and that. Kid was only sixteen. Using the brother's ID. We've all been there, right? Catch you later, mate.'

I wait til he heads off before I turn to Hopper. 'You're in.'

'Yeah.' He's a face on him like a slapped arse.

'What's up? You're back in the final.'

'Use your fucking noggin, Frank. I can't do it. Now I have my nose working, I can't.'

'Come here.' I pick up our glasses and drag him outside to a quiet corner of the smoking area.

Last Sunday when I, one hundred and ten per cent, did not want to go digging into the Da's past, after we left Rose's, it could've ended there. It was Hopper pushed me. I know it was partly cos he wanted to go for a spin in Ruth's car, but he did it for me as well. To get my arse moving. Now if I can persuade him he can't actually smell or taste, he's back in the game.

So I tell him about the placebo effect, the thing Bernie told me last week. Then I start making shit up about the powder: Rose told me Mrs EB makes up the remedies with herbs from the Kimchi House kitchen; ginseng is only the Korean equivalent of salt. I even come up with a whole list of made-up smells from the last few days: Oddsey was wearing women's perfume; the mussels tasted sweet like strawberries; a strange chemical smell coming off the Deadwood, especially in the car.

'You didn't smell any of those, Hopper, did ya?'

'No, but what about the fact I could taste those scallions?' he goes. 'And what I did smell. The sea and Mila.'

'Yeah, you got a little flavour of the scallions, alright, just memory from when you were a kid. It's all in your head. It'll start taking you in that direction, but you have to resist going the rest of the way. You have to pull yourself together. Believe me, Hopper. I know you cannot smell or taste.'

At least he's not arguing back; he's thinking about what I'm saying.

'Look,' I says, 'you said it yourself. The good smells were always in your brain. You get up on that stage and think of Jingle Bells.'

'What the fuck?'

'Your special smell: Africa, the nun. Dead people.'

'Myrrh. We Three Kings.'

'Whatever. Get a whiff of that. That's your personal . . .' I'm not sure where I'm going with this.

'My personal talisman,' he goes.

'Exactly.'

I think he's buying it. His shoulders relax and he shakes his body out, as if he's a boxer loosening up. I know that look; no better man to reboot the mojo. He raises his glass. 'Frank, I always knew it.'

'What?'

'If I've said it once, I've said it a million times, you've the magic touch. No two ways about it.'

As we're heading down the street, I think there's at least two ways about it, seven or eight ways, or six and a half, but, fuck it, at least we're sorted on the scallion front for now. And I'm seeing June tomorrow night. With a load of other people admittedly, but still and all. The Deadwood, the Da, is in some kind of happy ever after with Letty. Though you'd wonder what's ever after, especially regarding the Da? A new beginning at the end.

Whatever direction that thought was going in is completely drowned out by the sound starting to blast out of every speaker across town, bouncing against the walls, echoing off the river, lifting up into the sky. The sound of fifty little kids howling out the wolf chorus. Hopper joins in, shaking his head like a madman, and everyone around us picks it up, yowling and howling.

Stop thinking, Frank, I says to myself. Just do it, or be it. Or at least, get on with it. I throw my head back and do the same as Hopper, as everyone else. I'm the last wolf ever, howling my heart out, not knowing or caring if it's for the beginning or the end.

Love Is the Sweetest Thing

This is the tale that never will tire
This is the song without end

When your life ends up in a pile of smithereens, each shard becomes its own tale. One sliver takes a hold in someone else's story; your conclusion might be part of their beginning or maybe lodged in the middle. Another piece falls away; some drift upwards, catch the light for a moment, and we wonder what was that, what did we see?

Let the telling take you home. Eventually you yourself'll become surplus to requirements for the tale. You're a character now in someone else's memory, their imaginings. Words are bits of yarn; it's the listener pulls it together, makes of it what they will, adds their own pattern into it. That's some thinking by me, in the quiet here of Letty's bedroom. As Frank said, it's plain as a monk's cell, but what about it. We could be sitting up in the Gresham Hotel, Letty and me, having afternoon tea, or flying over Mount Leinster in a hot-air balloon, not a care on either of us now. It's our last go round together.

We have our own rhythm and routine. Spending a lifetime cleaning has dug a ditch in Letty's mind and all the words tumble and jumble over each other. They flow along, streams of confinement and sameness, til together the tributaries gather force and spill out to the open maw of the ocean. That's a quare abstract way of going on about work.

In truth, there's nothing as concrete as work, be it filling a pothole, building a wall, or wiping and mopping and tidying after other people. But it can become some class of prayer if you accept the traces; it lifts itself up to the skies, the honest labour of your hands when all else is taken from you. The over and over again; over the same, same over and over fills up the body, empties the mind and stills it, opening up a place and there you are, back again as beautiful as the first day ever I saw your face, I thought my heart would . . . her own self shining from the inside out, before her hair took to grey, the fingers locked inward, the crooked little back.

She lifts me off the dressing table onto the bed. There's a stack of cloths in her middle drawer for cleaning different yokes. For buffing my noggin, it's a cut-out square of an old green sheet.

Rocking back and forth, polishing the top of my head, rubbing my eye sockets as careful as if she were preparing a corpse.

There's variations of a life-tune singing out between us, voices from countless ages chiming in, at times as rough against each other as a rookery, but other times as sweet a harmony as you'd ever come by.

Her talking drifts around hundreds of same-same days, each one much like the one before or after. Always bells pealing and clanging for up and out and eat and pray and work and stop. Like a desert landscape, nothing stirring it seems and yet she hones in on a green shoot pushing its way through a crack in the dry sand. It could be a handful of petals she collected from the bouquet at St Thérèse's feet, hidden in the pocket of her apron; or the shine of the refectory floor, like the grandest ballroom. This morning, she returns to a particular Tuesday, after the hospital had closed down and she not long decanted into the cottage here. Decanted . . . puts you in mind of a pottery jug with blue glaze and little red flowers round the rim, wide-mouthed, red wine pouring down into it. At that stage, the nurses' home had been vacant for years, but they let Letty go back over once a week, to clean the uninhabited rooms.

Now in her mind she returns daily, and she takes me with her, through the side door, to the laundry room, collect the bucket full of cloths and rags, the polish and disinfectant walk the back stairs behind the refectory   start
at the top   work your way down
from the top down
                    top down
down
and all the words tangled come through me
        first the banisters and
  Pledge Waxed Beauty Instantly as You Dust   as it
was in the beginning now and ever   shall be
                another layer of polish to doorknobs that never
                turn to open never close
                            each bedroom much the
same the metal bedframe with iron springs and
              an occasional table
                    an open wardrobe

a lonely chair facing nowhere particular
wipe the bed frame *Brasso for Lasting Brightness* lasting
brightness brightness thou shalt
not brightness   not brightness
dreams caught in a duster   springs twisting
a cry of wanting
escapes   forgive me
lord   for I have sinned windows water
spots and rainbow streak chase them down with vinegar and
rags   beams and sparkles
I saw the light   no more darkness
another layer of wax to the floor another hour
polish the wooden handrail another hour
of dust and dust and remove another   another day's
worth   of dust to dust

another day and another

week year
years thou shalt not thou shalt not
statues in the stairwells clean the sky-blue robe
feet halos eyes   staring straight   ahead never meet
your eye   shine up those name plates   *Brasso Metal Polish
Wadding*
no fresh bouquets
today but a few hyacinths
from the flower beds at the back   run wild   put them in
a jar at the feet the virgin mary   fallen petals
sweep   mary immaculate
star of the sea catch a falling star of the sea pray for
the sinner
yellow roses st william   pray st

martin de porres   pray for us st carmel
fallen   petals sweep st anthony
                              pray for us
                      st francis where there is despair hope
hope hope pray for us
        bottom of the
              stairs the little flower
                        st thérèse a vase of brown stems wilted heads
fallen petals   put them in your pocket a pinny
                    full of fallen petals
                    hold them in your hands
                    all night long under
                            the cover
                    undercover
        yellow   water   stains
in the sink

                    disinfect   bleach and   disinfect

Women Who Know Use Clorox   who know women who
know   toilets scrub and flush   who knows

        who knows
        disinfect infect   infect who knows
        deliver us from infect dust drifts
              settles in the refectory buff the lino   circle the ballroom
              mop   the I was waltzing   with my darling to the
                    Flash Cuts Spring Cleaning Time in Half
cut in half half half half half half-light coming going
        through   the bars on the windows
                                        straighten up take
                                        a step one two

                                        three thou shalt not
                                        I was waltzing with
                                        my darling thou
                                        shalt not thou shalt
                                        not I was waltzing
        reflections in the pewter gravy jug   abandoned in the
corner
    back in Sweeney's   eyes in the mirror   meat
glistening and
            twinkling behind all that is seen and unseen   judge
the living
            and the dead   whose kingdom have no end
    no
end
                    No end amen

Come evening and she dons a royal blue bed jacket, props
herself up on the pillows for news of the weather and the
shipping forecast. I'm positioned beside the little radio. The two
of us listening out for all manner of climatic up and downs,
stories of Wind, his coming and goings

        The forecast for Irish coastal waters
                from Roches Point to Mizen Head to Valentia
        northwest winds will reach

    when you   give birth   to Wind he's everywhere
        Sunny spells   showers occasional mist or
drizzle, slight breeze otherwise fair   won't be can't be tied
down
    watch him escape over the hospital walls
testing his mettle against tree trunks a shed roof

pick up any auld bits of yoke to toy

with

steals a child's kite and fly me

to   the moon

outside the window

before he pegs it into the branches of our tree

along the Serpentine

Moderate to fresh and gusty west to

northwest winds risk of thunder   a risk of risk

of risk

arriving back to the ward

after a night chasing white-tops across the western lakes

rattling a window frame to let her   know he's home

Irish coastal waters from Valentia to Erris Head

to Fair Head visibility

generally good

occasionally moderate to poor   fruit of thy womb

now and at the hour of our death   walk the Serpentine to

the   end and back   sings   songs of branches

and leaves full   of grace fruit of thy womb

there's a lid for every pot

Wind and cloud

dancing cheek to cheek

bride and groom

stirring up a   storm

we forgive those who trespass against us forgive

trespass forgive

trespass

Northwest winds will reach gale force later
tonight on Irish coastal waters from Valentia to
        stormy weather, since my gal and I ain't together
Sustained winds at Malin Head have reached 62 mph
    storm of righteous anger   Wind reached *The*
Glen   heaved   against the gable end
   trespass against us crumbled it like an
             old
             dry
    wedding cake   since my gal and I ain't *fresh*
    occasionally strong   *southwesterly winds with gale*
    average temperatures   power lines down with us
               now and until the end of time
  South 13 knots, recent drizzle 5 miles 1016 falling slowly
  raindrops keep falling on my head
they ascended into heaven and are seated
               heaven I'm in heaven
    Clearer conditions heavy showers will follow   with
       a risk of for our salvation
  have mercy on us   keeps raining all the time
    have mercy   *Gale warning blustery showers some of*
hail with a risk of
     I believe in one god father almighty maker of heaven

     and earth
    and of all things visible and
    invisible *Slyne Head*
to Erris Head to Malin Head visibility moderate
    to poor   judge
  the living and the dead whose   kingdom have no end
      no end
    visibility poor

visibility poor mist four miles   1018   *rising   slowly*
                    visibility   *clearing*
          rising slowly
rising

                         it's a pleasant night across the country
                    it's a pleasant night
     across the country judge   the living and the dead
     no end

                    whose kingdom have no
                                        no no no

end

                    amen

     and rising

                              and rising slowly

Author Acknowledgements

My thanks go to my agent Gráinne Fox at Fletcher and Co, who got behind this story from the early stages. To Catherine Gough and all the staff at HarperCollins Ireland who worked on the book.

Thanks to the Arts Council of Ireland and the Tyrone Guthrie Centre. Also to Words Ireland for their support in connecting me with Lia Mills, a thoughtful mentor.

To Karin Whooley, Antoinette Clayton, and Carmel Winters, first readers of the manuscript.

To my writing friends: Nuala Ní Chonchúir, Eileen Kavanagh, Neil Hegarty, Suzie Perry, Bernie Furlong, Alice Redmond. To Declan Meade, for supporting my writing from the beginning and for his friendship.

In the first writing class I attended, I was very lucky to have Nuala Ní Dhomhnaill as my teacher, who turned me on to the joy of writing. Big thank you. I'm especially grateful to another inspiring writer and teacher, Claire Keegan, for her generosity in sharing her craft and encouragement.

Thanks to Siobhan Geoghegan and Ciara Fitzpatrick for their belief in the power of creative practice.

To my sisters Maria and Olivia and my cousin Caitríona for their constancy; to all my extended family, friends and neighbours who showed kindness to me in my writing efforts.

For all their love and care, thanks to my family Karen and Cúan.

Quoted Materials

'Begin the Beguine', written by Cole Porter

'I Believe', written by Ervin Drake, Irvin Graham, Jimmy Shirl and Al Stillman

'Dream Along with Me (I'm on my way to a star)' written by Carl Sigman

'The First Time Ever I Saw Your Face', written by Ewan MacColl

'The Deadwood Stage (Whip-Crack-Away!)' written by Sammy Fain and Paul Francis Webster

'Love in a Home', written by Johnny Mercer

'Tie a Yellow Ribbon Round the Ole Oak Tree', written by Irwin Levine and L. Russell Brown

'Don't Fence Me In', written by Robert Fletcher and Cole Porter

'We've Only Just Begun', written by Paul Williams

'Love Theme from "La Strada" (Travelling Down a Lonely Road)', written by Michele Galdieri

'Catch a Falling Star', written by Paul Vance and Lee Pockriss

'Only a Fool (Breaks His Own Heart)', written by Norman Bergen and Shelly Coburn

'When You Were Sweet Sixteen', written by James Thornton

'Love is the Sweetest Thing', written by Raymond Stanley Noble
'Stormy Weather', written by Harold Arlen and Ted Koehler
'Cheek to Cheek', written by Irving Berlin
'Mid-Term Break' by Seamus Heaney
'The Narrow Way' by Anne Brontë